Karna's Wife

Kavita Kané calls herself a true-blue Puneite, despite having been born in Mumbai and grown up in Patna and Delhi. Having studied and lived in Pune for many years, she considers herself as good as married to the city, where she now lives with her mariner husband, Prakash, two teenage daughters, Kimaya and Amiya, a friendly Rottweiler named Dude and a cat called Babe.

A senior journalist, with degrees in English literature and mass communication, Kavita is also a cinema and theatre aficionado. But writing, she confesses, is her only skill. *Karna's Wife* is her first novel.

Karna's Wife

THE OUTCAST'S QUEEN

KAVITA KANÉ

RUPA

First published by
Rupa Publications India Pvt. Ltd 2013
7/16, Ansari Road, Daryaganj
New Delhi 110002

Sales Centres:

Allahabad Bengaluru Chennai
Hyderabad Jaipur Kathmandu
Kolkata Mumbai

ISBN: 978-81-291-2085-4

Sixth impression 2014

10 9 8 7 6

The moral right of the author has been asserted.

Printed by Parksons Graphics Pvt. Ltd, Mumbai

This book is dedicated to my parents.

Aai, *who made me what I am today*
and
Papa, *whom I hope to be like some day.*

Contents

1

Karna

It was that man again. That man, with his thick mane, brooding eyes and twinkling earrings, walked towards her, his gold armour glittering so fiercely under the blazing sun that it was blinding. His intense radiance threw tormented shadows, the wind suddenly whirling away the figure made spectral by the shadows, and snuffing it abruptly while she stood there, her arms extended, against the vast emptiness of sand…

She woke up with a start, shivering slightly, her eyes wide, her breathing turning to quick gasps. She had seen the same dream. Again. Over and over again. And each time the persistently vivid dream spawned a haunted restlessness, pushing her into uneasy wakefulness.

The night was quiet, the marbled bedroom quieter still, but Uruvi could almost hear the raging turmoil within her. She looked down at her arms—stretched and trembling, as if trying to grasp the intangible. As intangible as the elusive man in her dreams. 'Karna,' she uttered the name softly, and whispered it several times over, convinced that this was the man she had loved since the day she had first seen him.

She recollected her first sight of him—striding into the arena of the archery tournament in Hastinapur. The contest had been arranged by the royal patriarch, Bhishma Pitamaha of Hastinapur, to highlight the archery skills of his great-grandnephews, the hundred Kauravas and the five Pandavas.

Against the flaming halo of the dipping sun, the young man had immediately attracted the attention of everyone present. The bustling arena went abruptly still and hundreds of eyes fell on the youth. He

1

looked serenely divine, swathed in an almost ethereal glow, his back straight, his head held high, his strangely golden armour gleaming as radiantly as his handsome face, while his earrings sparkled in the rays of the setting sun. He was tall—taller than Arjuna, the Pandava prince, but did not loom large like Bhima, the second Pandava and the strongest man in the kingdom. Lithe but muscular with broad shoulders and a trim waist, the young stranger with his thick golden brown hair appeared almost God-like to Uruvi. Saluting Guru Dronacharya, the royal teacher of the Kauravas and the Pandavas, and Kripacharya, the royal priest, he walked straight up to a plainly astonished Arjuna to announce grandly, 'I, Karna, shall perform every feat with the bow and arrow that have just been shown now, but with greater skill.' He then proceeded to do so with contemptuous ease.

As the Princess of Pukeya, Uruvi had a vantage view from the gold-leafed royal enclave perched majestically above the swarming crowd. Sitting amongst the regal entourage of the blind King Dhritrashtra and Queen Gandhari, Uruvi knew she had fallen in love with the stranger then and there—utterly and irrevocably. Mesmerized, she continued to stare at the handsome young man who was flaunting his phenomenal skills with more flamboyance than Arjuna. Uruvi was sitting next to Queen Kunti, the imperial widow of King Pandu of Hastinapur and the mother of the Pandavas. As her mother's childhood friend, Kunti was Uruvi's self-appointed foster mother.

'Who's he?' Uruvi excitedly turned to the Pandava queen, who looked unexpectedly ashen and seemed to stiffen at her question. 'Ma, are you not feeling well?'

There was no reply and Uruvi saw to her growing horror that Kunti had crumpled into a quiet faint. Thoroughly alarmed, and the stranger forgotten for the moment, Uruvi knelt over the prostrate figure, calling anxiously for help just as Vidura, the youngest brother and chief counsellor of King Dhritrashtra, took charge of the situation. Soon Uruvi was relieved to see her foster mother swiftly regaining consciousness. 'It must have been the heat,' murmured Kunti through parched lips, gathering her silken folds and her dignity quickly.

Reassured, Princess Uruvi peered down the gallery to watch what was happening below. The show was supposed to be a display of skills by the two groups of cousins—the Kauravas and the Pandavas. But this stranger, who called himself Karna, seemed to have stolen the glory from the Kuru princes, particularly Arjuna.

Uruvi watched Karna bow carelessly to the royal audience each time he strung his bow and effortlessly repeated the feats of Arjuna.

Prince Duryodhana, the eldest of the Kaurava brothers, looked visibly delighted, his swarthy face wreathed in a huge smile. For a man who rarely smiled, he looked unusually euphoric. He rushed to the young archer and embraced him like a long-lost brother, 'Whoever you are, fortune has sent you to me. My brothers and I are at your command,' he announced.

Events seemed to be happening too fast and decidedly not in his favour, realized an irate Arjuna. A promising and versatile warrior, he was the best Kuru archer. He blazed with an impetuous temper. 'Whoever you are, you are an intruder! You have entered uninvited and yet you dare compete with us! You shall sorely regret your arrogance the moment you taste defeat. I shall trounce you in a challenge.'

Karna gave a mirthless smile and replied evenly, 'What is the use of a competition if one cannot be compared with others? Talk is the weapon of the weak; release your arrows instead of hollow words.'

'This young man is a great warrior!' declared Bhishma Pitamaha in his deep baritone. 'He has surpassed each of Arjuna's feats.'

Arjuna looked almost apoplectic. Glancing at his mottled face, Princess Uruvi could not suppress a giggle. 'Spoilsport!' she dimpled. 'Can't face competition, can he?'

The mood of the tournament had radically changed; the air seemed to thicken rapidly with palpable tension. Having surpassed Arjuna's feats, the stranger, encouraged by Bhishma's pronouncement, was now challenging Arjuna to a duel.

Arjuna bristled angrily. He hurriedly bowed to his teachers, hugged his brothers and with his face flushed, stood ready for combat as Karna faced him.

The sun suddenly disappeared behind a huge dark cloud and it seemed as if it would rain.

'No, oh, no!' cried Kunti, getting up from her seat in nervous agitation. 'They cannot fight…oh, no, they shouldn't!'

'Ma, please, it's fair enough!' cried Uruvi, rising too in her excitement. 'If Arjuna is as good as that young man, or even better as he believes, what is there to be so scared of? And who is this young man anyway? He is absolutely wonderful. Oh, I am enjoying this! Now for the duel!' she chortled in glee.

Vidura gave her a stern look, clearly disapproving of her blood-thirsty idea of enjoyment. 'One of them could get badly hurt or worse, get killed because of immature egotism,' he spoke to his sister-in-law Kunti, the mother of Arjuna. Kunti was extremely agitated and seemed clearly against the duel.

Like Uruvi, the onlookers were wondering about the identity of this young man just as Kripacharya spoke to him. 'According to the rules of the game, only a kshatriya, a high-born warrior, can fight another kshatriya in a tournament,' he declared, placing himself firmly between the two young men. 'Arjuna, whom you have challenged, is a prince, the worthy son of King Pandu and Queen Kunti, the scion of the Kuru dynasty. Pray, who are you, son?'

Uruvi felt a sharp pain in her arm. Kunti appeared drained of colour while unconsciously gripping Uruvi's upper arm, her fingers biting into the soft flesh. She was staring at the youth with a strange emotion, as if his answer was of tremendous importance. The audience was hushed as everybody waited eagerly for an answer. Only the youth remained strangely silent, staring at the horizon where the sun was slowly disappearing. His handsome face was sapped of its radiant pride.

His lips were clenched and his noble head was bowed, as if in shame. The proud archer suddenly appeared lost.

'Why does he not say something?' Uruvi exclaimed edgily. 'Why doesn't he reveal who he is?'

The stranger was rescued from unexpected quarters. 'We all know this young archer outmatches Arjuna in skills. If the combat cannot take place merely because he is not a prince, I shall remedy it easily,' thundered Prince Duryodhana. 'I proclaim this youth King of Anga!' And with that, Duryodhana performed the required rituals to crown Karna the King of Anga on the spot. 'Now you are a king, a royal personage who can fight any duel or challenge any kshatriya,' proclaimed Duryodhana, handing the new king his crown, his jewels and the royal emblem.

Uruvi found herself smiling. Kunti, too, seemed happy that the situation had turned in favour of the stranger. 'That young man is certainly charming', Uruvi chuckled softly to herself. 'He has two women admirers already.'

Suddenly, the royal proceedings were interrupted. She saw an emaciated old man pushing through the heaving crowds towards Karna and, with a small cry, clasp the newly crowned king to his bosom.

'My son, my son!' the old man repeated over and over again, with tears coursing down his raddled face. Karna looked surprised and slightly uneasy for a moment before hugging the elderly man and touching his feet in solemn reverence.

The crowd gasped. Uruvi caught her breath; the sheer nobility of the act had stirred her. The Pandavas jeered with contemptuous laughter while the crowd grew restive.

Uruvi heard Bhima give a snort of derisive laughter. 'King of Anga indeed! You are but a son of our charioteer!' he sneered. 'Your father is Adhiratha, a charioteer in my uncle King Dhritrashtra's army. You are no prince, you are no warrior! You don't need a royal insignia or a bow. All you need is a whip to drive the horses! Or it would seem more appropriate if you had a brush in hand to clean the horses. You are fit to rule the stables, not the kingdom of Anga!'

Bhima's caustic words came like a whip, lashing the young Karna to steely silence. He seemed frozen, gazing intently at the sinking sun, his eyes twin dark pools of despair.

Taking Karna's sudden silence as a sign of weakness, Bhima pushed mercilessly further. 'You are no warrior, young man! You were strutting about so proudly a while ago—where has all that arrogance gone? You don't deserve the crown, or the kingdom given to you so undeservedly by my cousin here. Take your father's whip instead and help him out,' Bhima mocked cruelly.

The tide turned. The cheering spectators had gone mute, now that the great warrior had turned out to be no kshatriya at all but a lowly charioteer's son. But Uruvi reacted strongly to these hurtful words. 'Bhima is downright mean!' she turned furiously to Kunti, the mother of the tormentor. 'How can he ridicule the humble and the helpless? Does that pride and pettiness befit a prince? And why are the elders keeping quiet about this gross insult being heaped upon a defenceless person? Why does Bhishma Pitamaha remain quiet when Bhima is so brutally ridiculing the warrior? Did he not proclaim a moment ago that Karna was a great archer, better than even Arjuna?'

Below, Prince Duryodhana spoke up for the hapless Karna as well. 'Such speech is not worthy of you, Bhima! It is valour which defines a kshatriya, a kshatriya does not define valour. You are known by the deeds done; merit has no pedigree. Tracing one's lineage is pointless. I can give you hundreds of instances of great men of humble birth. The bloodline of heroes—like the source of a mighty river—is never known. Those born in the kshatriya clan have even become brahmins. Vishwamitra, born a kshatriya, became the greatest sage, obtaining the title of Brahmarishi from Lord Brahma himself. Our guru, Dronacharya, was born in a water pot—a drona—and Kripacharya of the Gotama race was born from a clump of grass. Let's not talk about parentage as the finger might point apply to you too...'

Uruvi saw Kunti flinch and she felt a frisson of anger against Duryodhana for his irreverent insinuation. It was an acknowledged fact that the Pandavas were the five sons of Queen Kunti and Queen Madri from five different gods. They were not fathered by King Pandu, who was forced into celibacy because of an ancient curse. King Pandu had requested his wife Kunti to make use of the boon Rishi Durvasa had once given her—that she could invoke any god and he would bless her with a son. That is how Kunti had conceived three of the Pandavas—Yudhishthira from Lord Yama, the god of dharma and death; Bhima from Vayu the god of the wind, and Arjuna from Lord Indra, the king of the gods.

'Awkward questions may be asked about your own origin,' Duryodhana continued derisively. 'Can a doe give birth to a tiger? Look at Karna—his golden armour, his shining earrings, his build, his confidence and the way he carries himself. He must be of royal blood. I am certain he is of celestial ancestry. We are talking about merit and skills, and Karna has more than proved that he is a worthy warrior. Unworthy of ruling Anga, did you say, Bhima? I consider that he is worthy of ruling this whole world!'

And with those contemptuous words, the Kuru prince took Karna by the arm, leading him to his chariot, and drove away into the dusk.

'What on earth is happening?' asked the blindfolded Queen Gandhari, mother of the hundred Kauravas, in rising bewilderment.

Uruvi answered cheekily, 'I think Duryodhana has got himself a new friend!'

She turned to look back at the departing chariot on the dusty road, carrying the man she had just fallen in love with away from her.

'And that was the first and the last I actually saw of him,' sighed Uruvi, her lips curling in an unhappy curve. Usually she wore a lovely, infectious smile. Either it was a flashing one which lit up her oval face, or a slow one suffused with an elfin charm. At the moment, she was grim, with a bitter ache in her heart for he was still a stranger to her and she wondered if her love was destined to remain unrequited. Her swayamwara, when she would follow the custom of choosing the prince she wished to marry, was being planned for the coming month of marghashirsha, in winter, and here she was dreaming about a man she had only seen, but never met.

His daughter's swayamwara would be more grand than Draupadi's, King Vahusha of Pukeya had promised himself. Not because he was one of the more powerful kings of the time. Not because he was a close ally of both King Dhritrashtra and Vasudev Krishna of Dwarka. Not because he wanted to outmatch King Drupada, the surly, rancorous father of the dusky, doe-eyed Draupadi, now the consort of the five Pandavas. But yes, because he wanted to flaunt his beautiful daughter at the most ostentatious swayamwara ever—to proudly present her to the world. She would eventually marry the most eligible of all her suitors—that fortunate one whom she favoured.

She was his little princess. Uruvi was the only daughter of the sixth King of Pukeya, the erudite Vahusha and Queen Shubra; an heiress to her father's legacy, his intelligence, and her mother's flaming beauty. Slender and petite, her loveliness was distracting, speciously masking her incisive wit. Though the burning fire in her eyes, the warmth of her smile, and the passion with which she articulated her thoughts were enticing, she was too spirited to be restrained, too proud to be cautious, and far too forthright to think of the consequences of her actions. She had a charming candour, a blithe audacity steeled with a stubborn resilience, which many admired but few appreciated. Most got carried away with her captivating beauty and her wit, and gazed at her in wonder.

King Vahusha was not apologetic about his adoration for his daughter. She was his only child—a gift bestowed on him a trifle late in life. He loved his wife, Queen Shubra, in an indulgent, unfussy way, as he did his mother and his various nephews and nieces, but he clearly idolised his daughter.

King Vahusha stood tall and imposing, thinking of the object of his paternal pride. With his spare form, his gentle eyes and aquiline nose, he looked more like a poet than a warring king, more fit to hold a quill than a sword, mace or a spear. With skin the colour of dull ivory and a shimmering silver mane, he looked more like a sage than a ruler.

He thought the world of his daughter. She was beautiful as she was brilliant, she was kind as she was brutally frank, she was loving as she was tempestuous. As a child, she had never given him a moment's uneasiness. She was naughty and defiant but never grossly disobedient; even in her mischief, there was an endearing impishness.

'She is my world,' he confessed simply to Queen Shubra whenever she gently chided him for over-pampering their only daughter. 'There are two types of children: one, whom you love naturally because they are your offspring and they become unconditionally yours the moment you hold them in your arms. But there is another kind, who besides this unreserved love heaped upon them, are enchanting because of their striking individual traits. Very early in life, this kind of child becomes an individual who is born to win over people by her innate character and distinctiveness. There are qualities in the child that are so endearing, so impossibly appealing, that you immediately fall in love with her. She completely woos you over with her charm and not just because she happens to be your offspring. Our Uruvi is one such child. Who cannot help but love her?'

There was truth in his statement, the mother agreed. Queen Shubra was a small, elegant lady with magnificent eyes, a straight, delicate nose and a pale smooth skin. Her thick, abundant black hair, tied neatly in a bun at her nape, had a silver streak. Her smooth face was still unlined, the occasional criss-crosses emerging whenever she frowned, which was often enough when it came to matters concerning her growing daughter. Uruvi could be a very trying child, Shubra sighed silently, not daring to voice her thoughts. The spirited daughter had inherited her mother's glorious beauty and her father's sharp mind, and both sizzled in her short flashes of temper.

No one remained unaffected by the little princess's vivacity and her inherent goodness. Even the sternest of the royal patriarchs— Bhishma Pitamaha—never hesitated to place her on his lap, and always offered her a basket of her favourite, freshly plucked jasmines each time she visited Hastinapur. The child was everyone's delight. 'Why do you always wear white?' she once demanded of the grand old man as she perched prettily on his lap. 'Even your hair is so white!

Don't you like colours? See what a brilliant pink I am wearing!' she said and promptly placed her bright stole over his broad shoulders, which were by then shaking with indulgent merriment. Each time, the little girl would make the otherwise grim, taciturn great-granduncle laugh uproariously through his luxuriantly flowing beard.

Or when she had irreverently asked the blind-folded Queen Gandhari about the piece of cloth tied around her eyes. 'Why do you wear that?' she had questioned the queen mother, softly tracing her dimpled little finger over the silken cloth. 'Do you like to play blind man's buff with Uncle? You should remove the fold and help him about instead!'

Queen Gandhari had giggled and hugged the child close.

'It's not often you see Gandhari smile, forget laugh!' Kunti observed quietly to Queen Shubra, her friend. 'Uruvi has an irrepressible naiveté about her which is so engaging! That little angel makes the whole world smile, whatever she does!' she gushed fondly. 'And I hope she doesn't lose that charm when she grows up! If she remains so delightful, you will have a handful to deal with, dear! One which I am ready to take on any time you want,' smiled Kunti. 'She is going to be my daughter-in-law one day, mind my words!' The smile had slipped from Queen Shubra's face when she heard Kunti's words, not wanting to think of the day she would have to part with her daughter.

Kunti loved Uruvi like her own child. 'Possibly because I don't have a daughter myself, and bringing up five boys can be quite demanding,' she had laughed lightly, and proceeded to proclaim that the dainty little princess would be the wife of one of her sons. 'That way, she'll be with me always!' Queen Shubra had readily agreed and the two friends had made a secret pact many years ago; one which both King Vahusha and Uruvi were aware of but treated with indifference.

Uruvi's father allowed her to break free of norms while her mother tried hard to restrain her from defying conventions. The daughter detested the unsaid decree which demanded that a girl of a good family should be hidden away till it was time for her to get married. She played with her friends in Hastinapur, sang and danced with her cousins, rode horses with the Pandavas and the Kauravas, and climbed trees with Bhima and Vikarna, the Kaurava prince.

A good many princes and young men, wealthy or noble, or both, had asked for Princess Uruvi's fair hand in marriage, but much to her mother's consternation, Uruvi had refused all of them. Her apprehensive mother worried that her daughter at sweet nineteen should still be single. She demanded why the girl was being so finicky; it was absurd to be so difficult.

Uruvi was charmingly obstinate. She found reasons to reject every one of her suitors. So her exasperated mother thought of the only reasonable way out—a swayamwara. She was pleasantly surprised when her otherwise mutinous daughter agreed to it. The mother hoped Uruvi would finally garland a suitable prince; hopefully, the soft-spoken, handsome Arjuna. Kunti might have been sweepingly magnanimous about Uruvi choosing any one of the five Pandavas, but Shubra confessed that she was most fond of Arjuna as a prospective son-in-law. He was surely the best choice—good-looking, kind and brave. They would make a good match—he so tall and handsome, she so slim and slight by his side. Heavens, she was already picturing them together. Shubra's smile fell, downed with a growing sense of unease. The future seemed so perfect but…it was this 'but' which kept coming between her best-laid plans and peace of mind.

'Have you asked Uruvi whom she wants to marry?' asked Queen Shubra somewhat sharply, turning to King Vahusha.

'No, but she will choose someone at the swayamwara anyway,' her husband reasoned amiably. 'Invitations to almost all the kings and princely suitors have gone out. We haven't missed any.'

'Don't you think it would be more appropriate if we knew whom she will choose instead of us playing this guessing game?' persisted his wife. 'If I know her well, she is likely to pick a boy whom I shan't approve of at all! She has an uncanny habit of annoying me.'

'Oops, don't tell me she has fallen in love with that fat Dushasana!

Now, that would be a very nasty surprise!' said her husband playfully, but his queen did not look too amused. 'She is more frank with you. Why don't you ask her yourself? In fact, I had assumed she might have confided in you by now. Girls do fall in love, you know,' she reminded him pointedly.

The King of Pukeya promised to be the responsible father and a conscientious interrogator.

Uruvi's sheltered life had been a pursuit of perfection, but her privileged world sometimes thwarted her. Uruvi imagined she came close to it as she painted beautiful forms of nature, but then she longed for more. In Karna she had found an appearance and personality so close to perfection that she could convince herself that her quest had been fulfilled. That man from nowhere had created a tumult in her heart each time he had strung his bow.

As a young woman in love, Uruvi saw in Karna all the qualities of a hero who was not being permitted to be one. His flaws made him more interesting. At Hastinapur's tournament when he had outdone Arjuna, he had been openly belittled as a charioteer's son and deprived of his right to duel with the Pandava prince. As the King of Anga, he was the inglorious ruler, looked down upon by royalty and the princes. As a noble warrior, he was cast off for not being a kshatriya. As an eligible suitor, he was disgraced for being of a lowly caste, a sutaputra—as Princess Draupadi had pithily reminded him at her royal swayamwara. No, it was not very hard to fall in love with Karna, however unsuitable a suitor he was condemned to be.

This man seemed to be born in adversity. Uruvi stared pensively at the small portrait she had painted of him and kept hidden in her bedroom coffer. As his tales of gallantry washed over from one kingdom to another, so did his saga of misfortune as the blighted man with a legacy of low birth, a sutaputra. The story of his life was a fairytale gone wrong. He was a beautiful orphaned baby, with bewitching kundals (earrings) and a golden kavach (armour) to protect him, who had mysteriously strayed into a river and into the lonely lives of Dhritarashtra's charioteer, Adhiratha, and his wife Radha.

The young Vasusena (or Karna, as he was better known, because of his sparkling earrings) nursed a smouldering ambition to perform and excel and earnestly believed he was destined for a better life. He did not wish to be a charioteer like his foster father, but a warrior, an archer. With this dream, the young Radheya, the son of Radha as he was also called, approached the best teacher of martial arts in Hastinapur—Guru Dronacharya—the guru of the Kauravas and Pandavas, but the guru refused to teach him because he was not a kshatriya.

Undaunted but deeply disappointed, he went to Parshurama, the guru of gurus in warfare and sought his blessings. Radheya soon became Parshurama's best pupil and showed the world his magnificent skills from a very young age. At the Hastinapur archery contest he outdid Arjuna, the rising star of the Kuru dynasty and the kingdom's most accomplished archer. But his moment of fame and credit crumbled when he was questioned about his birth and lineage. Once again, he was turned down for being a sutaputra, and had it not been for Duryodhana who in an unexpected burst of generosity had gifted him the kingdom of Anga, he would not have been what he was—the most formidable warrior in the country. Duryodhana had promoted the young sutaputra to royalty, transforming him from Radheya, the son of Radha, to Karna, the mighty warrior and the King of Anga.

Yet, pondered the princess, he was not allowed to bask in his well-earned glory. He was Karna, the King of Anga, the king with a crown of thorns, the king who was a sutaputra. He was a king not by birth, nor by worth. He would always be the sutaputra, the eternal pariah. And yet, she, Uruvi, the pampered Princess of Pukeya, loved this man most people treated with such scorn. It was easy to fall in love with Karna, Uruvi decided, but it was difficult convincing others about its judiciousness. She wished to wed him one day and if she dared to consider marrying him, she wondered what she was going to do about it. Or rather, how she was going to go about it. For one, how was she to get the discredited King of Anga invited to attend her swayamwara with the respect he deserved?

2

Her Father's Daughter

For the Princess of Pukeya, her father was her world. Though a kshatriya, King Vahusha was an eminent scholar as well, and in her quest to be like him, Uruvi found herself trying to learn mathematics and astronomy, the subjects her father excelled at. And it broke her heart and made her temper flare when she could not succeed. 'Why can't I get it?' she would weep in furious exasperation.

'Because you may be better at other things,' her mother often gently told her, wiping the angry tears from her glistening cheeks. 'Why do you insist on being like your father?'

Eventually, she had to accept that she could not be like him. She tried to be perfect in whatever she was good at, which was music and art. She was a natural artist, her strokes as well-defined as her sense of colour. Her love for nature blossomed and took her beyond the aesthetics of tints, shades and fragrance, leading into a scientific interest in plants and flora. She also grew to be an excellent horse-rider. Soon, she found herself going to the small gurukul (school) of Rishi Bagola, who opened a new, exciting world to her—that of Ayurveda and healing. She assisted him diligently in his work and learnt to listen carefully to absorb what he taught. While girls of her age were groomed to become dainty princesses, Princess Uruvi saddled her horse each morning to ride to the gurukul where she spent the day immersed in the world of medicinal herbs and other remedies.

Much to his disbelief, the rishi discovered that the child had a singular, unusual gift—that of healing. It was not just the sandalwood and herbal pastes that worked wonders on the soles of tired feet or on pulsating temples pounding with headaches. It was the cool, soft touch of her hand that worked marvels. Her fingers wove a relaxing spell as they rubbed into sickly skin and aching bones.

'Don't fret, O King, it's not a passing amusement for her,' the wise sage placated the worried father. 'She has a unique ability that even she is unaware of. Don't stop her from pursuing what she loves doing. It's her passion and it'll be her life's work one day.'

And soon King Vahusha found his daughter entering decrepit tents near scarred battlefields, nursing the torn limbs and bloodied bodies of wounded soldiers. With a tender smile and a caring touch, the princess would be busy assisting the other nurses to tend to the injured and the dying.

'Is this the fruit of war?' she once asked her father disconsolately. 'How can you feel so triumphant when you have hurt and killed so many? How can you gloat about your victory while trampling on other people's lives? What is it—insatiability, egotism, or self-importance—that goads you to go to war?' It was one of the few issues they furiously disagreed upon, and each time the father knew that his daughter, with her acute intellectual ability, had won the argument but lost the cause she was hopelessly fighting for. She loathed war and warlords and her father suspected that there were moments she hated being a kshatriya princess too.

Needing her father's approval just as a parched shrub thirsts for rain, Princess Uruvi did not forget even for a moment that she should never fail her father.

'If you push yourself so hard to please him, you'll topple over one day!' her mother frequently warned her with growing concern.

And now perhaps, that moment had arrived. Princes Uruvi knew she could not please her father this time, that she would fail him somehow. In her attempt to get her beloved as her husband, would she herself fall, bringing down with her the people she loved and the wonderful world she had lived in so long? Uruvi was full of despair at the thought of the hurt she would cause her family because she wanted Karna—yet, being Karna's wife was now her only aspiration, the only aim that gave meaning to her life.

As soon as he entered his daughter's room, the King of Pukeya sensed the tension. His otherwise vivacious daughter cut a still figure leaning against the carved column, espaliered with fragrant jasmine vines. Her effervescence seemed to have dried up. He watched her as she looked out unseeingly, the expression in her eyes reminiscent of that look of piteous pain when he used to leave for battle. He was uncomfortable with her silence. She seemed to have turned inwards, and the father in him was deeply moved.

'Is the idea of marriage so revolting—or is it that you are in love?' he gently asked.

Uruvi repressed her surprise at his perspicacity. 'How did you know?'

'Because a girl whose wedding is so near and is seen unhappily moping around could only mean that she is in love, my dear,' he reasoned. 'And because I can read you well enough by now. Who's the lucky fellow?' he asked heartily, hoping to lighten the strain.

She remained unusually quiet. Uruvi's silence gave King Vahusha an uneasy hint of a gathering storm, of the squall threatening to deluge them. 'If you don't tell me what's wrong, how can we solve your problem together?' he remarked, using his pet line of persuasion whenever his little girl turned rebelliously sullen. This time, however, she remained unmoved and silent, her fists clenched tight.

'I am waiting,' he said cautiously, instinctively crossing his arms as if to protect himself from what was to come.

'I want to marry Karna.'

There, she had said it finally; she heaved a sigh, her words wrenched out in a hoarse undertone. As he looked at his daughter with rising disbelief, King Vahusha's world hurtled down on him. Shock stunned him into brief silence. He wanted to shout at her in fury, in frustration, in despair, but could summon only a feeble 'No!' It was a cry of anguish, his eyes burning, his wan face paler still with the dawning comprehension of what his daughter's decision implied and the events it would set in motion. 'Do you realize the consequences?' he muttered in utter desperation. 'Not for me, nor your mother, but for yourself. If you marry him, you will marry doom!'

'I know,' she said quietly, looking at him with gentle equanimity. 'I know I love a man the world hates. I know I am hurting you and that I am asking far too much. And I know it's all so hopeless. But I needed to tell you the truth. Father, I could never marry a person you do not approve of. But it's also true that I cannot garland just any man at my swayamwara. For me, it is either Karna or no one. If I can't have him, I would rather stay unmarried.'

'Unmarried!' her father scoffed in sudden anger. 'You know that can never happen in the world we live in. Are you threatening me, child? Society will not permit me to keep you unmarried, nor will it allow you to marry a charioteer's son. You can't marry a half-caste. You wouldn't be as crazy as that. You are a kshatriya girl—you *cannot* marry a sutaputra!' he raised his voice and regretted his words the moment he uttered them. He realized with a sinking heart that his furious words would only impel his defiant daughter to become more rebellious.

'I will, I shall,' she said firmly. 'Am I doing anything dishonourable, Father? I am in love with a good man, who is honest and brave. I want to marry him. I am asking for your permission and want your blessings to do so. What am I doing wrong? Am I not allowed to choose the person whom I love?'

'But not the wrong man,' he argued.

'No, not the wrong man, the *wronged* man,' she corrected him immediately. 'A good man trapped in a bad situation.'

'You seem to know all about him, but what do you actually know of him?' countered the father. 'Agreed, he may be a fine young man, but does it make the circumstances any better? Or do you see yourself as the great leveller who is performing the noble deed of uplifting him from his humble background?' King Vahusha looked at her with a steadfast gaze. 'Face reality, my child. Do you think you will upgrade his status by marrying him? No, you will only worsen yours. You know how it goes in our society. Anuloma or the practice of marrying men of a higher caste is legitimate. But you are well aware that the reverse practice of pratiloma, that of marrying a man of a lower caste, is prohibited by the shastras. Karna is a sutaputra—the son of a suta—one who is born of a brahmin woman and a kshatriya father. The sutas traditionally served the kings and functioned as their rathakaras, their charioteers. There have been suta advisors to the kings, suta confidants of the king, but none of them have been treated as friends of the king or their equals. They weren't even provided with living quarters on the palace grounds. Not only did they endure such humiliation all their lives, so did their family and descendants. Have you ever heard of any suta being offered a brahmin or a kshatriya bride? That was the reason why the Princess of Panchala, Draupadi, rejected Karna at her swayamwara— for being a sutaputra, which makes him low in the social hierarchy. Duryodhana treats Karna as his closest friend—he has given him respect and identity, a royal recognition by crowning him a king. But has he offered him a kshatriya princess in marriage? He may be a good friend, but Karna can never be his kinsman. Please, child, don't do this—it will be no life for a kshatriya princess. It's a living death! Oh, Uruvi, forget him!'

He looked at his daughter's rebellious face, knowing his words were falling on deaf ears, but continued to persuade her to see reason. 'There are four examples of bad men these days, the dushta chathushtayam,' he said. 'One is Shakuni, Duryodhana's maternal uncle. The second is Duryodhana himself. The third is the malicious Dushasana. And the fourth, sadly, is Karna.'

Uruvi winced, but her lips tightened in a stubborn line. Since her childhood days she had heard of the evil uncle, Shakuni, poisoning the ears of his nephews, Duryodhana and Dushasana, against their cousins, the Pandavas. Rumours were rife that the trio had poisoned young Bhima once and tried to drown him. He had been saved in the nick of time. The latest attempt on the lives of the Pandavas and their mother was when their palace at Varnavat was gutted by an unexpected fire, charring six of its residents in a grotesque death. The scheming uncle and his two nephews were suspected of this crime as well, for the palace was later found to be made of lac, an easily combustible material, and the actual plan was evidently to burn the five Pandavas along with their mother, Kunti. Fortunately, the Pandavas, suspecting their cousins of their evil design, had already got a tunnel constructed under the lac palace and escaped through it. They lived incognito as poor brahmins for several years, hiding from the spies of Shakuni and Duryodhana. It was during their fugitive days that Arjuna, dressed as a brahmin, had won over Draupadi as his bride at her swayamwara. Strengthened by the political power of the King of Panchala, the Pandavas had eventually disclosed their identity and returned to Hastinapur with their wife, Draupadi, who was wedded to all the brothers because their mother had so decreed. Forcing a truce between the cousins by a deceptively fair solution by the elders, Hastinapur was divided between the Kauravas and the Pandavas, who were given the arid part of Hastinapur. With great effort and fortitude, they managed to convert this barren land into a beautiful city, which they called Indraprastha. In all these vile intrigues against the Pandavas, Karna was rumoured to have assisted his close friend, Duryodhana. But Princess Uruvi could never believe this to be true.

Her father voiced the same nasty misgiving. 'Out of his misguided attachment—his dhura-abhimanam—to Duryodhana, Karna too joined this triumvirate of evil,' he said, the warning in his voice unmistakable. 'Gratitude is a fine quality but in Karna, it is misplaced. By associating himself with evil, he will also get corrupted slowly but surely. All his good qualities will come to nothing. His great valour, his intelligence, his generosity, his fortitude, are tainted by this one single flaw—his blind support to the wicked. That is what I am trying to protect you from. Choose anyone but him, child.'

'I can't! What do I do?' she pleaded as she looked helplessly at him. 'I love him and I cannot bear to marry someone else! Could

I, in all fairness, wed a man approved of by everyone when I am in love with another? No, Father, you have taught me to be honest and I am trying to be just that now. Or, the other way out is to call off the swayamwara and I shall never think of marriage ever. Father, I cannot marry a man without your consent, which means I need your heartfelt blessings too. I cannot have a swayamwara in which my father disapproves of the groom. Unless you say yes, I shall not go ahead. I wouldn't risk a repetition of what happened to Karna at Draupadi's swayamwara. He was publicly jeered at as a sutaputra, not just by the bride herself but the attending guests as well. If Karna is invited to my swayamvara, can you assure me that he will be received with dignity?'

'You know my answer,' he said evenly. 'You are not leaving me with much choice, are you?' he gave his daughter a quizzical look, knowing that she had ensnared him in a no-win crisis. 'If I say no, you are the long-suffering spinster—and that's not an option. And if I say yes, you will be going into a life of misery and humiliation. Can I give blessings to either option?'

'Yes, Father,' she looked up squarely at the tall, dejected figure standing by her side. 'You brought me up to be what I am today; to make me capable, to look after myself and be wise enough to distinguish between the good and the bad. You were the one who encouraged me to make my own decisions and to stick to them and be brave enough to accept my problem. You told me to look into the mirror each morning and be proud of myself, to do nothing that I would be ashamed of. I am not ashamed to have fallen in love with Karna. And if it's going to be a mistake, I think I have enough courage in me to tackle the worst moments as and when I come across them one day,' she said quietly. 'Father, you taught me to honour and love the brave and good and I want to marry such a man. I want you to approve of him because I know I can never be happy knowing that I have hurt you. One cannot be happy at the expense of others' unhappiness, especially if they are those you love dearly. Father, I want your approval and your blessings and I want you to honour

Karna as you would any good human being.'

King Vahusha saw that he was losing the battle with his daughter. Yet he persisted. 'Karna is gifted, generous and righteous and the bravest of all warriors, but his loyalty to Duryodhana will bring about his downfall,' warned King Vahusha, the king in him dominating his paternal instinct for once. 'Karna may have all the sterling qualities a woman searches for, but they are nullified by the fact that he prefers to befriend evil. No one in the royal palace of Hastinapur has a good opinion of Karna. Duryodhana's mother, Queen Gandhari, resents her son's friendship with a lowly charioteer's son. Bhishma Pitamaha does not approve of Karna because of his arrogance. Nor does Dronacharya, who believes he is an upstart. For them, Karna is the bad influence on Duryodhana. What is Duryodhana without Karna? The Kaurava prince is simply riding on the ability and achievements of Karna. Duryodhana knows he cannot win any battle without Karna—if Duryodhana did not have Karna by his side, he would be too weak to face the Pandavas. You'll be alienating all these people whom you love and who love you dearly. You will be caught in a vortex and no one will be able to save you. Child, the Hastinapur court is a cesspool of deceit and intrigue. And by marrying Karna, you shall become a pawn in it as well. Forget him. There's a wonderful world awaiting you without him...'

'I will give myself to him,' she spoke with such simplicity, so much earnestness, that her self-surrender was touching, leaving her father overwhelmed. Eventually, he had to bow to her wishes.

Uruvi unhesitatingly turned away from the world her parents wished her to live in. When her mother got to know of her decision, she tried desperately to change her daughter's mind. She even resorted to locking Uruvi in her room and refused to talk to her disobedient daughter till she saw sense and listened to her parents' counsel. Days turned into weeks, and the doors of Uruvi's room remained as firmly locked as her resolution to marry Karna. Uruvi defiantly repeated that she loved Karna, even though he probably did not even know of her existence. This riled her mother even more. But she could not sway the princess, determined as she was to marry only the King of Anga at her swayamwara. The queen was too scared to call a family council, lest her daughter's adamant stand lead to a scandal. Even her closest friend, Kunti, was kept away from this family secret.

'How do we make her see reason?' Queen Shubra cried to her husband in exasperated fury. 'She is infatuated with him and what is the basis of her feelings? Only hearsay. She has not even met him to know what kind of person he really is! We have to free her from him by breaking the spell she is under. We have to pull her away from him.'

'We can't,' King Vahusha said, shrugging resignedly. 'We can't stop her thinking about him. We can't stop her from loving him. We can't do anything! She knows what she wants—and she knows exactly how to face the storm she has dared to churn up.'

'But she has to behave according to her status,' answered Queen Shubra heatedly. 'She has to realize her responsibility as a daughter and save herself from disgrace!' she wept bitterly.

'Speak as a mother, Queen Shubra,' the king placed his hands on his wife's shoulders. 'Is it easier to live an honourable life by murdering your daughter's happiness in the name of "honour" and family pride? Or is it easier to accept your child's decision, even if it's contrary to your wishes? Let's stop being so slavish to customs and think this over. It would be braver of us to live as the in-laws of the "dishonourable" Karna than be the honourable parents of an unwed daughter whose life has been forever blighted.'

The distraught mother tightened her lips, a gnawing ache choking her angry retort. Queen Shubra decided she needed to talk to her daughter again.

This time she entered her daughter's room with less antagonism, and she said more gently, 'I am so bewildered, I really don't know what to say,' Queen Shubra started, her voice inflected with a genuine distress. 'I came here again because I think your decision is drastically wrong. I wanted you to marry Arjuna as he is the best man any woman can have. Furthermore, I was comforted with the thought that you will be with Kunti. She's always been like a mother to you.

Everything was so perfect and you couldn't have had it better, my child. I admit I am disappointed. I hoped you would do great things...'

'By marrying Arjuna, you mean,' Uruvi lashed out, still clearly resentful. 'Mother, I do not love him and I will not marry him just because you and everybody else find it so appropriate!'

'It is for your own good,' her mother's passionate plea acquired an imploring tone. 'I can't watch you wasting your beauty, youth, talent and opportunities in this lamentable manner. Being Karna's wife won't be easy. He is not like us. He is not one of us. He is an outsider.'

'Don't be sad for me, Mother,' said Uruvi. 'I haven't failed, I have succeeded. You cannot imagine how I am looking forward to my new life. I shall live in the home of the man I love, looking after him and his family. There will be enough strength in me to be his wife and I shall be proud of that. I shall have him, I shall have his children. I shall have my work, my painting and my other pursuits. I shall live my life simply. When I am an old woman, I shall look back on a happy, peaceful life which I dared to choose and live the way I wanted to. What will I gain if I marry a man I don't love and lose my soul? With Karna, I will gain my life, my soul. I love him. I love him for what he is. I love him for what he will be.'

Further words were futile, Queen Shubra conceded. There had been far too much disagreement with her daughter and she didn't want to lose her forever. At last, her wounded silence and the father's gracious acceptance of his daughter's decision made way for Princess Uruvi's swayamwara to be held on the fifth auspicious day of marghashirsha that year. An invitation was sent to the King of Anga, just as it was sent to many others.

The King of Anga received the invitation with surprise. He was not the least impressed, either with the elaborate gold-embossed, graciously worded invitation to the swayamwara of Princess Uruvi of Pukeya. She did not interest him; she intrigued him. He was curious to meet the beautiful princess who, as everyone knew, would choose his arch-rival Arjuna at her swayamwara. Just like Draupadi once had.

3

The Swayamwara

The first rays of the early morning sun shimmered through the windows, over which a graceful tree cast its shadow. An immense creeper had draped around the filigreed balcony of Princess Uruvi's bedroom, making her feel as if she was living in a treehouse as she basked in the freshness of early dawn, the golden sky auspiciously cloudless. 'A promising way to start my wedding day,' she thought, with a sudden burst of happiness.

She had slept with the buzz of festivities humming around her and was roused with the droning still in her ears. She woke up to a delightful sight. The palace resembled a floral palanquin. Flaming marigolds and crimson hibiscus with fragrant jasmine flowers, strung together into thick garlands, festooned each cornice and corridor of the palace. The perfume of the threaded flowers merged with the fresh scent of the dew-moistened earth. She heard the soft twitter of birds, the rustle of the gentle breeze in the garden. Finally, she saw the crimson light signalling the birth of a new day, and stepped inside for her bridal bath. Kunti was waiting for her, holding a silver bowl of sandalwood paste.

Kunti looked extraordinarily happy. Uruvi would now be her daughter for keeps and in a short while would make her home in the new palace in Indraprastha. For a moment, a frown darkened her brows as she wondered anxiously how her daughter-in-law Draupadi would welcome her husband Arjuna's new bride. 'I got the bridal silks especially made for you,' she said instead, trying to erase the uneasy thought. 'It's a deep turmeric yellow—I know you love that colour, and you can wrap a red angavastra around,' she said as she clasped an exquisite ruby ornament around Uruvi's slender neck.

Uruvi was almost ill with the guilt swamping her. I can't deceive Kunti, she thought frantically. I have to tell her that, contrary to her expectations, I won't be choosing any of the Pandavas as my husband. Uruvi looked at Kunti and her heart swelled with emotion. She loved her so much but was about to hurt her so grievously. This was the woman whom she knew to be unbelievably patient, gentle and kind... and so giving. She thought she was a splendid example of a mother who had lived not for herself but for others. Suddenly, Uruvi asked her, 'When you look back on your life, do you have any regrets, Ma?'.

Kunti was visibly surprised. 'What a strange question! Is it a fit of bridal nervousness?' she asked, her eyes twinkling. 'And what's this about regrets? You're not having any qualms about this swayamwara, are you?' she added anxiously.

'No. No, I am not,' Uruvi replied firmly. 'I have been looking forward to this day for a long, long time. It's just that I felt like opening up to you. We haven't spoken for ages, and possibly, this will be our very last heart-to-heart talk before I get married,' she said under her breath. 'So, do you ever wish you had done anything differently?' repeated Uruvi, looking into Kunti's serene face.

'Yes, I wish I hadn't done some things! Hmmm, quite a few,' Kunti's voice trailed off, her tired eyes gazing at the rising sun. She slipped into a moment of wistful contemplation. Both the women settled into a companionable silence, not wanting to interrupt each others' thoughts. 'But let's keep all that for another day!' said Kunti, with her usual gentle smile.

'Whenever I look at you, I get the feeling you conceal your real self,' Uruvi revealed, sliding a jewelled hand in Kunti's soft, wrinkled one. 'It's like you are playing a role, living up to an image. You are what the person in front of you wants you to be. What are you really like? How could you accept it when King Sura, your father, gave you away to Kuntibhoja, his cousin, because he was childless? I would have been furious—how dare he!'

'Oh, dear, so many questions!' the older lady laughed lightly. 'Yes,

I was upset—I felt I was a doll being presented to another person. As Pritha, the daughter of King Sura of the Yadavas, I was given away to King Kuntibhoja to be brought up in his home as Kunti. I grew up without a mother but with many maids and nannies. It was fun sometimes!' she chuckled wryly. It was as if she was talking about someone else.

Uruvi looked at her closely and said affectionately, 'And that's how it has always been—you seemed to have everything, yet there was an emptiness in you. Ma, when will you learn to live for yourself?' Uruvi tried to voice Kunti's unspoken thoughts. 'You have played so many roles all your life. As the little Pritha who was given away by her father, you were made to renounce your name to become Kuntibhoja's daughter, Kunti! Kunti, the lovely princess, whom many princes wished to marry but who selected King Pandu at her swayamwara— only to lose him to his second wife, Princess Madri. Kunti, a wife who loved her husband so much that she let the childless Madri use the same boon she had been given by Sage Durvasa to invoke the divine twins, the Ashwini Kumaras, and give birth to Nakul and Sahadeva. Kunti, who would have preferred to have died with her husband, but lived to be a mother, not just to her sons but to the infant sons of Madri as well. Kunti, the queen who, in an instant, became a king's widow without a kingdom. Kunti, the queen mother, who lived for years in dread, worried about the safety of her five sons. Kunti, the queen mother, yet overshadowed by Draupadi, the daughter-in-law. You are that amazing mother who has always loved me as a daughter. A woman who has an enormous capacity to love and to give, but what have *you* earned in the bargain…?' Uruvi stopped as remorse sliced through her. She thought sadly, 'And like others, I too, will hurt you.'

'Stop dissecting me and tell me what the matter is. Why all these questions, dear? What's troubling you?'

The moment of truth was at hand. Uruvi knew she owed it to Kunti. She blurted out in wretched helplessness, 'I cannot marry Arjuna…I am in love with Karna.' She hated herself as she watched the colour drain from the elderly queen's face.

'No!' Kunti gasped in disbelief, a look of incredulity on her pallid face. 'No, oh, no! Not Karna!'

Uruvi knew she had hurt the person whom she loved the most after her parents. She tried desperately to stem the flow of pain her confession had inflicted on Kunti. 'I grew up with your sons. They are more like my childhood friends. And I do love them. I know you were hoping that I would marry Arjuna but I can't, I can't!' Uruvi realized it was futile giving explanations or self-justifications. 'I am sorry. So very sorry!' she cried, hugging Kunti close. The queen mother suddenly looked old and frail.

For a long time, Uruvi and Kunti held each other close. Then the older woman disengaged Uruvi's clinging arms and looked straight into her troubled face. 'Do you realize what you are doing?' she asked gently. 'Forget that I want you as my daughter-in-law. Try to foresee what this marriage may lead to. Karna is already married, with children. His other wife is a suta, of his caste, but you are not. You will be the outsider in their home. Can you ever live happily with him and his family? You don't even know what life is like away from these palace walls, and you are willing to give up everything to be just another woman in Karna's life, competing for his attention. Will you be able to deal with the problems such a marriage will bring?'

'I must if I have to,' Uruvi's eyes flashed with a familiar determined glint. 'I know I will be happy with him and I will make him happy,' she vowed.

Kunti stared at her for a long, wistful moment. 'Is that all? That you want to make him happy?' she whispered with a catch in her voice, looking searchingly at her.

'Yes!' cried Uruvi. 'And I am not ashamed of falling in love with Karna. Nor am I ashamed of what I am going to do,' she added slowly. 'My feelings for Karna struck me suddenly, leaving me defenceless. He probably doesn't even know I exist, he doesn't know that there is this crazy girl who is madly in love with him. My world turned upside down the moment I saw him at Hastinapur that evening at the arena...'

She heard Kunti draw in her breath sharply. 'You remember that day, Ma?' Uruvi turned excitedly to the older lady, her face elated. 'It was the most unforgettable day of my life!'

'I don't know why I care so much for him…but I do, very much!' Uruvi continued, her face flushed as she thought of the man who had unknowingly captured her thoughts, her life. 'I love him. I want him. I'll do anything to have him and I'll make him care for me! I'd even die for him…there, Ma, now you know!'

Kunti gave her a long, lingering look. 'You are so tempestuous, child,' she said finally. 'Who would believe that you just uttered those words? There's not an ounce of sentimentality in you—you have always been so down to earth…and there you go and fall in love! Now you are at once practical and passionate—not willing to let go of the chance you have to get what you want. I know you are capable of giving love. Most people can't…' she heaved a long sigh. 'If that is how you feel, both of you have all my love and my blessings. Never fear, child, I am with you,' Kunti tenderly kissed the bride's forehead, her tears falling fast and thick. 'May God give you the strength to lead the life you have chosen…the strength I lacked,' she muttered under her breath. Uruvi couldn't quite catch her words and frowned.

'Wipe that frown off, dear, you have a new life awaiting you!' Kunti smiled.

Uruvi was relieved that Kunti did not look miserable any more. In fact, Kunti's smile was one of happiness.

⸎

The city of Pukeya turned festive as the people prepared to witness the opulence of a royal wedding. The glorious carousing rang out for fourteen celebratory days, the sound of drumbeats loud and clear. Colourful fairs, full of entertaining games and shows, had been arranged and there were gifts for everyone. The princes and suitors were as nervous as the giggling maids-in-waiting, walking briskly through the marbled hallways of the new guest-houses handsomely designed to accommodate the swayamwara guests.

The marriage hall was as imposing as the enchanting gardens encircling it. Its walls were covered with wild rose creepers, covering every inch in scented luxuriance. Against the rising palms and the vivid flame-of-the-forest trees, the lotus-shaped marriage hall bloomed, beautifully decorated with marigolds, roses, hibiscus and Princess Uruvi's favourite wreaths of fragrant jasmines. 'This is going to be the best day of my life,' King Vahusha promised himself as he donned his royal robes, knowing it was probably his saddest day as well.

Princess Uruvi's swayamwara was well-attended with many brave kings, princes and noblemen of the country seated under the golden dome of the marriage hall. The hundred sons of Dhritrashtra were in attendance, as well as the five Pandava princes. Krishna was there with his elder brother Balarama, as were Dhrishtadyumna, King Drupad's son, Karna with his friend Ashwatthama (the son of Guru Dronacharya), Sisupala, the King of Chedi, and Jarasandha, the King of Magadha. The venerated triumvirate of the Hastinapur royal court, Bhishma Pitamaha, Guru Dronacharya and his brother-in-law, Guru Kripacharya, the chief priest, were present to bestow blessings on the couple, their dear princess who would surely choose everyone's favourite, Prince Arjuna. Besides the suitors and royalty, the hall was packed with eager spectators from all over the kingdom. And above the din of voices, the festive drums beat rhythmically in accompaniment to the notes of a hundred musical instruments.

Karna wondered what he was doing in this resplendent hall, crowded with the bravest and noblest of kings. He wanted to be far away from this madness. This swayamwara was a travesty, he thought wryly, the outcome of which was known to all—Princess Uruvi of Pukeya would choose Prince Arjuna as everyone had guessed, and they would live happily ever after. Karna heaved a long sigh, trying to shut out a memory that was wrenching his soul...Draupadi's swayamwara.

The marriage hall at Panchala had been as lavishly decorated as this one, he recalled, staring at the swaying garlands of marigolds.

And when, eventually, the Princess of Panchala had arrived in splendour, she had looked ravishing. Princess Draupadi had voiced a single condition for her swayamwara—she would only wed the best archer, the prince who could shoot his arrow on target to pierce the eye of a rotating wooden fish. He could aim only by looking at its reflection in a bowl of water, not directly at it. Each suitor would have one single chance to do this. Evidently, only the best archer could succeed, and Karna had felt a smug confidence at the time. This meant it would be either him or Arjuna. To win the hand of the beautiful princess would mean winning great prestige as well, Karna thought with a smile, as he had slowly walked up to the centre of the hall. He held the bow, lifted it easily and was about to string it when a sharp voice commanded him to stop. He turned. It was Princess Draupadi speaking to him, loudly and haughtily. 'Wait!' she ordered. 'You may be a king now, O King of Anga, but you are not of royal birth. I am a king's daughter and will not wed a base-born man. As Draupadi, the yajnaseni, the one born out of fire, I insist on being declared a veeryashulka, a bride to be won by the worthiest and the very best. I will not allow a low-born sutaputra to participate in the challenge. Please do not proceed.'

The entire assembly was shocked into silence. Stunned at her cruel words, Karna had flung the bow down and turned away with the words, 'O sun! Be my witness that I cast aside the bow, not because I am unable to hit the mark, but because the princess mocks me.'

Karna could still feel the agony of that moment. The humiliation still seared his pride, setting him aflame with anger. The memory remained a raw lesion that festered. It was not the first time that Karna had been taunted about his birth, yet Draupadi's words wounded him as nothing else had ever done. It stung him even now. Suddenly, the ringing tone of trumpets sounded and Karna was thrust into the present once more.

A grand procession of the princely guests from Srnjaya, Kamboja, Kuru, Kosala and many other kingdoms—with their different flags and gorgeously decorated elephants, chariots and horses, their soldiers in glittering uniforms—passed by slowly, with King Vahusha in the forefront. It was time for the princess to arrive for the ceremony and all her suitors took their seats, waiting eagerly. When at last, the princess dismounted from her elephant, conch shells, bugles, mrdangas and kettledrums blared. The ankle bells of dancing girls tinkled merrily to the music of vinas, flutes, gongs and cymbals, all rising to a crescendo.

Princess Uruvi entered the hall and for one electric moment, there was an awed hush. King Vahusha knew that no one could keep their eyes off her exquisite beauty, now enhanced by the bridal finery she wore. Confident and self-assured, Arjuna gazed at the princess he thought was his future bride, while Krishna looked pensive and Duryodhana leered. The observant Ashwatthama noticed that his friend Karna was mesmerized by the princess standing quietly, with her head elegantly bowed—he didn't seem as uninterested as he had pretended to be a few moments back, he thought. God forbid that this swayamwara erupts in violence like Draupadi's swayamwara, he shuddered involuntarily. If Karna was spurned by this haughty princess as well, Ashwatthama knew his friend wouldn't be able to take such an insult. Fearing a repeat of the previous fiasco, Ashwatthama's hand instinctively clenched his sword as he fervently wished he could whisk Karna away.

The bride looked ethereal, her face radiant like her flowing silks. Her dark eyes sparkled as brilliantly as the glittering jewels adorning her. With a magnificent garland in her bejewelled hands, her eyes downcast, she did not look up at the valiant princes in front of her. The priests solemnly chanted mantras invoking peace and blessings as King Vahusha led his most prized possession by the hand to the centre of the suddenly quiet hall.

'Hear all, O princes seated in this assembly,' he pronounced in a loud, clear voice. 'This is but an ordinary swayamwara of an extraordinary princess. There are no tests of valour, of bravery or skills. It is but the honest desire of the princess to garland a young man present here whom she wishes to marry. That man has won my daughter's heart and shall win her hand in marriage. Her decision will be undisputed and fulfilled with my blessings.' He turned to Uruvi and said firmly, 'Proceed, my child. May God bless you.'

Standing with her hands clasping the garland, Uruvi felt acutely vulnerable as she felt hundreds of eyes boring into her, observing her slightest movement. The princes were seated in a semi-circle. On her right, sat the Pandavas with Krishna; to her extreme left was Karna, seated between Duryodhana and Ashwatthama. She wondered how she could approach the man she wanted to garland. She could either head straight for Karna or walk the entire semicircle to garland him. Either way, she would be humiliating the Pandavas. She faltered as she took her first steps, feeling a moment's panic, her heart thudding hard. And in that moment it flashed upon her that she would indeed have to be brave to get Karna. For to have him, she would deeply wound many whose affection she cherished—her parents, Krishna, Bhishma Pitamaha and above all, Kunti, to whom she had divulged her heart's secret. She was burdened with guilt and pain instead of the joy she had anticipated feeling. She hung her head, a stab of self-deprecation knifing through her. Could she ever be happy by making those whom she loved most, so unhappy? She despaired, wondering why she had to lose so much to gain what she desired the most.

Now, she wanted to end this misery quickly. She found herself moving in Karna's direction and felt his eyes piercing hard at her as though into her very soul. Her feet seemed to have a will of their own, gliding towards the golden-armoured warrior. She lifted her head to look at him and her eyes remained riveted on him as she approached him, her steps slow but sure. As she walked towards him, he seemed to draw tantalisingly close and she could see the gold flecks in his tawny eyes. He had beautiful sunset—or were they sunrise—eyes. They were a molten gold, blazing with inner fire. Dark and brooding, they were shaded with long, thick lashes under well-marked eyebrows, while below them was an aquiline nose and a full mouth. She had not noticed all this before…oh, he was beautiful! There was a refinement and a strange spiritual quality in his face that was almost poignant. Surprise dawned in his eyes the moment she paused in front of him, proud and bold, but a quivering mass of nerves within. He sat still in his chair, looking at her with rising perplexity. The thick rose garland in her hand suddenly seemed incredibly heavy and her arms ached. She steeled herself, looked straight into his amazed eyes and leaned forward. She heard the sharp intake of his breath and saw him instinctively lower his beautiful head so that she could place the garland around his neck. Then, at last, he was hers!

A stunned hush enveloped the gathering; the silence was almost palpable. And the uproar that swiftly followed was riotous. Boiling rage and insults erupted from every corner.

'This is a public insult!' shouted Bhima, his disbelief curdling into a bitter wrath.

The assembly broke into pandemonium. 'A swayamwara means choosing a bridegroom from the same social class—a kshatriya bride cannot marry beneath her!' the princes raged.

'She has to choose one amongst us, a kshatriya,' Arjuna interjected pointedly.

'If she does not care to marry a prince, she should either remain a virgin or jump into a pyre.'

'It is vital that the social status of a woman is not lowered.'

'The princess cannot marry a man of a lower caste!' barked another incensed king. 'Pratiloma is prohibited by the shastras.'

'King Vahusha, how could you allow this outrage? How dare your daughter choose a sutaputra?'

'We cannot sanction this marriage—it's blasphemy!'

'And it's a sacrilege of the practice of swayamwara as well. We shall fight to protect it!'

A violent battle seemed about to erupt. In a quick movement, Karna pulled his sword out of its scabbard and held it up, the naked blade glinting in the noon sun. He was ready to take on the warring princes single-handedly. Duryodhana and Ashwatthama promptly unsheathed their swords too and stood by the side of their friend.

Duryodhana shouted menacingly, 'Not a drop of blood will go wasted!'

Arjuna and Bhima brandished their swords too, but were restrained by the warning hand of their mother, who shook her head in silent censure. 'It is her choice. Respect it,' she chided them softly.

Arjuna detected the reprimand in his mother's voice and wondered what he had done wrong. He knew that his mother was aware he had loved Uruvi with open devotion since she was a bratty little girl with wild, cascading hair and laughing eyes. As the besotted young boy, he was elated when his mother assured him that this teasing child would be his wife one day. Uruvi was meant to be his bride and he would fight for her as honour demanded. He felt a cold fury crystallise inside him and he swept a look of contemptuous dislike at Karna. 'Is that her choice? A lowly upstart, a pariah, an unwelcome outsider?' His voice was glacial.

'As Kunti rightly says, it is Uruvi who has selected her life partner and it's her choice,' Krishna's calm voice interrupted him. 'What she decides to do is going to determine her life. She has the freedom to choose whom she wants to marry. She chooses Karna—just as Draupadi selected you over Karna,' murmured Krishna.

Arjuna fumed. Was Krishna gently reminding him of Draupadi's swayamwara where the situation had been reversed? Then, it was he who had won Draupadi and Karna had been rebuffed. This time, it was he who had been set aside and Karna had won the fair bride. For an instant, Arjuna, drowning in the waves of humiliation and dishonour, recognised what Karna must have suffered when Draupadi had turned him down. Uruvi might not have been as maliciously explicit as Draupadi, but her unspoken rejection of Arjuna was just as devastating. Arjuna had never experienced rejection and wondered if he could live through this moment of utter shame. Mortification washed over him and icy rage froze in his veins. Uruvi could have spared him this public indignity, Arjuna swore, as he watched her stand close to Karna.

He felt another familiar emotion welling inside him. Arjuna recognised it as hatred, that single emotion he felt for this contemptible man, undiluted hate for this rival who was standing belligerently amidst the screaming crowd of angry princes. In the haze of hate, Arjuna did not see a noble warrior before him. He saw instead the charioteer's son who had, long ago, turned up uninvited and disrupted the contest at Hastinapur, performing better than him in each of his feats. This stranger was inflicting the same indignity on him now as well, snatching away what was rightfully his. Arjuna saw in him an insolent villain who had insinuated himself in the life of his cousin Duryodhana's, who, in turn, flaunted Karna's abilities in the royal court, annoying people like Guru Dronacharya and Bhishma Pitamaha, the two gurus revered by Arjuna. He saw him as an upstart suitor who had dared to think of marrying Draupadi. And now again, this usurper had dared to steal Uruvi—who was supposed to be *his* bride-to-be. Arjuna saw Karna as his sole enemy—an intruder who had marched brazenly into his life to mock him and divest him of his pride.

Arjuna recalled the moment he had first heard Karna's name— mentioned by Ashwatthama at Guru Dronacharya's ashram. Ashwatthama had described Karna as the best archer ever born. Even at that time, Arjuna had resented this unexpected praise. A few months later, that same wretched archer had publicly trounced him at the Hastinapur archery contest where Arjuna had been the favourite all along. This pariah had stolen his moment of glory. Then Arjuna's fury had swiftly turned into contempt when he learnt that Karna was but a lowly charioteer's son.

Jealousy had poisoned Arjuna. He burned with rage each time he caught sight of the sutaputra entering the royal court as the King of Anga, and resentment consumed him every time he was hailed as a master archer. He recoiled when people praised the friendship between his cousin and this commoner. Friend and cousin, both were despicable in his eyes; an enemy's friend was an enemy as well. But if he disliked his cousin, Arjuna loathed Karna violently, openly contemptuous of this low-born, self-proclaimed warrior. And right now, in the middle of the swayamwara hall, Arjuna felt the acrid taste of hate as he stood defeated this time too. He had lost, once again, to this man.

Feeling his eyes on her, Uruvi glanced at Arjuna, her childhood friend and the suitor she had publicly spurned. She sensed rather than saw the raw loathing in his eyes. She felt as if she'd been poisoned. She wrenched her eyes away from his venomous glare and turned to the scene unfolding before her. Uruvi appeared composed, but inside she was screaming at the world to let her be with her beloved. To just let them be. Although Karna's arm around her shoulders assured her of his protection, she was only too aware that her father and Kunti were right to warn her of the consequences of her action. Could she brave the terrible hostilities she had triggered?

She saw her father, Bhishma Pitamaha, Krishna and Balarama trying to mollify the infuriated princes. The Pandavas stood still, searing her with their collective anger. Kunti stood silently with them, her eyes appealing for peace.

'My daughter's decision is her own and I, as her father, stand by it completely,' King Vahusha declared loudly, his hands folded, his head bowed. 'She has selected Karna, the King of Anga, and he has won her hand in marriage. I appeal to everyone to respect the choice made at the swayamwara.'

But Duryodhana was not one to remain discreetly quiet. 'If a woman can get married to five husbands, can't a princess select a man of her choice as her husband?' he sneered, looking pointedly at the Pandavas. Others soon joined in the heckling. Arjuna drew out his sword, its sharp edge glinting in the sun. At this ominous moment, Krishna got up and asked the guests to hear him out. He said, 'King Vahusha invited all those he thought were deserving of the honour of winning his daughter's hand. And no one doubts Karna's valour and uprightness. This is a swayamwara and the bride-to-be has the final say. She has the right to reject any of the suitors for any reason; she has the right to choose whomever she wants. I am requesting all of you to let the wedding proceed.'

Though Krishna, the King of Dwarka, believed by many to be the avatar of Vishnu the Preserver, the supreme god, was not too well liked by some, he was unanimously feared.

'There have been instances of pratiloma marriages in the past, which had been resorted to in exceptional cases,' arbitrated Krishna, in a conciliatory tone. 'Emperor Yayati, one of the ancestors of the Pandavas and the Kauravas, married Devyani, the daughter of Sage Sukracharya, and this is only one example of a brahmin girl marrying a kshatriya prince. The shastras declare what is right and what is forbidden. They also say that once a marriage has been agreed upon in public, it cannot be annulled. Uruvi, by garlanding Karna, has chosen him as her husband—and I declare them married!'

His words worked their magic. Grudgingly, the suitors gave their consent for the marriage proceedings to continue. Uruvi flashed Krishna a grateful glance. He nodded his head elegantly. 'You were always a wilful child,' Krishna whispered as she bent down to touch his feet, bestowing her with his knowing smile and his blessings.

The marriage was celebrated with renewed aplomb and the city of Pukeya rejoiced with great fervour. It was decided that Princess Uruvi would accompany her husband, Karna, to his home early next morning, so the festivities continued late into the night, almost until the sun slowly lit up the sky to herald the beginning of her new life.

4

New Horizons: Karna and Uruvi

Standing at her balcony, Uruvi thought wistfully how this was the last night she would be spending in Pukeya, in the house where her first wakeful memories were centred. She stared at the darkening sky through the balustrade fringed with leaves, seeing moments of her childhood in a quick flashback. With a start she realized she had rarely cried in this house. The moments she recalled were full of innocent laughter and bliss—except those heart-wrenching times when her father had left for battle, which were often enough to snuff out her joy. Uruvi was suddenly swamped with a surge of sadness at the thought of parting from her home and her parents; yet, she was bursting with excitement at the thought of a new life with Karna, whom she had longed for so long.

At this moment, though, she sheepishly confessed to herself, she was nervous about coming face to face with the man she had seen vividly in her dreams almost every day. In her dreams he never spoke to her; now he would. Would he smile, would he laugh, would he touch her as she had wildly imagined? Or would he be cold and indifferent? And it was that look of uncertainty that Karna caught as he entered the bridal room. His new bride gazed at him, her mouth dry, overcome with a stifling shyness. He stood quietly, tall and distant.

They were two strangers meeting for the first time, yet they were bound together by marriage. She watched him approach her, his lips in a straight, almost stern line, his eyes dark and deep. She could not wrench her gaze off him, just as she hadn't been able to do during the swayamwara. She thirstily drank in the sight of him, parched with years of pining. It was his eyes—those twin spheres of molten gold that held a strange magnetism. From what she had seen of him, it was his eyes that flashed intermittently with either rage or resentment, or softened suddenly with unimaginable gentleness. But within them lay an unfathomable sadness that seemed to suffuse his being.

She felt him standing close to her, but not obtrusively so. It felt as if she had wished for this moment since eternity; she looked up at him through her veil, wishing that the moment would last forever, and her nervousness inexplicably vanished. But nothing prepared her for his blunt question.

'Why did you marry me?' he asked quietly, without preamble.

Famous first words, she thought wryly, and definitely not the most romantic either. 'Is this a game?' he rasped, a frown marring his handsome features. 'A new ploy? Or were you forced into this marriage?'

She wondered why he was so disturbed. She looked at him, her eyes gazing straight into his, undaunted and calm. 'I married you because I have loved you since the day I first saw you,' she replied with equanimity.

She had the small, irrational pleasure of seeing him look flabbergasted. 'But we have never met!' he breathed, barely managing to suppress his surprise.

'I fell in love with you even before I met you!' she confessed quietly.

'You can't have been in love with a dream!' he looked bewildered.

'At that day of the archery contest at Hastinapur, I decided I would marry no one else but you,' she said steadily, her eyes as unwavering as her voice. 'You seriously believe I was forced into marrying you after what happened at the swayamwara?' she countered with a dry laugh. 'On the contrary! What you witnessed at the marriage hall was just a small hint of what happened at home while convincing my parents. Frankly, they weren't too pleased with my choice either and certainly did not wish me to marry you,' she admitted candidly.

'*That* doesn't come as a surprise!' said Karna without resentment.

'I'm sure many people must have enlightened you by now about the fact that I am not exactly eligible!'

'I grew up loving you. I had decided to marry you a long time ago even though I know that I didn't even exist for you till now. And...'

'And yet you went ahead to marry me against all odds,' he quietly interrupted, '...against all that antagonism, opposition and disgrace.'

As he spelled out the words, the gravity of her deed hit him hard. It had struck him the moment she had started walking towards him, with the garland in her hands, at the swayamwara hall. He had wanted to get up and stop her then, had wanted to dissuade her, wanted to push her away, to make her flee from the terrible realities of his life. But he had been utterly mesmerized by the beauty of the moment, just as he was now.

Looking at the exquisitely lovely girl standing so close to him, he found himself helpless before her fragile beauty, a beauty infused with a fierce determination. He felt suddenly the attraction and magnetism of this girl. There was a tumultuous vitality in her, a forceful power. She was the kind of girl, he thought, a man could easily lose his head over. For the first time, he looked closely at the girl whom his rival, Arjuna, was supposed to marry. She was a picture of wistful charm. His inscrutable glance hovered hesitantly for a long moment over her soft lips, moved to her small, pointed chin, her tiny upturned nose, which accentuated her air of arrogance, to wander slowly over her petite figure draped demurely in bridal finery that could not sheath the seductive voluptuousness that lay beneath. His eyes travelled back up to her questioning, almost defiant face and their eyes locked in a lingering gaze.

But his doubt distracted him. He could not fathom why this princess had stooped to marry a social outcast like him. He persisted. 'Princess, you have decided to follow the hard path. I cannot promise you the life a royal princess deserves,' he began slowly. 'I am a wanderer myself, stuck in an eternal search. I am a vagabond who doesn't know where I am going. My past beckons my present, but I can see only a blurred future. All my life, I have been slighted as a person of low birth—and the stigma will rub off on you as well. Yet, I am not ashamed of who I am. I am proud to be Radheya, the sutaputra, the son of Adhiratha and Radha. As soon as my father found me, he held me close and took me home. From her selfless affection for me, my mother's breasts were filled with milk that very day. She has looked after me, loved me and tutored me. And I, too, will always regard them—Radha and Adhiratha—as my parents. I have been brought up in the suta tradition and have got married to a suta bride. I am a married man, happy with my wife Vrushali, the gentlest person ever. But you, you are a kshatriya princess. How will you be able to live with a sutaputra?'

'A sutaputra who was born to show valour and to achieve glory,' Uruvi corrected him gently, unfazed by his self-castigation. 'For me, that makes you enough of a kshatriya. You have attained fame and glory as a brave, formidable warrior. You are a good man, a generous, kind person. What more could I ask for? Honour is not in a name or status but what you carry in your heart.'

The princess argues well, Karna conceded with a reluctant amusement he did not dare reveal. 'You are kind, Princess, the world is not so generous,' he bowed. 'I have been reminded in more ways than one where I stand in society. I know it, I hate it, but I can't do anything about it,' he shrugged as if to brush off the burden of insults heaped upon him. 'And I don't want you to suffer the same humiliation because of me. You got a small dose of it today, but there'll be more to come, a more bitter medicine to swallow each time.'

'A medicine is supposed to cure,' she answered, her tone light. 'And if you have finished with my cross-examination, may I start with mine?' she looked up at him, a mischievous glint in her pretty eyes.

He tilted his head questioningly.

'Why did you come for my swayamwara?' she asked directly, unswerving in her stare. 'What game were *you* playing?' she mimicked him.

'A cat and mouse one—I wanted to see Arjuna's latest bride,' he admitted, a wicked gleam in his sunset eyes. 'But, seriously, I wanted to know who had dared to send me an invitation, knowing full well that I had stopped attending swayamwaras after what happened at Princess Draupadi's.' His voice hardened perceptibly. 'All my life I have endured taunts, insults and humiliation for being a sutaputra, but coming from a woman, a princess at her own swayamwara, was the most damning,' he said, the heat of suppressed anger burning through his voice. 'Draupadi proudly declared herself to be a bride to be won by the worthiest and the very best. I was neither, she reminded me. I was a low-born sutaputra who had dared to dream. She openly mocked me, saying that I could not be allowed to win her hand in marriage. I can never forget it—her words, her haughtiness, the people in the hall sniggering...I can never forget that hateful day. She was responsible for my son's death too,' he said, rage simmering in his voice. 'What I lost that day, besides my self-respect and self-worth, was also my son, Sudhama. He was killed in the scuffle after the swayamwara. And that haughty, heartless princess didn't turn a hair—she went off with her new husband Arjuna, without bothering to look back at the havoc she had wreaked. I will never forgive her nor myself for that,' he vowed, his eyes burning in fury.

Hearing him utter Draupadi's name, Uruvi's initial flash of jealousy was doused by a dawning comprehension—Karna loathed Draupadi. Her blatant rejection and her disparagement of Karna were like a raw nerve, reminding him painfully of the humiliation she had inflicted on him. Unrelenting in his festering hatred, was he the proud man scorned in love or was he the grieving father, inconsolable at his son's brutal death? Or, reflected Uruvi with a sinking feeling, were both emotions torturing him?

Karna's face was masked again in a brooding shroud, cocooning his cold, closed self. Uruvi wondered frantically how she could salvage the relaxed moment they had shared. 'I know what happened at Princess Draupadi's swayamwara,' she said evenly. 'But I invited you because you were the only one I wanted to marry. Had you not turned up, the swayamwara would have been called off and I wouldn't have married anyone else.' The finality of her words shocked him. He could not help being moved by her determination and love for him.

Watching the small, slight figure in front of him, Karna felt his rage subside. She was like a fountain of water, reviving him with the water of life and love. He felt a strange emotion, a surge of protective affection for this woman who had fought so desperately to get him. She had him, yes, she did, Karna thought with a sense of fond pride. He felt the first glow of her love and basked in it. He didn't want to ever see her hurt. He recalled the pain in her eyes when she had been insulted by the angry suitors at her own swayamwara. Anger flamed in his heart but a larger guilt tore him. It was because of him that she had to hear those terrible words. His conscience, always sensitive, was troubled. A pang seized him when he realized that their future would be an uneasy one; he would be responsible for many more bitter blows to her pride. He had experienced this humiliation himself and knew he still would, but from now on he would be dragging her along with him.

It was his turn to relieve the thickening tension between them. 'I would say I'm glad my curiosity got the better of me,' he confessed. 'When I received the wedding invitation from your esteemed father, I was naturally intrigued about why I was being invited to a swayamwara where everyone knew whom the bride was going to marry! I confess I was curious to see the bride. You were that perfect princess whom the perfect prince, Arjuna, was to marry. Instead, the iconic princess chose an interloper—it turned out to be a daring decision, which shocked everyone! And, dear princess, I was surprised too, amazed that you selected me over Arjuna.'

'Don't you think you are worth it?' she murmured, a smile in her whisper.

He dared not touch her. His bride looked so beguilingly beautiful. His eyes raked her body. She was small and slim but straight-backed, deep-bosomed and tiny-waisted, with flaring hips. His eyes caressed her dark hair, her oval face, her trembling lips. He could almost breathe in her fragrance. And then Uruvi saw his beautiful face melting into a small smile for the first time, like the sun coming out of the dark clouds, spreading light everywhere. His smile shone through the darkest pools in his sunset eyes, deep into her soul.

Although an upheaval had occurred in the lives of Uruvi and Karna, the palace of the King of Anga was still quiet. That late morning, when the news of Princess Uruvi's stormy swayamwara reached the palace, its tranquillity was rudely shattered, giving way to unaccustomed pandemonium.

The person to react most furiously to the news was Shona, Karna's younger brother. 'I am not against Karna bringing another bride home, but she's a kshatriya princess, a stranger, an outsider who will never be able to mingle with us. She is sure to disrupt the peace of this house. Worse, she may take him away from us,' he warned, voicing aloud his parents' rising trepidation.

The old parents, Radha and Adhiratha, looked visibly worried. Shatruntapa, or Shona as they fondly called him, disapproved of his brother's new marriage vehemently. Even Vrushali was unable to placate her angry brother-in-law. Her soft-spoken words made him more angry. 'As his wife, you are the one who is the most affected, yet you accept the situation so calmly!' raged Shona.

'If he is going to be happy, so be it,' she said evenly, smiling softly as she got ready to welcome the newly-wed couple who were on their way home. Shona glowered; it was characteristic of her to respond mildly. She would gladly suffer in silent despair, never allowing her emotions to show, even when matters concerned her so deeply. To Shona, her restraint showed her remarkable resilience.

It was in this atmosphere of doubt and distrust that Uruvi was given a traditional welcome as she entered the palace threshold, unaware of the hidden misgivings, but blissful that she was Karna's bride. They had driven for two long days from Pukeya, travelling along a road that ran by a river, flanked by thick trees. Now and then, she glimpsed the snaking river, smooth and blue. Her new home stood on a little hill, with a winding path leading to it. From a distance, she could see the sprawling sandstone palace, surrounded by a flower-filled garden. It was pretty, but was not as exquisite as her home in Pukeya.

The first person to welcome her to her new home was Vrushali, standing tall and elegant, holding a silver thali bearing incense, tiny bowls and other items used for the pooja, the customary prayers that would take place when the wedded couple entered the palace. Vrushali stooped over Uruvi, making the princess uneasily aware of being dwarfed. It was a sensation unfamiliar to Uruvi; she had always been cheekily confident about her diminutive size. It was her taller friends who eventually got uncomfortable, feeling like 'giants' next to her, as they often reminded her crossly.

Right now, Uruvi firmly overrode her momentary discomfiture. She straightened her back and looked squarely at the woman's calm face. But not for long. Uruvi found she could not hold Vrushali's serene gaze. She wondered if she could endure the scrutiny of the other woman as she performed the aarti, circling the silver pooja thali around her, the smoke of the flickering earthen lamp clouding the distance between them.

At last, Uruvi looked up to glance straight into her rival's liquid eyes, which were far-seeing and wise as if measuring the standards of others by her own scrupulous honesty. Uruvi felt like an intruder, trespassing on the happiness of the woman in front of her. She was emotionally prepared for the censure she thought would come from Karna's wife, or a cold silence expressing an unspoken displeasure in her conduct. But none came, and Uruvi felt her own defences melting away.

Behind her stood Karna's parents and a man who stood a little distance away, as if he did not want to be a participant in the ceremony. She wondered who he was. 'That's Shona, my younger brother!' she heard her husband whisper softly in her ear. The younger man frowned, mistaking the gesture as an open display of affection between the newly married couple.

Uruvi looked at the elderly couple who had nurtured Karna, the golden orphan, bundled in a basket afloat in the calm waters of the holy river Ganga. She felt a sudden surge of affection for them as she looked at them gratefully. Without these people, Karna wouldn't be at her side now. Both looked troubled but visibly happy to see Karna. Radha threw her arms around his neck and kissed him tenderly on his forehead. Adhiratha, radiantly happy, stroked his son's face with both his hands. 'You are back,' he smiled through his tears. He was a slightly built old man, exceedingly thin with a swarthy skin the colour of old ebony, his hair sparse, his tearful eyes full of hope and love.

Like most brides, Uruvi felt she was a guest in her new home, trespassing on unknown territory, amidst people she had just met but whom she did not know; with those whom she would learn to love, but not unconditionally as she did her parents. Stepping into her new home, she had stepped a rung higher into adulthood. Or, as some would remind her, a rung lower on the social scale, she thought wryly.

'Please feel welcome here, dear. I hope you will be comfortable,' said Radha, ushering her into her room, which Uruvi noticed was in the farthest east wing of the palace, at a considerable distance from Vrushali's room. Radha suddenly looked self-conscious. 'Please make yourself comfortable,' she repeated. 'We may not be able to give you what you are accustomed to...the luxury, the lavishness...we live a little differently,' she said contritely.

'You have given me Karna,' Uruvi's words were simple and sincere and Radha was struck by their raw earnestness.

'I heard there was chaos at the swayamwara when other suitors objected to your choice—you must have had a hard time...oh dear, I am handling this so badly,' Radha looked flustered. 'But don't worry, everything will be fine. You must love him very much to have taken this step, a decision difficult to make and, yes, somewhat unheard of!'

'Not terribly, I hope!' Uruvi and she laughed, the tinkling sound filling the room. Radha smiled back, relaxing a little.

'Radheya is special—I knew that the day my husband got him home from the holy river. He was such an enchanting baby, with a captivating smile and his ears adorned with earrings,' recalled Radha, her voice suffused with love. 'We were childless then...so when my husband found the baby, it was a wish come true. The whole incident was strange...the lost baby drifting along the river, the closed basket full of gold ornaments. The baby himself was so breathtakingly beautiful! Adhiratha says he resembled the morning sun, so bright and resplendent was he! He was covered with a golden sheath, like a warrior's armour. He was a wonder, a sight to behold! Adhiratha's joy knew no bounds, and he immediately got him home. He claimed the baby looked as if he was not only of royal blood, but of celestial birth. That's why he was sent to a childless couple like us. It is the gods that gifted him to us. After we adopted Radheya, good fortune came our way—we had children of our own soon. But Radheya is irreplaceable and we cannot live without him! His brothers love him unreservedly, especially Shona. For him, Radheya is God.'

'And so this child blessed with beauty, grace and splendour as well as God-given skills came to be known as Radheya, the son of Radha, and also as Vasusena and Vrisha,' added Uruvi, recalling the tales of bravery she had heard of her hero while she had longed for him.

Uruvi was momentarily overwhelmed with the intensity of Radha's emotions. His parents loved him completely, without restraint and reservation, and Vrushali worshipped him with an unwavering devotion. For the first time, Uruvi felt a sense of disquiet; a sliver of doubt pierced her mind as she wondered if her own love for him was as absolute as she thought it was. And more importantly, could he ever love her back, as completely and devotedly as he loved his parents, his brothers and his wife? Was her love magnanimous enough to accept the others' love for him as well? She would have to share him, not just with his parents and his brothers but his wife as well. She knew that sharing, as her parents had realized very early in her life, was not her strong point because as an only child, the love she gave and received was absolute, undivided and exclusive.

As she settled down in the palace, she seized any moments she could spend with her husband. When she heard his chariot wheels coming to a stop at the porch, a radiant smile lit up her face. Radha and Vrushali noticed this silent ritual and subtly saw to it that it was Uruvi Karna went up to meet first. Shona and Adhiratha often found the newly-weds talking quietly in the day, and did not hide their amusement at Karna's behaviour as an ardent husband.

Uruvi could spend hours chatting with her husband, although she did the talking and he did the listening. Her intelligent queries forced him to respond and he found himself discussing serious topics, which he seldom did with his mother and his wife. Uruvi was refreshingly different from all the other women he had known. As the days wore on, he became aware that what he already felt for her was not the sense of duty a husband reserves for his wife, nor just simple lust. He admired her. Mixed with her vivacity was an inner calmness, a composure, a serenity that relaxed him. He found himself talking to her freely about matters he usually kept to himself—his political affairs, his passion for archery, his boredom with the rich society that he at once despised and yet used to promote himself like a hungry scavenger. It was not mere knowledge, but her ability to comprehend even nuances with a quick, deep perceptiveness.

Barely a week after her stormy swayamwara, Karna admitted to himself that he was dangerously drawn to his new bride. There are very fine shades between love and longing, and need and desire, and Karna found himself uncharacteristically confused about his feelings. His fascination seemed to increase with each day—she excited yet soothed him; she was like a haven where he sought refuge and he knew he could never let go of her.

He had been married to Vrushali for many years. His marriage to the suta princess had been a duty, marked by a devotion which was an innate, instinctive part of his nature, his love for Vrushali being as deep as his love for Radha, like a calm ocean. But he was mesmerized by Uruvi, entranced by her beauty and intelligence. As a man of power and a creature of struggle, Karna realized he was crippled by the ethics he followed, trapped as he was by his own principles. He always kept his word, for one. For everything he did, there was a certain reason, a logical journey from aspiration to determination. He had wanted to be a warrior; he was one today. He was born an orphan but fate had willed him to be brought up in a large family where love and affection was bountiful.

And now, Uruvi had broken all his rules. She had won him; he had not acquired her.

Vrushali was mild-mannered, but a woman of spirit. She was tall, dark and soft-spoken, but with a firm lilt in her voice. She clearly kept the family together and Karna treated her with the utmost love and respect. Although not a pretty woman, her gentleness and natural air proved that beauty did not really matter. As the older daughter-in-law and wife, she treated Uruvi formally with the politeness expected from her. Whenever they met, Vrushali was always cool and unflustered, looking at her steadfastly, without emotion.

The two women got on reasonably well, with a cordiality lacking warmth. Uruvi did not feel comfortable with Vrushali, possibly because of her own sense of guilt for intruding in the older woman's marital paradise. Or perhaps the warmth was lacking because of Vrushali's innate aloofness—Uruvi could not really tell. They talked, they chatted, they lunched together, but Uruvi sensed a distance between them. For all their amiability they remained stubbornly unfamiliar, two strangers under the same roof, sharing and loving the same man.

Uruvi was sensitive about the impression she made on others, and beneath Vrushali's smiling, serene countenance, she discerned a certain remoteness. Her rival had already summed her up and Uruvi knew the conclusion was not an agreeable one. This disturbed Uruvi because she was used to the approval of others. It vaguely annoyed her that she had not impressed the other woman as favourably as she had intended to. Uruvi could not pinpoint the cause, but she knew that the older woman did not think well of her.

Shona was a master of cold praise. Uruvi soon realized to her dismay that he disliked her, but she couldn't do a thing to change his poor opinion of her. His innate civility and the affection he felt for his older brother kept him from making a direct statement, but his expression showed his disapproval of her plainly enough. He tried to avoid her, and was so excessively polite when he came face to face with her that it bordered on curtness. However, in spite of himself and grudgingly so, he had come around and probably did not consider her a threat to his sister-in-law, Vrushali, whom he was fiercely protective about.

Unlike their older daughter-in-law, Karna's parents seemed to hold Uruvi in open awe, as if she was a goddess who dared to tread the mortal path. These conflicting responses to her made Uruvi feel lost in her new palace, bereft, without the warmth of the family and friends she missed. She remembered how her father had watched her with a tender smile, her mother's indulgent look as she played the sitar, Kunti's delighted outpouring of affection each time they met, Bhishma Pitamah's tolerant smile as she argued vehemently with him, Bhima's relentless yet affectionate teasing...she was so used to the affection which they all so obviously felt for her, and expressed in pampering her. Uruvi had a naïveté, a charm and an eagerness that was captivating. There was a generosity of manner, guilelessness and a natural affability which could not but make people take to her. When she did not get the same affection in her husband's home, Uruvi felt perplexed.

Days flew by fast, but Uruvi got to know her husband very gradually. Karna was attentive and devoted, just as he was with each family member. But Uruvi sensed a certain detachment in his devotion.

'I find something missing...he is with his family, yet apart. Although surrounded by people who love him, Karna is so alone, never satisfied. It seems that he is always searching, always wondering who his natural parents are...,' she told herself.

She noticed that no day would start without Karna paying

obeisance to the early morning sun and then touching his parents' feet with quiet reverence, followed by giving alms to one and all, whoever visited him at the palace. Despite his outward calm, there seemed to be a constant turmoil in him, as if he were in quest of his true self. 'And neither I nor anyone else can help him out,' Uruvi admitted defeatedly to herself. His life had been one long bitter struggle which he did not allow himself to forget. It was distressing to watch him steeped in his angst, yet arrogant in his conviction about his innate worth. He valued his merit but it was not enough for him until he was recognised and consecrated by society.

As the King of Anga, the first duty Karna had taken upon himself was an oath. He swore that anyone who approached him with a request at midday, when he worshipped the sun, would not go away with his request unfulfilled. That was the reason why he would never allow anyone to leave empty-handed. Uruvi wondered, is that why he gave away alms so generously every noon? Was that unquenchable thirst for social recognition turning him into the most magnanimous of gift-givers? Was his philanthropy kindled by his need for self-glorification? Or was it an identification with the sun god and the inherent generosity of Surya? Or, more aptly, was it a driving need to imprint an unforgettable impression on society?

He was the caring older brother to Shona, who clearly hero-worshipped him, the formality in their relationship tempered by a certain indulgence on Karna's side. 'He is still a child,' he used to gently defend his younger sibling whenever Radha grumbled about him. 'He is more like a son to you,' she would retort, and both mother and son would laugh together.

Uruvi was witness to Karna's sporadic flashes of dry humour, especially among people who could understand his witty remarks. Karna was amusing and spirited if he allowed himself to relax— he had a fabulous memory for a funny story and was whimsical, sometimes indulging in pure fun.

If Karna could make Uruvi laugh—and he did—she knew he could do the same with Vrushali too. Each time Karna glanced at

Vrushali, Uruvi, despite herself, felt a red-hot jealousy and she hated herself for it. Watching them, she felt her eyes burning in their sockets, like burning coal. Gripped by envy, she could not speak as she watched them talk to each other softly one afternoon. He was the person she loved most wildly in the world, yet she hated him now as he listened to what his older wife had to say. As if sensing her eyes on them, they turned to look at her.

Abashed, she stepped out of the room, ashamed of her own angry feelings. Anger was not a novel experience for her, but this flaming, searing jealousy was. She painfully reminded herself she was the interloper, not Vrushali. To her jealous eyes, they seemed much too comfortable with each other. Ururvi had not known a more devoted couple, but she could see that they had no dreams, no goal-driven desires. They were happy with each other, with their sons and the family and did not crave for the wealth and status they did not have. But with her, the equation took a turbulent swing because Karna never let her forget that she was a kshatriya princess, part of the elite.

Off and on, Karna's moods swung between being volatile or merely dutiful, but nothing he did ever upset Vrushali's amazing placidity. Vrushali could calm him with just a look or a word. They never disagreed, which seemed to be in keeping with an unspoken pact. Once Uruvi had asked her husband if he ever quarrelled with Vrushali. 'No,' he shrugged. 'We do not seem to have anything to squabble about. Vrushali has the temper of an angel.'

'Possibly,' Uruvi retorted, bristling a little. 'But you don't. You are at times arrogant, aggressive and moody.'

'Am I? You are the first person to say so. If I am all that and worse, it means that she suffers me...as you do.'

'I had quite made up my mind never to fall in love with an insensitive boor,' she dimpled.

'Are you sorry you did?' he asked, his eyes twinkling.

'I was a perfect fool that I did. That bit of luck, or chance or fate or whatever poked in and took the matter out of my hands!' she frowned at him. Her dark eyes had that look again, somewhat teasing, sometimes tender, that made his heart lurch. Her lips were slightly parted in a sigh.

'You are irresistible!' he breathed softly, and kissed her parted lips.

∫

It was with his sons—Vrasasena, Shatrunjaya, Dvipata, Sushena, Satyasena, Chitrasena and Susharma—that Karna shrugged off his armour of polite reserve. Uruvi often watched them scrambling down the steep path in front of the palace in the mornings, racing their way to the grove of trees on the banks of the stream flowing by. As they splashed in the warm, shallow water, Karna was in his most elated spirits. She observed them with a small smile, the girl in her surfacing momentarily, longing to jump in and join them as well. She saw Karna laughing, shouting and singing boisterously. He might have been thirteen—as old as Susharma—and at no other time had Uruvi seen him so happy and vulnerable. There was such an appealing breeziness in him that Uruvi was amazed. These were such beautiful moments that it was like experiencing heaven.

'You seem to have enjoyed yourself enormously,' she said one morning when he returned to the room.

'I always do. They are my best moments,' he smiled, and Uruvi felt he had allowed her to enter his secret space. She smiled back at him, her eyes shining.

When she was alone, Uruvi longed to express her wonder about her new relationship with her husband, to pour out her restlessness, but there was no one to confide in. She was surprised to find herself missing her mother acutely. She had always assumed she would miss her father intolerably but, instead, she found herself wishing that she could rush to her mother and vent her emotion of the moment, whether it was anger, frustration or happiness, or just engage in idle talk.

Though she longed for her parents and her opulent palace at Pukeya, Uruvi found herself fascinated and considerably charmed by her husband's loving family and the frugality that was practised in the household. She took some time getting accustomed to both. Uruvi toned down her lavish ways, self-conscious about being extravagant and ostentatious at times. She loved the hill on which her home stood, the teeming wilder of the forest, the birds with their colourful plumage and the brilliant butterflies fluttering by. She timidly began lending her personal touches wherever she could in the palace, arranging flowers in vases and decorating the rooms with artifacts, while Vrushali looked on tolerantly.

For her, it was beautiful being married and being Karna's wife. It was fulfilling to run his home, with kindly suggestions from Radha and Vrushali, to potter around, read her texts and wait for her husband to return each evening. Most of all, it was wonderful not to brood about the future.

Except for her jealousy, which sometimes surfaced, Uruvi knew she was extremely happy with her husband. They enjoyed each other's company, teasing playfully and laughing a lot every now and then. Even when other people were present, their eyes often met, exchanging a little private message. It was quite touching, even to the cynical Shona, and their relationship was blessed by Radha and Adhiratha.

5

The Pariah's Wife

When news of the extraordinary turn of events in Princess Uruvi's swayamwara reached the royal palace of Hastinapur, some rejoiced, but most were dismayed that Princess Uruvi was Karna's wife and not Arjuna's bride. Vidura was saddened. He immediately went to King Dhritrashtra to give him the news. 'O King, the daughter of King Vahusha has become the wife of Karna, and not our daughter-in-law as we had all wanted. Our family has lost a good ally.'

'No, no, Vahusha will always be our ally; he is our close friend. By becoming Karna's father-in-law, he is not lost to us. Karna is close to Duryodhana, which means that Vahusha will also have to side with Duryodhana and not Arjuna. You bring me great news, Vidura. Go and welcome Uruvi. She is our daughter-in-law all the same.'

Reacting to the turn of events more happily than his uncle Vidura, was Duryodhana, for only bad news had come his way since the disaster of Draupadi's swayamwara. The Pandavas had risen from the ashes, and had not been burnt alive in the lac palace after all. To aggravate matters, the marriage alliance of Arjuna with Draupadi had strengthened the ties of King Drupad and the Pandavas. And worst of all, his father had not just welcomed the wandering Pandavas back with their common bride but had also handed over half the kingdom to them. They had prospered, naming their golden city Indraprastha, and their popularity had amplified. They had got mightier by the day through goodwill and marriage alliances, thought the Kaurava scion vengefully.

But for Uruvi's unexpected decision, Vahusha's kingdom of Pukeya would have been friendly territory for the Pandavas. But Uruvi had completely turned the tide in favour of the Kauravas, reflected Duryodhana with immense delight. Uruvi was his new trump-card and he would have to play it carefully; just like he had done with Karna when he had first seen him perform better than Arjuna during the archery contest at Hastinapur years ago.

He had been secretly delighted when he had finally found a match for Arjuna in this golden youth. He considered himself equal to the mighty Bhima and could even beat him at wrestling and a mace fight. But his deepest dread was Arjuna. He had always feared that no one could challenge the Pandava archer. In the foreseeable tussle for the throne of Hastinapur, he wanted a supreme archer on his side, and in Karna, he immediately recognised his strongest chance against the Pandavas. This was the real reason why he had promptly offered Karna the throne of the kingdom of Anga. His selfish generosity had been mistaken for magnanimity. With that move, he had Karna entirely and eternally by his side—but getting Uruvi on his side would be much tougher.

Duryodhana knew Uruvi felt only contempt for him. She had been exceptionally opinionated even as a child, and Duryodhana grinned as he recalled the frequent tiffs he had had with that chit of a girl who dared to play with, and boss over, boys. He recollected one incident in particular, when the little princess had nearly clawed his eyes out when he had pushed Nakul, one of the Pandava twins, down from a high branch one quiet afternoon. She had leapt at him and scratched him mercilessly, leaving him with a bleeding face and murderous scratches on his chest, arms and legs. She was quite a spitfire, he thought, but she had been always loyal to the Pandavas, which is why her choice of Karna over Arjuna had come as an unforeseen jolt to those who knew her. Savouring the unexpectedness of Uruvi's choice, Duryodhana was struck with another thought— that there was more to that tempestuous princess than her temper. And now, as his best friend's wife, she would certainly behave more congenially with him, he supposed, with a grim smile.

If Uruvi had not been so immersed in her love for Karna, she would have realized earlier that her contentious marriage had prompted many tongues to wag nastily. Noblewomen looked at her inquisitively wherever she went, handmaids glanced at her furtively as she passed by, and royal ladies put their heads together to discuss her behind her back. Most asserted that the marriage was a scandal, some thought it was a pity, others said it was an unpardonable disgrace.

'She is a fool! But it's too late to do anything now...'

'She doesn't know what she is up against. Someone ought to have knocked some wisdom into her. How did Queen Shubra allow the marriage to happen?'

'There's no bigger fool than a woman in love. When such a woman has made up her mind to make a laughing stock of herself and her family, there's nothing stopping her.'

In time, the truth slowly seeped in and Uruvi knew would be treated as the wife of a pariah. It steadily dawned on her that all the ladies she knew were ignoring her, barely acknowledging her except for patronising nods. Queen Gandhari did not invite her for a formal post-wedding feast, while Yudhishthira's wife, Devyani, was openly cold to her, not even glancing at her when they met. The aunts and uncles at whose homes she had been accustomed to lunches and family feasts also treated her with frosty disdain.

Initially, Uruvi was so happily centred in her own private heaven that she barely noticed the scornful glances that came her way from the royal ladies assembled at social occasions. Her appearance at these gatherings caused a certain awkwardness because of her new, low status but she was happily oblivious to it all. She was as affable as always but she soon saw that things were dreadfully amiss.

She was made cruelly conscious of her unpopularity and her fall from grace. Even when she was unmarried, royal princesses and noble ladies had secretly been wary of her, resenting her air of superiority and arrogance. But the reality was she had never been one of them, because she was more interested in art, literature and medicine than in idle gossip. And she would often make fun of them with her sharp wit, leaving them fuming with indignation.

The royal women had always misunderstood her. She was perceptive and effervescent, her warm, brown eyes shining with laughter often. While she spoke to people she didn't like with a biting wit, barely concealing her scorn with a smile, she could chat amiably with the wives of soldiers, charioteers and visiting merchants.

Now her marriage to this unsuitable man provided them with just the suitable weapon to wound her. Now they seized the opportunity to look down on her as the wife of a wretched sutaputra. She was now the outsider, the inferior one, and they made sure she never forgot this. She was neither the Princess of Pukeya any more nor would she ever be accepted as the Queen of Anga.

At a family lunch that her mother hosted, Uruvi noticed many relatives did not attend and the few who were present, stared at her, giving her the cold shoulder. Not able to bear the embarrassment on her mother's face, Uruvi rushed home quickly, promising herself she would never make her mother suffer such ignominy again. But she could not run away from the humiliation of such a life, and each snub forced her to recall her mother's words of caution, warning her of how people would treat her after her marriage to Karna. She felt a strange stirring in her heart. It was bruised pride.

'Now you will know who is your friend and who is a fake,' her mother consoled her, saddened to see her daughter hurt and smarting. But her words were a gentle warning of what was to come. 'You shall find, dear, that the world is full of two-faced people and phonies.'

And Uruvi was to discover a cruelly superficial world, which she had failed to recognise. She was incredulous when she did not find herself included in the hallowed guest list of Queen Vibhavari, her maternal aunt, for the gala Sankranti festival feast, when the regal dowager flaunted her impressive collection of glittering jewels and family heirlooms.

Uruvi's reversal of fate and fortune meant social chastisement.

'Friends' like Princess Ruta and Princess Usha fast disappeared from her life like a whiff of smoke, leaving behind a distastefulness that was hard to dismiss. Uruvi could not quite get over the sudden impertinence of her old friend, Princess Gouri, who had turned out to be a spiteful gossip. By ingratiating herself with Uruvi in the hope that she would be introduced to the right people to achieve fame as a budding poet, Gouri had shown how she was manipulative and insincere. Her father had tried to warn her about this opportunistic girl, but Uruvi was hopelessly duped.

Gouri had pretended that she was very upset about the disgrace that had befallen King Vahusha and Queen Shubra due to Uruvi's unprecedented marriage. 'What a downright shame,' she would say to people she met, fuelling the raging fire of controversy each time she found someone she could recount it to, garnished with spite. There was nothing that thrilled Gouri more than the misfortunes of her friends. Their unhappiness was her happiness. Their business was her business. Her other business was penning excruciatingly pedestrian poetry.

Uruvi knew she had to use the royal ladies as pawns in her new game of survival. Whenever she came across them, she walked up to them and laughed with them, putting on an act of cordiality. With a chuckle, Queen Shubra told herself that her daughter treated them as if she were tolerating fools. Her daughter was wonderfully capable of dissimulation and her act came easily to her.

It wasn't really in Uruvi's nature to look down on people, but she often caught herself thinking the royal ladies were abominably dull, without any intellectual interests that made life so fulfilling. Most were smug about their wealth and status, but capable only of mediocre thoughts. Though they were mothers, their intellectual level remained unfailingly stupid.

They read nothing that was worthwhile. They liked to talk more often about themselves or the latest piece of jewellery they had got for themselves. These pitiable women were devoured by petty jealousies and obsessed by pettier rivalries. They were malicious. Cushioned by wealth and power, they were pathetic in the smallness of their minds. What did it matter if they looked down on her now? Uruvi dismissed them in her mind, knowing that her acumen was far greater. When she smiled, she asserted herself as a winner. She was clever and beautiful and she had married the man she was in love with, something the preening ladies could not boast of—yet secretly envied her.

It was tiresome that she had to pretend to be kind to them. Most often, she was mischievously mocking since they did not deserve her attention anyway. She chatted with them brightly as if she did not have a care in the world and was contemptuously amusing while taking care to be pleasant, which irked them. She took a delight in observing that they resented her when she was so cloyingly nice to them, thinking that she was putting on airs or that she was poking fun at them. They were not wrong—she was.

'Courage is very odd,' King Vahusha told his wife gravely. 'Any other person would have locked herself in her home to hide from this deliberately cold treatment and the unkind remarks. But not my Uruvi; she's a lioness all right!'

The men were slightly more polite, but she did not fail to notice that they tried to cover their embarrassment by exaggerated courtesy. Bhishma Pitamaha was one of them. At first, Uruvi dreaded meeting him face to face, so she avoided Hastinapur's palace as much as she could. Then one grey day, on an impulse, she went to meet him.

Bhishma Pitamaha raised his silver head as she entered the room. His eyes looked pained. For a few long minutes neither of them spoke. Uruvi wondered how she would begin the conversation. She was too uncomfortable to voice her thoughts as volubly as she otherwise would have.

'I realize you are not too happy with what I have done,' she began slowly, her voice soft and sad.

For a moment, Bhishma Pitamaha did not reply. Then he turned gently to look at her and smiled softly. 'No, dear, I was not happy, but if you wished to marry Karna, you have my blessings.'

'But you don't approve of him, do you?' she blurted out frantically. 'Perhaps you couldn't be expected to because Arjuna has always been your favourite. You have the same prejudice as the others have about him because he is a charioteer's son. But Karna is an extraordinary man,' she spoke quickly, her words tumbling over one another in impassioned heat. 'You proclaimed him yourself as a formidable archer. He is generous. He is kind. He accepts others for what they are and he accepts himself as well. He makes no secret of the fact that he is a sutaputra and is not ashamed of it. He has not forsaken his family and is as devoted to them, even now as the King of Anga. I love him. Is it unnatural that I should have married him?'

'It will only end up in you losing the distinction between right and wrong,' the grand old monarch replied quietly. 'One day, you will have to answer this question yourself—is Karna a bad man doing good things or is he a good man doing bad things? You will need to remove this confusion and know the difference between the good and the bad.'

Uruvi smiled slightly, but her eyes were grave. 'Perhaps we make too much of the difference between one person and another. The best of us can be worse, and the worst of us can be good. Who can say?'

'Are you persuading me to believe that white is black and black is white, dear?' There was sincere affection for her in his voice.

'No, sir. Karna is a warrior by his deeds but each time, whenever he and Arjuna were compared, Arjuna has won because of his noble birth and not because of his merits. Is *that* not so unfair, that it has blown up into a huge wrong?'

Bhishma's reply was exceptionally blunt. 'Have you ever wondered why such a fine young man as your husband joined up with the Kauravas?' he questioned quietly. 'He is one of them now—he is their heart and soul, their comrade, their brother. Yes, Duryodhana is an opportunist and found in Karna the one person who could counter Arjuna. Besides which, he has enough charisma to woo over anyone if he decides to do so.'

'His generosity might be selfish, but he was the only one who stepped forward to help Karna. The Pandavas never did,' Uruvi reminded the veteran warrior, her voice sharpening. 'Neither did Guru Dronacharya and Kripacharya. Or you,' she dared to say, looking at him accusingly. 'Did you reprimand Bhima when he insulted and humiliated Karna by calling him a man of low birth, when what really mattered was the deed, the merit, and not the birth? If you had intervened, Karna probably would not have been with the Kauravas at all!' she charged, trying to temper her accusation with some politeness.

The old man remained undaunted by her words. 'The fact is that Karna was drawn to Duryodhana, irrespective of Duryodhana's charisma as a leader and his generous gesture,' he explained to her. 'Karna's greatest hunger at that time of the archery contest, and, my dear, remember this—a hunger that shall remain forever in him—is for acceptance, for social recognition. This young lad with every sign of aristocracy in him, and signs of a divine birth with his kavach, his natural armour and his kundals, the earrings that he seems to have been born with, knows that he is not the son of his adoptive parents. He guesses that his parents are high-born, which is also why he is so arrogant. Keep him away from evil company. A noble and generous warrior like Karna will suffer grievously because of the company he keeps—Shakuni, Duryodhana and Dushasana. Are they the kind of friends a wise man would have? How do you decide what is good and bad? The one who sees the bad in what is good is a bad man. Karna is a good man, but he sees good even in what is bad. His seeing it as good doesn't make the bad good, but makes his goodness look bad. Being constantly with Duryodhana, I fear, has made Karna vain and blind to evil too.'

'And Arjuna is not vain?' Uruvi flashed. 'Arjuna is full of conceit and self-importance. He cannot believe that anyone can be better than him—but Karna is. So he hates him. Being your favourite, as well as Guru Dronacharya's and Krishna's, Arjuna has always been privileged as the blue-eyed boy whom everyone loves. Unfortunately for all of you, I don't love this Prince Perfect. He may be brave, dutiful, good and wise, yes, but he is weak. If not for Krishna, who is he? You and many others would have preferred—and had planned accordingly—that I marry Arjuna. I did not heed your wishes and for that disobedience, I have come here to apologise.'

'But you are not sorry for what you have done.' There was no reproach in Bhishma's voice.

'No, I am not. But I am sorry for hurting the people I love most with my decisions and actions.'

'You did what you had to,' he sighed, and suddenly looked old and painfully tired. 'And you have my blessings. Just a word of caution, child. Karna is valiant and righteous. So is Arjuna. But Karna is on the side of evil and Arjuna is on the side of truth. Karna can never win against him.'

Uruvi kept silent as she silently agreed with the old man. 'True,' she murmured. 'But you cannot deny Karna is a superior archer than Arjuna.'

'Individual skill is only a part. Victory in battle is a whole. The part, however great, cannot win against the whole. Remember this, my child, and make Karna understand this. Or else he will move towards doom...'

Uruvi did not hear the words he muttered under his breath, '...and eventually, so will you.'

It was his blazing kavach and his sparkling kundals that first attracted her to him, Uruvi had often insisted to her husband. Karna's typical reply was a small smile broadening into a grin. The golden armour her husband was said to have been born with spread across the huge expanse of his chest, from his wide shoulders down to his trim waist. She could never resist teasing him about the armour and the glowing orbs he was born with.

'They say you are the best-looking man in the country right now. Each morning when you go down to the river to have your bath, the women of Hastinapura go crazy!' she said one night, with a naughty sniff. 'You should either start bathing at home or stop showing off!'

'And here I thought I was popular for being the bravest warrior!' Karna replied with a smile. 'But even as a child I had problems with my kavach and kundals. I used to keep pestering Mother and ask her why Shona didn't have them as well. Poor lady, she had no answer! But I realized as a child that they were a blessing. Whatever I did, I never hurt myself. I fell off a tree once and I was unhurt! It was always Shona who was all bruised and black and blue all over!'

Uruvi gave the golden sheen on his chest a deliberate, hard look. 'Well, it doesn't hurt you but it's causing a lot of harm to many! It's all because of your kavach and kundals that you draw such a huge fan following of women,' she said, hoping she had induced the right whine in her voice. 'They can't keep their eyes off you.'

'Well, what do you suggest? I rip it off? I can't remove it. So you better suffer it and your husband with it!' he said, pulling her close against him.

Uruvi recalled Bhishma Pitamaha's words about Karna's birth. She rested her chin lightly on his glistening chest to look up at the twin twinkling orbs. 'I agree with your good friend Duryodhana when he said that this is what marks you from all the others. They are proof that you are special, exceptionally special. That you may be of…let's say…celestial birth?' she teased, her eyes twinkling.

'No, dear, you have the wrong man. I have no godly genes. How about your husband being a lowly mortal instead?' he whispered, his lips close to her ears, his warm breath fanning her face.

She allowed a fleeting pout to play on her lips. 'A mere mortal? Is that all I get?' she said and raised her shoulders in a little shrug. 'But I love this lesser mortal nevertheless!'

She flashed a quick impish look at him. She could hear the steady thud of his heartbeat as she nestled close against him.

When the morning came, she roused him out of a deep sleep with a sprinkle of kisses all over his face. It was her morning ritual. The early rays of the sun slanted into the room on his golden armour, lighting him with an ethereal glow. He woke up quickly, his eyes wide and lustrous, and pressed her close to him as he always did when he woke up.

Later in the afternoon, Karna was with Shona, discussing a minor matter of the court. But Shona soon noticed that his brother's mind was elsewhere. A tinkle of laughter chimed in the quiet afternoon hour, prompting them to look down at the garden from the wide verandah. Karna's lips lifted in a small smile, his eyes softening. His wife was playing with his sons below. Shona saw he could not take his eyes off her; he had never caught his brother looking at Vrushali in that manner.

Uruvi's laughter rang clear, blending naturally with the happy squeals of his sons. A soft smile played constantly on her lips, her eyes bright, her long neck bowed towards them. It was a charming laugh, rippling and gay like a young child's, tinged with a joyous abandon that was infectious. She laughed constantly, and when she was not laughing, a bantering smile tugged at her lips. Her soft eyes shimmered with the joy of living, the happy warmth spreading wherever she went. It was her sheer vitality that was Uruvi's most shining trait. The pulse of life gave her a glow that dazzled him. He could not forget the impression she made on him at her swayamwara when he first saw her, breathtaking in her loveliness.

She was like a goddess in the land of the ordinary. She had strength and sensitivity and, although simple and unaffected, was proud, her bearing showing a nobility that befitted a princess. If she was charming to everybody, she was also barely courteous to those whom she disliked. Karna frowned when he recalled Uruvi's glacial curtness when she spoke to Duryodhana. Otherwise, she was endearingly uncomplicated—but she was caring only to those whom she liked or loved. Oh, yes, she was loving, so tenderly loving…he remembered her soft, supple body against his and his face flushed.

'Radheya, are you in love with Uruvi?' asked Shona abruptly, walking up to him from behind.

Karna walked further to the edge of the verandah and looked intently at the blue magic of the early morning sky. There was a slight smile on his face when he turned back to Shona. 'Yes,' he answered reflectively. 'I do not love her the way I love Vrushali, who I know you are utterly devoted to. I will never hurt Vrushali, if that's what you are afraid of. I know that's the reason you are asking me this question. I respect her too much. She is a very good woman, with a sweet, gentle nature, who can make everyone happy. Uruvi, on the other hand, is like a wild exotic flower in a desert who must be sheltered from the bitter winds. I want to protect Uruvi; she has fought the world to be with me. No one need think of protecting Vrushali for she is too capable and self-sufficient. I think Vrushali loves me for myself and not for what I may become. Whatever happens to me or whatever I do, I shall never disappoint her. But I am not good enough for Uruvi.'

'She doesn't think so. She adores you, as does Vrushali.'

'I admire Vrushali more than any woman I have ever known,' said Karna gravely. 'But Uruvi is much too good for me. She has a wonderful intelligence; she is as good as she is lovely. I love her enthusiasm, her lively humour, her ambition to work as a healer. She is interested in everything and has a lot of knowledge and good sense. There are very few topics she cannot discuss. She is an extraordinary creature of opposites—there seem to be two women in her, one rational, the other emotional. I am entirely unworthy of her.'

'What utter rubbish! When have you started getting daunted by love and beauty?' Shona scoffed.

'It's not just love and beauty as you so dismissively say. Uruvi has taught me a lot of things…'

'Oh? How? What has she taught you?' Shona asked, bewildered.

'She has taught me to live…'

Shona laughed scornfully. 'Really? Is she teaching you how to be more of a kshatriya? No, the question here is—is she worthy of you? Is she suited for you, for our family?'

'She is. She has already passed her test…but I have yet to do so.' Karna had his back to Shona so Shona could not see his face. Was it possible that Karna had smiled when he said those words?

6

Friends: Ashwatthama and Duryodhana

At the King of Anga's palace, a visitor who often came by was Ashwatthama. Uruvi was a little intrigued by this unusual friendship, because Guru Dronacharya's disdain for Karna was as notorious as his undying affection for his famous disciple, Arjuna. Ashwatthama, the 'brahmin warrior' and the only son of Guru Dronacharya, clearly did not follow his father's sentiments, Uruvi gathered, with a mirthless smile. And neither father nor son made any pretence about their feelings for Karna. Dronacharya's dislike of Karna was equal to the loyalty Ashwatthama pledged to the same man. Dronacharya's distrust of Karna went a long way back—as long as Ashwatthma's burgeoning friendship with the young Karna when the sutaputra had dared to visit the guru's ashram so many years ago.

'It soon became clear to us that Radheya was obsessed about learning warfare rather than taking up a charioteer's profession like his father,' sighed Radha, when a curious Uruvi asked her how Karna and Ashwatthama became friends. She never once called him Karna, Uruvi noticed with amusement; he was always her Radheya, the son of Radha.

'One day, bowing to Radheya's demands, Adhiratha decided to take him to meet Dronacharya, then an established teacher in the art of warfare who taught the Kuru princes. But Dronacharya, on realising that Radheya was Adhiratha's son, rudely refused to accept Radheya as his student because Adhiratha was a charioteer. He only taught kshatriyas, he insisted. Angered by the guru's insolence and being dismissed so indifferently, and seeing his dream crumbling before him, Radheya was a little more impolite to the guru than he meant to be.'

'Oh, what did Karna say? I know that Dronacharya was so piqued that he has still not forgiven Karna,' Uruvi asked, intrigued.

'Radheya has always been a rebel against caste and the social hierarchy,' her mother-in-law said, after a brief pause. 'He has constantly been cruelly reminded that as a sutaputra, he cannot aspire to more than he deserves, but he believes in his own worth and is contemptuous of those inferior to him in merit. And he did not hesitate to ask Drona, who had refused to train him with the Kuru princes, why he could not be taught by him. He asked why the royals were so privileged—were they blessed with special gifts like a hundred arms? Why do they get this importance? Moreover, if Dronacharya taught only kshatriyas, then how did his son, Ashwatthama, a brahmin, qualify to learn the art of warfare from his father? Radheya's impertinence infuriated Dronacharya and he was curtly told to leave the ashram. But Ashwatthama, who had witnessed this conversation in mute admiration, was clearly impressed with Radheya. From that day, they became close friends. In fact, it was Ashwatthama who informed Karna about the celebrated archery contest at Hastinapur, and persuaded him to participate in it.'

'Karna could not stop himself from going there uninvited, so he gatecrashed at the contest at Hastinapur,' Uruvi sighed deeply, remembering that momentous day, the day life changed so irrevocably for her...and for Karna.

'Yes, I was so worried that I sent Adhiratha to see what was happening, and he followed Radheya to the grounds where the contest was being held.'

Because of his foster father's unsolicited presence there, Karna had to admit to his lineage and was publicly heckled by the Pandavas. The incident still rankled in Uruvi's mind and she was enraged when she recalled the humiliation Karna was forced to suffer. If it could upset her so much even today, Uruvi wondered how intensely it must have affected Karna. Ashwatthama could have done little to help his friend, and the saviour of the moment had been Duryodhana instead. After that, a lasting friendship between Karna and Duryodhana began, which few could fathom but most disapproved of, she being one of them. Uruvi pursed her lips tightly in rising frustration.

Like Duryodhana, Ashwatthama befriended Karna unconditionally, without any bias or reservation. Karna and Ashwatthama were strangely similar—both were loved dearly by their families but not socially accepted. Ashwatthama's parents loved him exceedingly, yet he was ignored by others for no fault of his own, and he had no friend to boast of except Karna, who was an outcast himself. Perhaps that was why they empathised with each other so well, Uruvi deduced. His father's staunch disapproval of the friendship did not deter the son.

She recalled Ashwatthama as a young lad, a serious, quiet boy, always courteous and obedient. Being older than the Kuru princes and her, he did not join in their games at the palace gardens. And as far as she could remember, neither the Kaurava princes nor the Pandavas treated him too well; they were flippant with him, as if they tolerated him just because he was their guru's son. He used to watch them with his solemn eyes, his face always grave and impassive. She recalled him revealing some emotion only when he looked visibly displeased at the blatant favouritism his father showed for Arjuna. If the guru frowned on the friendship between his son and the sutaputra, the son resented the strong bond between his father and Arjuna, the proud guru and his devoted shishya (disciple).

As the only son of Dronacharya and Kripi, Ashwatthama was the centre of their existence. But as Dronacharya was dreadfully poor before he came to Hastinapur, the son bore the brunt of their poverty. Ironically, it was their great love for their son that strained the relationship between Dronacharya and his wife Kripi. And it was because of his great love for his son that Dronacharya earned a sworn enemy in his once-upon-a-time friend, King Drupad of Panchal.

The story about Ashwatthama, which had been told to her by her mother, was a curious one. It seemed that the couple was so poor that they did not own even a cow, in spite of being brahmins, and little Ashwatthama had never tasted milk as had the other boys in the brahmin neighbourhood. One day, a very fretful Kripi, tired of fooling her little son with rice powder and water, which she gave him instead of milk, taunted her husband Dronacharya about the great gap in wealth between the two friends—while one was a king, the other remained a poor brahmin who could not afford milk for his only son. Angered and shamed by her words, Dronacharya left home, promising he would only return with wealth and fame. Recalling King Drupad's promise to share his kingdom with him, Dronacharya approached his friend for help. But that promise turned out to be empty and the arrogant King of Panchal not only refused to help him out, but did not acknowledge the guru as his friend either. 'Friends are among equals,' he said scornfully, and offered to give him alms befitting a poor brahmin. Humiliated, Dronacharya took the insults silently—but he vowed revenge.

As the guru of the Kuru princes in martial arts, Dronacharya told them that they had to fulfil one important command. He asked them to bring King Drupad to him in chains as guru dakshina, the gift customarily given to a teacher by disciples. At once, without further ado, all the Kuru princes set out to capture King Drupad—but it was Arjuna and the Pandava princes who defeated the swelling Panchala army. The victorious Arjuna captured King Drupad and brought him to his revered guru. In his moment of triumph, Dronacharya told the defeated king that by taking half his kingdom as he was entitled to, he could become his equal, but being a brahmin, he was neither interested in kingdoms nor in becoming a king. Saying this, he contemptuously returned the kingdom to King Drupad and set him free. The humiliated King of Panchal swore revenge on his friend and performed a special yagna (sacrifice) from which sprang a son, the sword-wielding Dhrishtadyumna, born to kill Dronacharya, and a daughter, the dark, sultry Draupadi, who would marry Arjuna, Dronacharya's favourite disciple. The stage was set for the king to pit the shishya against the guru.

It was ironical that Dronacharya had earned himself another enemy through Arjuna, besides the wrathful King Drupad. And that was Karna. Dronacharya, because of his extreme affection and pride for his favourite disciple, Arjuna, had rejected two potential rivals, both worthy opponents, of Arjuna. The first one was Eklavya, a tribal prince and a master archer who was asked to give his right thumb as guru dakshina. When he heard the guru's command, the devoted Eklavya cut it off and offered it to him, knowing that he could never string a bow ever again.

The other contender who challenged Arjuna's prowess in archery was Karna. Realising that the young sutaputra might better his favourite student some day, Dronacharya rejected Karna outright on the pretext that Karna was not born a royal warrior. Karna, smarting under the snub, then swore that, one deciding day, he would challenge Arjuna and defeat him. In this way, Dronacharya had set two worthy archers against each other and inadvertently began a terrible rivalry between Karna and Arjuna, one that was to reverberate throughout their lives, Uruvi thought bitterly.

The relentless Karna meanwhile persisted and sought knowledge of weapons and martial arts as the student of Parshurama, the guru of Bhishma Pitamaha. But even as he rose to become the star pupil of the formidable and hard-to-please Guru Parshurama, Karna did not allow himself to forget the sting of Guru Dronacharya's insult. 'The seeds of discontent continued to grow as a life-long resentment against the Kurus' guru,' sighed Karna's mother wretchedly.

The last to fall prey to Dronacharya's love and extreme partiality for Arjuna was his own son, Ashwatthama. In his relentless pursuit to make Arjuna the best warrior in the world, the guru overlooked his own son. Perhaps that was another reason why the two connected so well, Uruvi supposed, as she saw Ashwatthama wait for Karna at the steps below her balcony. Their common opponent was Arjuna, courtesy Guru Dronacharya.

'It has been ages since I saw you last,' Uruvi welcomed Ashwatthama with a smile. 'How is your mother?'

'She is doing fine, thank you,' he replied politely, his voice low, almost a whisper. 'She told me to give you her congratulations. I also want to wish you a happy life together,' he added shyly. 'Karna is a lucky man. And you are a very lucky lady.'

Uruvi had not heard Ashwatthama delivering such a long speech before and she was touched. 'Next time, please take me to visit her. I would like to pay my respects to her as well.'

Ashwatthama bowed formally and walked away towards her husband who was coming down the marble steps after his morning prayers to the sun god. He looked dazzlingly handsome as always. Uruvi felt herself basking in that unusual warmth she always felt when she gazed at him. Watching them together, she felt how physically alike they were as well. If Karna looked magnificent in the glittering kavach and kundals he was born with, Ashwatthama, too, was blessed with a glittering, precious gem on his forehead from birth. As the wearer of this jewel, he was blessed with immortality and was free from the fear of death, disease, hunger and war. The two men were quite inseparable, the guru's disapproval notwithstanding. Dronacharya and Kripacharya, Ashwatthama's maternal uncle and the royal family chief priest, maintained a cold disdain for the charioteer's son who ranked low at the royal court.

'Radheya could never get over Dronacharya's rejection of him,' revealed Radha during one of the many chats she had with her new daughter-in-law. 'For days, he burned with anger at the sheer injustice of it. And I could do nothing to calm that storm within Radheya who, till now, cannot understand why he was not allowed to be trained with the Kuru princes. He strongly believes in being fair. In his righteous indignation, Radheya considered Guru Dronacharya failed as a teacher—he should have been fair and just to all his students.'

Radha paused, looked distinctly troubled, but continued with her recollections, wanting Uruvi to know what her son had gone through. 'After being rejected by Guru Dronacharya, Radheya decided to practise martial arts on his own. And he took his brother Shona's help. He gathered information about various ayudhas (weapons) in the day and then after sundown, practised them. He soon surpassed everyone in skill and strength through self-discipline; but not for a single moment did he allow himself to forget those painful moments of humiliation poured on him. I can understand his bitterness, but he must rid himself of it. I haven't been able to help him, so will you try, dear? It's like a slow poison, slowly corroding him, his soul...'

At this point, Shona silently entered the room and overheard the conversation between them. He interrupted sharply, 'No, Mother, it's those insults that goad him into doing the extraordinary.' He turned to Uruvi, who was surprised that Shona was actually talking to her. 'Pain is a part of Radheya, just like his kavach and kundals,' he said testily. 'Without the pain and mortification he has suffered so long, he would not be what he is today. A bold warrior, a kind man, he can never forget his roots. He wonders about his birth yet cannot forgive his natural parents for deserting him. If he thinks he is the best archer, he has a reason to believe so. The fact is—he is, so when he says he is unsurpassed, it is neither boasting on his part nor arrogance. The manner in which he prepared himself for the archery contest of Hastinapur is just a small instance of his sheer self-belief and his convictions...' he sighed. 'One day, Radheya heard from his friend Ashwatthama how the previous week Guru Dronacharya had decided to test his students—the Kuru princes—in their skill of archery. He hung a wooden parrot from the branch of a tree and then summoned his students. He asked the first one to aim for the bird's eye but not to shoot just yet. He then asked the student what he could see. The student replied that he could see the garden, the tree, flowers, and all that was around him. Dronacharya asked him to step aside and not to shoot. He repeated the same procedure with a few other students. When it was Arjuna's turn, he told his guru that the only thing he could see was the bird's eye. This satisfied the guru, who allowed Arjuna to shoot the bird—and Arjuna successfully hit the eye of that parrot.'

Shona continued, his voice heavy with admiration, 'After listening to Ashwatthama's anecdote, Radheya told me that if Arjuna could hit one eye of the parrot, then he could hit both eyes in a single shot! Both Ashwatthama and I laughed his claim away but soon he proved what he said. Since we practised at night, Radheya decided to shoot both eyes of the parrot that very same night with the help of an ordinary lamp. I followed Radheya's instructions closely. I suspended the wooden parrot high above the tree and held the palita beneath. Radheya strung the bow with two arrows slightly changed their position one after the other and as soon as he got the signal from me, aimed at both eyes of the bird. His aim was so accurate that he achieved his target in a single shot!' Shona's eyes sparkled with unabashed pride as he talked about his older brother. 'He had barely practised and yet he could do it so effortlessly! This just shows that Radheya *is* the greatest archer in the world and frankly, he doesn't need to challenge Arjuna to prove his merit. This is the same man who was denied tutoring by Guru Dronacharya and not given entry to the archery contest... all because he was a charioteer's son. Lineage matters over merit and Radheya cannot lay claim to it. His lineage is considered ignoble, so his merit has been consistently ignored.'

What Shona revealed came as no surprise to Uruvi. 'What dharma does Dronacharya talk of?' she sneered. 'Some may call him loyal to the Kuru throne but has he been really fair to others besides Arjuna? Both Karna and Eklavya were ruthlessly swept aside to make way for Arjuna as the best archer in the country. Dronacharya's treatment of Karna was as malicious as the pitiless suppression of Eklavya's talents—not just because Eklavya was a tribal but because he would have been a threat to his favourite disciple, Arjuna. Like Karna, Eklavya was rejected and callously cast aside so that Arjuna could feel secure and become successful! Is that the dharma of a teacher?'

That it was this teacher who had derided her husband consistently, without fail, and kept on disparaging him even now, made Uruvi furious and she felt a sudden antipathy for this same person whom she had respected so deeply all the years she was growing up. 'The validation of this supposed great teacher is anything but teaching and education. How can he be the perfect guru if he is so blatantly partial?' she asked derisively. 'If he is not humble and honest himself, how can he teach his students those virtues? Instead of teaching

Arjuna humility, he pampered him and encouraged him to believe he was the best. The only justification for his presence in Hastinapur is not training the Kuru princes but seeking his own vengeance—to destroy King Drupad through Arjuna, who is his ace card. He is going to exact his revenge through Arjuna. All he actually wants to accomplish is to settle scores with his oldest enemy.'

Radha looked at Uruvi, awed by her perception, but her eyes were troubled. 'Shhh, girl, there are spies everywhere...' Shona looked unfazed, secretly enjoying his sister-in-law's tirade but not showing it. She was talking like a true princess in a regal rage, but the princess seemed to have forgotten she was now in the house of a suta.

'Spies? That's something Dronacharya started in this kingdom! And pray, how can he harm me or you, Mother?' she asked scornfully. 'The damage has already been done—he has harmed Karna enough. And what of his dharma as a brahmin? It is imparting education justly. But how fair has he been? He is no devotee of truth,' she stated angrily. 'Why, he is said to have secretly trained Ashwatthama but then Arjuna got furious and wouldn't allow it!'

'Hush, child, don't say a word more! There will be trouble!' beseeched Radha. She was almost hysterical with worry and fear and was relieved to see Radheya entering the room. She gave him a pleading look, hoping he would be able to handle his tempestuous wife.

'Don't worry Ma, I know how to silence her,' he said airily and waved them away. To Uruvi's rising astonishment, his brother and mother took the cue and left the room, but not before Uruvi noticed a smile playing on her mother-in-law's face. She looked reassured and amused too.

'My little woman has quite a temper!' Karna drawled and without waiting for her retort, he placed his hand on her mouth. 'Peace, lady!' he ordered and replaced his hand with his lips. Astonishment gave way to pleasure and Uruvi allowed herself to melt until she realized he was trying to distract her. She pushed him away.

'What did I say that was wrong?' she demanded.

'Are you going to get angry and abusive with all the people who have behaved badly with me?' he asked smiling.

'Yes! I shall!' she said fiercely. 'I can't bear it if anyone hurts you. And that insufferable guru insists on being rude to you—I can't help resenting that!'

'Let him be. And if that's your parameter, then, Princess, you will have to fight almost everyone!' he murmured, a smile in his voice. 'And I would rather have you with me than let you waste your words on others! Do you always do what you like?'

'Always.'

'And how do you avoid doing what you dislike?' he asked with a grin.

'Simple, I don't do it.'

'Hmm...I pity your parents...you must have given them a terrible time while you were growing up!'

'I did!' she agreed impishly. 'I tormented them when I tried to convince them that I would marry only you. I told them over and over again that I wouldn't dream of marrying anyone unless I was madly in love with him! And it's the same hell I am giving you now...'

He laughed softly. 'It gives me great pleasure...this hell.'

⌣

From now on she would look at Ashwatthama with new eyes, Uruvi decided, for she felt a deep respect for the shy son of the conceited Guru Dronacharya. Ashwatthama was the only person, besides Duryodhana, who openly acknowledged Karna's greatness and who considered his close friend as the finest archer, far superior to the supposedly insurpassable Arjuna.

It was Duryodhana who had lifted Karna from the throes of indignity to social glory by declaring him his ally. Ashwatthama and Duryodhana, two of Karna's closest friends, were different as individuals yet in harmony in their choice of Karna as a friend. Karna loved them unreservedly, his amity peppered with the right mix of respect and courteousness; he knew where he stood in the chain of command. With his innate need to be socially respected, Karna had reciprocated the affection displayed by Ashwatthama and the generosity shown by Duryodhana.

For a man who carried in his heart the wound of unrecognised greatness, their acknowledgement gave him support, cushioning the hurt he felt when others looked down on him. Karna, Uruvi decided, was such a contradiction. If he was respected as the mightiest archer in the kingdom, why was he defeated so often by giving in to his sense of inadequacy? Why was this king, known for his generosity and benevolence, not so generous and kind to himself? Beneath his fierce pride, his self-image could not reconcile to the low social status thrust upon him, the niggling insults piercing his impassive composure. And he continually rebelled against this injustice, combating the world, battling the conflict within himself, yet never hesitating to be faithful to his friends. His loyalty to them was like blind devotion, almost sublime in its intensity.

Whenever Karna praised Duryodhana or when people mentioned Duryodhana's wonderful friendship with Karna, Uruvi was attacked by an angry helplessness that was almost stifling. Her father's and Bhishma Pitamaha's warning words kept echoing dully as an ominous prediction. So intense was the bond of friendship between Duryodhana and Karna, that once Bhishma Pitamaha had told her father that if there was one good quality in Duryodhana, it was his profound fondness for Karna, his closest friend. Uruvi was fearful about their closeness; she watched in exasperated anxiety each time she saw them together. She was wary of Duryodhana and almost terrified of how Duryodhana had manipulated Karna since the day they first met.

Against the setting sun that evening, the martial exhibition at Hastinapur saw the dawn of an extraordinary, unexpected friendship. Duryodhana was the sole person who openly condemned the discrimination demonstrated by Guru Dronacharya and Kripacharya and likened Karna, the worthy warrior, to the sun. On behalf of his new-found friend, the Kuru prince argued fiercely that the sun does not need to prove its brilliance—its identity lies in its power to illuminate the world and Karna had a similar power. From that moment on, Duryodhana gave Karna his hand in friendship and honoured his friend with a new identity.

Uruvi could not understand why Duryodhana bothered to be pleasant to her; he knew she resented him. He knew that she did not spare him and seldom lost a chance to berate him. It was true that they had known each other for more than a decade, but she thought him coarse, brutal and devious. She was puzzled that he did not try to avoid her. Instead, he made a show of friendliness, especially at their wedding when he vociferously raised a toast to them and celebrated the occasion with deliberate gusto.

Karna's daily presence at the royal courts notwithstanding, Duryodhana, like Ashwatthama, often stopped by to meet his friend at home. 'This is a recent development,' observed Vrushali archly, watching the Kuru prince step down from his chariot. 'I am surprised he knows the way to our house—he never used to visit us before! Not that he is welcome in the house, anyway,' she shrugged and abruptly turned to Uruvi, a sudden beseeching look darkening her usually calm eyes. 'Please do me a favour. Neither I, nor Mother, Father nor Shona have ever been able to convince Karna that his friendship with Duryodhana spells nothing but doom. Will you try to do something for me? Something that I have not been able to do for so many years? Keep Karna away from this detestable man!' With her unusual entreaty still ringing in Uruvi's ears, the older woman flounced from the room.

Vrushali's urgent words troubled Uruvi, disquiet sweeping over her. The anxiety made her frostier than she otherwise would have been when Duryodhana entered the room. He was a heavily built man, almost as huge as Bhima, with great broad shoulders and ungainly limbs. His face always wore a sardonic expression; his features were hard, large and heavy. He constantly pulled at his thick moustache, a gesture that Uruvi found faintly annoying.

'You wanted to speak with me?' It was more a statement than

a question, but Duryodhana seemed unruffled by her brusqueness.

'Yes, all I want to say is that it pleases me that you are Queen of Anga rather than the Queen of Indraprastha.'

Duryodhana's words had a ring of honesty, but Uruvi was unsure about how true they were. She preferred to misconstrue his statement. She let herself get riled, to provoke anger in this man whose friendship with her husband left her so helplessly furious. 'Ah, Indraprastha...I have heard it's the most beautiful city existing today,' she replied pleasantly. 'The barren Khandavaprastha has been converted to Indraprastha, the city of gold, I hear. The Pandavas have so wonderfully re-established the ancient capital! The ruins have been transformed into such a wealthy city,' she gushed. 'The Pandavas are ruling Indraprastha, bringing back all its glory. The credit, I must say, besides the resourcefulness of the Pandavas, goes to your father who came up with this fine demonstration of fairness and justice by halving the kingdom and giving away the arid part to the Pandavas.'

Uruvi knew she had struck a raw nerve. Duryodhana flinched. 'Are you provoking me, dear Princess?' he asked softly. 'I won't pretend that I am happy with my father's decision. He was forced to obey Bhishma Pitamaha and Guru Dronacharya,' he replied shortly. 'They would like to believe that the Pandavas are entitled to half of the kingdom. I don't; nor does Karna. We differ with their opinion and agree that the kingdom shouldn't have been divided. Karna, though, believes in battling out. His suggestion was—and I fully consented to it—that we launch a surprise attack on the Pandavas and King Drupad before Krishna joined them with his Yadava army. His argument was that we attack the Pandavas before they grow stronger and more friends join up with them. I, frankly, would have preferred something more subtle and less direct than an open battle, but Karna staunchly believes we should fight and take a more aggressive way out.'

'Why are you telling me this, Duryodhana?' she asked coldly, her voice freezing. 'From when has any woman been informed or asked for advice on court politics and family intrigue? Besides, neither Karna nor I are part of your family to interfere in the affairs

concerning your relatives. Please keep us out of your family feuds.'
She tossed her head and got up to leave the room.

Duryodhana's next words stopped her. 'Karna is part of my family. He is my closest friend, as dear to me as Dushasana and my other brothers. He is like my brother, Uruvi.'

'But he is *not* your brother!' she pointed out vehemently. 'He is not and never can be. Leave us alone, Duryodhana. Don't involve Karna in your family disputes. You have a long-drawn-out problem with your cousins. Solve it in your way but do not drag my husband into the familial mess. Your family already resents his presence in the royal court—they find him too interfering, which in a way, is not unfounded. Karna should not be meddling in your family affairs but he does because you allow him to. You want him to.'

'He speaks as a true friend for a friend in need. And in my hour of trouble, I need him by my side.'

'You said it,' she said scornfully. 'How would you define your "hour of trouble"—your fight with the Pandavas or your deep grouse against them? That resentment exists since your childhood. Why should Karna help you fight your war with your cousins? Isn't that why you made him the King of Anga in the first place? So that he is forever indebted to you? It's no friendship you claim, Duryodhana, it's a devious arrangement, it's emotional extortion!' she lashed out. 'You are playing on his loyalty and his deep sense of gratitude,' Uruvi flamed with passion, seething with anger against the man who was smiling tolerantly at her. 'Can you deny that you see him as the only worthwhile opponent against Arjuna in the battlefield? Do you deny that Karna is just a pawn in your game against the Pandavas? Do you deny that you are neatly playing up the rivalry between Arjuna and Karna to your advantage so that they hate each other as you had planned? And now you want to place me in the plot as well. Don't make me say more harsh words than what I have already uttered... but please, let him be!'

Her eyes glittered dangerously in her pale face. The man smiled inwardly; he had purposely provoked her this time and had won the round. 'Whatever I may say, you are not going to believe me because, you too, like others, are too prejudiced. But please understand this; Karna is the only true friend I have. I respect him and I love him dearly—don't ever question that,' he pronounced quietly, biting hard into each word for emphasis. 'You ask me to let him be. Though unwilling, I am sure I could,' he said. Uruvi could not understand why a flicker of a smile crossed Duryodhana's face when he seemed to agree with her.

She soon found out.

His eyes gleaming with triumph, he went close to her to say softly, 'But will *he* let me do that?'

7

...and Foes: Shakuni

'You ask me to let him be. Though unwilling, I am sure I could...But will he let me do that?'

Duryodhana's words rang in Uruvi's ears. She knew she could not reply to Duryodhana's hateful question. She had the answer but had to leave it unspoken. A few days later, that answer was put into words by Karna sooner than she had expected. The occasion was a grand feast hosted by Duryodhana and his wife Bhanumati for the newly wed couple. Karna looked pleased when he informed his bride about it but noticed she did not look too thrilled about the invitation.

'You don't look very happy about the feast.'

'I am not comfortable with those people,' she started hesitatingly, but decided to mince no further words. 'Why is Duryodhana inviting us when his mother had made it plain that she dislikes us? Queen Gandhari cold-shoulders me and she doesn't even speak to you civilly! Moreover, has Duryodhana ever invited you and Vrushali together to his palace?' she asked bluntly.

'No, he hasn't. But that's because you have a different equation with Duryodhana; you have known him since childhood, but Vrushali barely knows him. And where Queen Gandhari is concerned, I know she disapproves of my closeness with her son. I am way too beneath them.'

Uruvi looked impatient. 'She doesn't affect me, but Duryodhana does. Like her, I don't understand why you need to be so close to him. No one likes him—not your mother nor your brother. Vrushali disapproves of him. And so do I,' she flashed. 'I wasn't particularly fond of him in our childhood either. He was mean and manipulative then; he is still so now.'

'I know you dislike him. But that does not change my feelings for my friend,' Karna replied evenly. 'I am not telling you to change yours nor can you change mine. All I am telling you is that we have been invited for a lunch feast and propriety demands we graciously go.'

Uruvi tried to sound sensible. 'I shall go for the feast, but just this one time. Please do not expect me to socialize with a person I do not like, and whom, frankly, you need to stay away from. Karna, Duryodhana is not a good man,' she added weakly.

Karna smiled wryly and Uruvi looked sharply at him. 'I am serious. It's not just me—no one who loves you is pleased about your close association with Duryodhana. All of us are worried. He is known to be a power-hungry wolf, and is using you as his strongest weapon against the Pandavas. And worse, he is dragging you into his private war with his cousins. It's a family feud and it's best you stay clear of it. What I am telling you...'

'...is what so many others have warned me about often as well. But, it goes a long way, and I cannot *not* be his friend because of his flaws. You accept a friend with his faults, however bad.'

Uruvi responded, saying bluntly. 'His faults will be your undoing! You are *not* one of the Kauravas. You are *not* family. You are *not* like him.'

'He was the only one who has helped me at all times. Always,' he repeated quietly.

'By crowning you King of Anga, has he bought you body and soul, Karna? Are you so indebted to him that you are blinded with gratitude? A friend is one who advises the other when he goes wrong. Have you ever told your friend that he is wrong? That he was wrong when he tried to poison his cousin Bhima? That he is wrong when he does not give what rightfully belongs to the Pandavas—their share of the kingdom? That he was so wrong when he tried to kill the Pandavas and Kunti in the lac palace?'

'That's not true...it's a wicked rumour!' Karna lashed out angrily.

'You did not tell him all this because you, like him, believe he is right,' she pursued relentlessly. 'In your blind love for your friend, you cannot see nor distinguish between good and bad, right and wrong,' Uruvi softened her voice, trying to be placating. 'You refuse to believe the worst about your friend. He is influencing you the same way he himself was so evilly influenced by his uncle, Shakuni. Duryodhana, sadly, is a poisoned man, nursed on hate and envy since childhood. I don't blame him—he has been brought up to consider the Pandavas as his enemies. Why do you patronize such bitterness in a man whom you call your friend?'

'Because whatever his nature may be, he is loyal. And he is my friend,' replied Karna calmly. 'It was Duryodhana who helped me when I was being publicly disparaged at the archery contest, it was Duryodhana who first acknowledged me as a worthy warrior, it was Duryodhana who made me a kshatriya, by merit if not by birth. When I was ridiculed by Draupadi at her swayamwara, it was Duryodhana who stood by me, it was Duryodhana who challenged King Drupad and Dhrishtadyumna and questioned their intentions at the same swayamwara. It is Duryodhana who sides with me whenever Dronacharya and Bhishma Pitamaha are dismissive about me, it is Duryodhana who has given me the respect that I am worthy of. No one else has done that. Rejected by all, I have found honour among the Kauravas. For all this and more, I shall be eternally grateful to Duryodhana.'

'But he does all that because he needs you,' she argued, a desperate plea in her voice. 'He needs you to fight his final battle with the Pandavas. Without you, he can never win against them. Without you, the Kauravas are nothing. Assured of your unwavering loyalty, Duryodhana can afford to be arrogant and forceful. He can claim all rights to the inheritance, even though the elders believe at least half of it, if not all, belongs to the Pandavas. That is why Dronacharya and Bhishma Pitamaha resent you—because it is through you that Duryodhana is so flagrantly powerful. Duryodhana has been spurred by his father's unfulfilled aspirations, a father who is blinded by the ambition to be king. And on your part, Karna, you are indebted to him for the social sanction and the kingdom he has bestowed on you. But you are bound to a person who is not worthy of either your love or your friendship. Duryodhana cannot be anyone's friend. He is simply using you against his cousins. The Duryodhanas of the world will seek you out because they need you to serve their interest. You are his best ace against them—can't you see through him?'

'I will always stand by him, whoever and whatever I am against,' Karna's words were deceptively soft, his face a mask of cold inscrutability. 'Duryodhana gave me the kingdom without my asking for it and I shall give him my undying friendship in return. I promised him I shall serve him till my last breath and I am committed to him for life. Only Duryodhana offered me an opportunity to prove myself—to be a king, a warrior and an archer—and I took it.'

'And sold your soul in the bargain!' she countered angrily. 'He is violating your conscience! You are wasting your loyalty on a person who has no integrity, no dharma...' Uruvi implored, realizing her words were being drowned by his unflinching loyalty.

'He could be; but for me he is simply a friend, a saviour, who stood by me in my worst hour. Uruvi, he may be evil but I see his goodness too.'

'But that doesn't justify his vices. O Karna, he is dragging you to a certain no man's land! Where is all this hate and intrigue and revenge going to lead?'

'To conflict—that is inevitable, isn't it? Where is power ever without politics and conflict?'

'But you have never been greedy for power—you don't want it!' she argued, twin angry spots on her cheeks. 'Power can never corrupt you for you have never hankered for it. And the tussle is not for power—it's one-upmanship between the cousins. They seem to be fighting for the throne, which Duryodhana does not believe in sharing. But with you it's never been this lust for the throne or the crown...'

'All I ever wanted was respect, Uruvi. And Duryodhana has given me that,' Karna said quietly. 'I aspired for nothing else. I wanted to be recognised for my merits. Not for what I was born as. Not for my lineage—or rather, lack of it.'

There was an unaccustomed harshness in his voice, his rigidity contrasting starkly with the helplessness she knew he was actually feeling. 'Yes, Duryodhana has given me the respect and honour that I strived so hard for, and when I look at him, I feel blessed. He has everything yet he has nothing. I have a family who loves me unconditionally. I am Radheya, proud to be the son of Radha, but is Duryodhana proud to be Queen Gandhari's son? He has a mother, but has never known the warmth and selflessness of maternal love. He has a father, but has King Dhritrashtra carried out his responsibilities towards him? Instead of guiding his son, he is lost in his own unfulfilled ambition and unrequited hopes, groping in vain for kingship. Duryodhana seems to be born in hate, for hate. Did Queen Gandhari ever forgive King Dhritrashtra for forcing her to marry him? That resentment percolated to her son as well. She was so disappointed that Duryodhana was not born before Yudhishthira that she was ready to abort him!' said Karna scathingly. 'I was dumped by my natural mother after I was born but here is a mother who was ready to kill her son before his birth. How then, can he *not* be branded with hate and evil? As a baby, was he ever held with love and affection? His father was blind, so he could not see his first newborn, but his mother did not remove her blindfold even to have a glimpse of the son she had so desperately wished for. She rejected him solely because he was not born early enough! Oh, Uruvi, he has been brought up in heartlessness—within the confines of indifference. His mother never really bothered about him; his father saw him only as an heir, not a son to be loved and cared for. He has been brought up on hate—by his uncle, who seeks revenge for the injustice done to him, his father and his sister by the Kuru clan. Shakuni seeks his revenge through his nephew, slowly poisoning his mind and soul to make him the puppet he wants him to be. Duryodhana was doomed before he was even born...he was born a child of hatred and lives to hate...'

Uruvi listened to him in silence. She absorbed his words almost unwillingly, trying to understand what he was saying. He was like a brave soldier battling against the whole world, which was in conspiracy against him, yet he was fighting hard for his friend. His heart was full of sorrow for his condemned friend, understanding him because his own life had been a long struggle against desperate odds. People had treated him shabbily, fate had consistently played foul with him, and yet by sheer grit and genius he had overcome all with grace and humility. He now stood by a man who had defended him. Allegiance prevailed; loyalty won.

'And yet you prefer to live in hate? And thrive in revenge? Is that the price you are paying for the good he seems to have done for you? Can you ever be happy, Karna?' The anger had evaporated from her argument her words gnawed by sadness.

'I *am* happy,' he said quickly. 'I am lucky I have you. I am proud I am Radheya. I am blessed that I am loved. And if I can give a little of that consideration for Duryodhana who has never got love, I think I am doing him a little good...' he sighed deeply. 'My dharma is to be with my friend. I owe it to him. My passion is archery. And it is your love, the love of my parents, my children, Vrushali and Shona that fills my heart. These will guide my life and lead me to glory. I don't aspire for anything else, Uruvi. Except Arjuna's defeat—by me,' he finished softly.

If Karna disliked Arjuna, it was because of the resentment and rivalry between them. But the utter loathing in Karna's heart was reserved only for one man—Shakuni—the person both Uruvi and Karna abhorred. Uruvi wondered if anyone did approve of the man except for his hundred Kuru nephews. The only one of the old king's sons who hated Shakuni was Yuyutsu, who was King Dhritrashtra's son from a low-caste handmaid, and was, therefore, treated as a pariah, just as Karna was. It seems even Shakuni's blindfolded sister Queen Gandhari was not too fond of her brother and was mistrustful of his continuous presence at Hastinapur. With her silken blindfold around her eyes, the sister tried to steer herself far, far away from the tussle of power, politics and intrigue—the three games her brother loved playing.

Shakun presence at Hastinapur was a mystery that few could fathom and even Bhishma Pitamaha was unable to get rid of him. As the brother of the queen, he had no reason whatsoever to stay in the kingdom of his sister's husband. But he had an impelling motive. If rumours were to be believed, it seems the root of the problem had been Bhishma Pitamaha himself. Shakuni's burning resentment against Bhishma Pitamaha was that but for him, his sister could have wed Prince Pandu, the heir apparent, instead of the blind Prince Dhritrashtra. He could not forgive the treachery behind this marriage. Neither could he forget that by marrying off his sister to a blind king, Gandhari and her children had been forever deprived of the kingdom that was rightfully Dhritrashtra's. It had been Prince Pandu he had wanted as his sister's husband, not Prince Dhritrashtra who had lost out on his claim to the throne because of his blindness. Shakuni could never forgive the ecclesiastical old man or the entire Kuru dynasty for having swindled his sister Gandhari and his father King Subala into what he believed was a farcical marriage. They had been made to think that Gandhari would be marrying the King of Hastinapura—and that was King Pandu. But Bhishma Pitamaha had other plans which, though well orchestrated, did not fall in place the way he had intended. The terrible fall-out of this miscalculation was to prove the biggest blunder, shattering the peace of the Kuru clan forever.

Bhishma Pitamaha's intentions had been noble. Realising that Prince Dhritrashtra had lost out on his throne because of his blindness, the grand uncle decided to compensate by marrying off the older prince early, hoping that the first child would be the heir to the Kuru crown. That was why he had hurried King Subala of Gandhar and forced him to to give his daughter, the beautiful Gandhari, in marriage to Prince Dhritrashtra. Their first-born child would be the

King of Hastinapur and justice would be reinstated for the blind prince. But these grand designs did not turn out as planned.

It seems that even Queen Satyavati was unhappy that Bhishma Pitamaha had enthroned King Pandu instead of the older son—Dhritrashtra. Unlike the last time decades ago, when as the new stepmother of young Bhishma (or Prince Devvrata as he was known then), the ambitious Queen Satyavati had forced him into his terrible vow of celibacy to protect her and her children, Bhishma remained stubborn and did not yield to her arguments. The explanation given to her was that as Dhritrashtra was blind, he would not be able to look after the affairs of the state—that was the reason why the throne was best suited for Prince Pandu, her grandson and the younger son of King Vichitravirya.

By choosing to get the blind prince married before Pandu was wedded, Bhishma Pitamaha had planned to enthrone Dhritrashtra's son as the heir to the throne. But it was not to be—Yudhishthira was born before Duryodhana and that mantle fell on him. A livid Shakuni swore vengeance when King Pandu was crowned king. His sister showed her protest more subtly. She accepted her fate with a smile on her face and a silk cloth around her eyes, so that she would experience the world in darkness, just as her blind husband did. The revengeful brother, watching his sister's self-flagellating blindness, promised himself he would sink the Kuru kingdom into an even deeper darkness than what his sister had plunged herself into.

Always clad in dark silks, Shakuni sported a white beard, which was a rather unexpected contrast on his round, jolly face. This evil genius always wore a smile, appearing deceptively cheerful with his bright grin and a perpetual glint in his eyes. Many mistook it for a merry sense of humour. He had otherwise small, undistinguished features and his eyes were tiny. His fleshy face matched his corpulent body, the belly protruding oddly to give him an almost comical look. But that, again, was as deceptive as the man himself.

Whenever he met Uruvi, the elderly uncle never failed to greet her with a warm smile and an exaggerated bow. 'Ah, the Princess of Pukeya! Good day to you, Princess,' he would say sarcastically, emphasizing her royal designation, which never failed to make her uneasily aware that she was no longer a princess but a sutaputra's wife.

One day, she decided to take him on. 'Good day to you, sir,' she returned with a sunny smile. 'I appreciate the fact that you do not forget to call me "Princess"—how can I ever forget whose daughter I am? Just like you are the Prince of Gandhar, staying in Hastinapur, I am the Princess of Pukeya living in Hastinapur as well!'

Uruvi saw his eyes going frosty, but the smile did not slip from his face. The arrogance behind his jovial facade never let anyone forget that he was the Prince of Gandhar, the son of King Subala and the only surviving brother of Queen Gandhari, living for one nefarious goal—the fall of the Kuru dynasty. He loved the game of dice, and never could be seen without his twin dices, which he constantly rubbed in his hands. There was a gory story that the dices he caressed so lovingly were made from his father's thigh bones.

Uruvi shuddered at the thought of it, and recoiled at the gorier tale she had heard of this evil prince. On the advice of astrologers, the lovely Gandhari was married to a goat before she married the prince of Hastinapur, as her astrological charts declared she would be a widow and only her second husband would survive. When her husband, King Dhritrashtra, discovered this, he flew into a rage and imprisoned his father-in-law and brothers-in-law, banishing them to dank dungeons, where they were given only a fistful of rice to share every day. Knowing that they would starve to death, the old King Subala gave only his youngest son the meagre meal so that he would survive and avenge their deaths. That youngest son was Shakuni, who was released only when Gandhari pleaded with her husband. And that was why he had stayed on to plot his revenge and hasten the end of the Kuru clan. With the dice in his hands, he soon made King Dhritrashtra, Duryodhana and Dushasana his unwitting pawns in his game of revenge and retribution. His sister, blindfolding herself from this awful truth, remained oblivious of his motives.

'He is so shrewd, he can see through people's flaws—that's how he plays his game of manipulation,' remarked Karna to Uruvi when rumours of the Kauravas' attempt to kill the Pandavas in the lac palace at Varanavata refused to die down. 'He plays on the weak points of his foe and corners him in his own trap. He is preying on Duryodhana's weakness, which is his jealousy of his cousins. Similarly, he plays on the weakness of the Pandavas—their mildness—and has managed to pit the two groups of cousins against each other. He intends to destroy both. He is vile, he is wicked. He is a rat, who doesn't have the courage to face his enemy upfront, but would rather devour them through stealthy nibbling. He can cause untold destruction, and would be the first one to escape from it. An evil coward, that's what he is!' Karna spat, livid that he was powerless to make his friend see through the malevolence of the sinister uncle whom he loved so devotedly.

Uruvi could not have agreed more with her husband but she thought there was more to Shakuni's plot, something even more devious. She wondered whether King Pandu had been spared from his treachery. King Pandu was said to have died of Sage Kindama's curse—but had he? Or had he been murdered by Shakuni's spies?

Once, when King Pandu had gone hunting, he shot down a deer but the wounded animal was actually Rishi Kindama who had taken the form of a deer while lovemaking. The dying sage cursed the horrified King Pandu that he would die if he were ever to consummate his marriage. Once, in a moment of weakness, King Pandu made love to his second wife Queen Madri, and the king died in his wife's arms. A grief-stricken Madri then jumped into her husband's funeral pyre.

Why, Uruvi always wondered, would Queen Madri consign herself to the flames, when no queen before her had joined their husband in the funeral pyre? Moreover, why would the mother of tiny, helpless six-month-old twins, Nakul and Sahadeva, kill herself and leave them orphaned and under the care of her husband's first wife? It was strange. Had Madri, too, been mortally wounded like her husband, King Pandu, when they had been attacked? Had she been able to talk to Kunti before she died? Had Shakuni played up the curse of the sage to his advantage after all? If he could instigate

Duryodhana to burn the Pandavas and the Queen Mother in the lac palace, he would not have any qualms in murdering King Pandu too. The only person who probably knew the truth was Kunti—but she was an evasive lady who knew how to keep her secrets. Uruvi recalled how she had pestered her on her wedding day about whether she had any regrets, but had got nothing out of her.

Uruvi, however, had never dared to express such thoughts—neither to Karna nor Kunti. She didn't want to add to the atmosphere of suspicion at the royal court where treacherous mind games were being played.

Shakuni had always seen to it that he played his cards right, ensuring that Dhritrashtra remained the King of Hastinapur. First through the blind king and now through Duryodhana, he had secured greater power for himself. Unlike his sister who had turned away from the politics of power, he revelled in it. He lusted after power; the power to destroy his enemies.

Uruvi recalled her father's words and his definition of dushta chathushtayam—Shakuni was one of the wicked four with Duryodhana, Dushasana and Karna, the one she had willingly married in spite of this slur on him. The epithet stuck, but Shakuni was the most wicked, the most vile of them all. And as honour among villains goes, it was ironic that out of the four, two loathed each other. Karna was at his arrogant worst whenever he was near the devious old man and Shakuni never missed a chance to remind Karna that he was a king only through the blessings of his nephew Duryodhana.

Dushasana did not bother to give Karna the respect he expected. In greeting, he always bowed low to Uruvi, but he never bent his head or folded his hands for Karna. Karna noticed this but remained silent.

'Why do you take their insults so easily?' she blurted out one day, when she couldn't bear to see the hurt in his face.

'Because I don't want to hurt Duryodhana. They are his brother and his uncle,' he said simply. 'And how much can Duryodhana protect me? It's how it's always been. I have got used to such unpleasantness. I have lived with it long enough, and I'll have to live with it till the end. But you, Uruvi, you will have to toughen yourself too. You will have to learn to live with this humiliation.'

'I try to...oh, why do we live in this hell?' she cried.

'I didn't have a choice. I was born into it. You had an option, but you chose to marry an outcaste like me,' he said, his lips tightening slightly.

'No, I am not regretting my decision, if that's what you mean... but yes, it hurts. It hurts badly. Till now, I didn't realize the world could be such a cruel place.' She had said these words in a whisper, her voice deadened with a strange hopelessness. Karna recognized this and gave a deep sigh. Uruvi said plaintively, 'How could you live like this? It's torture! Why can't you get away from them?'

'You know well I cannot.'

'Anything is better than this. This is a life of degradation, of humiliation, and worse, knowing that you are the wrong person in the wrong place with the wrong people doing the wrong things...oh, Karna, don't you ever think it so?' she implored, her eyes glistening with despair. He could not look at her, the desperately expectant look in her eyes was too much to bear. Timidly, she stretched out her hand to touch his. He covered her hand with his and squeezed it tightly, as if clutching at the last vestige of hope.

'I want to make you happy. You are all I have got. I love you. But I can't forsake that one man whom you want me to renounce for you.'

She released her hand from his and stood up. She went over to the long mirror at the end of the room and said, 'It's about time we got ready...your parents are expecting us downstairs.'

As the wife of Karna, Uruvi had resigned herself to the reality that she had to live with enemies. Her father had cautioned her; so had Kunti. It was not just a word of warning, it was their last plea to protect her from certain lifelong misery, from the relentless ill-treatment she could not escape from. By not obeying them, she had hurt them as much as she had hurt herself.

She detested being known as the wife of one of the dushta chathushtayam, a description that filled her with shame. 'No!' she cried, 'he is not wicked. Karna is not a villain. He is good, he is noble, and I love him for that.' But the world was not listening to her silent cries. She would have to carry the burden of this stigma as well. Since her marriage, she could not look at the Pandavas straight in the eye, especially Arjuna, whom she had spurned for his arch-rival. With her parents, she was always on the back foot, knowing that they were experiencing her hurt and humiliation as well. The same guilt swamped her whenever she was in the presence of Krishna or Bhishma Pitamaha. She avoided them or glanced at them covertly as if wanting to rush off and hide.

She found it difficult to reconcile herself to this apologetic way of living. But she had to endure it. She had to suffer the way people looked at them, at her, at Karna, the false sympathy she had to often put up with. The embarrassment that deluged her often made her hate herself. Nor could she stand the contempt people showed for Karna. She sometimes wished she was more thick-skinned, so that she could see nothing, feel nothing. It was misery that forced her to chat, to laugh off their scorn and remain agreeable even when the nastiest tongues wagged. She had to learn to survive, and the only place she could hide was in the recesses of her thoughts, her silent tears slipping softly down the shadowy contours of her face, dripping into the darkness.

8

Indraprastha

King Yudhishthira, the worthy Pandava king, was known as ajatashatru: one who has no enemy. It was because of that sterling quality that all men, gods, kings, sages and saints were happy at the success of the Rajasuya yajna—the sacrifice made by King Yudhishthira to declare himself as the emperor of all kings—except Duryodhana. Yet, neither he nor Karna protested against Yudhishthira's grand title openly.

Uruvi voiced her doubts to Karna. 'This is the best chance Duryodhana has to prove his might. If he resents Yudhishthira's claim as emperor, he should fight Yudhishthira in an open battle.'

Karna frowned, his voice troubled. 'But he insists on doing otherwise. He says he will be vanquished by his cousin as the Pandavas have the support of all the major kings. I tell him, what does it matter? He has me, and I am sure Bhishma Pitamaha and Dronacharya will take his side out of family loyalty. Why doesn't he fight the Pandavas and get what he wants? He couldn't have had a better opportunity...' Karna looked perplexed.

'Because he doesn't think the way you do. He is a coward,' Uruvi could not hide the sneer in her words. 'He would rather win Yudhishthira's share of the kingdom through deception than an open combat. He is wily, not valiant. He has Hastinapur, yet he covets Indraprastha—the barren half of the kingdom that was handed out to the Pandavas. Now that they have managed to successfully convert it into a land of wealth and prosperity, Duryodhana regrets that the Kauravas were forced to part with it. Today the Pandavas are ruling Indraprastha in full glory and your friend has become insecure again, right, Karna?' She didn't wait for her husband's reply; he was looking at her wordlessly.

'Worse, with Yudhishthira performing the Rajasuya sacrifice, he has declared himself the emperor of all kings. Yet, Duryodhana doesn't have it in him to challenge the Pandavas and oppose their growing might,' she said disparagingly. 'He would rather plot deviously and yearn for what is not his. Why can't he live in peace and let others live in peace too? He is itching for a fight but a mean, sly fight—not an open battle at all! The wicked are never satisfied. As a friend, why don't you restrain him from this madness?'

Her tirade made Karna restless, though he fought hard to hide it. What Uruvi said was true. 'I cannot stop him, understand this, Uruvi. No one can,' he replied quietly. 'Duryodhana is like this because he has been mentored by the evil Shakuni far too long. He believes his right to be a king has been usurped by his cousins who, frankly, he has never considered his cousins at all. He has never acknowledged the sons of Kunti and Madri as the sons of Pandu. To him, the tales relating to Kunti's boon are all eyewash. His resentment for the Pandavas stems from there. He sincerely believes that since he is the eldest son of the eldest king, he is the heir apparent to the throne of Hastinapur. His father, in spite of being the eldest son, had to renounce the throne in favour of King Pandu because he was blind. He wants to take back that throne which he thinks was always rightfully his, but which has been given away to Yudhishthira instead. He believes that this was blatant favouritism.'

'And you believe what he believes in?' she asked. 'Can't both of you see that it was deliberately done to avoid a clash between the Kauravas and the Pandavas over the whole Kuru kingdom?' Uruvi reminded him pointedly. 'Why can't he be content with what he has been given? He remains jealous of the Pandavas. And he always hated Bhima the most! Poor Duryodhana, he was beaten up so badly by Bhima each time they quarrelled! I remember those hideous fights well, when Bhima used to pummel him black and blue!'

'The hate runs much deeper now,' Karna agreed solemnly. 'Bhima is his eternal opponent in mace warfare. Bhima dominates the Kauravas in sports and in various skills with his immense physical power. Both Bhima and Duryodhana possess exceptional physical strength, and have been equally well-trained by Balarama in mace fighting and wrestling. But if Bhima has the power, Duryodhana wields more skill with the mace.'

'A rivalry similar to the one you have with Arjuna,' Uruvi thought silently. 'How can I forget that Arjuna and Karna are on par? Both are remarkable archers, both competed savagely for Draupadi's hand, and again, at my swayamwara, I made them adversaries. But it is getting more dangerous than mere ego clashes. Both Karna and Arjuna have a deep bond with the Kauravas—one through friendship and the other through blood. What they have chosen to do has shaped them and their families, accentuating the importance of obligation and responsibility. But each incident has impelled the situation towards a climax—the invincible friendship between Duryodhana and Karna is as strong as the seething rivalry between Karna and Arjuna. Moreover, the antagonism between the Pandavas and the Kauravas is getting as virulent as the growing hostility between Karna and Arjuna.' She shivered at the thought of the implications of this enmity.

'Why do you hate Arjuna so much?' she asked abruptly, her words rushing out before she could stem them. She regretted them instantly. Karna gave her an inscrutable look and said blandly, 'Not because of you, dear. I am afraid I am not a very jealous person.'

'If not me, then is it because he won Draupadi?' she hit back, hurt to the quick, the stab of jealousy going deeper than she would have imagined.

Karna paled. 'Have you lost your sense of humour, woman?' he said with vehemence. 'It's got nothing to do with you or Draupadi. You give her more credit than I can claim!' he added dryly.

There was a long silence which Uruvi was suddenly afraid to break, scared that it would shatter the easy camaraderie between them. What madness had prompted her to mention such a forbidden topic! Or was it her jealous heart overwhelming her usually rational mind?

Karna's next words were calm as if the storm had passed. 'Our rivalry goes beyond women, dear,' he said slowly. 'Arjuna has always been thrown at me as a comparison for the qualities I supposedly lacked. He is said to be my superior—but I don't think so. I am not less of a warrior than him, considering all the disadvantages I had to live through while he sailed smoothly with all the benefits of being a prince! And it's not just an ego clash; the resentment is far too deep. I guess we were born to be enemies,' he shrugged, the expression on his face composed. The enormity of the rivalry clearly did not ruffle him.

'Coming back to where we started, you rightly mentioned that now, especially with the city of Indraprastha blooming into a more beautiful and prosperous place than Hastinapura and with Yudhishthira proclaimed as its emperor, Duryodhana is, of course, enraged! Yet he refuses to confront the Pandavas!'

Uruvi took the cue and continued the discussion. 'It's possible that he hoped the powerful King Jarasandha of Magadha would have vanquished the Pandavas,' she remarked thoughtfully. 'But Krishna shrewdly had the king killed in the duel with Bhima before the Rajasuya yagna, and now there is no one to object to Yudhishthira's assumption of the throne, not even Duryodhana. He either fights him valiantly or accepts the reality, however distasteful it is to him. Anway, Yudhishthira on his part is full of humility, as he always is. I hear that the Rajasuya celebrations are going to be magnificent and that Yudhishthira has involved all the members of the Kuru family, even Vikarna, Duryodhana's younger brother, besides Bhima, Arjuna, Nakul and Sahadeva.'

'Lord Krishna is in charge of washing the feet of all the guests,' said Karna with deep reverence. 'It seems that all the duties had already been assigned to others, so Krishna offered to take up this task most humbly. "Am I so unworthy that I cannot do this task?" he is said to have asked Yudhishthira. "Work is honour and there is dignity in any kind of work."'

'Yes, there is!' chuckled someone, making them turn in surprise. It was Krishna, who had suddenly turned up in person. Uruvi was astounded to see the most powerful king and ally of the Pandavas at Karna's palace, and her surprise clearly showed, for Krishna remarked with a smile, 'Wonders do not cease to happen! But has Karna told you the meatiest bit of news? He is part of the preparations for the celebration too. Since Karna is so well known for his generosity and charity, Yudhishthira has handed him the responsibility of looking after this part-charity! In fact, I am here to discuss a few matters about the Rajasuya.'

Karna gave him a reverential bow. Uruvi turned a delighted smile on her husband. 'You are helping out too?' she looked visibly elated.

'Uh, er, yes, it's for a good cause...and I couldn't turn down Yudhishthira's request,' he muttered self-consciously. His face had turned scarlet, and Uruvi could not help beaming more broadly. Her face was radiant, her eyes twinkling in a sudden burst of cheerfulness. That he would be together with Krishna and the Pandavas filled her with happiness. It would not last long, she knew, but she wanted to revel in the moment. Krishna observed the glow on her face and smiled knowingly.

'I hope, dear, that I have not earned your disapproval by killing Jarasandha,' mocked Krishna, giving her an exaggerated bow. 'Am I spared your sharp tongue and haughty glare? Karna, how can you live with this shrew?'

'He is leading a charmed life, don't worry,' she laughed and added in mock anger, 'Are you here to create problems between me and my husband? With Jarasandha, you played it very safe as usual! With him dead, you have rescued the eighty-six princes he had imprisoned. And best of all, Yudhishthira's Rajasuya yagna can be held peacefully...'

'Don't be too sure of that! There are still quite a few who are not happy about Yudhishthira declaring himself as the emperor. What do you say, Karna?'

'Those who are unhappy about it should challenge Yudhishthira in a battle,' Karna replied flatly. 'Accepting tributes and allegiance from all the kings is what the yagna is all about. By performing the Rajasuya sacrifice, Yudhishthira will have crowned himself the emperor and impose his imperial authority.'

'Spoken like a true warrior,' commended Krishna. 'What else can the worthy pupil of Parshurama advise?'

Though she was supremely happy watching her husband's camaraderie with Krishna, Uruvi found Karna's observations a little jarring. 'That is giving sanction to the annexation of other kingdoms in the guise of imperial authority. Shouldn't a king concentrate on his subjects and rule his own kingdom in fairness, in prosperity? Rather than expanding his empire though war for personal greed or to gain power, he would be better appreciated by his subjects if he looked after them!'

'A king cannot live without ambitions, it's his noble virtue,' argued her husband. 'Heroic deeds are what make a kshatriya illustrious. Whatever his other qualities, it is heroism that makes a warrior. What is life without effort and enthusiasm? We should build our strengths and use them as weapons to lead a successful life. Failure often happens because we fail to recognize our strengths and our weaknesses.'

Krishna looked delighted at Karna's words. 'O pupil of Parshurama, what you say is true. Death comes to all, the hero as well as the weak, the brave as well as the cowardly, but the noblest duty of a kshatriya is to be true to his faith, to overcome his foes in righteous battle, and to win glory.'

'At the cost of peace and prosperity? That's hollow reasoning!' countered Uruvi spiritedly. 'Why should a king not be satisfied with ruling his kingdom and making it a peaceful, prosperous state? He forgets that's his responsibility too—he owes it to his people and his subjects. If each king thought this way, there would be no war, no conflict, no confrontations.'

'That is idealistic, if not futile thinking, dear. Man is not a peaceful being,' Krishna said gently. 'You are a kshatriya's daughter and hearing you speak such words of the faint-hearted is strange.'

'I am saying this *because* I am a kshatriya's daughter!' she retorted, her words sharpening not so much with anger as with the pain that clouded her mind. 'I have lived with it all through childhood, tormented by constant worry, and I have seen my mother do the same, and my grandmother before her as well. It is easy starting wars; ending them is not in your hands because the end is always terrible. Each time my father went for battle, I lived in the fear that he would not return. And if he had died, it would have been a heroic death on the battlefield, wouldn't it? But what good would it have done for me or my mother? That she was a hero's widow and me a hero's fatherless child? What good has war done except give satisfaction to those seeking vain glory?'

She became dejected, the anger suddenly dissipating, punctured by an unusual anxiety and a fearful apprehension of what was to come. Would she be struck with the same terror for Karna's life each time he went to war? Krishna smiled at her bowed head, her face averted to hide the pain tearing through her. He quietly beckoned to Karna and they left the room. Uruvi was oblivious of their absence, and when Karna returned later, he noticed Uruvi staring vacantly into the distance. 'Why are you so upset?' he asked gently.

She turned to him. Her face was ravaged with grief. 'Because I fear I shall lose you. I live with that dread, I sleep with that fear, I wake up with that thought,' she whispered, a sob in her voice. 'And what will take you away from me is war, a bloody, pointless war. I can foresee it. O Karna, leave the Kuru princes—then we can be much happier.'

Karna heaved a long sigh and placed a hand on her shoulder. 'We live with our choices, and we choose to live in a certain way,' he said gently, drawing her close. 'I choose to be a kshatriya, a warrior. I choose to be with the Kauravas. You choose to be with me as my wife. We have made our decisions. Neither of us can turn back, can we? What had to happen has happened. What is to happen will happen anyway...' he nudged her slightly. If you look so pale, what will your parents and Kunti say? That I have not treated you well!'

At the mention of Kunti, and the prospect of meeting her parents soon, Uruvi forced herself to brighten up, smiling through her fears.

'You didn't tell me you were helping the Pandavas with the Rajasuya event. How do you feel about being with them?' she asked instead.

Karna smiled. 'I know what you are getting at—but this is a temporary arrangement, Uruvi. I won't be with them forever.'

'I wish you would!' she blurted before she could restrain herself.

'I couldn't even if I wanted to,' Karna sighed. 'The Pandavas have never accepted me.' There was a resigned ring in his voice. 'All I wanted to do was devote my life to archery. That is what I am good at and what I know best. And all I want is to spend my life perfecting this skill. It was only Duryodhana who gave me this chance to do so. He made me a warrior, an archer and a king, although the last I don't really like, frankly. The Pandavas didn't give me any chances. And that's how it is—me with Duryodhana and Arjuna with Krishna.'

'If you had chosen Krishna, glory would have been yours too,' she said. 'People like Duryodhana will always seek you out because they need you to serve their selfish interests. But with Krishna, you will have to seek—with the love and devotion your heart is so full of. If you had gone to him, he would not have refused you.'

'Dear Uruvi,' Karna answered with a weary smile. 'You want me to befriend Krishna, but if I do so, won't I be self-serving like Duryodhana whom you accuse of being an opportunist? I love Krishna, I respect him. I bow to him. And I want to be like him in my small way. Like him, I want to give everything I can to one and all. And when Duryodhana asked for my hand of friendship, I gave it to him, no questions asked. Uruvi, Duryodhana *needs* me, just the way Arjuna needs Krishna. Arjuna asked for his help, so Krishna couldn't refuse. Duryodhana asked for my help, and I cannot refuse either. Perhaps, one day, I might go to Krishna for help, or possibly, Krishna himself will come to me and there may be something I can do for him.'

Uruvi fell silent, wondering if she should welcome or dread that day.

Like Bhanumati, Duryodhana's wife, Uruvi was eager to visit the beautiful palace built by the Pandavas. One of the reasons why she agreed to attend the Rajasuya yagna was to satisfy her curiosity. There was an interesting story about the palace. Indraprastha had been built where the Khandava forest once stood. A dangerous forest where no humans could live, it was infested with snakes and other feral creatures. With the blessings of Krishna, Yudhishthira requested Agni, the fire god, to burn down the forest so that he could build his dream city, but Mayadanav, a demon who lived there, was scared when he heard the forest was going to be destroyed. He begged for sanctuary, and was given permission to stay on, but on one condition: that he would build them a city and a grand palace that the world would look up to in awe. Mayadanav, a protégé of Vishvakarma, the architect of the gods, willingly agreed. He constructed the city of Indraprastha for the Pandavas, which was so beautiful that it had no rival in its splendour either on earth or in heaven. But the pride of Indraprastha was the imperial palace with its fantastic design, and this was where Kunti took Uruvi to show her around.

The moment she entered the palace, Uruvi was struck by its air of mystery. Nestled in a beautifully landscaped garden of fruit trees and scented creepers, the palace rose gracefully from the luxuriant greenery. It was beautiful but perplexing to Uruvi. The strangely ornate workmanship faintly annoyed her; it seemed to have been overdone. Though the palace befitted the grandeur of the king of kings and the greatest of princes, it breathed beauty but lacked soul. Uruvi preferred not to voice her thoughts to Kunti or anyone else—no one would have agreed with her, she smiled wryly. All the guests were too impressed with this marvel of supernatural architecture.

'Why this fantastic play of magic? This is to be your home, not a museum!' remarked Uruvi. Kunti gave her a small smile. This girl was as tactless as ever. Clearly, neither marriage nor its responsibilities had blunted her thoughts or her tongue.

'Where's Draupadi? Why is she nowhere to be seen?' Uruvi asked curiously.

She was busy with the Rajasuya preparations, Kunti hastily explained and ushered Uruvi into her bedroom. Uruvi was not taken in by Kunti's show of exuberance. Something was definitely amiss. Arjuna had been exceptionally frosty with her and barely civil to Karna, only as much as the occasion forced him to be. She could understand his cold resentment, but what puzzled her was Draupadi's strange behaviour, for she seemed to be avoiding them completely. Uruvi had not yet been formally introduced to her and had not seen her the entire day. Was this Draupadi's way of treating her as a sutaputra's wife? Uruvi felt the clammy hand of a cold snub. And with a sickening realization, she recalled that she had not even received a formal invite—it was Kunti who had coaxed her to visit Indraprastha and the new palace. In contrast to the cold dismissal by his brother and his wife, however, Yudhishthira's inclusion of Karna in the Rajasuya preparations was indeed a warm, kind gesture. Uruvi dismissed her disturbing thoughts, determined to enjoy herself. Her parents were here and so was Kunti, the people who mattered most to her.

'So, child, what are you wearing for the function?' Kunti interrupted her thoughts.

Uruvi burst out laughing. 'Oh, Ma, what does it matter?' she answered with a shrug. 'It's not my event. It's yours and Draupadi's. You are the hosts!'

'And you will always be my guest of honour!'

Uruvi was as anxious to meet her parents as were they to meet their daughter. Queen Shubra was particularly apprehensive. The moment she caught Karna and Uruvi together, she felt like a stranger between a lovesick pair. It was easy to see that her daughter was madly in love with Karna. But what made the Queen of Pukeya heave a huge sigh of relief was that her son-in-law was obviously in love with her daughter as well. There was a light in his eyes that was unmistakable; he could not take his eyes off Uruvi and found an excuse to be with her all the time. Her daughter blushed often, her lips slightly parted in a sigh when she looked at her husband. They looked like lovers who would rather walk off into the sunset, hands entwined, searching for a place to be with each other. It was exciting, even a little moving, and the mother felt her hostility for the son-in-law slowly melting away.

The Rajasuya yagna was a success, as predicted. The morning saw King Yudhishthira, in a dazzling chariot, enter the hall with Draupadi. Uruvi had not seen Draupadi till then, but had heard enough stories about her to make her curious. At the very first sight, Draupadi was arresting—tall, dark and voluptuous. Her magnificient eyes were heavily kohled, yet luminous. She had a fine nose, her mouth red and generous, curving slightly downwards. Her skin was smooth, and her coal-black wavy hair tumbling down her rounded shoulders, was, crowned with a tiara of diamonds and other glittering gems. She had not tied her thick mane in a bun as most women had at the event; clearly, she knew it was her best feature. She wore a heavily embroidered crimson silk sari, her slim feet bare beneath tinkling anklets. She was not a delicate woman, but like a goddess of summer, exuded raw sensuality.

Draupadi's eyes were not demure or downcast as she sat for the yagna besides Yudhishthira. They were stealthy and searching, as she scrutinized the guests around her. As she did so, her eyes met Uruvi's, but she looked indifferently away when Uruvi smiled. This woman doesn't like me, Uruvi thought with amused surprise. She wondered why. Because of Arjuna? Because she was supposed to have married Arjuna and Draupadi was still angry about it? Uruvi could not fathom why the Pandava queen had coldly ignored her and it bothered her a little. The Pandava queen had not come down to meet her when Uruvi had visited Kunti at the palace either. Or was it because she was a sutaputra's wife? It was that horrible feeling again. Her face flamed with the heat of feeling outright rejection.

The ceremony was in full swing. The priests, religious heads and brahmins were performing a sacrifice and loudly chanting the Vedic hymns. The princely guests from many kingdoms, like Madri, Panchala, Chedi, Pukeya and Kosala, were present in full regalia. In order to observe the great ceremony, wives of the nobles and queens of the royal family arrived, gorgeously dressed, in fancy palanquins. Queen Bhanumati was among them, and catching sight of Uruvi standing near one of the marbled pillars, rushed to her side, smiling and waving to her.

'Am I late?' she gasped, catching her breath.

'No, well in time,' Uruvi smiled. There was something utterly adorable about this blundering girl. One had to like her, even though she was Duryodhana's wife. Karna treated her like his baby sister, indulgent and teasing alternately.

'The yagna has just started,' Uruvi held her hand affectionately. 'There's the couple doing the pooja,' she said pointing at the Pandava king and queen. Yudhishthira was closely following what the priest was saying, but Draupadi looked distracted. She was staring straight into the distance, a soft almost caressing look on her face.

Curious, Uruvi's eyes followed Draupadi's to see who Draupadi was gazing at. Then Uruvi's heart skipped a beat, her body going suddenly tense. It was Karna. Draupadi was looking pensively at Karna, her otherwise dark, flashing eyes soft with immeasurable tenderness. Uruvi paled. She looked towards her husband. He was chatting with Ashwatthama; they seemed to share a joke for, suddenly, Karna threw back his head and laughed. Karna's laughter seemed to break the spell for Draupadi and Uruvi saw her hurriedly glancing at Yudhishthira instead.

Uruvi stared at the rising flames of the yagna fire. She couldn't forget the look of longing Draupadi had given Karna. She felt a prickle down her back and her throat had gone dry. It came to her with shattering suddenness—Draupadi was in love with Karna. It was such a surprise, such a shock that she could not cope with it. It couldn't be! It just couldn't be! Uruvi found herself shaking her head, trying to ward off the impossible. It couldn't be that Draupadi loved Karna. But Uruvi had seen Draupadi's expression—and she knew. There was no mistake, no illusion about the intensity of the look and what it meant. She felt no jealousy. She felt no anger. Just plain amazement. It couldn't be possible, she breathed painfully. But it was. If Draupadi loved him, why had she humiliated him at her swayamwara and thrown away her chance to marry him? She knew he would have passed the test, yet she had not allowed him the opportunity to win her at her swayamwara. But why? *Why?*

And what were Karna's feelings for her? The thought jolted her. Did her husband harbour a secret love for Draupadi as well? Cold fear caught at her heart. Could it be so? For Uruvi, the long hours of the yagna turned to sheer torment. Her eyes kept shifting from Karna to Draupadi and back, searching for tell tale signs. Draupadi kept glancing at him furtively whenever she could, but Karna seemed oblivious to her, cold and inscrutable as he always was. But the fear did not leave Uruvi's aching heart.

'You look so disturbed. Aren't you feeling well?' Bhanumati's chatter broke through her thoughts. 'You seem so oddly quiet. We have hardly spoken!'

Uruvi gave her a wan smile. She knew she could not leave the function midway. Following the Rajasuya sacrifice, there was the Vedic ritual called patni-samyaja, a sacrifice performed by the king and his wife, and also by priests. When Queen Draupadi and King Yudhishthira had their avabhrtha, a holy dip in the river, citizens of all the varnas—the brahmins, the kshatriyas, the vaisyas and the sudras—followed them. With everyone refreshed after bathing, the guests dressed in their best silks, adorned with ornaments and garlands, the women with golden girdles around the waist and vermillion tilakas on their foreheads. The men and women of Hastinapur and Indraprastha were rejoicing, but Uruvi barely registered the happy commotion around her. She wanted to run away, far from the crowds and her disturbing thoughts.

As the ceremony came to an end, all the guests began to leave. King Yudhishthira persuaded his close friends and relatives, including Krishna, Duryodhana and Uruvi to stay back. They could not refuse the request of the king and Kunti, especially, coaxed Uruvi to stay on. Uruvi wanted to rush back home to the comforting confines of her own room but she forced herself to listen to Kunti. She agreed to stay on for another day although her instincts warned her not to do so.

The next morning, Uruvi sat in the verandah with Kunti and Subhadra, a soft-spoken lovely girl rumoured to be Arjuna's favourite wife; she had consented to elope with Arjuna under the very nose of her suitor, Duryodhana! So, that was another slight Duryodhana was unlikely to forget. Uruvi heard chatter downstairs and saw Duryodhana being shown around by the royal couple, Yudhishthira and Draupadi. Karna was with them. Uruvi bit her lip. He kept a distance from the couple, and lagged behind the group. Draupadi this time though, looked through him and was treating him as if he was invisible. Uruvi could almost feel the icy coldness between them.

A retinue of handmaids appeared and lined up before the guests. 'This way, brother-in-law,' Uruvi heard Draupadi tell Duryodhana, indicating that he walk though the encircling wall. Duryodhana looked suspiciously at Draupadi as if she was poking fun at him.

'I'll use the door instead,' he said and banged straight into a solid wall. He was so dazed that he had to be steadied by Karna. Uruvi suppressed a giggle but her eyes danced with merriment. So did Subhadra's. Kunti hushed them warningly.

'You should have listened to me, brother-in-law,' said Draupadi, amiably. 'In this palace, what appears to be is not what it actually is.' She and Yudhishthira moved towards the courtyard, which was an intriguing piece of architecture. The surface of the left side seemed like a ripple of water. On the right, though, the floor of the courtyard appeared to be polished granite. The maids walked across the rippling surface of water in the courtyard, while the royal guests looked on, speechless. Draupadi walked across the shimmering water surface herself and requested them to follow her. 'I'll go the other way,' said Duryodhana, and before anyone could warn him, he took a step on the 'granite'. There was a loud splash and Uruvi saw Duryodhana waist-deep in water, drenched and dishevelled. Uruvi clapped a hand to her mouth and stifled a giggle but Draupadi could not control herself. She burst out laughing. 'Oh, the blind son of a blind father!' she exclaimed, merry tears streaming down her face.

Karna was helping his friend up. So was Yudhishthira, apologizing profusely. Duryodhana went white with fury, and looked crazed enough to hit Draupadi. Had it not been for Karna's restraining hand, Uruvi realized in horror, Duryodhana would have done just that. Instead, he gave a cry of rage and stormed out of the palace. Uruvi saw Karna give Draupadi a venomous glare. 'I hope we can contain the situation,' he muttered to Yudhishthira and rushed after the Kuru king. The usually gentle Yudhishthira was pale, and he frowned angrily at his wife. 'Do you realize what you have done?' he asked in exasperation, and followed Karna out of the courtyard.

Draupadi was still smiling mockingly. She did not know that it would be her last smile for a long time to come.

9

Draupadi

It was the thought of Draupadi that now tormented Uruvi. She could not forget the look of intense yearning she had seen in Draupadi's eyes, her gaze lingering on Karna. She shut her eyes to block the image but it was impressed on her mind. The restlessness within her grew; it besieged her through the day and ravaged her through the nights. The raven-haired, black-eyed, smiling Draupadi seemed to taunt her in her dreams. It was almost the same vision she replayed each night…

She heard a husky laugh. Draupadi was strolling down a path, the movement of her swaying hips lissom and lazy. She was alone, walking towards someone. Uruvi turned her head to see whom Draupadi was going to meet, her steps quickening, eager and rushed. It was Karna, tall and smiling. He got up to greet her. Draupadi looked more beautiful than before, almost luminous in her loveliness. Her skin was silky and smooth, her face glowed, her thick hair cascaded down to her slim waist. Her lips were full and smiling, her eyes smouldering with desire. Karna drew her close and Draupadi flung her arms around him. She stood there laughing, held in his close embrace, the tinkling sound similar to her laughter when Duryodhana had walked into water in her palace. Uruvi's terrified eyes saw an approaching fire behind the embracing couple, burning everything, everywhere, as the sound of anguished screams rent the air. She recognized a huge battlefield, blood-soaked and full of heaped corpses and…

The shrieks pierced her into wakefulness. She shut her ears to cut off the weeping howls, her eyes shut tightly to erase the lingering image imprinted in her convoluted thoughts. Would Draupadi's unkind laugh spark off a raging fire of hate, war and bloodshed?

The consequences of her taunting laughter had been enormous. Duryodhana had left for Hastinapur more livid and resentful than he was when he had arrived there. He ranted and raged for days after that, and Uruvi wondered when the terrible inferno of hatred would flare up some day, obliterating everything. Karna tried to placate him, but in vain, as his words only worked like inflammable oil over a smouldering fire.

'Let him be. He just cannot bear the success of the Pandavas, Indraprastha and the lovely palace,' Uruvi said dismissively. 'And Draupadi's malicious remark scratched a raw wound. It'll burn, it'll bleed, but you can't do anything about it. As you once said yourself, Duryodhana has gone too far down the path of hatred and jealousy. He'll do anything to get what he wants. And he wants the Pandavas out—preferably destroyed. And you, inadvertently, will be part of his plot, Karna. That will be the day.'

Uruvi had resigned herself to the fact that she could never weed out the deep-rooted hold Duryodhana had over her husband. It was too firm an allegiance, but she tried to convince Karna to see how his friend was on the path to destruction.

In her turmoil of worry, jealousy and suspicion, Uruvi discovered that she had something to look forward to in her life. She was wildly happy—and disgustingly sick—each morning. She wanted to break the news to Karna, but each time she faltered, either out of uncharacteristic shyness or because she simply did not consider the moment as the right one.

One late morning he found her looking piteously pale as she lay down in bed.

'Are you unwell?'

'No. I am pregnant,' she retorted as blood rushed to her cheeks.

He couldn't believe his ears. He stood still for a long time, staring at her with a happy disbelief, and then swept her into his arms.

'Oh, Uruvi!' he sighed, holding her close. She looked up at his face, his eyes shining with joy, his smile wide and warm. 'Why the excitement? It's not the first time for you!' she teased.

'It is the first good news after such a long, long time,' he replied fervently.

For five days, Karna did not leave Uruvi's side, and for those five days and five nights, he thought of Uruvi and the child she would bear. He was worried. Nothing seemed to be going right. He was having a trying time keeping Duryodhana calm after the fiasco at Indraprastha. He was thirsting for revenge—and Karna was aware that the Kauravas were hatching a plot though he was discreetly kept away from the hushed meetings between Shakuni and his nephews. Not that he cared but he was sure something dire was afoot and they did not want to include him in their plans. Karna grew restless; why did Duryodhana not confront his cousins and finish the feud once and for all? He could not understand the deceit and subterfuge—he loathed it.

He looked down at the sleeping form of his wife by his side. There were times when their arguments got too tempestuous and Karna knew it was because of a certain external factor—Duryodhana. She seemed gripped by some inner fear that Karna had not been able to understand. Since they had returned from Indraprastha, Uruvi's vivacity had sobered to a strange sullenness. She had often been moody, sometimes morose and petulant. But the baby in her womb had swept away all that.

He knew he had her love. And it made him feel happier than he had ever felt in his life. He wanted to take her in his arms, to stroke her hair and kiss those tear-stained eyes whenever she cried furtively, hoping he would not see. He wanted to comfort her, wanted her to smile at him and to see those deep, flashing eyes sparkling with mischief and mirth. When he was with her, he felt happy and calm; the adoring affection he saw in her dancing eyes always touched him. On an impulse, he bent his head to give her a long, lingering kiss. Drowsily, she returned his kiss and slowly woke up, rising to his passion. He took her small face in his hands, 'You are soon going to be fat and clumsy, little woman. But I can't help loving you,' he muttered thickly.

A wave of passion swept over her, and she was moved by the raw fervour in his voice.

She gave a shaky laugh, 'I can't think what it is I see in you.'

He chuckled. She took a childish delight in puncturing his ego and it was a characteristic answer.

One afternoon, Karna left for the Hastinapur royal court as Duryodhana had urgently asked for him. Uruvi impatiently waited for Karna to return—she had never needed him so badly.

She resented Duryodhana for meddling in their lives in the insidious way he did. She had learnt to live with it, yet she could not suppress the prickle of annoyance or the stab of absurd fear whenever Duryodhana called for Karna. She knew that she was expecting the worst. She retraced her steps to her chamber with a vague feeling of foreboding, a queer formless dread of something about to happen.

She could not have guessed, or never could have imagined, what that something was going to be.

When that day dawned, it was deceptively calm. Everybody went about their work as usual and Uruvi was unaware that this day would bring one of the most decisive moments of her life.

In the late afternoon, her maid came rushing into her room. Her frightened expression struck terror in Uruvi's heart, and when the maid told her the news, she quivered with shock. King Yudhishthira and the other four Pandavas had been invited to play a game of dice at Hastinapur. Playing against Shakuni, who had resorted to trickery by using loaded dice, King Yudhishthira had lost badly. In desperation, he lost game after game, gambling away his entire kingdom, his wealth, his army, his four loyal brothers and even his wife, Queen Draupadi in a series of gambits to retrieve one by staking another. Worse, when Draupadi was gambled away, the unthinkable happened. Karna had encouraged Duryodhana's brother Dushasana to drag Draupadi into the court and disrobe her. Having won her in the game, the Pandava queen became the property of the Kauravas, right down to the clothes she was wearing. Announcing this with a leer, Dushasana had attempted to strip the weeping queen in the large hall with everyone, including the elders, looking on helplessly. But amazingly, a miracle happened, for as Dushasana unwound Draupadi's sari, it seemed endless, stretching into expanses of cloth—until, at last, the exhausted Kaurava prince gave up, despairing at the never-ending length of the sari.

'The Pandava queen had fainted but it was the Almighty who saved the poor woman from the wicked Kuru princes,' sniffed the maid, in righteous indignation.

The maid rattled on with all the lurid details of the shameful event, and Uruvi was in shock. Her legs gave way and she sank to her knees. She felt drained. She wanted to scream but a wordless shriek choked her. This is the start of the finish, she thought. The obliteration, the end, she registered dully in her mind, and closed her eyes in despair. A tear slid down her cheek, but she wiped it away determinedly. She shook herself as she waited for her husband to come back. She needed all her strength, she needed all her calm. And never had the wait been so long, so wretched, so painful. But it gave her time to get a hold on herself and weigh the situation.

She did not hear Karna return, but sensed his presence late that moonless night. The palace was silent; his footsteps as soundless as the prevailing stillness. The room was dimly lit when he entered their room. He gave a start when he saw her, awake and sitting up straight.

'Are you feeling unwell?' he sounded alarmed. She heard the note of worry in his voice. She forced herself not to think of the tenderness in his query; his concern swept over her, leaving her even more distraught. She held on to herself to stop herself from crying.

She bit her lip and said evenly, 'I stayed awake to let you know that I shall be leaving for Pukeya tomorrow morning.'

'For how long?'

'I don't want to stay here. I am leaving you. I just wanted to let you know my decision.'

'What are you talking about?'

'You know what I am talking about,' her voice was icy. 'I am talking about the devious plot, the game of dice that you helped devise with your friend Duryodhana to usurp the Indraprastha throne. It shows that you are as conniving as he is. I am talking about how Draupadi was so shamefully dishonoured at the palace. Do you want me to go into the details or would you be courteous enough to spell them out yourself?'

He looked at her in mute anguish.

Rage leapt to her throat. 'Tell me, Karna, in your own words what happened there. How you instigated Duryodhana to drag Draupadi to the hall. How you encouraged the Kauravas to strip her. How you called her a whore. How you watched shamelessly as Dushasana pulled at her sari. How you were the hero?'

Her fury rose, her words knife-like, 'Did it make you feel proud, great warrior, to pull a woman by her hair and haul her through the royal hall? Did it make you feel proud, great warrior, to strip her of her pride? Did it make you feel powerful, great warrior, to disrobe her? To deride her as a prostitute? Did it make you feel happy to hear her beg and weep? What sort of a man *are* you?' she cried. 'How could you do what you did? How could you say that as a wife of more than four husbands, she is nothing but a "whore"? That the Pandavas were like sesame seeds removed from the kernel and she should now find other husbands?'

Karna's lips tightened a little but he kept quiet. His silence incensed her further. 'How can you be so complacent, so pleased with yourself, seeing everything? How can anyone be so shameless, so depraved? Answer me, damn you, answer me!' she shook his arm violently.

Karna stood still as her words poured over him like lava. His eyes tortured, he turned away from her.

'I want you to speak out! Talk to me! Tell me how you could behave so shamefully!' she wept, in pain and in wrath.

'I have no answer,' he said at last. 'I have no explanation. I cannot justify myself.'

'What do you mean you cannot justify yourself?' Her voice trembled in cold fury. 'If that is so, your whole life is a pretence, a lie. You talk about dharma, but what sort of righteousness is that which cannot rise above your wrong sense of obligation to your friend Duryodhana, knowing fully well that his evil intentions have no limits? You are so fixated about your negative status and low birth, and yet, it prompted you to call Draupadi a harlot; it instigated you to order her to be stripped. You are deceiving yourself if you think you are this kind, good and noble person when you are not! You never were! You are as despicable as Duryodhana and Dushasana. It is not Yudhishthira but you who lost everything at the Hastinapur hall. You have given away everything, all that you were proud of, all that you were so righteous about. You have let yourself down, you have let me down, and you have let all of us down! It was my fault. I set you up on a pedestal, thinking you were the best of us. You were nobler, braver, wiser and better than everyone else. But you weren't, were you? You were none of all that—you turned out to be just a contemptible cad!'

Karna flinched. His breath came out in a dry, swift gasp. 'I will not defend myself, for what I have done is disgraceful. Yes, I have been a brute and a beast and done the lowliest thing possible. I hate myself for what I did. And I know it's been terrible for you. It was endless madness! It was as if something within me broke the moment Yudhishthira staked Draupadi and lost,' his voice rose in passion. 'And I recalled Draupadi as she was at her swayamwara—hateful, haughty and taunting. I remembered how her words hurt me and I think I went completely crazy after that. All my loathing for her welled up in me and I was beside myself...yes, it was me who instigated the Kauravas, telling them that Draupadi be brought to the hall. Dushasana did what I had told him to do. He dragged her by her locks and threw her across the floor. I watched—and, yes, I felt elated. That mad jubilation drove me to do more...I wanted her to be humiliated the way she had publicly shamed me in front of all those kings. I wanted her to suffer the same ignominy, that same indignity. And then I said those terrible words. I called her a whore, I called her a woman available for all!'

His voice was dead; his eyes closed tight in agony. 'Uruvi, believe me, it was the immense hatred that made me insane for the moment, and the moment went on and on and on. And I was enjoying it like a sadist does. I wanted her to beg for mercy and turn to me for help. But she did not,' he whispered hoarsely. 'She looked at me with pure contempt and that made me more angry...so I told Dushasana to pull at her clothes. Oh God, I said it, I said those terrible words!' he groaned. Defeated, he fell to his knees, his face tormented. His features were twisted in misery. For her, it was horribly painful to watch his abandonment in grief, the shame on that beautiful face.

Was it passionate love he felt for Draupadi, or was it passionate hate? Uruvi wondered bleakly. It seemed to her that there was a fine line between love and hate. 'I loved you, God knows how much I love you,' she heard herself say, the anger suddenly spent, swallowed now in an engulfing pain. 'For years, I have worshipped you. You were everything to me. I believed in you. You were my god,' her voice broke. 'But now, after knowing what you did, and what you are capable of doing, I am shattered. I have died a little today, Karna. It is like you twisted my heart out and crushed it. You killed me. You have killed my love for you. And now I believe in nothing; neither in you nor in me.'

He did not answer, the colour draining from his face. Slowly, his handsome features began to crumble, distorted in grief. 'Forgive me, forgive me,' he whispered brokenly. 'Oh, Uruvi, allow me to forgive myself.' His eyes, appealing and bright with unshed tears, sought hers. And then the tears fell, pouring down his face. He came towards her with his arms spread as if in surrender and fell heavily on his knees. 'Help me absolve myself, Uruvi. God help me!' Sobbing, he tried to hold her close, weeping unrestrainedly. The self-abasement of a noble, dignified man was demeaning, yet moving, stirring emotions she had promised she would not allow herself to experience.

'Don't, Karna, don't!' She pushed him away.

'Don't go. I love you too much. I was wrong. I acted unethically. And I sinned. So help me.'

For Uruvi, his obvious torment was unbearable to look at, but she steeled herself.

'No, Karna, you cannot make me change what I feel for you now. I cannot forget what you did. I can't! I *can't*. I can't bear you touching me. It's odious! It's like you actually touched Draupadi yourself and ravaged her!' She saw him flush deeply. 'No, I can't bear it! My mind is quite made up. I have thought it all over so much that I am exhausted. I have been brooding since I got the news, and all I have felt is repulsion. She'll always be there between us,' Uruvi came out with what she was struggling to say. 'Oh, it's loathsome. I think of you looking at her with that angry lust in your eyes. It's so physical, it's degrading!' She clenched her fingers in agony and her voice was getting shrill. 'I can't make myself forgive you. I have tried. Let me go, I beg you, don't make me stay...' Her heart thudded wildly, the pain almost unbearable. The tears she had restrained so long flowed copiously and she wept broken-heartedly. Karna went white; he had never seen her cry so openly before.

'I wouldn't force you to stay here against your wishes,' he said hoarsely. 'Strange, that's what I felt too, but oh, so differently!' his voice was dead, his eyes lifeless. 'I had this horrible image in my mind at the time—it wasn't Draupadi whom Dushasana was stripping but you! In that huge hall with all those people there, I suddenly saw that it was you who was being assaulted, not Draupadi. It was you who was molested, not Draupadi. It was you who shrieked for help, I could hear only your voice screaming in agony. And that was when I regained my sanity but it was too late! I was lost! I was worse than the worst. I was doomed!'

He had sunk down at her feet, his face buried in his hands. He was crying painfully with deep sobs that tore his chest. The sound was heart-wrenching. 'Draupadi deserves her revenge; and I deserve the death she has cursed me with.'

Uruvi stepped away from him and put her hands to her ears to shut out the painful sobs and the terrible words. Blindly turning away, she collapsed on the bed, tears streaming, wishing for the morning to dawn and whisk her away from the enclosing darkness.

10

Draupadi's Revenge

'I will slay Duryodhana and Dushasana, Arjuna will slay Karna and Sahadeva will slay Shakuni, that gambler with dice. I also repeat in this assembly these proud words which the gods will assuredly make good: if ever we engage in battle with the Kurus, I will slay this wretched Duryodhana in battle with my mace, and when he lies prostrate on the ground, I will place my foot on his head. As for the other wicked person, Dushasana, who is audacious in speech, I will drink his blood like a lion!'

This terrible oath of Bhima was not only the words of an avenging man, it was a war cry signalling the beginning of the annihilation of the Pandavas' enemies. His oath resounded through the city of Indraprastha as the Pandavas prepared to leave for their exile the next morning. Having losing Indraprastha in the game of dice, the Pandavas were to go into exile for thirteen years in the forest. Duryodhana had shrewdly made the last year of the exile all the more difficult for his cousins. In the thirteenth year, they had to remain incognito, else they would have to go back into exile for another thirteen years.

The Pandavas and Kunti were shocked to see the visitor who had come to their palace that morning. Kunti was about to step forward to greet the unexpected guest, when Arjuna, his face flushed with rising fury, strode towards the silent figure, with a deep frown.

'What have you come here for? How dare you come here!' he barked. He had gone pale with anger. 'Leave! Leave before you are rudely shown the door!'

It was Uruvi. She had decided she had to meet one person

before she left for Pukeya. And she knew that person would not welcome her. Yet, a meeting was essential, however much Draupadi resented her. Draupadi was not to be seen in the room, but Uruvi's eyes frantically searched for her. She knew she would not be welcome but she had not anticipated such virulent hostility. She shivered, but before she could utter a word of explanation, Arjuna erupted, 'You have the gall to come here after what your husband has done! Get out, Uruvi, leave at once. You lost your respect in this family a long time ago, but after what happened yesterday, you and your husband are my sworn enemies. Go!'

Yudhishthira and Bhima were too stunned to react to Arjuna's burst of brutal words. Uruvi begged, 'Please no, hear me out…!'

A sharp voice broke through her panic. 'Arjuna! Stop it. Stop it at once!' Kunti's sharp words were like a whiplash. 'Is that the way you treat a guest? How dare you talk to her in that manner?' Kunti turned upon him angrily. 'Is this how you treat a lady? And you talk of the behaviour of others!'

'Ma, after what happened yesterday, I am being fair and decent. You forget how Karna treated Draupadi!'

Uruvi paled and saw Kunti visibly flinch.

'That doesn't justify what you are doing!' snapped Kunti. 'You call yourself a great warrior, but you could muster enough courage to abuse a defenceless, pregnant woman. Is that chivalry?' her voice was dangerously soft. 'And what wrong did Karna say? That a woman with more than four husbands is a public woman? Our law states that, Arjuna. Did you know that I, too, had argued on the same assertion used by Karna? When your father, King Pandu, requested me to seek the divine blessing of a fourth god to provide him another son, I had cited a similar definition of a whore to your father—a woman who has more than four husbands. Be it your mother, or your wife Draupadi, the definition sticks.'

Arjuna was shocked into an aggrieved silence. Before an upset Kunti could utter any more angry words, Uruvi interposed hastily. 'Please, Ma, don't be annoyed!' Uruvi beseeched, taking the old lady's hands in hers. 'I don't want to cause more trouble. I came to see you before you left for the forest. I had to meet you. I need your pardon. I beg your forgiveness for what happened to your sons and Draupadi. I am sorry, I am so very sorry...' she cried, sinking to her knees. She touched Kunti's feet, her face wet with tears. 'I know my words can never be enough. They cannot undo what you have gone through. I ask for forgiveness. From each one of you! Please!'

In utmost humility, Uruvi bent forward to touch Yudhishthira's feet.

Arjuna controlled his anger and said in a gentler tone, 'What are you asking forgiveness for? *You* haven't done anything wrong!'

'But my husband has wronged you,' she whispered, her face downcast with shame, her eyes pleading.

'And for that he will pay dearly, Uruvi, whatever my mother's justifications are,' Arjuna retorted, his tone harsh, his face set. His eyes were flashing again and his pale face whitened in his emotion. 'Thirteen years from now, I shall kill him. When I return from our exile, I shall kill Karna in battle,' he swore, his face a mask of cold hatred. 'Your child will be an orphan thirteen years from now, and you a widow!' he pronounced with freezing finality, each vicious word slicing through her, predicting the days of doom that lurked ahead.

The silence was heavy with menace. Uruvi looked at Arjuna listlessly and said, 'Yes, I know you will kill Karna one day. All of us will have to pay the price for the shame at Hastinapur. Bhima has vowed to kill Duryodhana and Dushasana. But how many more are fated to die with them? What sort of war will this be?'

'Stop this drivel!' cried Kunti. 'There will be no war, no killings. Haven't we gone through the worst already? How can we talk about war and death so easily? Duryodhana and Dushasana will pay for the humiliation of Draupadi but not by death. They are my nephews and Karna is my...' she stopped short abruptly, '...my Uruvi's husband. He is like my son.'

'Oh, he's like a son, is he?' a shrill voice interrupted the heated exchange of words. Uruvi turned around slowly to see Draupadi enter the room. She quivered with wrath as she said, 'That same son, who publicly called your daughter-in-law a whore in the presence of elders and so many others! Who said that the Pandavas were all like sesame seeds removed from the kernel, and that I should now find some other husbands! Are you going to forgive him and your darling nephews for what they did to me that day? Answer me, Ma. I deserve justice. And I want revenge. And if war is the answer, so be it. Is that too much to ask? Is it, O powerful Bhima? Is it, O brave Arjuna?' Her scornful questions were punctuated with venom. Then, with one bitter look, she haughtily flounced from the room.

Uruvi appealed to Kunti and Arjuna. 'Please let me talk to her,' she pleaded. 'I promise not to upset her. She needs to be consoled, or her rage will take all of us into devastation and disaster. Let me bear the brunt of her fury.'

For the first time, Uruvi saw Arjuna's face soften and he nodded his head. Uruvi swiftly followed Draupadi to the inside chamber. Draupadi was weeping, tears of pain, sadness, anger and scorn coursing down her face. 'What do you want?' she hurled at her fiercely. 'Leave me with some dignity...go away!'

Uruvi could not look at her for long. The hurt and anguish in Draupadi's eyes was more than she could take. This was not the haughty, regal queen Uruvi had seen at the Rajasuya yagna. This woman, with her face swollen with crying, was cowed down and broken. In the grip of turbulent emotions, her entire body trembled, her face white.

'I want your help,' Uruvi said simply.

'My help?' questioned Draupadi with a harsh laugh. 'I thought I was the one who needed that! How would I help you?'

'Please help me. Help us to get out of this hopeless situation,' she entreated, swallowing her pride. Help us get back the life we all had, give us some way out...some hope...help me to rid myself of this feeling of doom, this hatred, anger and loathing in my heart—and in the hearts of so many others,' entreated Uruvi. 'I need you to make me strong once again. Draupadi, you are the only one who can stop the insanity that is about to begin—it will destroy all of us eventually!'

'How can I save anyone when I couldn't save myself? Who can salvage *my* lost honour?' Draupadi flung her words at Uruvi viciously. 'Who can give me back my prestige? You ask me to be a saviour when I am the victim. For all I know, you may be secretly revelling in this situation. Is it your crowning moment to see me sobbing and weak before you, like it was for your husband?' her voice broke. 'What more do you want from me?'

Timidly, Uruvi stretched out her hand and touched Draupadi's quaking shoulder. 'I want your forgiveness.'

'Never!' she said violently, shaking off Uruvi's hand from her shoulder. 'Are they so scared of what they started that they have sent you as a peace emissary? Let all those who made me suffer burn in the hell of hate, pain and humiliation, as I am burning now. I shall make each one of them endure the worst.' Her cheeks were flushed and her eyes full of grief. 'The assault was theirs; vengeance is mine. You cannot snatch it from me with your righteous pleading.'

'I cannot offer you words of comfort. No words can soothe the torment you are going through. The situation has no solution,' said Uruvi. 'But I feel responsible...' her voice trailed off uncertainly but a moment later, she gathered her courage to say what she wanted to. 'I feel responsible for what Karna did—and he did the unpardonable. I am sorry, I am dreadfully sorry.'

Suddenly, Draupadi's haggard, tear-streaked face lit up with a smile, and at that moment, her courage shone. 'You need not be sorry, I am ready to fight back! I have to, my determination is my lifeline. It's my sustenance!'

Uruvi was moved. 'There's no doubt about it,' she said. 'You are a very brave woman.'

'You call it courage? I think it's the only way I can survive,' said Draupadi. 'We have to deal with the consequences of what happened on that fateful day. Is there any other way out?'

There was no way out, and both the women knew it. Uruvi dreaded it while Draupadi seemed to welcome it with hungry vengeance. The tragedy which was to follow her humiliation at Hastinapur could no longer be averted. It was a definitive moment. Uruvi turned to look at Draupadi, and she, feeling her eyes upon her, turned too. There was a small harsh smile twisting her lips.

'They tried to break me in every possible way,' she said, her eyes far away and vacant, yet seeing each moment of that day. 'I couldn't believe it when Prathikami, the charioteer, came to me with the message that day. My husband had wagered and lost everything— even me, his wife—and upon Duryodhana's command, I was ordered to appear at the court as a maidservant to the Kuru princes. I was born to the great King Drupad, I am the daughter-in-law of the famous King Pandu, I am married to the Pandavas who are powerful warriors and I have given birth to sons who will be heroes. How can I be a servant?' The arrogance was back in her voice but just for a fleeting moment. Draupadi turned to Uruvi, her face ravaged with pain. 'Which man would pledge his wife, Uruvi?' she cried. 'Did he not have anything else to pawn? He didn't! He had lost his kingdom, his wealth, his brothers, his pride and himself. And finally—me!' she said tremulously.

She went on, her words harsh, her face hard. 'I told the charioteer-messenger, Prathikami, to return to court and ask Duryodhana a question: if Yudhishthira had lost himself first, he could not offer me as a stake. I told him to ask if King Yudhishthira first offered himself or me as a stake. I demanded an answer and I got it, but how! Duryodhana ordered Dushasana to drag me to the court. To my utter shock, he forced his entry into my room and said mockingly, "You are now ours!" I could only stare at him in horror. I was almost in a state of undress, clad in just one piece of cloth…'

Uruvi winced. Women wore a single sari only when they were menstruating, and they remained inside the more private section of the living quarters during those four to five days. The Kuru prince, with his brazen intrusion, had broken all possible barriers of decency. 'He grabbed me by my hair, which was loose down my back, and started dragging me all the way to the royal hall. I tried to wrench free and run away, desperately pulling away towards Queen Gandhari's room where I could get refuge, but I couldn't. He dragged me by my hair right up to the court, and then, in front of everybody, threw me on the floor,' her voice was now flat, devoid of emotion.

'They were all there—Bhishma Pitamaha, Dronacharya, Kripacharya—and Karna...' Draupadi's voice turned into a hoarse whisper, with a tremor that troubled Uruvi. 'I realized I was at the mercy of the Kuru princes, and the only ones who could help me out were the other people present. I begged. I pleaded with them that if they believed in God and their dharma, they could not forsake me and leave me in a plight worse than death. But there was not a sound from them—they were quiet. I appealed to them and I argued. I was desperate, but my words fell on indifferent ears. I questioned how my husband had the right to pawn me when he himself had lost his freedom; since he was no longer a free man, he had no claim over me. I screamed, "Where is righteousness? Where is justice? If that does not exist here, this court ceases to stand for morality, for lawfulness. It is run by a gang of rascals!", but no one heeded me.'

Draupadi narrated each horrifying moment, recalling vividly what had transpired. 'And do you know what the mighty Bhishma Pitamaha, the noblest and supposedly the most just, said to me then, Uruvi?' she asked scornfully. 'The patriarch of the Kaurava family and the most formidable warrior, had only this explanation to offer to me, "The course of morality is subtle and even the most illustrious, wise people in this world fail to always understand it," he said, but he didn't raise a finger to help me.' She stared ahead, her face set and frozen. 'Nor did my noble husbands. I appealed to them with these words: "My father had faith in the strength of your mighty arms and thus gave me to you. In an open assembly, I am being dishonoured, but you sit with folded arms. Are you not ashamed?" But they kept quiet...they could not even look at me.'

Draupadi gasped, 'How could my husband Yudhishthira, who had lost himself, stake me at all? None of the elders, so learned and proud of their dharma, could give me an answer. They sat there with lowered eyes like dead men with no life in them!'

'It got worse,' she continued tonelessly. 'Duryodhana kept taunting me and was as lascivious as he always is. He was provoking the other four brothers to disassociate themselves from Yudhishthira's authority and take their wife back. But none of them dared to be disloyal to their elder brother. To goad them further, Duryodhana bared his thighs and patted them as if to invite me to sit on his lap. Now Bhima proclaims that one day he will break that very thigh of Duryodhana in battle. Yet at that time, neither he nor anyone else in the assembly uttered a word of protest. And then I heard Duryodhana say derisively, "As the Pandavas are now our slaves, I command them to disrobe Draupadi."'

Draupadi said slowly, 'It was only Vikarna, the Kuru prince, who stood up for me. He tried to plead that the wager was manipulated. But Karna disagreed,' she paused, taking a deep breath. Then she continued, 'Karna argued that Yudhishthira, as a free man before the dice game had even started, had forfeited whatever he possessed, which included me as well. To emphasize the point, Karna further maintained that even the clothes we were wearing were Duryodhana's property and told Dushasana to seize them. My husbands flung their uttariya, their shawls, away. I couldn't, could I? I was wearing the ekvastra, the single robe, that day. Dushasana moved towards me and I knew then that the Kuru princes would not hesitate to strip me in public. Yet all the elders were silent and my husbands sat with their heads hung low, silent and accepting!'

Draupadi's proud head bowed in shame as she said these words. 'And then to my horror, Dushasana snatched my sari and started to unwrap it. I was being stripped in public—amidst the elders and the nobles and the kings—yet no one stopped him from committing this atrocity!' she raged. 'With no one to help me, not even my husbands, all I could do was pray and think of Krishna then, for he was the only one who would come to my rescue. I prayed to him, I trusted in him to help me and that miracle, which everyone is marvelling at today, is solely because of him. All the great valour and righteousness of my husbands could not protect me, but Krishna did!'

Uruvi did not wish to interpose; she allowed the Pandava queen to pour out her anguish. 'I shall recount a small incident which occurred years ago,' said Draupadi, and for the first time, Uruvi heard a smile in her voice. 'Once, during Sankranti, all of us were enjoying sugarcane juice with Krishna. As was the custom, the gopis offered him some freshly harvested sugarcane. He was breaking one with his hands when he cut his finger on its sharp edge. Krishna's wife, Satyabhama, ordered the gopis to rush for some medicine, but I knew I had to stop the bleeding. So I quickly tore off a piece of my sari's pallu and bandaged his finger. It's ironical isn't it, it all boils down to the sari!' she smiled mirthlessly. 'Perhaps that's why he blessed me with the never-ending sari, to repay me for wrapping my sari that day around his bleeding finger.' She smiled tenderly, her face softened by her evident affection for Krishna.

Her expression hardened, almost immediately, as she remembered where she was, and continued to chronicle her saga of shame. 'Dushasana finally stopped unwrapping yards and yards of the sari, which did not seem to end. It was only then that Bhima vowed that he would tear open Dushasana's chest and drink his blood one day. And I promised myself at that moment that I would not tie my hair unless Bhima washed my hair with this man's blood. It was my moment of a terrible decision,' she breathed, a deep colour dyeing her pale face. 'And I shouted it to the world. I would have revenge. I would destroy those who destroyed me!'

Draupadi was in a frenzy of hate. But she suddenly quietened down, barely giving Uruvi a distant glance, the shadow of a cruel smile flickering across her set mouth. Uruvi had an uneasy impression that she was staring at her as though she was not a person, but a statue—she seemed to be transported to a different world from hers.

'It will be obliteration,' Uruvi shuddered as she heard herself utter the terrible words. 'It means total destruction on an unending scale, not just personal vengeance.'

'So be it,' Draupadi declared with calm equanimity. 'Hearing my curse, Bhishma Pitamaha, Dronacharya and King Dhritrashtra, fearing that the chain of events was leading to disaster, at last brought a stop to the horror. It finally dawned on the old king that he had to undo the wrong. He tried to appease me, saying he would grant me any boon. I looked at him and at those present in the assembly and wondered what a persecuted woman should now hope for. Justice? Revenge? I finally asked for my husbands to be freed of their bondage to the Kauravas. The old king begged me to ask for the kingdom we had lost. I looked at my husbands with their bowed heads and raising my head high, I proudly told the king that they would win back the kingdom that was rightfully theirs by their own efforts. I did not need an endowment from them,' she added scornfully.

'When I rescued my hapless husbands from slavery, even Karna, who had earlier flung such terrible words at me, could not help exclaiming that no woman had accomplished what I just did. That like a boat, I had rescued my husbands who were drowning in a sea of sorrows,' she murmured, the memory of Karna's comment melting the harsh, angry lines of her face.

She loves him! Uruvi's last doubts about this revelation were cleared. The mere mention of Karna's name made Draupadi's face go warm and tender. There was no rancour, no anger. Somehow, Uruvi got an uneasy feeling that whatever happened between Karna and Draupadi at the Raj Sabha was something very personal, almost sacrosanct for Draupadi. She cherished it and it allowed her to forgive him.

The cold contempt was now reserved for her husbands alone. The Pandava princes surely deserved every lash of her wrath. Her five husbands had given her enough reason to disparage them. She, Uruvi reflected sadly, was the Nathavathi Anathavat, suffering the agony of a woman who had five husbands but with no one to protect her, who is alone and uncared for. She had married the Pandavas— the mightiest warrior-princes of the kingdom—but all they could do was make her their queen. They could neither protect her nor give her the respect and honour that a woman, wife or mother should get. Married to them, she remained alone, unaided, undefended, uncared for and even unloved. Was that why she pined for Karna even today?

Uruvi forced herself to stop thinking about Karna and dragged herself back to what Draupadi was telling her. 'And after taking King Dhritrashtra's blessings, I turned to leave the hall where I had been shamed so wickedly,' continued Draupadi, 'I bowed before all the elders present in the Raj Sabha and announced with as much sarcasm as I could muster, "One duty remains, which I must do now. I could not do it before. Dragged by this great, mighty hero, I almost forgot. I was confused. Sirs, I bow to all of you, all my elders and my superiors. Forgive me for not doing so earlier. It wasn't my fault, O gentlemen of the Sabha." And saying that, I left the hall with my head high, even though my honour was in shambles.'

Uruvi could not but admire Draupadi. Even in her extreme humiliation, she had the courage to strike back at her offenders. But the Panchala princess would waste neither time nor tears on regrets. She thirsted for her revenge. The men had played a treacherous game and she would never let them forget it. In her aggrieved fury, it was she, now, who wielded her clout. It was she, Uruvi realized, who was making the decisions and turning the course of the flow of events to come, deciding not only her own fate but that of generations to follow. Uruvi felt the stark difference between her and Draupadi— both were princesses, but while she had been cosseted in love by her parents, Draupadi had been born out of anger and revenge. She would live and make others live in the same fire she had lived through. The hatred and vengeance that almost consumed her were what she would bestow on her world as well. She knew the time had come to wield her power. She was a yagnaseni, the princess who leaped out of the sacrificial fire her father had invoked to seek revenge on his friend-turned-mortal-foe, Dronacharya. She was born to be the avenging angel, and today, she was determined to wreak retribution on her foes. She would live with a fire burning in her till she sought reprisal—even if it meant war, which Uruvi knew was inevitable.

Ironically, Draupadi had become a pawn in her own game. By her scornful rejection of Karna because of his low birth, she had sown the seeds of hate and humiliation. By her malicious remark, echoed by her sneering laugh, she had provoked Duryodhana into a frenzy of feral hate. If her impulsive behaviour proved to be her undoing, her revenge would be the nemesis of all those who had harmed her, Karna included, Uruvi reflected.

Draupadi was moving around the room, clearly preparing to leave for the forest the next morning. She looked resigned to the fact because she was not yet defeated. She was biding her time—and when her chance came, it would be she who would hit back.

Draupadi gave a weary sigh. She looked calm now but it was deadly calmness. 'I don't know why nor do I want to. But what I do know is war is certain once we return. They cannot avoid it. And if my husbands do not declare war, I shall make my father and brother and my sons fight for me.'

Her words echoed with a bleak finality, yet Uruvi heard a pang of longing in it. It was not just longing for her lost love for Karna, her yearning for him, it was a longing for all what she had lost—her self-respect and the honour and protection she expected from her husbands. It was a longing for a normal, uncomplicated life, for a simple existence with a home, husband and children, a life without politics, intrigue, war and ruin. It was a longing to be treated as a self-respecting woman, and not as a pawn to be used as her father and her husbands had done. She did not want to be perceived as an object of lust as Karna, Duryodhana and Dushasana had done, or as a means of revenge as Karna had been guilty of doing. Draupadi's life was diametrically opposite to Uruvi's more sheltered journey. Yet, both women knew they would have to struggle to deal with the extraordinary nightmare their lives had turned into.

The wheel of misfortune was turning slowly, trampling their lives. 'Karna and I might be the first to be destroyed,' Uruvi realized with sudden bitterness. As if reading her thoughts, Draupadi gave her a gentle smile, the anger and hate wiped clean from her face. She looked almost serene. Draupadi had nothing more to say and Uruvi knew she should go.

'I think I should leave,' she said lamely, shuffling her feet.

She was stopped abruptly by the next words uttered by Draupadi. 'Don't be harsh on yourself—or your marriage,' the Pandava queen said mildly. 'Neither of you deserve it. You came here to apologize for what your husband did. But Karna did what I possibly would have done myself were I in his place. I remember what I said when I pleaded with all those present at the royal assembly. I had said, "To be dishonoured is to die." I died a little that day. And I realize now that I, too, must have made Karna die a little that day at my swayamwara when I insulted him in the presence of a full royal court. He did not retaliate. He merely kept a dignified silence, put the bow back in place and looked skywards at the sun—as if seeking an explanation for why he had to suffer such humiliation. Uruvi, now I know what it is to be dishonoured. You feel sullied, shamed. I did the same to Karna once and I have been punished for what I did to him.'

Uruvi looked at Draupadi with rising incredulity; she could not believe her ears. This woman who had endured such excruciating ignominy was ready to forgive her oppressor! She was condoning his behaviour! How could she absolve him for his cruel words, his foul abuses? She, as his victim, was ready to exonerate him, while Uruvi, as an angered observer, could not bring herself to pardon her husband.

Uruvi wondered what this woman was all about. As a suitor, Draupadi knew that Karna had desired her as a woman, a lover and a wife, but the Panchala princess had been reluctant to break the norm and accept him as her husband. Knowing fully well that he was capable of winning her, Draupadi had insisted on rejecting Karna for his low birth, depriving him of his chance to win her at her swayamwara. She preferred rejecting him, rather than accepting her feelings for him. For him, that humiliation was like a piercing arrow that stuck deep in his heart. Seething, he had waited for the slightest opportunity to retaliate—and the dice game was his one big chance to humble Draupadi. So he did. He crushed her. She bore it with as much brave dignity as she could, for she believed she had reaped what she had sown, that it was her hurtful words that had sown the seeds of revenge in Karna.

Human nature is odd; the emotion called love odder still. Was Draupadi's love for Karna so great that she could absolve him so easily? Or was it that Draupadi's love was greater and more large-hearted than hers? This was the second time she had this feeling of being a lesser mortal, a failed lover. First, it had been Vrushali who had made her feel insignificant, and now, Draupadi evoked the same feeling of worthlessness in her. She somehow made Uruvi feel her love was not as profound. Was her love for Karna so feeble, so frail that unlike Vrushali and Draupadi, she could not forgive his faults? Did Draupadi love Karna so selflessly that she lost her sense of self so completely?

Draupadi knew that though she loved Karna, she could never marry him. She had been born to be the consort of Arjuna, the favourite disciple of Dronacharya, her father's arch-enemy. By choosing to marry Arjuna, she had unwittingly offered herself as the wager in the political crossfire between the Kauravas, the Pandavas and the Panchals.

Besides Karna's low birth, his disgrace at her swayamwara was also because of her brother's outright rejection of Karna as her suitor. Perhaps it was her fear for her brother's life that had prompted Draupadi to insult Karna so scathingly that he was forced to opt out of the swayamwara. Her disapproving brother Dhrishtadyumna would have been no match for the warring skills of Karna, an athiratha, a warrior capable of fighting sixty thousand foes single-handedly, and would have been easily killed in a duel between the two. To save her brother, in all likelihood, Draupadi sacrificed her love. She had to marry Arjuna while she longed for Karna. Uruvi looked at Draupadi, beautiful and proud in her pain, and she knew that Draupadi was broken-hearted. Like her birth, Draupadi's life too was predetermined by a singular goal—the annihilation of the Kurus. And Karna would be one of the casualties in this path of devastation.

'You came over here to try to save his life, didn't you?' asked Draupadi softly. 'You love him that much?' She looked at Uruvi with such an intense sadness that Uruvi could feel her pain; they seemed connected in this moment of shared suffering. 'You were so desperate that you were ready to bear Arjuna's rage and my wrath.'

Uruvi nodded slowly, wringing her hands in nervous anxiety. 'Only you can save him,' she whispered brokenly. 'I knew it was too much to ask. But I am so afraid I shall lose him—I don't want him to die!' she caught a sob.

'Don't say that! Don't torment yourself,' Draupadi said gently. 'If you love him so much, why are you so angry with him? If you are angry for my sake and if it makes you any feel any better, let me say this—I am more hurt than angry with him. Karna is known for his goodness, his kindness, his righteousness. And honestly, the one person whom I thought would come to my help would be him. But he did not. I didn't expect my husbands to get me out of the situation—for they had got me into this nightmare in the first place. But yes, Karna, I thought, would be my saviour. Not my husbands, not Bhishma Pitamaha, not Dronacharya, Not anyone else. But his behaviour was in retaliation for my rejection of him. So, we are even now!' she added. 'But I am not angry with him. He insulted me in a moment of heat! Love knows how to forgive. Love is blind—to faults, to flaws. You are fortunate to have him...keep him, don't lose him.'

Her voice trailed uncertainly. Draupadi was almost confessing her feelings for Karna to her. Uruvi dared not utter a word to break the moment. Draupadi looked bereft, the longing on her face obvious. Her hands were clenched into tight fists as if she was trying to restrain herself physically. 'There is no way out. And I can't help you, however much I would like to...' Draupadi said tonelessly, her shoulders sagging under the burden of pain she was carrying. 'Do you know how much Arjuna despises Karna? He has made a vow of abstinence until he kills Karna...'

Uruvi paled. Arjuna, in his undiluted hate for Karna, was inflicting the same punishment of celibacy on himself and Draupadi that Uruvi was exacting on Karna and herself. Was she being too harsh on Karna and too righteous?

'Uruvi, this is the last time we can meet, because the next time it will be war,' Draupadi saw the sadness in Uruvi's face and guessed her thoughts. 'Stay with Karna, Uruvi. What had to happen has happened and all of us are going to suffer for it. You came to me hoping I could salvage the situation. I cannot. I cannot save him, Uruvi. The situation is out of my hands. I am not the reason why Arjuna has sworn to kill Karna in battle. There's more to it...' she said tiredly. 'But it is in our destiny to watch helplessly as bloodshed rages between our husbands. And we know who is going to lose the war and his life,' she said hollowly.

Both the women knew that the two men would bring this terrifying, personal rivalry to a closing battle of immense proportions. And neither of the two women could save Karna from his imminent death at the hands of Arjuna. Karna's parting words kept ringing in Uruvi's tormented mind. '*Draupadi deserves her revenge; and I deserve the death she has cursed me with.*'

11

The Separation

The Pandavas left for the forest the next morning, leaving behind their mother, Kunti, who did not accompany them for the exile this time. She had decided to stay back at the palace of Vidura and his wife, Parshavya.

Other unexpected news was the arrival of Sage Narada at Hastinapur. 'Thirteen years from today, the Kauravas will be annihilated because of the crimes committed by Duryodhana,' he declared to the stricken old king and Vidura and vanished from sight, leaving behind a pall of gloom in the palace and the city where the magnificent Rajasuya celebrations had been held just a few months ago. Uruvi felt crushed under the dread; the bleakness of the future seemed to stifle her.

She was determined to follow her plan. However much it broke her heart, she had to leave Karna. Distance would probably make her stronger and for that, she would have to leave for Pukeya. The thought of parting from Karna was unbearable, but then she remembered, the outrage at the Kuru hall and shuddered with renewed shame and horror, reminded that she could not respect the man she loved any more. Perhaps she was being heartless, cruel and unreasonable, and after hearing what Draupadi had to say to her, a new bewilderment troubled her. She was torn between her moral indignation and being loving and forgiving. She wanted to turn back and flee into the world she had once belonged to, hungry to catch a glimpse of Karna again. She wanted desperately to say one last word of comfort and tenderness, once more to ask for his understanding, strength, love and kindness. She was struck numb with pain, her hands stretched

137

as if to bring him back. She wanted to rush into his arms, forget the growing nightmare and to continue to live as contentedly as she once had.

Dawn was creeping along the river mistily but grey clouds still hovered above the dark trees along the way. Restless and in a state of distress, Uruvi reached the beautiful palace that was her childhood home. It was as imposing as ever, the garden sprawling in front, welcoming in its lush greenery. She stepped down from the chariot and slowly walked inside. Everything seemed the same—her mother's surprised smile, her father's warm eyes, her excited handmaid, the carved armchair in the wide verandah, the ancient banyan tree in the garden. But she had changed.

When Uruvi entered the house, pale and troubled, King Vahusha saw at once that something dreadful had happened. He knew what she was going to say before she spoke.

'Father, I have left Karna.'

He took her hand gently and embraced her. She broke down and wept unrestrainedly. Hot tears coursed down her face, unchecked and uncontrolled. 'I am tired,' she murmured brokenly.

Queen Shubra, dismayed, opened her mouth to speak, but her husband motioned her to be silent.

Uruvi did not utter a word of explanation and her father knew that she needed to be left alone. She went to her chamber upstairs and watched the day advance slowly from her balcony as the sorrow—undeserved, bitter and overwhelming—seeped in. Her head pounded and in her disturbed state, she could not read, converse or eat. She walked in the grounds to tire herself out. At sunset, she returned to her room, spent and listless. The night was silent; her room was still. She could not think any more and her turbulent mind had gone strangely vacant. Soon, she heard a discreet cough.

'Who's there?' she cried, startled and annoyed.

There was a pause. She turned to the threshold and saw her father come into the room. He quietly said, 'I know something is very wrong. Do you want to talk about what happened?'

'I came home because I knew I could count on you. And your sympathy,' she answered, looking a little sheepish.

'It was bound to happen...'

'Was it, Father? Were you expecting this?' she cried.

'I suppose so. You couldn't hope to keep him always for yourself, dear,' he reminded her gently. 'He is destined for other things...'

She could not have agreed more. In bits and pieces, in fits and starts, in between sobs and gasps, she recounted what had happened, most of which he already knew through hearsay and the rumours flying thick and fast in his kingdom.

'Are you sure you want to leave him?' he asked finally. 'You couldn't live without him before—will you be able to now?'

'I have to,' she murmured.

'Why do you have to? Is this some sort of a punishment you are imposing on yourself or is it a way of punishing Karna?' he asked sharply. Then, in a more kindly manner, he continued, 'Listen, child, do what your heart tells you, not your pride. You are too proud to accept that the person you so wholly loved could go wrong. Your judgement has taken a knock and you cannot bear the fall of your idol. But that was your mistake, not his. Karna didn't ask to be your god.'

She raised her eyebrows slightly. 'Father, are you defending him or are you justifying what he did? You sound like a saint, not a king.'

'Evil is everywhere. But so is good—and you need to recognize it when you see it,' her father gently reminded her. 'It is easy to single out the faults of others, chastise the wicked, but how many realize their own flaws and knowing them, are repentant? How many make amends? At least, Karna has that integrity in him.'

She kept silent, confused, clenching her hands agitatedly. 'I want to go back to him—but not now! I need to think! And I am not sure if I am right or he is wrong, or whether he is right and I am wrong. What makes me so terribly sad is to think of his unspeakable degradation! I thought there was no one like him. I admired him so much! He was the world to me. Was he a sham or was he my illusion?'

'Do you think all of us are perfect, dear? For you, it's agony that the person you believed in so totally, you considered so angelic, should be so flawed and hollow. What is hurting you is that the person you thought to be the epitome of goodness should fall so suddenly.'

Uruvi shrugged her shoulders. 'After this, I thought my love for him was killed in a flash. But that is not so. I love him in spite of everything,' she admitted, grudgingly.

'It is your sense of honour which defines what is right or wrong and it need not be correct always. What Karna did was deplorable, but what made it highly offensive for you was that your hero had feet of clay. It is your personal disappointment in him that you find a betrayal. But he has not betrayed you. He was a man scorned and sneered at and he hit back in anger when he got a chance to hurt the woman who did it. Whether it's a man or a woman is immaterial. Dishonour can kill decency in anybody. You have never experienced it, dear, so you wouldn't know how one reacts to it.'

'Have you ever been humiliated?' she asked curiously, surprised to see this side of her father.

'Oh, yes, several times!' he laughed lightly. 'That's why most wars are fought! Wars are often a personal vendetta, not impelled by noble reasons. It is easy for the ego to get dented any time, by anyone. Another mistake you are committing is clubbing Karna with Duryodhana and Dushasana. Karna retaliated out of vengeance; they behaved as they did in sheer spite and lust.'

'But that doesn't condone what he did,' she countered swiftly. 'It was wrong, simple!'

'And what gives you the right to be so judgemental?' her father looked annoyed. 'Morality be damned! A scruple which causes so much grief and turmoil is not worth it. Morality is not a rigid formula of mathematics. No standard of it can be laid down for all times, and for all situations. Even legal experts like Bhishma could not find a solution for the quandary posed by Draupadi. You are not being righteous; you are running away from the problem. Face it. And tackle it in a less extreme manner!'

'There is something called conscience!' she cried vehemently.

'Are you his conscience-keeper? If so, show him the way. Don't condemn him and flee in righteous horror. Don't close your eyes to the flaws and reality—or it will be you who will stumble and fall in a deep void. Condemning and condoning are two faces in the mirror; but it takes more courage to forgive than to criticize someone. Are you brave enough to pardon Karna?'

Would she be as magnanimous as Draupadi? Uruvi asked herself this question remorsefully, knowing that Karna's prey, though broken and bruised, had enough strength in her and love in her heart to absolve him. Her father looked at her meaningfully. 'You need to be brave to forgive,' he repeated. 'Are you strong enough to accept his imperfections? You are disillusioned because your hero fell from your eyes—but he will only soar higher after his nadir. A weak man goes downhill, but Karna is a strong person. His stumble will never be his fall. He will heave himself up and go higher. And you need to be there with him then.'

Uruvi gave him a helpless look, and with an abrupt movement, sprang to her feet. 'The problem is that I am just as much in love with him now as I was then,' she said and paused. 'Does love make you so vulnerable and powerless, Father?'

'No. It makes one strong. It has given you forbearance and courage. It is not what has happened or what will happen that is relevant; what you do in the *now* is significant. That defines your karma.'

Surprisingly, her mother backed her father's advice. Uruvi remembered, with a twisted smile, when her mother had come face to face with her son-in-law at the swayamwara hall. Uruvi had expected her to give him a frosty greeting but her mother's face had shown a gamut of fleeting emotions. Royal breeding clashed with her animosity, her social grace battled bravely with the contempt she had for the young man, but then an expression of affable welcome veiled her dismay and dislike admirably. Uruvi had wondered if Karna had been able to catch how unforgiving her mother's expression was, concealed by the facade of politeness. She was assessing him. Her mother wore the same look now. She was trying to assess her.

'So you have decided to leave and not face the consequences, have you?' She was passing the verdict already. She paused and added gently, 'But Uruvi, you couldn't be happy without him, you can't exist without him! You said that no woman could want a better husband—and you went ahead to prove to us and the world that's how it was. And this I have to admit, Karna has always been kindness itself to you. He is a decent man. And you loved him madly once.'

Uruvi looked at her mother squarely. 'I still love him, Mother. It's not that I have left him forever—our society wouldn't permit me, would all of you? I only came here to rethink,' she stopped abruptly, suddenly weary of explaining her actions and confusion. 'I just need some time, some space…Mother, please, I don't have the will to argue with you. You were right; I was wrong,' she sighed deeply. She passed her hand over her eyes.

'No, I think you were correct and I was wrong all along,' her mother refuted quietly. 'Neither Arjuna nor any of the Pandavas would have been right for you or for any woman for that matter!'

Uruvi was startled; her mother was in the throes of intense anger, her cheeks glowing an angry red. 'Mother, what do you mean?'

'I am thankful now that you refused to marry Arjuna…or it could have been you, instead of Draupadi who would have been disrobed at the Hastinapur royal hall!'

'Mother!'

'I keep thinking that had you been Arjuna's wife, what could he have given you? Disgrace? Humiliation?' Queen Shubra asked heatedly. 'The five Pandavas put together could not protect Draupadi in her hour of distress. The cowards kept quiet and watched the outrage!' her mother said with disdain. 'I am grateful that I did not give my daughter to a man who cannot defend his wife, and I am sorry to say that I did not realize this earlier. You were smarter than I thought, Uruvi.'

Uruvi was completely taken aback; her mother's tirade left her speechless. She was surprised that her mother was now endorsing her decision to marry Karna.

'Was I, Mother?' Uruvi looked disconsolate. Slowly, she glanced back at her mother, and in her eyes, unmistakably, gleamed a look of irony. Her mother was vexed and disturbed. Uruvi thoughtfully touched the bangles on her wrist. Her coolness troubled her mother, so she stopped in front of Uruvi and faced her, taking her hands in hers.

'You condemn Karna for what he did, but Uruvi, can't you see what the Pandavas so shamefully allowed to happen at the Kuru hall? People insist that it was devious of Duryodhana and Shakuni to swindle poor Yudhishthira in the dice game. But how morally correct was Yudhishthira when, as a king, he pawned his kingdom away? What right did he have to play with his kingdom and his subjects? Worse than that, as a husband, he staked his wife for a game. And when she was being stripped, he kept shockingly silent just as her other husbands did. Spineless wretches, how could they allow it? *That* is shameful! And as a mother, I am happy that I was wrong about those Pandavas! On that day, I thanked God that you were Karna's wife and not Arjuna's!'

Uruvi's impassive face twisted into a sardonic smile. 'It was a hall of shame, Mother,' she murmured desolately. 'Each one of them was morally wrong—Bhishma Pitamaha, Guru Dronacharya, Kripacharya, King Dhritrashtra, Vidura, the Pandavas—and yes, my husband—every one of them! They were guilty of participating in a heinous offence. They watched and preferred to do nothing, neither protesting nor protecting Draupadi. The only one who did not transgress is possibly Vikarna, who was sensitive and brave enough to warn the others that what was happening was so awfully wrong. The others silently watched a crime happen in front of their eyes and did nothing. They simply turned their heads away. All of them behaved shamefully, Mother.'

'Yes, all the more reason for the Pandavas to have stood up for

Draupadi. Why didn't they? What could have happened? Not anything worse than what actually did take place! I would have respected the Pandavas more had they picked up their weapons and challenged the abettors of the crime. In the cloak of nobleness and virtuosity, they favoured silence and servility instead. Cowards!' she said fiercely. 'I admit Karna was not the husband I would have wished for you, but over the months, I accepted him, the sole reason being you were so happy with him. And that's what matters. He loves you in his own odd way, and more importantly, he keeps you happy. After hearing about what happened at the Kuru Raj Sabha, I don't think Arjuna or any of the Pandavas could have made you happy. The important factor for any parent is that her child is contented with whomsoever she marries and I confess Karna has emerged more suitable than I could have ever imagined! That's why I shan't allow you to wallow in needless condemnation. As a wife, would you have pardoned your husband who doesn't have the guts to defend you or would you excuse a man who dishonours a woman in a vindictive payback? I think you are being foolishly upright. Don't be so heartless and don't be so hard on yourself. And think of the baby.'

Uruvi winced—she couldn't let herself forget this reality. 'What kind of world am I going to bring my child into, Mother?' she asked despairingly. 'The future seems so bleak!'

'The future is never ours to see,' Queen Shubra placed a placating hand on her daughter's shoulder. 'You can never know what is going to happen. But you can steer the present forward in such a way that it gives you enough dignity and courage to face your future, however unpleasant it may be. Make your present a better way of living. That makes the world easier to live in too,' she added in a soothing tone.

After her mother gave her this sensible advice, Uruvi decided to give herself some time. She tried to push Karna from her thoughts but he kept haunting her. She missed him but she concentrated on her unborn child instead. Her days spent at Pukeya waiting for the baby to arrive were probably more restful than the emotional turmoil of the last few days. She was considerably at peace now; she knew what she needed to do. She gossiped with her mother and laughed with her father. She gathered enough cheerfulness within her to giggle with her friends about becoming a mother soon.

But the rawness in her heart was intolerable. She couldn't help thinking about Karna and the turbulent days, weeks and months that had separated them. She wondered how he had reacted to her sudden flight to Pukeya. A wisp of unease troubled her. Would he be on the lookout for her? Would he come to Pukeya? Had he given up on her or did he think she would return soon? She looked out of the window almost every hour of the day.

Then one early morning, she saw his chariot racing down the dusty path. Her heart leapt with unbridled joy and she realized with a start how much she had longed to see him. She saw him leap down from the chariot and stride purposefully inside. She scanned the corridor anxiously. He was taking ages to come up the stairs. What was he doing? Was he talking with her father? Was he being castigated by her mother? Uruvi could feel herself getting increasingly agitated and she wanted to race down the stairwell to meet him. But pride and prudence stopped her and she decided to wait for him instead. She could not see him anywhere, so she paced restlessly in her room.

And then, all at once, he was there—in all his splendour. He was coming up from the landing when he saw her. His fleeting glance of amazement was followed by an expression of delight, to be swiftly traded by his usual shuttered look. Uruvi wanted to rush to him and throw her arms around him. But she sat rooted to her chair, her eyes drinking him in thirstily.

No thoughts filtered through her mind, no words emanated from her lips. She looked up at him instead, her eyes clear and steadfast, her lips frozen. He looked bewildered, but comprehension slowly dawned on him. She was resolute in her stance; with her head held straight and high, her chin jutting out proudly, she looked ominously calm.

'You are still very angry with me?' he asked squarely.

She looked at him with clear, candid eyes. 'Never. Ever. I realize I can't be angry with you for long. It's my failing.'

He whispered hoarsely, 'I have come to take you back. Have you forgiven me?' There was a desperate plea in his voice.

'I don't blame you. I now understand a little.'

'Don't be so kind, Uruvi. I probably don't deserve your pardon either.' He gave her a rueful smile.

She stared at the floor and seemed to ponder deeply. She looked pale and thin, her face pinched, and he could see she did not look too well. Her imminent maternity gave her a mature poise. Deep in her eyes was a solemnity that sobered the usual sparkle in her eyes. She didn't show any bitterness in her behaviour towards him, and instead, seemed happy to meet him. He had not missed the passionate flare of joy lighting up her eyes just a moment ago.

He wanted to gather her in his arms again but something about her stopped him. It was as if, suddenly, they were two strangers in a room. His attempt at reconciliation had left her uncertain and he had not expected much from their meeting anyway. Perhaps it was better to leave her alone, but he wanted her to return to him. He knew he must give her enough time to calm her feelings. After all, she knew how much he loved her; and he knew how devoted she was to him. Perhaps she was still fighting her conflicting emotions, but Karna knew that the moment of truth had arrived. He had seen that glint in her eyes. The look in her eyes scared him; he saw fear in them, yet she was serene, in an almost frozen way. Her calmness frightened him and the fear in her eyes puzzled him, intensifying into a state of agitation. He wished she would make a scene, hurl angry words at him, scream at him; he could cope with that. He couldn't handle her inscrutable tranquillity. It was better to have it out.

'What is it, Uruvi? Tell me,' he said evenly, preparing himself for the worst.

Uruvi glanced away. Her face grew a trifle paler. 'I can live with you as your wife, but never as your lover again,' she looked at him steadily. 'I can't stay away longer for that would create another scandal. Yes, I shall come back with the baby because that is expected of me. And I shall return because I love you—I can't help myself. I can't stop loving you. But solely as your wife and the mother of our child.'

It took some time for her words to sink in his mind. His heart thudded and he felt himself change colour. He stared emptily from her bedroom window at the clouds floating in the long distance. Dark and thick, they hid the sun, moving slowly with a sluggish deliberateness. 'Are you punishing yourself or is it a penalty for me?' he asked softly. 'Doesn't it mean anything to you that I love you?'

'I love you and that's why I have the courage to do this. I want to tell you again, Karna, that I am not condemning you; you did what you thought appropriate at that moment of time—be it in anger or in the desire to take revenge. I realized this soon enough. That's why I took time to think in retrospect. My common sense tells me I am over-reacting. But this is not about common sense; my whole mind, my heart and my soul is in torment. I can't deny and neither can you, that Draupadi will always be there between us. In fact, she was always there but I just didn't realize it.'

She ignored Karna's small gesture of protest and continued relentlessly, 'In some way, you belong to her. And each time you touch me now, she'll be there, between us.'

She waited for Karna's denial but it was not uttered. There had been an underlying rationality in her foolish fear after all. 'I can't rid myself of that certainty. I thought I would get over it, but I can't and never shall. Please help me,' she beseeched sadly.

Exhausted, Karna leaned back against his chair, his eyes shut, the pain distorting his features. It was heart-wrenching to watch the grief on that beautiful face. He buried his face in his hands for a long time and then, at last, looked up at Uruvi despairingly.

'Oh, my dearest, please don't look at me like that!' she cried. 'I am sorry, I have shattered your life! But I have broken my happiness too...' He thought her voice trembled slightly.

'But you loved me. I know it. That's one thing I believed in more than I believe in myself—that you loved me completely. Can you just stop loving someone?'

'But I never stopped loving you,' she said softly. 'I love you but with love comes respect and that respect has gone.'

Her words crushed him completely. He knew what she had said, what her words meant.

For some minutes, they just sat there, without a word, the silence full of turmoil, the stillness of the night closing in on them. At last he said, 'I shall go now. Goodbye…until I come to see our baby.'

He did not even touch her hand when he walked away. He stopped, turned and threw a last look at her. She wanted to say one word of comfort, to ask for his forgiveness once more, to soothe him, but she steeled herself and remained silent. He left the room, and she threw herself heavily on the bed, staring with dry eyes at her room, a place where she had once been so blissful, but now was so wretched.

12

Kunti and Uruvi

One day, as Uruvi sat at her dressing table staring at her reflection in the mirror, she heard a commotion in the patio below her balcony, but did not bother to see what was happening. Downstairs, Queen Shubra was delighted to see that her friend, Kunti, had come on a visit. She was meeting Kunti after a long time, but Queen Shubra knew that the visit would not be without a reason. Kunti never indulged in pleasure trips. She, too, wanted to talk to her about Uruvi, who had behaved obstinately again by refusing to return home with her husband.

Kunti smiled as they embraced each other but Queen Shubra noticed that she looked unusually worried. It wasn't like her. Even in the worst of circumstances, Kunti's iron will to tide over trouble was astounding. Each time she had emerged stronger, even though a little sadder.

Queen Shubra remembered Kunti as the cheerless little girl, Pritha, who had come from her father's house to the palace of King Kuntibhoj. That was when and where they had become friends. Kunti had always been strong while Shubra had been a wilful child, so their rivalry centred on who was tougher. The edge of competitiveness continued over the growing years and Kunti had eventually won, but she had once told her, 'You have had a happier life, Shubra, and the best part of it is Uruvi. She is your ultimate gift.'

Kunti had always reserved a tremendous affection for Uruvi, which was reciprocated in equal measure by the child. Queen Shubra was not a jealous woman and did not resent their closeness. But she did wonder about their unusual bonding. In spite of being the mother of Yudhishthira, Bhima, Arjuna and the foster mother of the twins,

149

Nakul and Sahadeva, it was to Uruvi that Kunti was utterly devoted. 'She reminds me of myself!' Kunti had laughed as she swung the little girl in her arms. Shubra knew that Kunti was happiest when she played with Uruvi. She reminded her of the young Kunti deeply in love with Pandu, the handsome prince of Hastinapur she had eventually married. Just like Uruvi had married the man she loved. Shubra was again struck with the similarity of the two—both were enormously self-willed and they usually got what they wanted.

Queen Shubra could guess why her friend had hastily rushed down to Pukeya from Hastinapur. It must be because of Uruvi, or more exactly, her refusal to return home with Karna. Gossip must have already made its malicious rounds when Uruvi had unceremoniously left home for Pukeya. The fact that she had not gone back with her husband, even when he had gone to fetch her, must have stirred another thunderstorm in Hastinapur. And since Uruvi was pregnant, it made the situation seem a lot worse, Queen Shubra thought worriedly. She was doubly relieved now that Kunti had arrived. She hoped Kunti could knock sense into this stubborn child of hers. She was probably the only one who could.

The two friends did not sit down for their habitual chat. They did not exchange a word, their apprehensive glances revealing their worry. Without bothering to rest after her journey, Kunti headed straight to Uruvi's room.

Kunti had expected Uruvi to rush into her arms as she always did, but this time she did not. She got up instead, more out of decorum, and looked at her expressionlessly. The last time they had met had not been in the best of circumstances. It was, unforgettably, one of the worst times, Kunti recalled with a silent shudder.

The same anxiety was running though Uruvi's troubled mind. She could not find the words or the emotion to greet the elderly queen as she used to. She stood stiff, her fists tightened. Kunti hugged her and wrapped her arms around her thickening waist, feeling the tension emanating from her.

'Have you still not forgiven yourself for what happened at the Raj

Sabha?' Kunti asked gently, coming straight to the point. 'Oh, child, how much will you suffer about this? Let it go.'

Uruvi listened to her in complete silence. Kunti frowned. It was not like Uruvi to be so withdrawn and silent. She would have preferred an impassioned debate with her.

She decided on her next move, which she hoped would provoke a reaction from the silent girl. 'Is your love for Karna so shallow that you cannot forgive him for what he did?' she began. 'Forgive him, dear, for your own sake. If you do not forgive him, you will end up hating him! He will always be the wicked transgressor who broke your dreams and happiness. Worse, you will not be able to forget this unpleasantness. By not forgiving him, you are not forgiving yourself either. Yes, he said those outrageous words to a woman, but so be it. He is repenting—and suffering too. Why are you jeopardizing your marriage for what happened? Try to forget, dear, and accept what you cannot change. It is only then that you will get peace.'

Uruvi looked at her, an unmistakably cynical expression on her face. Kunti was vexed; Uruvi's coolness almost angered her. 'What is it that Karna said that has affronted your fine moral principles, Uruvi?' she asked, her voice sharpening perceptibly. 'That he called Draupadi a whore? What did he say that was wrong? Draupadi is the wife of five men and that fact remains unchanged, doesn't it?'

Uruvi flinched.

Undeterred, Kunti went on. 'You are shocked again, I notice. But Karna, in a moment of anger and pique, was actually quoting the scriptures correctly. They claim that a woman who gives her body to a fourth man is a wanton woman, a swairini. And a woman who has had sex with five men and more is a whore. So, by being the wife of five husbands, Draupadi becomes, theoretically, a whore. Karna merely drove home this point.'

'What he said was contemptible!'

'Possibly,' Kunti argued in a detached tone. 'But at that moment he believed he had a right to insult her because she, too, had once humiliated him in public. Uruvi, it is an issue fraught with emotion.

The matter's delicate and personal. They both said what they did to preserve their pride and vent their anger—all was said in the heat of the moment. Get over it. It happened, yes, but it's a moment that is now in the past. Don't relive it.'

Uruvi looked aghast, her face pale with anger. 'How can you defend what he said? It's crass, it's despicable! And how can you, as her mother-in-law, justify the use of the word "whore"? She's the wife of your sons!'

'Because I have gone through it myself!' Kunti asserted calmly. 'I have been called a whore and worse when I became the mother of the Pandavas. Everyone knew my husband, King Pandu, was cursed, that he could never consummate his marriage, and yet, I was the mother of three boys. I was never allowed to forget that discrepancy ever! Why do you think Duryodhana still refuses to recognize the Pandavas as his blood relations? Because they were not the sons of King Pandu. They were the sons of Kunti and Madri—never King Pandu's.'

Uruvi fell silent again, looking at the senior queen with steady, alert eyes. She was watchful, careful not to miss out on a single word.

'Like you, Uruvi, I fell in love and was fortunate enough to be able to choose my own husband. You, too, fell in love with a man and were determined to marry him. And I think we were lucky to be allowed to get away with our freedom of choice. Which queen in my family got to choose her husband on her own? Satyavati did not select King Shantanu as her husband—he chose her as his queen. Nor did her daughters-in-law, Ambika and Ambalika, who were kidnapped by Bhishma Pitamaha and forced to marry Satyavati's son Vichitravirya. Gandhari, too, was forced to marry Dhritrashtra by Bhishma Pitamaha, who also made King Pandu marry Madri after I had married him. Subhadra has been fortunate like us—she was in love with Arjuna before she got to marry him. But did Draupadi marry the man she loved?'

Here, Kunti deliberately paused for a fraction, and in that moment, Uruvi realized that the older lady knew Draupadi's secret as well—that her daughter-in-law had loved Karna. Her cryptic look said it all but both of them did not dare to voice the unspeakable fact.

'Draupadi did not pick and choose Arjuna at her swayamwara,' Kunti continued smoothly. 'He won her. Uruvi, we are the lucky ones. Karna did not win you—*you* chose Karna. As I chose King Pandu. Not that I ever regretted that decision. Do you regret marrying Karna, Uruvi?'

'No.' The answer came out in a flash, destroying any doubts she ever harboured about the depth of her feelings for Karna.

'Nor did I regret marrying King Pandu,' smiled Kunti. 'Not even when I discovered that the handsome man I had fallen in love with and married was sickly, suffering from frequent bouts of ill health. Even before he was cursed by Sage Kindama, he could rarely make love to me,' she whispered in a savage undertone. 'I could never have his children. And then, he married the exquisite Madri,' she raised a tortured face. 'But I loved him so much, Uruvi. I could accept him with whatever flaws he had. It hurt when Madri intervened in our life but I consoled myself and accepted her as I knew he loved me and that he had been forced to marry Madri as a gesture of political goodwill. You are to Vrushali what Madri was to me. Yet, did that make your love weak and insecure?'

Uruvi shook her head, recalling the jealous anger she felt each time Karna was with Vrushali but her intense love had overridden it. What must Vrushali have felt when she, Uruvi, insidiously entered Karna's life to threaten her marital bliss?

Kunti gave her a knowing look. 'That's what I mean when I say love is sublime—it gives us enough strength to face the fiercest odds. Mine was the cruel fact that my husband had to stay celibate. It frustrated him greatly, especially the awful reality that he could have no heir for his kingdom. Yet, the three of us as the newly married young king and his queens lived happily, until one fateful day.'

Uruvi knew that Kunti was telling her something she may have not revealed to anyone else. The fact that she was disclosing it meant that there was a purpose behind it, for Kunti did not act or speak without a reason. Uruvi wanted to know that reason. She heard Kunti continue in a deceptively flat voice. 'And then one morning, that awful day dawned. King Pandu had gone hunting and killed a deer with his precise aim. The hunter had struck his target but the prey was not what it seemed to be. The deer in actuality was Rishi Kindama who had taken the form of a deer while making love to his mate. The dying rishi then cursed King Pandu, warning him that he would die if he were ever to consummate his marriage with his wife. Forced into abstinence, the young king gave up his throne to his older brother in despair. We left for the forest, but even there our closeness tortured him relentlessly. He had two wives but could not touch them!' she said thickly.

Uruvi saw that Kunti was finding it difficult to continue but she did not tell her to stop. 'It was in the dark forest that I revealed my dark secret to my husband,' the old queen whispered. 'Before my marriage to King Pandu, Sage Durvasa had visited my father's house. I had been warned by my father that he was an insufferably irascible sage but I had to see to it that he was served impeccably. He was not to be displeased in any way—I did as I was told. The old sage was so pleased with my devotion and efficient hospitality that he granted me a strange boon. It was as if he knew that one day I would marry a man afflicted with the curse of sexual abstinence. The revered rishi granted me a chant—a mantra—to invoke whichever god I wanted to and ask him to bless me with a son—a son especially endowed with his own godly virtues.'

Kunti stopped, a faraway look in her eyes. Uruvi wondered whether there was any point in what she was telling her. But she did not risk interrupting Kunti as she recalled her painful past. 'On hearing that this boon was bestowed on me, King Pandu, instead of being upset, was delighted and he requested me to use the boon to provide Hastinapur with an heir. He saw a glimmer of hope of being a father of sons—but whom he could not have fathered. He knew they would not be from him, but he was beyond caring about that. All he wanted was an heir to the throne. And he came up with a solution for all his problems. He exhorted me, he appealed to me, he pleaded with me to use the mantras. Through the mantras, I was to beget his children and follow the custom of niyoga, the practice of offering one's body to another man with the husband's consent.'

When Kunti saw Uruvi's shocked expression, she laughed harshly. 'Oh, yes, it happens. It happens in most royal families though it's kept as the best-known open family secret,' Kunti said derisively. 'It happened with me and before me, with the two queens of King Vichitravirya, who was an impotent husband—Ambika and Ambalika. They were two out of the three Kashi princesses whom Bhishma Pitamaha had kidnapped for his half-brother, King Vichitravirya, the younger son of Queen Mother Satyavati.'

Suddenly, there was a cold draught in the room and Uruvi shivered. Kunti collected her thoughts and wrapped her shawl around her tightly. 'After King Vichitravirya's sudden death, his two widows, Ambika and Ambalika, had to offer themselves to Sage Vyasa, under the orders of the queen mother, who was desperate for an heir to carry on the Kuru dynasty. Earlier, she had asked Bhishma Pitamaha to perform niyoga with the widows but he refused adamantly. Then she called in her illegitimate son—Sage Vyasa, whom she had conceived through Sage Parashara before she married King Shantanu, the father of Bhishma Pitamaha and King Vichitravirya.'

Uruvi was dumbfounded at the royal intrigues Kunti was revealing so faithfully. 'Ironically, none of the three sons conceived through Sage Vyasa—Dhritrashtra, Pandu and Vidura—were of Kuru blood; they were not the sons of King Vichitravirya at all!'

Why was Kunti tracing the Kuru bloodline for her? This puzzled Uruvi but she wanted to know more. The revelation that neither Dhritrashtra nor King Pandu were 'pure' royals was a mockery for Uruvi. 'Bhishma Pitamaha is said to have refused Queen Mother Satyavati's request of niyoga on just one reasoning: he said intercourse with the wives of others was a grievous sin. Moreover, niyoga was permissible only at the instance of the husband and *not* of the mother-in-law. Defeated, the queen mother called for her long-forgotten son and that was when Sage Vyasa was brought in.'

The tale got more sordid. 'The widowed queens had no option: they could not refuse or choose who would perform niyoga,' recounted the elderly Pandava queen. 'It seems Queen Ambika shut her eyes in sheer terror when she was alone with the highly renowned but hideously ugly sage and out of that union was born a blind son—Dhritrashtra. Queen Ambalika suffered a similar horrifying experience. She was said to have gone as white as a sheet during the niyoga with the sage, which is why King Pandu was born anaemic and pale. Ambika was ordered to have niyoga with the sage again by her mother-in-law. But the young widow sent across her maid instead to the sage and the consummation was a relatively satisfactory one—and so Vidura, a healthy boy, was born. He was the queen mother's favourite but since his mother was a maid, he was considered not "royal" enough and was always snubbed as inferior. Just like Karna is,' added Kunti quietly.

Hearing his name, Uruvi felt an ache in her heart. She realized soon enough why Kunti was telling her this tale of the Kurus. In some odd way, it was connected with Karna. 'Vidura was always considered a Kshatta, or more politely, as a kshetraja, the son of a low-caste woman and a brahmin.'

'So that was how niyoga flourished in my husband's family—it was not new for him!' said Kunti dryly. 'When he came up with the suggestion, I initially refused. It was only when he went on his knees and begged me with folded hands that I reluctantly gave in—but completely on my terms. When I agreed to subject myself to niyoga, I said I would decide who the man would be, and King Pandu had to agree to it,' the mother of the Pandavas flushed darkly. 'Eventually, I invited a god rather than a brahmin, as he had suggested.'

Uruvi had heard from her mother the cruel rumours about the birth of the Pandavas and the subsequent humiliation Kunti often had to suffer at the hands of relentless gossips and spiteful tale-tellers. 'And that was how Yudhishthira was born first, from Lord Yama, the god of dharma and death. From Vayu, the wind god, I had Bhima, and lastly, I gave birth to Arjuna, the son of Indra, the king of the gods. After I had given three children to King Pandu through niyoga, I stopped. When he asked me to offer myself again for niyoga, I refused outright for I knew the scriptures allow niyoga only up to a maximum of three times. And that was when I quoted to him what I told you just now—the woman who gives her body a fourth time is a swairini, a wanton woman, and one who does so a fifth time is a kulta, a whore. I did not want that stigma, so much to my reluctance, I agreed to share the mantra with Madri. She invoked the Ashwini Kumara twins to beget Nakul and Sahadeva. Thus, the five Pandavas were born!'

Uruvi's patience was gradually wearing thin; she wanted Kunti to hurry to the most crucial part. 'Did King Pandu die because of Rishi Kindama's curse or was there another cause?' she asked as tactfully as she could.

'What other reason could there be?' Kunti looked puzzled. 'I found them later. He was dead by the time I arrived and Madri was sobbing away hysterically, blaming herself for his death!'

'You didn't see him die?' Uruvi asked instantly, little realizing that she sounded heartless.

'What are you getting at, Uruvi?' Kunti looked distressed. 'Madri saw him die—he died in her arms! She was mad with grief and barely coherent. We quietly arranged for his funeral in the forest...'

'Why didn't you inform Hastinapur?'

'We were in the middle of a thick jungle—it was better to perform his last rites as soon as possible. But how was I to know that the frenzied Madri, mad with grief, would jump into the funeral pyre too? It was a nightmare I have never talked about till now—all I wanted to do was take the small children with me and return home. When Madri died with King Pandu, it was up to me to bring up the five boys and I returned to Hastinapur to stake my claim to the kingdom.'

'You have been fighting all through your life, but have they given you your rights, Ma? I wonder if ill-luck is hereditary too or is it the curse of victims like Ambika and Ambalika, or even Queen Gandhari, that has made us see what is happening now?' Uruvi said sadly. 'Gross injustice has been heaped upon these women. It was rape, though all of you would like to call it something more polite!' said Uruvi. 'Offspring born of adultery—vyabhicharodbhava—can never be the source of happiness for anyone. King Dhritrashtra was born blind, but worse, he was blinded by power and the ambition to become a king. He believes his right to the throne was usurped and given away to his younger brother. The brother could not have children of his own and sought niyoga from his wife. His children were never his blood children. As for the third child of King Vichitrvirya, social norms would not accept Vidura or his sons ever as inheritors as they are said to be low-born. What inheritors did Queen Mother Satyavati get from her legacy of ruse and intrigue? Her grandchildren who can hardly boast of the "royal" blood of King Shantanu, her husband, are today fighting amongst themselves and heading for a destructive war!'

Kunti heaved a weary sigh but remained quiet, and Uruvi saw her as a forlorn, sad figure who refused to stop fighting the battles of her life.

'Why didn't you go to your father?' Uruvi asked instead.

'Again, dear, I have not been as fortunate as you are,' Kunti remarked somewhat dryly. Uruvi flushed, reminding herself she was in her father's palatial home. 'As a widow with five young boys, I could not turn to my father for help. I had two fathers—King Sura of Vrishni who gave me away to his childless friend, King Kuntibhoj, my second father, but both disowned me in my worst hours,' Uruvi heard the bitterness which Kunti could not hide in her voice. 'Neither of my two "fathers" came forward to provide shelter or support to me. I turned to that one person who I knew would help me—Vidura, Queen Mother Satyavati's favourite grandson. He has proved to be more than a friend and a protective uncle to my sons. It was he who saved them from being burnt alive. And it is in his home that I have now sought shelter when my sons have gone on exile. I returned for the sake of my sons to give them their rights, and even today, I am still doing that. I could have gone for another exile this time too, but I did not. I sent Draupadi instead. I stayed back to remind King

Dhritrashtra and Queen Gandhari that injustice has been meted out to me and my sons all these years. I intend to subtly reproach them with my silent presence, which will remind them of my sons' violated rights. I am a patient woman and I won't give up.'

'You are now fighting for your sons' rights, but what about your daughter-in-law's violation in the royal court?' asked Uruvi softly. 'In spite of everything, you could not save yourself from nasty tongues, could you? Then, is it not tragic irony that you made your daughter-in-law, Draupadi, suffer a worse humiliation by marrying her to your five sons? And isn't it worse fate that it was my husband Karna who, on the basis of this very assertion, called Draupadi a whore?'

'Yes, I should have foreseen this,' replied Kunti dully. 'It was an oversight on my part. I believed that if Draupadi were to marry the five Pandavas, she would bring them closer and they would be united and strong in the fight for their rights for Hastinapur. I thought marriage to five different women would have scattered them. I feared a split that would weaken the goal.'

Uruvi saw Kunti in a new light, as a woman she had never before witnessed. She was appalled. 'And you used Draupadi as a weapon for the purpose?' she retorted bitingly. 'She was only a means for your sole purpose of bonding the brothers forever. You wanted their lives and ambitions governed by, and revolving around, a single woman. Five wives would have created chaos and differences between the brothers, is that it? What a price for her to pay, Ma! How could you be so coldly calculating? Was I part of your great plan too, but which did not materialize?' Uruvi sounded hurt.

'No, dear, you were not! But even though you did not marry Arjuna, I am glad that you chose Karna as your groom. I mean it, Uruvi. I couldn't have been happier! About your other accusation—yes, probably I did and I am guilty as charged,' Kunti said evenly. 'I wanted you to marry one of my sons because it would have been for the best for all of us, just as I considered it worthwhile that Bhima should marry Hidimba, the rakshasa (demonness) princess who was madly in love with him. They have a son now—Ghatotkacha—the strongest man on earth right now.'

'And who will aid you in case there is a war, right?' Uruvi guessed shrewdly. 'So, with all your daughters-in-law, it was your stratagem and cunning all the way. But in my case, things went a little wrong, didn't they?'

'Yes, you married Karna and as I said earlier, I couldn't have been gladder!'

'Why? I hurt your son when I married Karna—doesn't that rankle? I know your sons, the Pandavas, hate me for what I did and can never forgive me for my decision to marry Karna and reject Arjuna. They have not forgotten nor forgiven me for it.'

'I supported your decision about Karna because he is a good man. A very good man,' Kunti murmured softly.

'A very good man who doesn't always get it right! He is doing the most wrong things. Don't absolve him of his faults.'

'I am not. I am telling you that he, like others, is not perfect. It is you who should accept his failings as well. Do not be so self-righteous or disparage him to a point of an ugly confrontation. He humiliated Draupadi for an altogether different reason. He simply wanted to hit back at the woman who had once publicly scorned him.'

'You always seem to have all the right answers. But what if it had worked the other way round?' asked Uruvi irreverently. 'What if, instead of uniting your sons, Draupadi had been a spiteful, vengeful woman and had split the brothers by playing one against the other? She could have played the seduction game with your sons as well as you played the game of intrigue with her.'

There was a sudden flare of tension between the two women. 'But my strategy worked wonderfully, especially with Draupadi,' Kunti answered sharply. 'With Draupadi also came the Panchala power and the Yadava wealth through Krishna, which increased the power of the Pandavas. Instead of labelling me as a scheming mother-in-law, did you know that the Kauravas planned to destroy the Pandavas' unity by sending across a bewitching beauty to seduce them? It was Karna who pointed out their folly. He explained to them that as the

Pandavas were married to an extraordinarily beautiful woman, who also was their common wife, this ploy was sure to fail.'

Again, at the mention of Karna in the context of Draupadi, Uruvi felt a stab of jealousy. Kunti noticed the gleam of anger in Uruvi's eyes, detecting the storm raging within Uruvi. She had provoked her successfully, she thought, and continued with her relentless but subtle harrying.

'Answering your last question about why Draupadi did not turn against us, Uruvi, you well know by now, dear, that Draupadi is not an avenger,' she replied smoothly. 'Or would she have forgiven Karna so easily?' Kunti gave the younger girl a shrewd look. 'If the offended has pardoned the offender, the case is closed, right, Uruvi? And that's how it should be. The chapter is closed. Don't turn back the pages.'

'I don't need to turn them back; they keep flipping back with the winds of time,' answered Uruvi resignedly. 'I am not leaving Karna, if that's what you fear. I will return to him once the baby is born.'

'But your relationship is not as good as it was before, is it?' the older lady persisted.

'I can't make myself forget and forgive what he did, it's not easy!' she cried in despair.

'Nothing is easy,' Kunti retorted briskly. 'I told you my story because I wanted you to realize a few things. That you should know when to give in and when to hit back. This time you are hitting the wrong person for the wrong reason. It's Draupadi, isn't it? It is she who is coming between the two of you.'

I must be painfully transparent, Uruvi thought with dismay. The one secret she was trying to hide so frantically was now stripped bare. She could not avoid the issue any longer with the older lady. 'Yes, Draupadi is an insidious presence...' she agreed slowly. 'Somehow I think I have already lost Karna in a way. And you realized it too, and that's why you came here to reassure me, didn't you? You know Draupadi loves Karna and that's why she has forgiven him so simply, so effortlessly. But what about Karna? How am I to live with a man, knowing he is in love with a married woman? Each time I feel like going near him, I recall his words to her—that she is nothing but a whore who has bedded five husbands! It is as if he regrets he wasn't one of them! He said that she should find other men to cohabit with—it was as if he has been waiting and lusting for her all along! I can't get rid of that horrible, hideous image of the two entwined together,' Uruvi shut her eyes in tight fury. 'It torments me, keeps taunting me. I can't sleep, I can't think any more!' she wept, burying her face in her hands.

Kunti could not bear to see Uruvi's anguish, and wanted to assuage her pain. She went up to her and embraced Uruvi gently, as if to wish away the sorrow welling inside. The tears still streamed down the girl's pale face. Kunti allowed her to weep out the agony she had buried inside her so long. She had been shocked when she saw Uruvi at her doorstep on the day her sons and daughter-in-law left for their exile. When Uruvi had insisted on meeting Draupadi, she had wondered what the two women had spoken about, but she had not got a chance to talk with Uruvi after that day.

She had known something was hugely amiss and had been anxious about Uruvi since then. Karna looked jaded and unhappy each time she saw him at the royal court. And there seemed to be no news about Uruvi, except that she had left for Pukeya. Finally, she had decided to visit Pukeya to find out for herself. She had been very worried and now, with the girl sobbing disconsolately in her lap, Kunti felt her own eyes wet with tears, although she rarely let herself cry. Kunti knew obscurely that it was better for her not to put what she felt into words. But Uruvi, she reflected, hardening her heart, had to face the reality she was running away from.

'Have you asked Karna about his feelings?' she asked, as Uruvi's bout of weeping abated.

'No,' Uruvi murmured brokenly. 'I don't dare! I fear his reply. What if he admits to it? I know he can never lie to me…but I wouldn't be brave enough to take his honesty.'

'You have two options—but both are difficult,' warned the older woman. 'Either question him openly and accept the situation gracefully or…'

'Do I have the luxury of another "or"?' Uruvi questioned harshly.

'Or,' Kunti said deliberately, 'believe in your love and trust him. Believe that he loves no one but you. Loving is not just believing; it is also accepting the worst. Uruvi, he does love you. I have seen him with you; he is a contented man. Don't ruin what you have. Your doubts, your suspicions, your somewhat misplaced noble moral fortitude can do you more damage than good. You have been lucky to get your man. Keep him safe with you. Don't stretch your luck too far. It might just swing back hard and harshly. Marriage is about working on what has changed, not what you once believed in.'

Uruvi gave her a strange smile and Kunti was, for once, nonplussed. Had she ruined or bettered the chances for Uruvi and Karna? She was not too sure.

13

The Birth of Vrishakethu

Uruvi did not hear from Karna for a long time after his visit. Kunti's warning words kept resonating in her mind and all she wanted to do was run back into Karna's comforting arms. But she knew she could not; she would not. The baby was due any moment and as she waited for the day her child would be born, her thoughts kept drifting to the man she loved. She pined for him and even though she was still distressed about what he had done, she desperately hoped she had not lost him. This tussle between her heart and mind never seemed to end.

Karna did not write to her and neither did she. It was as if an invisible, impenetrable wall had divided them. All she got to know through Vrushali's letters was that Karna stayed away from his home, spending weeks at a stretch on the battlefield. After the Pandavas left for their exile in the forest, Karna had taken upon himself the duty of expanding Duryodhana's empire in his mission to declare him the emperor of the world. Commanding a huge army marching to different parts of the country, Karna subjugated many kings and made them swear allegiance to Duryodhana as the king of Hastinapur or forced them to meet his army in combat. Karna won all the battles easily. And in this military blitzkrieg, he, as the mightiest warrior, forced many rulers and clans to surrender—the Vangas, the Nishadas, the Kalingas, the Vatsas, the Ashmakas, the Rishikas, the Kambojas, the Shakas, the Kekayas, the Avantyas, the Gandharas, the Madrakas, the Trigartas, the Tanganas, the Panchals, the Videhas, the Suhmas, the Mlecchas and even the ferocious forest tribes. Pukeya remained vulnerable, and Uruvi wondered what her father would do if Karna attacked his kingdom. But she knew he would not.

When the time for the birth of her baby arrived, she was as prepared as a soldier is ready for war. Late at night, she woke up with a sharp pain stabbing her body. She was trembling as she called out for her mother, who came into her room immediately. Her last coherent thought was that their baby had arrived in good time. He was as punctual as his father.

The baby was born early in the morning, before dawn broke into the light of another day. By mid-afternoon the baby had three early visitors. Kunti apologized profusely for not coming in earlier. And then, the baby's father arrived. He was warmly greeted by a visibly pleased Queen Shubra and an overjoyed King Vahusha.

'It's a boy!' Queen Shubra smiled with delight. 'Congratulations, son, you have another boy!'

Karna stood stiff and silent, yet his impatient eyes kept wandering towards his wife's room. For a moment he let himself relax and Uruvi's parents could see his joy. He asked huskily, 'He was born with the sunrise, so he ought to be lucky. How's Uruvi?'

'Doing as well as can be expected,' his mother-in-law replied with a huge smile. 'She was well prepared; her labour pains began in the middle of the night and by dawn, it was all over!'

Radha, who had accompanied Karna, smiled quietly at her son's evident eagerness to see his child. 'You are behaving as if it's your first born, Radheya!' she smiled.

'He is *our* first child,' Karna murmured. 'The first child always has an amazing effect on one. May I meet her?' He looked appealingly at his mother-in-law. 'If she doesn't want to see me, it's fine,' he added hastily. 'Don't let me upset her. But I would like to hold my baby for just a moment.'

'She's awake and I think she wants to meet you. She wants to show you the baby herself! Come. Let's go meet her,' Kunti gave him a long, lingering look and gently took him by his hand to lead him to Uruvi's room. She pushed him inside, letting go of his hand reluctantly. Karna turned and bowed to her.

'Go, son. Go in. Meet your child. And your wife. Bless you,' she murmured softly, her eyes tender with mixed emotions.

As Karna stumbled into the chamber, he was arrested by the sight of his wife, smiling slightly, nestling the baby closely in her arms; he had imagined them so often like this that it was a warm familiar sight. It was a sublime vision, a transcendent moment he knew he would cherish till the last day of his life.

She wore only a single sari and she looked wan. Her long hair, dishevelled and damp, clung to her head and hung down her shoulders in cascading wisps. She was deathly white, but the moment she saw him, he could see the colour seeping into her cheeks. Her soft lips broke into a small smile.

Then Karna held the baby in his arms, feeling an indescribable happiness. His son was beautiful, huddled snugly in his strong arms, his head already covered with soft, golden hair and his huge dark eyes gleaming softly.

'He has a lot of hair and it's as fair as yours,' Uruvi whispered, her eyes sparkling brightly.

'But his eyes are like yours—dark and oh, so very huge!' He kissed the baby's broad forehead.

'He'll be just like his father,' she said warmly.

'No! No, he won't,' Karna pronounced quietly. 'I don't want him to be like me. Ever. I wouldn't say I am a very good role model—let him chalk out a better path for himself. Have you thought of any name for him?'

She shook her head, lowering her eyes to hide her turbulent feelings. He was sitting so close to her that she could inhale his scent, could feel the strength of his body. She wanted to touch him, wanted to feel his arms around her but that wall between them was still there. Her pitiless words, once uttered so calmly, still kept them apart.

'Then we shall ask the family priest to choose the best name according to his horoscope,' Karna leaned over smoothly and returned the baby to her. 'You have always given me more than I can ever ask for. I hope I deserve him,' he said abruptly.

'You are a father any son would be proud to have.'

'And as your husband, Uruvi?' he pressed. 'When can I be your husband again? Can you ever forgive me? Please tell me. Tell me how I can make you respect me, love me as you once did.'

'I do love you,' she said tenderly. 'Let me happily remember the time when we were together. Let me have that forever.'

In his silence, he assented.

Karna stayed on for a few more days till the naming ceremony of the baby. King Vahusha spared no effort to make the ceremony memorable, with music, dancing and the choicest of eats for the guests who came in hundreds. The baby was named Vrishakethu and he seemed rather happy about his name as he chortled away all through the ceremony conducted by chanting priests.

'He's a good child,' Queen Shubra stroked the soft cheek of her first grandchild. 'Usually, it's either the baby or the mother who gets cranky at such occasions! He seems to be so accommodating!'

'He's just like Radheya,' gushed Radha, joining them to gaze adoringly at her grandson. 'He never gave me trouble, even as a baby. It was as if he was born to be wise and considerate. This one will be the same.'

'That's what every parent hopes for—the best for their child. Sadly, very few children realize that parents always keep their best interests in mind. They would never wish harm for their child, would they?' said Queen Shubra.

Uruvi agreed, recalling her mother's concealed concern, which she had masked so magnificently during the swayamwara, and how vehemently she had opposed her marriage to Karna. Now that Uruvi had become a mother herself, she felt a strange, unaccustomed affinity with her mother, understanding why her mother had reacted as she did—it was only because she wanted the best for her daughter. Uruvi was glad she had her mother close to her, and felt a small pang at the thought of leaving her soon.

When it was time to leave Pukeya and return home to Karna, Uruvi was ready with a smile and a wise gleam in her eyes. Holding her baby close, she waved to her parents and turned away resolutely. Her father watched her walk to the chariot with her husband and her baby. The air was still mild and spring-like and above the palace towers, small white clouds sailed leisurely in a sheer blue sky. She held herself straight. She was still slim and lovely and he could not help staring at his child, who had become a woman now. He thought that it would not occur to anyone that his daughter was putting up a brave front. She carried herself proudly, with her head held high, a tiny smile on her lips hiding a broken heart. Yet, he knew, some part of her loved and hoped still.

Days went slowly by, stretching into weeks. The nights were achingly longer. Each evening, Karna retired to his room and Uruvi slept in her huge bed alone and miserable, yet proud and unyielding. Women, Uruvi thought wryly, could conceal their feelings so wonderfully. No one could have guessed what she was going through. Karna was distant towards her—he looked strained and in his eyes was a hungry, haunted look. Uruvi tried to ease the tension as best as she could but constantly found herself torn between longing and despair. She was withdrawn when he was with her, her vivaciousness subdued, but they played chess together, chatted and discussed various topics. The difference was that they rarely laughed together as they once did.

The family did not seem to notice any change in their relationship. Even if they did, they kept a discreet silence, hoping the cloud would soon pass. 'She'll come around one day,' Radha assured her husband. 'She loves him too much and he cannot survive without her. You saw the state he was in when she went to Pukeya? He had gone to pieces. Give her time. The baby will help to put everything right.'

Uruvi engrossed herself in the baby to distract herself from thoughts of Karna. She refrained from bringing up any contentious issue and avoided talking about Duryodhana. She never spoke to Karna, except when he questioned her directly, and often retired to her own room quietly. But Karna noticed that she was in radiant health. There was a soft glow about her, a healthy colour in her cheeks, and in Karna's eyes, she never looked more beautiful, with the baby cradled in the crook of her arm as she murmured softly to him. He was filled with love whenever he gazed at her. She averted her eyes but not before he saw the longing lingering in them. Oh, she was proud and still so fiercely belligerent. Each time he left home for the battlefield, he couldn't forget that look in her eyes and he remained hopeful that she would come back to him as the bride she once was.

One morning, on one of the many days Karna was away, Uruvi met Vrushali as she rushed up the stairs. 'Careful, dear, you need to be more cautious,' she greeted Uruvi with a small smile. 'You are still not very strong.'

Uruvi promptly stopped. 'Thanks, I keep forgetting that!' she laughed self-consciously.

'As is often the case,' Vrushali said dryly and Uruvi detected a subtle undercurrent in her words. 'But as a mother now, you will have to be less impulsive and much more responsible. Are you tired?' she asked, rounding off her disapproval with a gesture of concern.

Uruvi stared at her. She had never got down to knowing this woman at all. She was cold yet polite, distant yet solicitous, greeting her but never making her feel welcome. Uruvi felt a frisson of irritation rise within her but she calmly asked instead, 'Any news of Karna?'

'He's gone to the battlefield again,' Vrushali sighed. 'Ever since the Pandavas went into exile, Radheya has rarely been in Anga. Perhaps since you left, he prefers to stay away from home.' Vrushali almost sounded accusing. 'He is busy with his campaign for Duryodhana, collecting as many crowns for him as he can,' Uruvi heard the slight sneer in her voice. 'He and Shona went off three weeks ago but should be back in a day or two,' she said and began to move away.

'He's gone with Shona?' Uruvi sounded surprised.

'Our whole family is fighting for the Kurus these days—Shona, Vrasasena, Shatrunjaya, Dvipata and Sushena are Radheya's little army for his dear friend. Thankfully, Satyasena, Chitrasena and

Susharma are too young to be on the battlefield,' Vrushali said bitterly, resentment lacing her words. 'An entire full-blooded family is fighting somebody else's war!'

Feeling weary, Uruvi suddenly wanted to sit down. 'Let's go to my room,' she suggested, 'or I'll have to sit on the steps!'

'Yes, I was coming upstairs to see Vrishakethu,' Vrushali smiled in gentle agreement.

It was the first time Vrushali had ever stepped into her chamber. Uruvi peered into the cradle. The baby was fast asleep so she continued talking to Vrushali. 'Has the situation worsened so much?' Uruvi asked almost apologetically, but she already knew the answer. All the men in the family were on the battlefield and that is how it would be from now on. Karna saw himself as a pioneer, a crusader for the Kuru family, and his sons, who were young and enthusiastic, had caught on to their father's sense of purpose in expanding the frontiers of the Kuru kingdom. They and Shona were too devoted to Karna to disobey him.

'I have already lost one son, my Sudhama, needlessly,' Vrushali's usually serene face was creased with pain. 'We haven't yet recovered from that tragedy at Draupadi's swayamwara, but Draupadi has managed to cast her spell again!' Vrushali looked uncharacteristically virulent. 'She and that wretched Kuru prince, Duryodhana! Radheya will never free himself from Duryodhana! He is with the Kauravas but he is not like them—and they know this well! They fooled him into thinking the dice game was without any great stakes. Knowing full well that Radheya was against the dice game right from the beginning, Duryodhana and Shakuni had warned Dushasana not to allow Radheya to enter the Kuru Raj Sabha when the game was on. But somehow Radheya managed to get in and clearly, on that day, he was the wrong man in the wrong place.'

Uruvi blanched. She did not want to hear of the episode again. Blood rushed to her head and her breathing oppressed her. 'Oh, that Panchala princess has cast a spell on him since her swayamwara!' Vrushali fumed, ignoring Uruvi's discomfiture. 'She humiliated him publicly and we lost our son because of her! I know that when he saw her vulnerable at the Raj Sabha, it brought all those terrible memories back and he got a chance to get even with her. Calling her a whore because she had five husbands was right, in a way, but morally, he lost out, didn't he?' She looked pointedly at Uruvi, prompting her to reply. Uruvi did not bother to answer; she had no intention of getting into a debate on Karna, Draupadi and herself.

Vrushali seemed to be enjoying her awkwardness for some strange reason. 'Despite all his righteousness, Radheya could not bring himself to forgive that woman. The fact that he refused to help her in her moment of need shows the depth of his resentment and loathing!' she remarked with malice, a quality no one would have attributed to the mild-mannered Vrushali.

'Did he discuss the incident with you?' Uruvi asked quietly.

'No. Karna doesn't ever talk about what bothers him; he prefers bottling it all up!' Vrushali shook her head sadly. 'I cannot believe he is the same man whom I married so many years ago! He seems to have changed so much. Whether it's a sign of corruption or maturity is something I fail to understand.' Vrushali paused for an instant, fingering the mangalsutra hanging around her slender neck. 'Radheya has only one measure of right and wrong—his blind loyalty to Duryodhana in any situation. Even when he is wrong, Radheya supports him—that's all that matters to him, fully realizing that it will be his downfall one day. Truth and lies, right and wrong are all a matter of perception. Radheya believes he is right in standing up for his friend; we think he is wrong and his devotion is misplaced because it is for a man who has no integrity. He believes what happened at the Kuru hall was wrong, but he eventually ended up being part of it and now he berates himself silently,' she sighed.

Vrushali spoke calmly, measuring each word with a certain nonchalance. She persisted in the same vein, 'I have known him since both of us were very young and, over the years, I have seen him changing—often for the better, sometimes for the worse. I have watched him slowly get sullied. That decadent Kuru prince tried to get him into the habit of drinking, womanizing and gambling, but Radheya, after his initial surrender, retraced his steps fast enough to get back on his feet again. Since then he has been part of Duryodhana's coterie, yet his heart is not in it. I can see he's getting sucked into the palace intrigues as well. I guess I lost him a long time ago.' Vrushali sounded wistful. 'First I lost him to Duryodhana, then to Draupadi...'

'Draupadi?' Uruvi asked sharply.

'Haven't you realized it yet, dear? He is utterly fascinated by her and the fact that she rejected him goads him into further madness. It is a horrible love–hate relationship. You wonder whether he loves to hate her or hates to love her.'

What a crazily spinning world I'm living in, Uruvi screamed silently. Here I am so completely in love with a man obsessed with another woman, a woman who loves him too, with the same untamed passion. She glanced at Vrushali, hoping desperately that she was wrong.

Then Uruvi heard her say, 'And finally, I lost him to you.'

There was a long, deliberate pause, forcing Uruvi to feel uncomfortable. Vrushali looked at her squarely, her eyes clear, condemning her openly. 'He has gone so far away that he is not mine any more. He stopped coming to my chamber a long time ago. Why are you turning crimson, Uruvi?' asked Vrushali with evident amusement at her rival's unease. 'Seriously, I was jealous of you once, but no longer. I know where I stand. And that's certainly not coming between you lovebirds. I knew I had to step back—and watch you being his wife and lover, which was a difficult task at first!' she gave a humourless laugh. 'You are realizing it finally, aren't you, that it is rather hard being Radheya's wife?'

Uruvi looked back at her thoughtfully. 'Who has had an easy time, Vrushali? Ask my mother or ask our mother-in-law. Bhanumati, too, knows it is not easy being Duryodhana's wife; Draupadi and Subhadra or even Queen Gandhari and Kunti have faced difficult times in their marriages. We all have married men so complex, and we can do nothing but watch helplessly. That is what is so frustrating!'

cried Uruvi violently. 'Vrushali, Karna's worthiness and ability are not enough; they have to be accompanied by wise decisions too. He is the bravest, the most kind, the most wonderful man we know but perhaps he is making too many misjudgements and moral errors.'

'Yes, he is, and I can't ignore that any longer!' Vrushali replied. 'Living in false hope and illusory expectations is not optimism, Uruvi. It is living in denial. Perhaps I am no longer in love with the man Radheya is today...' she trailed off unhappily.

But I still am, Uruvi thought with despair. And I can't let go of him. She knew she loved him to distraction. Was he her weakness?

'Oh, what would I do to bring back the old days at Champanagari where we first met and married!' cried Vrushali in sudden frustration. 'You rushed to Pukeya when you couldn't handle the situation here, Uruvi. Why? Because, you wanted to go back to your roots to make sense of your life, to deal with the madness engulfing all of us. There comes a time when we need to make sense of our being, of what we are. You are lucky to have your Pukeya.' The older woman was crying and she buried her face in her hands to muffle her sobs.

'No, no dear! All is not lost! We have him, we love him and that is our greatest blessing!' Uruvi tried to reassure the distressed woman, moved by the appeal in Vrushali's cry. 'That's because he is a man who hungers for social respect. He is seeking his identity, which has been denied to him. He wants to be known as a worthy warrior!'

'At what cost, Uruvi?' she flashed fiercely. 'He is sacrificing himself and his family to a selfish society that has not hesitated to remind him every now and then of his low birth and his inferiority. It kills me, it's killing him and it will eventually destroy our entire family,' Vrushali looked pointedly at the rocking cradle. 'Save your child from this meaninglessness, Uruvi.'

'Would it make any difference?' Uruvi shrugged her shoulders. 'In spite of having us, his children, and a family that loves him so unconditionally, Karna is so remote. I always thought a family was a refuge in a merciless world but does it hold true for Karna? He is always so alone, ever unfulfilled, constantly haunted by the unresolved ambiguity of his true self. Till he finds it, he will remain a restless soul, searching for his ultimate truth. But by then, it might be too late—for him, for all of us.'

'It is too late for him, isn't it, Uruvi?' she asked gently. 'You have not forgiven him for that one fault of his.'

Vrushali was forcing her to respond. Uruvi got up impatiently, as if to shake off her angry thoughts. 'I can't make myself forget that it was Karna who instigated the Kauravas to disrobe Draupadi in court,' Uruvi's voice trembled as her pain struggled with shame. 'After the Pandavas lost everything—their kingdom, their own freedom, their queen in the game of dice, it was Karna who said she was nothing less than a whore. It was his words that prompted Dushasana to start pulling off her clothes. Until Karna uttered the unspeakable, no one in the Raj Sabha had dared to think of stripping Draupadi! It's so horrible, Vrushali! As a woman, can't you feel the pain and humiliation of Draupadi? And what I cannot accept is that it was our husband who did that to her!'

'Yes, he spoke out of hurt and anger! But can't you see his repentance, Uruvi?' retorted Vrushali. 'The shock of your flight broke him. He asked me to intercede for him, to implore you to return. I refused as I believe what's between the two of you is too private. And so, he went to Pukeya to get you back. But you did not relent and he returned the very same day. Since then, he's been occupied with Duryodhana and his military plans. His loneliness is intolerable to him, and like a driven man, he's running away from home and all of us, to drown himself in his work and despair. He's willing to promise you anything—hasn't he abased himself enough, Uruvi? I have grown up with his faults and I love him in spite of those. I have forgiven him a thousand times over, because each time he changed. I learnt that loving is giving. And forgiving. I only hope that by the time you do it, it is not too late…for you and for him.'

14

Uruvi and Bhanumati

One day, Sage Maitreya arrived at the court of King Dhritrashtra and stayed on for a few days at Hastinapur. Uruvi, as well as many other noble ladies, were summoned by the king to pay their respects to the eminent rishi.

'Revered sir, I heard you met my dear nephews, the Pandavas, in the forest. Are they well? Will there be love and peace in our family again?' King Dhritrashtra pleaded, yearning for the blessings of the great man.

'Yes, I met Yudhishthira in the Kamakhya forest with the other sages who accompanied me,' Sage Maitreya acknowledged with a brief nod. 'I heard about the shameful episode in the Hastinapur Raj Sabha and I could not believe it was allowed to happen when you, Bhishma and Drona were present.'

The three stalwarts, Uruvi saw with undisguised satisfaction, had enough grace in them to hang their heads in shame as they had done in this very hall, months ago. She looked hard at Bhishma Pitamaha, her eyes gleaming viciously, but he averted his face.

Turning to Duryodhana, the sage said, 'Answering your father's question, I think the answer lies with you. For your own good, I advise you to make peace with the Pandavas. Feuds in the family are destructive. Moreover, not only are the Pandavas popular and strong, they have very strong allies in Krishna and King Drupad.'

Duryodhana reacted with more pompousness than expected. Clearly, Karna's ongoing victorious digvijaya, his military campaigns, had given him a swollen head and he was revelling in their success. When he heard what the sage had to say, the Kuru prince burst into a loud, contemptuous laugh and slapping his thigh in disdain, shrugged the remark away rudely.

Uruvi heard a collective gasp of horror in the assembly. Duryodhana's insolence was as monumental as his mistakes. The rishi then flew into a rage and stood up menacingly. 'Your arrogance will bring you down one day. You slap your thigh in scorn but one day, the same thigh will be torn and broken on the battlefield and you will die a slow, agonizing death,' he predicted, uttering his words like a curse. He turned to leave the court but was stopped by a visibly upset King Dhritrashtra.

'I beg of you, please forgive my son. He is immature, he is ignorant! O revered sir, please take back your curse,' he pleaded, falling at Sage Maitreya's feet.

'If your son decides to make peace with his cousins, my curse will not work. If he persists in his hostility, he will not escape his doom,' he declared and strode out of the crowded Kuru hall. Bhanumati's face was ashen, her eyes wide with dawning horror. She threw Uruvi a glance of desperation.

Many sages and brahmins visited the Pandavas and when they returned to Hastinapur, King Dhritrashtra made it a point to meet each one of them. All had one story to tell—of how the princes, born in pampered royalty, were enduring life in the wild jungles and facing several hardships. The old king seemed moved, but not his son. His face remained grave, but in his eyes there glinted a devilish delight. He loved listening to these anecdotes with perverse pleasure, enjoying a vicarious glee in hearing that the Pandavas were suffering and would do so for many long years.

One late morning, Uruvi learnt that Karna had been called in by Duryodhana to go to the Dwaitvana ranches with a huge Kaurava army. She was perplexed. 'Why does one need an army to check the herds of cows, bulls and calves?' she asked Bhanumati in rising bewilderment, when the younger woman had dropped by with her son, Lakshmana.

The little prince had wanted to see the new baby. He was a quiet, solemn boy, unlike the endearing, animated Abhimanyu, Arjuna and Subhadra's son. He stared at the baby for a long time, then went out quietly to play in the garden. Uruvi saw him soon sitting on the bench, playing with his ball, and she marvelled how this soft-spoken, taciturn little fellow was the boisterous Duryodhana's son. Lakshmana was fair, almost pale, and very grave for his age. He never ran about noisily like other boys and only played solitary games.

Bhanumati noticed Uruvi staring at her son. 'He is such a good boy,' she sighed, the pride and joy unmistakable in her voice. 'Coming back to your question, Uruvi, if I know my husband well, he has gone there to trouble the Pandavas—and not for any stock checking,' Bhanumati replied dryly. 'Dwaitvana is very close to where they are now. My husband would be most happy if he were to actually see them suffering. He wants to gloat, that's all! Oh, why does he do that? He has heard the curse of Sage Maitreya and yet he couldn't care less!' cried Bhanumati. 'He has Indraprastha and a chunk of the Pandavas' kingdom. He need not burn any longer with jealousy and yet he pursues them with such cruel relentlessness.'

Uruvi decided it would be wiser to remain quiet. She watched her pacing the floor and wondered how this lovely princess of Kamboja had agreed to become the Kuru queen. The bubbly younger sister of the first queen of Duryodhana, who had died at a young age, she was selected by Guru Dronacharya as the next bride-to-be for the crown prince of Hastinapur. Her father, the King of Kamboja, readily agreed because the guru was his friend. Uruvi was amazed at the way the young princess had adapted to her life as the queen of one of the most disliked kings of the kingdom. Probably that was why Bhanumati tried to be extra nice to everyone, trying to make up for her husband's unpopularity. She had a compelling desire to be liked and was very sensitive about the impact she had on others. She lavished affection on everyone, but Uruvi suspected that the fear of rejection lingered in her. Uruvi had noticed the look of uneasiness in Bhanumati's eyes when her effusiveness was often reciprocated with a cool slight. This reaction was ironical, considering that Bhanumati, as the queen, could either reject overtures of friendship or condescendingly confer favours to a selected few. Uruvi recalled one instance when Bhanumati gave Vrushali a cold brush-off, showing she could be mean to the underdog. Vrushali had been instantly dismissed and not considered worthy of Bhanumati's time, Uruvi recollected wryly, so it was surprising that she had accepted and acknowledged Karna as part of her coterie. Right now, the Kuru queen seemed to be disturbed and Uruvi knew it would be best to allow her to do most of the talking, especially when it concerned Duryodhana, a subject she didn't like to discuss anyway.

Bhanumati was pacing in the room like a caged tigress. 'He hates the Pandavas so much that it's as normal as breathing to him. When it comes to them, the evil in him is never satiated—it keeps fermenting to poison him and all those around him. He turns into a monster, a sadist—he enjoys the unhappiness he causes them and likes to watch them suffer,' she asserted. 'Uruvi, would you believe me when I say that otherwise he's a normal man getting on with life? He is a fabulous father, a benevolent king, a brave warrior—he is so good and kind to most people, but he abhors the Pandavas with a passion! And his hatred is so bigoted that he cannot tolerate anyone favouring them either. That's why he keeps clashing with people like Bhishma Pitamaha, Guru Dronacharya and Vidura.'

Was that why Karna showed his dislike for the Pandavas as evidently as Duryodhana did? Was that Karna's way of impressing Duryodhana? Bhanumati's next words took away her doubts about Karna's integrity. 'You and Karna fail to understand him because you measure him according to your own high moral code,' she said. 'In fact, the only person who can dare to defy Duryodhana is Karna. He is the only person Duryodhana genuinely respects—and that is because Karna always speaks his mind unhesitantly and fairly. He does not mince his words,' she remarked. 'Karna has won battles for him yet my husband thinks only of keeping the Pandavas in misery. Karna is not greedy for a kingdom or wealth, but Duryodhana is. As a mighty warrior, Karna conducted the victorious digvijaya for

Duryodhana, not for himself but for his friend. But even after he has won an entire empire for him, is Duryodhana happy? He will always yearn for that share of the Pandavas and more. He loathes his cousins—that's ingrained in him and nursed further by his Uncle Shakuni. They haunt him and he will hunt them down—he won't rest in peace until he can find a way to destroy them.'

Distraught, Bhanumati spread her arms helplessly. 'Oh, Uruvi, I loathe his wickedness and his warped insecurity! He seems to be insatiable when it comes to the Pandavas. Karna has handed him great power—he is the emperor today. Yet, he wants to watch the poor Pandavas in their misery—a misery he inflicted on them. Initially, I dismissed it as the usual jealousy found in most families, but it's a mounting paranoia with him. He has done every evil deed possible— he even tried to kill his aunt and his cousins, usurped their throne, humiliated Draupadi in the worst possible way—could he stoop lower? What else am I to bear as his wife, Uruvi? I hang my head with shame but he has no sense of shame or remorse whatsoever when it comes to the Pandavas. He is a demon whom no one can stop—not even Karna! Who can I say all this to, except you?' she cried, wringing her hands in restless frustration.

'Stop torturing yourself.' Uruvi tried in vain to calm the other woman. 'We are both suffering the same pain.'

'No!' she protested fiercely. 'Don't ever make the mistake of comparing Karna with Duryodhana! Karna is too noble and whatever you consider he is doing wrong is for the sake of his friend. In fact, he is one of the few good men here and don't ever forget that, Uruvi. He might be making all the bad choices but he is a righteous man. He is keeping a promise he pledged to himself. He might be Duryodhana's closest confidante but he is not like him—and you know that. He is guided—you can call it misled perhaps—by his strong sense of loyalty.'

'And that's going to be his ruin,' Uruvi finished quietly. 'He knows it but he will remain loyal. I have realized well enough now that you cannot advise a person who stubbornly believes that he is right though he knows, rationally, that he is wrong. Bhanu, we have to live with it. We cannot change our husbands any more than we can alter what is happening around us. We think we can, but that again, is extreme optimism. The only power we seem to hold is on ourselves—we can but modify ourselves. And the sooner we do it, the better for all of us,' she added tiredly. Seeing the grim look on the other woman's face, Uruvi chaffed lightly, 'And hey, are you defending Karna because he's the best sparring partner you can get to play your game of dice?'

The harshness on Bhanumati's face melted away at Uruvi's words. 'Oh yes, I do! He is the best in the game, and yes, he is my favourite person too, besides being the best-looking man in the kingdom right now!' she grinned wickedly. 'And though I know you don't approve of their friendship either, he is the best thing to have happened to Duryodhana. Duryodhana loves him more than he does anyone else, probably even more than himself or Lakshmana! If there is one good quality in my husband, it is his deep, genuine love for Karna. He considers him more than a friend, Uruvi. And he trusts and loves him completely.'

Uruvi got up restlessly. It was her turn to get agitated. 'Karna is Duryodhana's best weapon against the Pandavas,' she heard herself arguing, even though she had been trying to avoid doing so. 'If a war starts between the cousins—and you know very well that it will, once the Pandavas return from their exile—Karna is Duryodhana's biggest hope for victory. He knows that the only one who can fight Arjuna—the most powerful of the Pandavas—and defeat him is Karna. It's self-interest not friendship.'

'Like everyone else, you don't like my husband much,' sighed Bhanumati with a rueful smile and added, 'But both of us have seen to it that it doesn't come in the way of our friendship—and neither should we try to break theirs. It would be futile. But please, Uruvi, understand that the bond between Karna and Duryodhana is too intense, their friendship is unique.'

She hated to admit it but Uruvi knew that Bhanumati was right. The friendship between their husbands was strengthening day by day. People admired it and considered it a comradeship to emulate. Even though Duryodhana was an emperor, they gushed, he never considered Karna his inferior. He would make the court poet and the street bards compose songs in praise of his friend and his great achievements. As if reading her thoughts, Bhanumati voiced them aloud. 'Karna, as a king, warrior and friend of Duryodhana, is now an integral part of the court of Hastinapur, however much you resent it, Uruvi,' she said quietly. 'Why, Karna has won his friend, besides several kingdoms, even princesses! Like Bhishma before him, Karna brought home the princesses of Kashi as wives for Duryodhana. He seized the princesses while challenging the kings and princes to take them away from him if they dared. None of them could. Karna again helped his friend marry the princess of Chitragandha. She had rejected him at her swayamwara, but refusing to take no for an answer, my jilted husband had carried her away by force in the presence of other kings like Jarasandha, Sisupala, Dantavakra, Salya and Rukmi. They chased him, but Karna intervened and defeated them single-handedly. In fact as a token of his appreciation for Karna's courage, Jarasandha gifted Karna a portion of Magadha.'

'But again, was this action of Karna right? In the guise of helping his friend, what did he do?' questioned Uruvi, righteous anger creeping back in her voice. 'He kidnapped and helped to abduct these princesses, even though they were reluctant brides in the first place. How many more crimes is he going to commit in the name of his friend and for the sake of their great friendship?'

'Duryodhana values Karna as a friend because he knows he is a better person than he is,' Bhanumati continued quietly. 'He admires his strength of character, his righteousness, his honesty and his loyalty. I need to tell you about one incident, which I haven't revealed to anyone else. One day, Karna and I were busy playing a game of dice in my private room—and the fact that we were permitted to do so, shows how much Duryodhana trusts his friend. Karna, as usual, was winning the game, and though I am a good player, I am quite a bad loser. Just then, Duryodhana entered the room and I made a move to get up as is the custom. Karna's back was towards Duryodhana, so he hadn't seen him enter the room. He thought I was running away from the game and made a move to grab me. His hand tugged at my pearl girdle and it gave way, pulling my angavastra along with it. I was aghast and seeing my expression, Karna realized something was amiss. He turned around, only to see Duryodhana approaching us. But my husband wasn't angry. Unfazed, he coolly picked up my angavastra from the floor and re-adjusted it on my shoulder, chatting casually all the while about this and that, as if nothing untoward had occurred! Which husband would react in such a way if he found his best friend and his half-attired wife, together in his bedroom?'

Uruvi, for once, found herself at a loss for words. Bhanumati had silenced her perfectly. She recalled that time-stopping, crystal-clear moment when she had realized Draupadi was in love with Karna. But to date, Uruvi was still not sure about Karna's feelings for the Panchala princess. Was the jealous, resentful suspicion she nursed about Karna's feelings for Draupadi warping her logical way of thinking? Had she allowed herself to surrender to unreason? Had she permitted an unwarranted doubt to twist into an irrational conviction? That was one question she dared not ask her husband—she was too afraid of the consequences for she knew Karna could never lie to her. She was not yet brave enough to hear her husband confess that he loved another woman, a woman who happened to be his arch-rival's wife. Had his love for Draupadi turned into a lifetime bitterness? Oh, if only Draupadi had acknowledged her love for Karna publicly! She should have married him, instead of pining away for his love, that longing which had smouldered within him, turning into a vengeful hatred. It was her rejection of Karna as her suitor that had altered the course of events to come. Had she accepted him, there would have been no dice game in which she was gambled away and assaulted in the Raj Sabha.

The insult of Karna and the violation of Draupadi were symbiotic; they were inescapably entwined. Had Draupadi married Karna, there would have been no fear of war or the horror of the future annihilation. But where would have that left her, Uruvi told herself sourly? If Draupadi had married Karna, would he ever have appeared at her swayamwara? He would have been too happily married to the Panchala princess to consider an invitation to an unknown princess' swayamwara! With a start, Uruvi realized that she was in a better position now than she imagined, for she would have been the one shrivelling away in the sadness of unrequited love. Draupadi may be pining for Karna, but withering in love she was not, Uruvi inferred with grim perception. She was, instead, stoking the fires of a horrifying conflagration that would burn all of them alive.

Not for the first time, Uruvi wondered if she had been fair to Karna...and to herself.

A few days later, there was shocking news. Duryodhana had been seized by Chitrasen, the Gandharva king, at Dwaitvana. Karna and the Kaurava army had been vanquished by the magical weapons of the angry Gandharva king and had to retreat in haste. Uruvi was secretly pleased that the fiend seemed to have taught Duryodhana a lesson at last, hoping that he had met his match finally. But her glee vanished abruptly when she got to know that Duryodhana's rescuers were none other than Bhima and Arjuna, who had come to their cousin's aid in his hour of distress. She was flummoxed and so was the entire city of Hastinapur when they heard how the two Pandavas, on Yudhishthira's orders, had rescued the evil Kuru prince from the clutches of Chitrasen. So much for real goodness, Uruvi thought in exasperation.

Karna's return home was a sombre one. Uruvi fathomed a deep restlessness in him. In his anguished self-flagellation, he was punishing himself for not being able to protect his friend, for failing to rescue Duryodhana from the Gandharva king. He had never felt as crushed and routed as he did now, not even when he was cruelly ridiculed by Bhima at the archery contest at Hastinapur. 'What sort of a friend am I?' he said aloud in a tormented voice. 'I could not help my friend in his darkest hour. Fighting the Gandharvas on the other side, I was too late to save him. My friend might forgive my blunder but how can I ever forgive myself?'

Duryodhana's homecoming was equally tortured and turbulent. Writhing in shame, the humiliated Kuru king declared his wish to fast unto death. He locked himself in his room and refused to come out for days. He even offered his crown to his brother Dushasana, saying he could no longer face the world as a disgraced king. And Uruvi had never seen her husband so troubled. He devoted all his waking hours to his disheartened friend, dissuading him from such idle talk. 'This is not the way a king talks,' he told him. 'What is the use of fasting to death? That is not the way out of disgrace. There is no sense in dying; it's only when you are alive that you can do anything worthwhile. Rise and fight instead!'

Karna was also tormented by the fact that it was Arjuna who had rescued Duryodhana. Uruvi recalled Bhishma Pitamaha's words. He had said that Karna, the blazing, brilliant sun, was eclipsed by the worthy Arjuna each time solely because he was blotted by the dark clouds of the Kauravas. Had Karna finally realized that he was doomed never to win any battle against his most bitter foe, Arjuna? Yet he fought on with his never-say-die belligerence.

She had to be just to Arjuna too. Her blind love for Karna did not permit her to recognize Arjuna's inherent qualities. She had not played fair with him either, but he had never retaliated with either unkindness or cruelty. He had been cold and unfriendly but never aggressive. She remembered him as a young boy. He had been gentle, kind, dutiful, singularly brave and highly principled. Those were the reasons why he was everyone's favourite, particularly of Krishna, Bhishma Pitamaha and Guru Dronacharya, much to the chagrin of Duryodhana and the other Kuru princes. She had felt and experienced the animosity between the Kauravas and the Pandavas all those long years ago. Had it been squashed by Bhishma Pitamaha and the parents of the cousins early enough, the hostility could have died out. But the scheming Shakuni had fanned the resentment instead, allowing it to grow into a vituperative hatred that would eventually consume the Kuru princes.

Arjuna's real asset was his sincerity, which pushed him to chase perfection. Though born in a great family of warriors, he did not allow himself to be content and self-satisfied like his brothers. He did not rest on the laurels of his illustrious family but drove himself harder to become the greatest archer and the mightiest warrior. He was a little vain about his achievements, but even Uruvi had to concede that he had never abused his huge power as a popular prince, but remained gentle and kind. He fought against the wrongs done by the evil Kauravas with spirited resilience, and yet, he hesitated to take definitive action against them because his strong sense of loyalty could not make him disown his blood relatives. His animosity for Karna, however, was not tempered by any such sentiment for he was not a blood relation—he was his implacable foe.

Karna and Arjuna had inadvertently begun a terrible rivalry years ago which was to pan through their lifetime. Guru Dronacharya had refused to accept Karna as his disciple, upon which Karna had sworn to prove himself. It whetted his resentment against the collective ranks of kings and nobility and Arjuna in particular.

Karna's first confrontation with Arjuna at the archery contest at Hastinapur was as bitter as the others to come. Karna lost Draupadi to Arjuna; Arjuna lost Uruvi to Karna. And now this outrageous episode of Draupadi's disrobing at the Kuru hall, where Karna had stripped Arjuna and Draupadi of the last vestige of self-respect, turned out to be a point of no return. Both were waiting impatiently for an open fight. And now it deeply irked Karna that he had not been able to save his friend Duryodhana. Instead, it had been his hated rival Arjuna who had won the round by capturing the Gandharva king and Karna had lost face.

The days passed with excruciating slowness. In the sprawling palace of the King of Anga, Karna's family watched him suffer with remorse. He was like a man haunted, trapped in the helplessness of his friend's misery, Uruvi mused. He could not bear to watch

Duryodhana's desolation and lashed out at himself for the unseemly situation his friend was in. Uruvi could see that he was battling emotions that were crushing him.

'I shall vanquish the Pandavas!' Uruvi heard him shout in fury. He was talking to himself, his face a shadow against the blinkered rays of the setting sun. 'O Duryodhana, I shall conquer once and for all the cause of your despair. I swear to you that when the Pandavas' exile of thirteen years is over, I shall kill Arjuna in battle!' And with those words, he touched his sword and bowed his head to seal the terrible oath.

As his words floated down to her, Uruvi heard an incensed Arjuna's vow echoing in her ears. 'I shall kill Karna one day in battle,' he had told her in his rage. Uruvi closed her eyes in despair, her husband's vow reiterating the other terrible oath she had heard long before.

15

Karna's Vow

Uruvi was to hear the terrible words uttered again by Karna in the royal assembly of Hastinapur when Karna publicly declared his oath once more. The grand occasion was the Vaishnava ceremony organized by Karna in honour of his friend as the emperor of the newly gained, extensive empire. The rites of this ceremony were considered the ultimate war sacrifice. The king performing the sacrifice—in this case it was Karna, on behalf of Duryodhana—would have openly dared the kings in the empire and forced them to either accept his supremacy or fight him. If the king returned after defeating all the other rulers, the performance of the sacrifice would send him to the highest abode of Lord Vishnu, the supreme god. Karna had accomplished even this task for his friend, Uruvi thought bitterly.

Duryodhana had wanted to perform a Rajasuya sacrifice, similar to the one King Yudhishthira had held the previous year. But he was advised by the brahmins to perform the Vaishnava sacrifice instead—according to them, while King Dhritrashtra and his cousin Yudhishthira were alive, Duryodhana could not hold the Rajasuya sacrifice. Fortunately, in unexpected good humour, Duryodhana accepted the brahmins' advice and went ahead with the Vaishnava celebrations in splendour.

.'I shall kill Arjuna in battle. If anyone—even Death himself—intervenes to protect Arjuna, I shall slay him. Until I have destroyed Arjuna, I will not eat meat or drink wine,' he announced in a sombre tone. 'And I promise not to turn down any requests and to grant favours to anyone who asks me after my morning prayers—just as I have done for a long time.'

His solemn vow evoked the expected response. The sons of King Dhritarashtra, except the kind-hearted Vikarna and the wise Yuyutsu, shouted with joy and the old king could not stop smiling. Karna was their strongest ally; he was their supporter, unequivocally and indisputably. War was imminent and death a certainty, for there would be no truce between the Kauravas and the Pandavas. Peace had never stood a chance.

Uruvi saw the dreams of possible harmony crushed in the shattered faces of Kunti, Guru Dronacharya, Vidura and Kripacharya. She glanced at the one man who still had the power to stop the war. But she saw the last hope dying in the aged, weary eyes of Bhishma Pitamaha as well. The old hostility had been revived to begin the prelude to the finale. It was all so hopeless.

Uruvi was seized with a helplessness she despised herself for. She felt powerless to stop the unavoidable momentum of events, which would end in needless tragedy. She feared for her future—and that of Karna's. She loathed the fact that it was Karna who was instigating a confrontation; a conflict, Karna argued, that was inescapable and would, sooner or later, turn into a war between the cousins.

She rushed out of the Raj Sabha, her hasty exit observed by Kunti, Duryodhana and Bhishma Pitamaha. But she would not spare her husband; he was pushing for a war she dreaded. She desperately wanted to salvage a losing battle but did not know how. More worried than angry, Uruvi confronted Karna the moment she could talk to him in the quiet seclusion of her room.

'Are you aware that Arjuna, too, has sworn to kill you in battle?' she asked, her belligerence sharpening her tone.

Karna made a gesture of indifference. 'Yes, I have heard so. Does it make a difference?' he shrugged. 'Just as war between the cousins is inevitable, so is the final face-off between him and me. I have been waiting for years for this. I have lived for this moment.'

Uruvi felt a familiar rage rising within her. 'What sort of madness are you living in?' she lashed out in fury. 'Are you beginning a war to serve your end—to fight Arjuna? How can you ever win when you are backing evil? Why are you not on the side of Truth? Karna, you may be virtuous, but oh, you are so very wrong! There will be war, there will be total destruction. Why are you hell-bent on being so stubborn? Why, oh, why are you so unwise? You talk about killing Arjuna but with Krishna by his side, he is invincible. He will not allow you to win. Never. A war with Arjuna means certain death for you.'

'I know.'

His quiet affirmation shocked her into silence, robbing her of further speech. Uruvi stared at him in disbelief. Perhaps that was his way of admitting that he was accepting the inevitable. He seemed to cruelly taunt her—that she had been right all along. She had won, he had lost. But was she supposed to be happy? She had been defeated, too, and was about to lose the one person she loved the most.

'I know I am going to be killed by Arjuna in the war and it is not just because he says so,' Karna continued, his voice hard and relentless. 'It is because I am a cursed man, Uruvi. I should have told you this earlier, but I didn't have the heart nor the courage to reveal my secret to anyone. I want to tell you the truth.'

Terror froze her. She wanted to scream at him to stop; she did not want to hear any more bad tidings. But he began to speak slowly, his face as expressionless as his voice, 'I have been living a cursed life—I carry the weight of curses spelt out by different people at different times. Years ago, rejected by Guru Dronacharya because of my low birth, I sought the tutorship of Guru Parshurama, the warrior sage who taught martial arts to everyone, except kshatriyas. I was forced to lie for I did not dare tell him that I was a sutaputra. Claiming I was a brahmin boy, I devoted myself to learning how to use the Brahmastra, the deadly weapon, a missile created by Lord Brahma himself. With my devotion to him and determination, I soon became his favourite disciple. One day, while my guru rested his head on my lap, a bee burrowed into my thigh, stinging me,' Karna recounted, a clinical detachment in his voice. 'It hurt terribly but I bore the excruciating pain silently so that I would not disturb my guru. On waking up, my guru noticed my blood-mottled thigh—and swiftly realized that only a kshatriya could withstand such intense pain. Incensed at the deception, Guru Parshurama cursed me, saying, "You will forget the Brahmastra and all that I have taught you at the moment you need it most." I tried to explain that I was not a kshatriya, but was a sutaputra who yearned to become a warrior. He calmed down a little and even regretted he had cursed me in a moment of anger, but said he could not take back the curse. Instead, to recompense me, he gifted me with the celestial weapon, Bhargavastra, along with his personal bow, the mighty Vijay, which I carry with me to this day—it has helped me win so many battles and wars. He blessed me with everlasting glory and fame. But each time I look at my bow, I remember his curse—that I shall forget all that I have learnt in my darkest hour. If that is not death, what is, Uruvi?'

Karna did not want to stop; it was as if a dam had burst within him. He wanted to tell Uruvi everything and she could feel his desperation. 'On my way back home, in utter despair, I practised the 'Shabdavedi Vidya', the ability to hit a target by listening to sounds. But unfortunately, I shot an arrow, from the mighty Vijay bow my guru had just gifted me, at a cow, mistaking it for a wild animal,' he continued tonelessly. 'The arrow killed the helpless cow and its incensed owner, a brahmin, cursed me, screaming that I would die a similar death, that I, too, would be helpless in my last moments. And that is what fate has in store for me, Uruvi. I might not die a hero's death in the battlefield, after all. This is what I fear most in my life. I dread my death for this one reason!'

Karna's handsome face contorted in pain and before she could interrupt, he went on relentlessly, exorcising his own fears and suffering. 'Once, a few years ago, while riding through my kingdom, I met a child who was sobbing because the milk in her pot had spilled and she was too scared to return home because her stepmother would punish her. Feeling sorry for the little girl, I squeezed milk from the wet soil back into the pot. While the girl skipped home happily, I suddenly heard the agonized cry of a woman in pain. It was Bhoomidevi, the earth goddess. She was furious and spelt out a curse that one day at the most crucial battle of my life, she would trap my chariot's wheel with the same deathly grip, just the way I had wrung the soil and that would be the cause of my death. So, Uruvi, I am a dead man already. Arjuna need not kill me in battle.'

She went cold, gripped by the icy grip of dread, defeat and impending death. And in that moment Uruvi knew she would lose Karna forever. She felt an intense empathy with his unending torment and it broke her heart. She had never loved her husband more. She saw him look sadly back at her, and felt her eyes smarting with sudden unshed tears. Overcome with emotion, she knew she could not fight her husband any more. She wanted their war to be over, once and for all.

She walked slowly towards him and placed her head gently on his chest, her arms going round his waist. She felt him stiffen but he didn't push her away. They stood still, locked in each other's arms for a long time. There was no need for words; their pain and longing bound them together.

He bent his head down as she looked up to his beautiful eyes. His face was so close to hers that she could feel his breath on her upturned face. She moved closer to him. 'Please stay. Don't go away,' she pleaded. Her lips trembled. The thought that she would lose him was unbearable. She clutched at his arm, her nails digging hard into his flesh. 'I love you. I love you. I love you so much,' she said softly in despair, holding him close to her. 'I don't want you to die,' she cried. She allowed her pain to surge into a mounting passion. She threw herself at him with abandon, seeking his lips. She had forgotten all her bitter thoughts in the joy of holding him again. She clung to him, feeling in that moment all the anguish of their parting, the terror of the future, and the rapture of their reunion.

'Don't leave me...ever.'

'I can never leave you. You know that.' He tightened his arms around her, feeling her soft body melt against his.

He faltered. He could taste the salty tears on her face. She made no sound. He drew away and wiped her tears. 'Hush, dear, everything will be fine now...'

'I fear I am going to lose you forever. But I don't want to lose you before the time comes,' she wept. 'I am afraid. I am so scared I have already lost you. And by pushing you away, I am doing exactly that. Damn my rules and my moralizing...! I care more for you than ever and I want you with me. I am sorry for what I put you through...it was pride, it was my foolishness. I can't go on without you any more!'

He took her hand. 'I know you better than you know yourself. You did what you thought was right; it wasn't malice. You are my conscience-keeper, reminding me whenever I am wrong. Even though I rarely heed you, you don't give up either. You are the bravest woman I know and I love you for it.'

'You don't know what I go through each day, dreading what is to come,' she sobbed brokenly. 'There won't ever be peace; the harmony is forever lost. There is going to be war—and I hate it. I fear it. I don't care who wins or who loses, all I want is you by my side. I had always thought that I would grow old with my husband but I fear this can never be...oh, why can't we give up these thoughts of war and go somewhere else?'

'If you are not brave today, it'll be worse tomorrow. Trying to escape is not the route of the heroic. Face the truth and brave the consequences. The test of courage is not to die but to live. And live with dignity and conviction every single day.'

He was silent for a moment, gazing at her drenched face. He gently pulled her close. His greatest fear had been dispelled—she would not leave him; she would be by his side through all the trouble that lay before them. He had lived in this dread for so long. She had gone away once, and those had been the most empty days of his life. He had wanted to run after her and bring her back home, to beg her till she forgave him, but he could not find the moral strength in himself to do so. He had instead distracted himself in his military campaigns. He had not dared to hope she would come back to him ever again. But she had, mercifully, although with a condition; a condition more cruel than the torture of living in the hellish void of her absence. He had mutely complied, consoled himself with the thought that she was close to him; that he could love her by simply looking at her and live by keeping her by his side. Karna hoped that they would be together for as long as possible—but he knew there was not much time.

Vrushali liked to watch Karna and Uruvi with their son, who was now almost two years old. She saw them walking in the garden with him. Uruvi took Vrishakethu out in the early morning, each day, and they were soon followed by Karna. They spent an excited half-hour teaching their son to walk, run, play and hold his father's mace. The toddler beamed up at his parents as they stood a few metres away, urging him to waddle between them. Every time the baby hurled itself into his father's outstretched arms, Karna whooped with joy and hugged him tight as though he could not bear to let him go.

Vrushali saw them from the shadows of her verandah. They looked so content and blissful together that words would have shattered the tranquillity of the moment. It warmed her heart, and yet, it hurt her to observe the affection Uruvi so obviously felt for her handsome husband, who hovered possessively close to her. It was a touching sight. Karna often tucked the wisps of her curls behind her small ears as she tried to keep pace with his long strides. Every now and then, he looked down at her; they had eyes only for each other, except when the occasional chuckle of the toddler reminded them of reality.

Vrushali could not look at them for too long. Not because, she told herself, she was jealous, but she felt she was intruding on their private moments. She loved Karna no less because he loved Uruvi. She could not envy them their happiness. She was content being his closest friend, giving him the words of advice and the patience he expected from her. Vrushali knew that she enjoyed his confidence and with a tinge of sadness, she exulted at the happiness she was allowing the man she loved. Both she and Uruvi were desperately in love with him but she could not miss how his eyes rested only on Uruvi. Her gracious acceptance of their love would be the best for all of them, she thought resignedly, and moved away from the verandah into the comforting confines of her room.

'He is a brave lad!' Karna declared proudly, placing his son on his shoulder and holding his small fists with his arms outstretched. He looked at his wife, walking closely by his side, below Vrushali's verandah. His eyes were tender. 'It was when I knew you were going to have a baby that I realized how much I loved you,' he said. 'Till then, you were just a beautiful fairy who had entered my life and made my world suddenly wonderful with your magic.'

'Aha, are you confessing your love for me after all this while?' she asked with a laugh.

'At first, I could not believe that a person like you would choose me as a husband. It was such a shock! Don't you see what I mean? I had you, I almost lost you and you are with me again. Our child means everything in the world to me. I don't know how to put it across…I feel a new emotion for Vrishakethu, which I don't understand myself. He is our future, isn't he?'

She looked at him keenly and there was a soft wetness in her eyes. 'I thought of him—and you—all the time, even when I was on the battlefield,' Karna said wistfully. 'I was scared you would never come back and I would eventually lose both of you. I wanted to hold him in my arms, and I wanted to teach him to walk. And I am doing all that right now because you came back, Uruvi. I cannot thank you enough.'

Uruvi flushed deeply. She clasped her hands tightly together around his arm, afraid he would go away from her again.

'And as he grows up, I'll teach him all I know. I'll teach him to ride and I'll teach him to shoot with the bow and arrow. I am going to be the proudest father in the world.'

'You already are one!' she reminded him warmly. 'Your oldest son, Vrishasena, has turned twenty now and has grown into a fine young archer himself! He is as formidable as you! And your other sons are picking up too. Why, you have a fine in-house army!'

He gave her his disarming smile. She wanted to capture this moment forever...but she frowned as a thought struck her. Karna noticed her change of mood immediately.

'Anything troubling you?' he asked quickly.

She looked at him directly in his eyes. 'Either give me an honest answer or do not reply if you so wish...' she began hesitantly, but continued more firmly as she saw Karna nod, his face suddenly solemn. 'I have been trying to run away from this doubt but I ended up running away from you instead...' she sighed and gathered courage again to voice her words. 'Karna, did you ever love Draupadi?'

He went white first and then colour flooded his face. He flushed darkly, his lips pursing into a severe line. Uruvi wondered, with a swift pang, if she had made a mistake. But she knew she needed to erase the last shadow which lurked between them.

'Yes...' he replied eventually.

She had been anticipating this answer, dreading it, but the moment he said it, it was—much to her surprise—an enormous relief. She was suddenly free of the misgivings, the jealousy that hounded her and the treacherous thoughts that harassed her.

'Yes, I loved her...once,' he said evenly, accentuating the last word. Crazy hope surged through her. 'It was a mad infatuation that died as fast as it was born. It was born the moment I saw her at her swayamwara and died the moment she shamed me in public,' he answered slowly but deliberately. 'She is a bewitching woman...and I could not resist her, I admit. I was certain in my arrogance that I would win her at the swayamwara. I was more in love with *that* heady feeling than with her. The thought that I could possess the most beautiful woman and that I could win the woman the world wooed was like winning a prized trophy. Draupadi is the woman whom I was once attracted to, long before you entered my life. You have no reason to be jealous of her, Uruvi. No, it wasn't love, it was intoxication, which sobered the moment she hurt my pride. And when she married Arjuna, she was someone else's wife. I couldn't have looked at her in any other way—she was not mine any longer. I respected her as a married woman—except for that one instance at the Raj Sabha...' he admitted. 'I hated her then but even now that hate is spent and turned to ashes. I am the one who is now burning in shame. I regret those terrible words I said to her and I know I can't ever take them back. If there is one thing I wish to undo, it's that. What I said and did in the heat of the moment was unpardonable. I only hope that some day I have the courage to beg for her forgiveness...'

Uruvi almost blurted out that Draupadi had forgiven him a long time ago but stopped herself just in time. She had extracted the truth from him but she could never spell out the Pandavas' wife's secret feelings for Karna. 'Repentance, like forgiveness, is divine—it purifies the soul,' she said softly, hoping her words would make him feel cleaner, lighter.

There was nothing more to say. They walked together in silence, grateful for the peace of the moment and finding solace in it.

16

Kunti and Vrishakethu

From the time Vrishakethu was a baby until he was almost in his teens, Uruvi took him to visit Kunti at Vidura's palace. The queen seemed reluctant to go to the Anga palace, citing one excuse or the other to avoid it. During the long, painful years when the Pandavas languished in their exile, their mother found a new means to divert her loneliness—Karna and Uruvi's child. Spending an hour or two with the baby gave her immense pleasure.

Initially, if Karna was displeased about this, he did not show it. Taking his silence for his sanction, Uruvi continued with her visits to her foster mother and not once did Karna utter a word of protest. But one day, cornered by Shona's clear disapproval and Radha's possessiveness where her new grandson was concerned, Uruvi decided to confront him.

'I want to know if you mind me visiting Kunti,' Uruvi began the topic with some unease, finding herself sounding slightly defensive.

'No, she is like your mother and it's but natural you would like to meet her.'

'You're sure it doesn't trouble you?' she asked, uncertain because she knew Karna was not saying what was actually in his mind.

'What I am saying, dear, is that *I* don't have any objection,' he smiled.

'But some others do?' she persisted.

'Frankly, what does it matter to me or to you if Queen Gandhari and Duryodhana aren't too happy with the fact that you are close to Queen Kunti?' he shrugged. 'Go ahead, but come back before it gets dark!' and with a quick hug, he pushed her out of the room.

Uruvi suddenly felt happy on her way to Vidura's palace. She found herself smiling idiotically, and realized that what Karna thought of her meant a great deal to her. She yearned for his approval like parched earth for cool water.

Each time Uruvi went to see Kunti, she found her eagerly waiting for them, or rather, waiting for Vrishakethu, Uruvi corrected herself. She would rush forward to pick up the chubby child and hold him close to her for a long while. The boy always hugged her back, lisping her name in his endearing trill, which never ceased to delight the elderly queen. As she had once lavished love on little Uruvi, Kunti pampered Vrishakethu.

One afternoon she said wistfully, 'He's so enchantingly beautiful!' her eyes moist and tender. 'He's just like Ka…,' she broke off suddenly, coughing hard, and Uruvi hurried to get her a glass of water. '…he's so much like Abhimanyu when he was a baby!'

'You miss Abhimanyu awfully, don't you?' Uruvi asked gently, sensing the old queen's sadness.

'Life is full of compensations,' she murmured, kissing Vrishakethu softly on his cheek. 'At the moment, though, I am glad to have a grandchild playing on my lap!'

'How is Abhimanyu?'

'Subhadra and Abhimanyu are at Dwarka. Krishna did not want them to accompany Arjuna during the exile.'

'Neither did you accompany them this time.'

'Draupadi is there to look after them…' she said vaguely. 'And there needed to be someone here to remind the old king of the justice denied to my sons,' Kunti's eyes were hard. 'Memory is selective and it's so convenient to forget wrongs if there is no one to remind the perpetrator of them.'

'And you and Uncle Vidura are seeing to that?' Uruvi questioned her dryly. 'And does it have any effect? The old king is so blinded with his own ambition that he seeks its fulfilment in his sons. Shakuni knows this and he plays his game skilfully with both the father and the sons. Karna resents him and firmly believes that Duryodhana wouldn't have been so evil if it were not for that wicked uncle of his.'

'That's so true but unfortunately for the Kauravas, their uncle has been with them since they were born, seeing to it that their hatred remains deep and their political appetite whetted.'

'Strange,' frowned Uruvi. 'It is as if the brother and sister came as a pair to Hastinapur and changed the very scenario of the place in their own different ways...'

'Oh, let's not get into all that...let me enjoy my grandson!' said Kunti impatiently. Uruvi stood by watching, smiling at the growing fondness between the older woman and Vrishakethu.

'He does look a lot like Karna, doesn't he?' the elderly queen asked a little tentatively.

'Yes, without the kavach and kundals!' Uruvi replied with a quick smile.

Kunti did not speak; she looked quite pale and her eyes widened in a confused expression. Uruvi thought she looked almost terrified.

'Ma, what's wrong? Did I say something wrong?'

'Don't ever speak so lightly of them, child,' Kunti looked quite gaunt, the skin of her cheeks stretched taut across her face. 'The kavach and kundals are a godly gift—they are a boon to your husband.'

'How would *you* know?' Uruvi asked curiously.

'But isn't it obvious, child?' Kunti had regained her usual authoritative composure. 'It would only be a fool who would not recognize their uniqueness.'

Uruvi flashed a quick smile. 'Yes, I keep saying the same thing to Karna—that they are godly and he must be of celestial birth.'

'Does he talk about his biological parents?' Kunti asked hesitantly, with a strange eagerness in her voice.

'Well, he doesn't discuss this topic much—he cursorily mentioned it once. He does wonder who his mother is and why she abandoned him so easily,' said Uruvi. 'It is his kavach and kundals that make him believe he was born an aristocrat. But the fact that he was so carelessly cast in the river might well mean that he was an unwanted child of a distressed mother. Or he may be a child of a callous noblewoman who ruthlessly left him—and that hurts. It's a paradox. He wants to know his identity, which he often suspects of being royal, yet he is disparaging about it. It's his weakness, which anyone can exploit. Call it his failing, his limitation or his disadvantage, but he has suffered enough from it!'

Kunti interposed quietly. 'I think that's why he hates Draupadi— she exposed his weak point at her swayamwara and he could never forgive her for that!'

Uruvi was proud that she could remain unaffected at the mention of Draupadi's name. 'Karna loathes his true parents,' she sighed. 'He wants to have nothing to do with them! He doesn't miss them emotionally because, fortunately, he has been blessed with the love of both Adhiratha and Radha, who adore him! In fact, the one person whom Karna loves most, with utter devotion, is his mother Radha. She is his lifeline. His brother Shona worships him and, of course, Vrushali is his biggest comfort, but the bond he has with his mother is special. Karna knows that though he was an abandoned child, he has received more than his share of love and respect from a family who love him unconditionally. So in that sense, I don't think he misses his natural parents. He doesn't need them.'

Uruvi noticed that Kunti was sitting stiffly, with her back straight. She was listening to Uruvi's words with her hands clenched in her lap. 'Go on, dear. I want to know more...'

'He has no love for his natural parents but society will not allow him to forget his parentage,' Uruvi continued, her delicate brows furrowed in a frown. 'His dilemma is his identity, which he would love to forget about but cannot because no one will allow it. It keeps haunting him because of barbed insinuations from people and constant social criticism. He has to prove himself all the time because he is always asked about his lineage. That's what eats into him; it's not his ancestry but the way people see him. Frankly, he does not really care who his real parents are but he is not allowed to forget the fact that he doesn't know where he came from. I have no respect for his natural parents. They deserted him and worse, left him at the mercy of a ruthless society. I loathe them!' she spoke so venomously that Kunti blanched. 'I am proud to be known as the wife of a worthy sutaputra rather than of some worthless prince!'

'They must have had their reasons...' Kunti mumbled.

'That's a justification for their selfishness. They were supposed to be responsible for the baby, not just think of themselves!' Uruvi retorted scathingly. 'When I hold my baby in my arms, I often wonder how Karna's mother could have let him go! Oh, she must have been heartless!'

The older woman looked at the fuming girl, and a deep colour dyed her sallow skin. Her emaciated hands, lying on her lap, started to tremble a little. She thought of the words spoken with such vehement feeling.

'Had it been not for his close family, Karna wouldn't have been the fine person that he is now. *They* are his true parents, he insists, and he can never give them up. He is more fulfilled being called Radheya than Karna. What more can one say?'

As she spoke, Uruvi realized that Kunti had made no reply. It was as if she could find no words to voice her unspoken feelings. Uruvi saw that she was silent, as if she was struggling with an indescribable emotion. Kunti picked up Vrishakethu and hugging him close, buried her face in his soft curls.

⁓

Her friendship with Bhanumati was decidedly ambiguous, Uruvi told herself with a cheerless shake of her head, very different from the friendship their husbands shared. Just as this thought crossed her mind, Bhanumati suddenly appeared. The queen of Hastinapur looked agitated enough for Uruvi to usher her into the quiet privacy of her room. Uruvi did not need to ask what had happened for she burst out, 'It's Jayadrath! He has come home with his head shaved, with just five tufts of hair left on his head.' Bhanumati was so distressed that she could hardly speak coherently.

And then the story slowly came out through Bhanumati's

tremulous lips. Jayadrath, the King of Sindhu, was Duryodhana's brother-in-law and the husband of Dushala, the only sister of the hundred Kaurava princes. He had come across Draupadi in the Kamakhya forest and had tried to kidnap her but she was more than a match for him. As he grabbed her, she kicked him hard till he fell to the ground, then sat in his chariot and calmly ordered a quaking priest standing nearby to call her husbands over. They rushed to the spot immediately. When Bhima was told about Jayadrath's evil intentions, his rage knew no bounds and he was about to leap on Jayadrath to kill him—but it was Draupadi who stopped him. She reasoned she did not wish Dushala to become a widow, especially when her husband would suffer such a pitiable death. Treat him like a slave instead, the Panchala princess insisted, so Bhima shaved off the hair of the king of Sindhu. 'Here is that unworthy son of the unworthy father, the sinful Sage Vridhakshtra!' announced Bhima, leaving five clumps of hair to remind Jayadrath of the Pandavas. Then Bhima set him free. His ignominious return had sparked an inferno among the Kaurava princes.

Another reason for the Kauravas to scream murder, Uruvi sighed inwardly. 'Each time that damned woman is the reason for some bad news!' Bhanumati snapped viciously. 'First, it was her swayamwara, which was catastrophic enough! Karna lost his son Sudhama, besides being publicly insulted, of course! My husband was intending to start a war then and there but it was Karna who restrained him, yet again! Then, she made my husband stumble and fall in that wretched palace of hers, and had the cheek to call him the blind son of a blind father!' she seethed. 'Her disrobing at the court assembly was a result of her arrogance. What is it in that woman that brings out the worst in a man?'

'How fair is it to blame Draupadi for every mess? Did she ask Jayadrath to abduct her?' retorted Uruvi, but without malice. 'Haven't the Kauravas brought ruin upon themselves? Draupadi is the catalyst who will precipitate what the Kauravas have initiated. It's a vicious spiral, which will destroy everything.'

'Oh, don't say such horrid things, Uruvi! It's scary...'

'But can't you see it coming, dear? So why blame poor Draupadi? She is a victim of her own charms, her unusual beauty, which makes men desire her. Do you deny that Duryodhana and Jayadrath have lusted after her?' And Karna as well, Uruvi thought bleakly. 'And in her sensuous beauty, she attracts violence along the way. That's her deadly appeal.'

'That she lives with five men is bad enough...'

'She is happily married to them!' Uruvi corrected her sharply. 'As a wife, she has accomplished the astonishing task of keeping all her five husbands happy—a fact Satyabhama, Krishna's wife, is insanely jealous of as she prides herself as the perfect wife! Draupadi inspires her men; she holds them together. Otherwise, in sharing her, they would have been at each other's throats. Did you know that after giving a son to each of her five husbands, she distanced herself from them to allow them to take other wives? She isn't even jealous, except perhaps of Subhadra—Arjuna's apparent favouritism infuriates her!'

Uruvi realized that she was talking a little too lightly about the famous hostility between the two wives of Arjuna—Draupadi and Subhadra—and she bit her tongue in quick regret. Another person who had been livid when Subhadra had eloped with Arjuna was Duryodhana, the suitor Balarama, Krishna's older brother, had selected for his sister but whom she had rejected because she preferred his cousin. Balarama had wanted his favourite disciple, Duryodhana, to marry his sister, but Krishna favoured Arjuna as his future brother-in-law. As expected, Balarama's Duryodhana lost to Krishna's Arjuna. It was still a sore point with the Kaurava king. Bhanumati knew her husband nursed a soft corner for Subhadra, but she had taken it gracefully in her stride.

'And here I can't manage even one husband!' scoffed Bhanumati with a brittle laugh. 'But I guess you are right, Uruvi. Draupadi is more maligned than she deserves. She seems to bear the brunt and be the cause as well of all troubles!'

'She is too spirited for everyone's liking!'

'Like you are, Uruvi?' quizzed her friend with an affectionate look. 'You know, you are quite like Draupadi yourself, so frank and forthright—is that why you like her so much? She doesn't like you though...' she added slyly. 'I caught the look she gave you at the Rajasuya ceremony—it was really nasty! If looks could slay, you would have been dead a long time ago!'

Uruvi knew why Draupadi disliked her. Earlier it had amused her, but now, knowing exactly where she stood in the triangle of love, life and deceit, Uruvi dreaded Draupadi's jealous dislike of her. Had Bhanumati seen Draupadi's furtive glances at Karna as well? Bhanumati was pretty shrewd. Did she realize that Draupadi was in love with Karna? Uruvi knew why she defended Draupadi so strongly. As Bhanumati had mentioned, Draupadi was an inextricable part of their lives. The fact that she loved her husband no longer troubled Uruvi, but she felt an unreasonable guilt that she knew Draupadi's worst secret. And the pressure of hiding it from everyone was testing.

Uruvi realized that Bhanumati was awaiting her reply. She preferred to ignore Bhanumati's jibe and continued easily, 'More than a personal liking for her, I admire Draupadi,' Uruvi smiled, but with an effort. 'You find us similar? I couldn't disagree more. If both of us are outspoken, it's because of our circumstances, which are so strangely dissimilar. I am frank because I was encouraged by my father to be so—I was quite the pampered child! But Draupadi speaks her mind because conditions have forced her to be cruelly blunt. It is her only means of self-preservation. She is a born rebel, fighting and clawing for what she wants. I got almost everything I wanted readily on a platter. I was brought up as a princess and so was she. But she had to fight her way out, even with her parents. She was, in a way, unwanted as she came second to her brother. Her father had held a holy yagna to ask the gods to give him a son to avenge him and kill Guru Dronacharya. He was granted a son—Dhrishtadyumna—but he got a daughter too. She was Draupadi, who arose from the fire, but who was all fire and brimstone herself. She was born out of hate and revenge, of the hatred her father King Drupada harboured for his friend-turned-foe, Drona. Arjuna was Drona's favourite disciple, but she became the consort of all the five Pandavas. But what have they given her? They made her their queen yet made her suffer the worst humiliation. She looks after their interests, but in return has got nothing but indignity and shame. Yet, she was forgiving enough to spare Jayadrath his life because of her compassion for Dushala, the sister of the man who was responsible for her disrobing at the Hastinapur Raj Sabha.'

Bhanumati had the grace to look embarrassed. 'Uruvi, you know where and when to hit back! But sadly, Draupadi's kind generosity has gone to waste! Jayadrath is seething in mortification and is planning revenge on the Pandavas right now with my husband at the palace. He swears revenge and is thirsting to kill the Pandavas.'

'He should be happy he has been spared!' Uruvi jeered. 'But again, Yudhishthira and Draupadi have made a mistake by pardoning him. Bhima should have killed him but I am not surprised that, as usual, Yudhishthira intervened and made peace. That man is priceless! He treats Draupadi like a rag doll and a prized trophy rolled in one. He dared to stake her at the dice game and now, when a man attempts to molest her, he lets him go free!' she said in anger at the wrong done to Draupadi. 'Jayadrath will make a deadly enemy for the Pandavas now,' Uruvi warned but realized she was telling the wrong person. 'Ah, yes, everyone's preparing for battle. Clearly, the Kauravas do not intend to return Indraprastha to the Pandavas, which is their lawful inheritance. They are bent on war.'

'And so is Karna,' intervened Bhanumati.

'Karna will do whatever Duryodhana says,' Uruvi said mockingly. 'After all, Duryodhana is the ultimate king and Karna is just his employee!'

'Sometimes I think I hate you too, as my family does!' cried Bhanumati, annoyed. 'You, too, have rubbed many people the wrong way—my father-in-law, for instance. I guess he only tolerates you because it was Karna whom you married and not Arjuna, which he sees as a winning card. Dushasana hates you, so does Shakuni.

Both have warned me many times to stop meeting you. Why, even Queen Gandhari is a little wary of you and doesn't mince her words about you!'

'Yes, I have heard she doesn't approve of me much—or the fact that I tend to wounded soldiers rather than queen it over others at home!' Uruvi gave a short laugh. 'Her Highness doesn't consider it suitable that a kshatriya princess should work in the rehabilitation camps for the wounded. But then, I am but a lesser mortal, a sutaputra's wife—so where does social snobbery come in? I am a lowly person mixing with the lowly soldiers. Anyway, her dislike of me goes a long way back...'

Uruvi shrugged her slender shoulders. 'It seems that when I was a child, I had impudently asked her why she remains blindfolded when she ought to be helping out King Dhritrashtra. I didn't know then that she wore the blindfold as a mark of silent protest to make Bhishma Pitamaha feel guilty for forcing her to marry a blind prince,' she said. 'But then there are some people like Kunti, who insists that this is all vile talk. Married to a blind man, the young Gandhari, Kunti maintains, decided that she would not enjoy the gift of sight denied to her husband and from then on kept a silk scarf tied around her eyes. Kunti considers her the devoted wife, but I see in her a masochistic person of such stubborn resolve that she deprived her husband of seeing the world through her eyes. Queen Gandhari refused to cooperate in every way and she made her displeasure at becoming his wife pretty clear. She was never the wise, comforting life partner for her blind husband. Neither has she looked after her children well. They were allowed to be brought up by her wicked brother who nursed them on hate and vengeance.'

Uruvi sighed briefly, 'Anyway, she didn't take my childish comments too kindly then. Though my argument still remains the same. The old king is physically blind, but she remains blind to the faults of her sons and refuses to perceive the enormity of what's happening around her. Had she not allowed Shakuni to stay put in Hastinapur and poison Duryodhana's ears, I wonder if the situation would have worsened between the cousins. Didn't she ever realize her brother was evil? Doesn't she see that her brother is thirsting for the destruction of the Kauravas as revenge for the raw deal he and his sister got?'

'As you rightly said, she preferred turning a blind eye,' Duryodhana's wife agreed weakly. 'Duryodhana just does not listen to anything she says. He respects her, yes, but is too impatient to hear her out.'

Uruvi looked at her friend and asked her if she knew her mother-in-law's story.

'Yes, my mother told me how she was married off to the blind prince because Bhishma Pitamaha wished it,' concurred the daughter-in-law. 'And she is still bitter about it. But she is more resentful about having no hold over her sons. When I see her, Uruvi, I stop feeling sorry for myself. She was forced to marry a blind prince but never really could be a wife nor the real queen. She could never enjoy queenhood as Queen Kunti did as the wife of King Pandu—for however short a while. I think she transferred that burning wish to be queen into becoming the queen mother, the mother of the oldest Kuru prince. But that, too, was not to be.'

Dragging herself to the present moment, Uruvi tried to gauge the enigma called Gandhari, the person whom Kunti loved so unconditionally. It must have been a nasty shock for Queen Gandhari when she discovered that she was beaten in the race to motherhood. Uruvi could well imagine the grim picture. From the wild stories she had heard about the Kuru queen, one of them was that the Gandhar princess had been so disappointed that Kunti gave birth to Yudhishthira first that, in her fury, she had tried to abort the foetus. It was only through the blessings of Sage Vyasa, who transformed the foetus into a hundred children, that she became the mother of the Kauravas. Another tale about the enigmatic mother of the Kauravas was her intense dislike for Yuyutsu, the illegitimate son of King Dhiritrashtra from a maid. What must her plight have been when she saw Yuyutsu, a handsome, healthy boy, unlike her still-born foetus? It was not unsurprising that Yuyutsu was on the Pandavas' side rather than his own brothers, who never treated him well anyway. Queen Gandhari echoed similar sentiments possibly because she still smarted from her husband's sexual misdemeanour. Uruvi supposed, but she did not voice her thoughts aloud.

'Your mother-in-law proved to be too weak to stand up to the might of hatred, probably,' Uruvi said, trying to be solicitous. 'As a mother, she is a puzzle. She is as indifferent to her children as they are to her. They really don't care for her or respect her opinions. She complains to you that she has no control over her sons, but it was she who allowed them to grow up wild, unrestrained and thoroughly spoilt, unlike the way the Pandavas were brought up almost single-handedly by Kunti. Can you imagine the Pandavas daring to go against Kunti? It's because she is their world. But that's not so with the Kauravas; their mother is not a figure of maternal kindness nor is she the guide, philosopher or the strict disciplinarian a mother should be. Did they heed her when she repeatedly pleaded with her sons to make peace with the Pandavas? She was ineffective. Just as she was unsuccessful in preventing the public shame Draupadi suffered in the royal assembly. She is largely responsible for the mess that exists today. Had she thrown out her brother, Shakuni, in the first place and reined in her sons Duryodhana and Dushasana, matters would not have been so grievous!'

Bhanumati sat silently as Uruvi analytically castigated her mother-in-law, but hearing the disparaging way she spoke of her husband, she could not restrain herself any longer. 'According to you, the root of all evil and unhappiness is my husband!' she snapped. 'He is a great king, a good husband, a good father, a generous friend, and yes, he is a terrible foe—he hates the Pandavas because he doesn't consider them his cousins anyway. Why do you hate him so much? Because he is so close to Karna? Believe me, Uruvi, Karna means everything to him. Karna is the person whom he loves without reservation, without any expectations. Karna is more precious to him than even Dushasana or any of his brothers and that says something for a man whom you consider selfish and calculating. Surprisingly, he doesn't dislike you. He admires you and not just because you happen to be the wife of his dearest, most cherished friend. He insists you were the best thing that could have happened to him. And he means it. Just as I think that Karna is the best thing that has happened to my husband. But you evidently don't agree. Why don't you accept the fact that the two of them are such close friends that they would die for each other?'

'I can't speak for Duryodhana, but I do know that Karna will one day die for his friend,' Uruvi replied quietly, her fists clenched. 'And I am scared. I dread that day. I cannot accept the fact that I can't change what's going to happen. All I can do is to watch weakly—just as you will, Bhanumati. Duryodhana wouldn't have been an emperor were it not for Karna and neither would Karna be a king, had it not been for Duryodhana. Their friendship will be their downfall, but I admit, it's a bond that is strong and everlasting.'

17

Karna's Kavach and Kundals

While Karna was a warrior, Uruvi was a healer. The battlefield spelt two different connotations for them, two diverse worlds. For Karna, it was the sacred ground to fight for honour and truth; for Uruvi, it was a wasteland where the dead and wounded fell.

As Karna won more wars, subjugated kingdoms and forced kings to surrender, Uruvi practised the art of curing, of soothing the suffering of others. With Vrishakethu growing up into a strapping young boy who did not need constant care, Uruvi devoted more of her time to help those injured in war. It was her calling and she worked at it with passion. With battles erupting often in those days of strife, she found herself and her team of nurses working day and night in makeshift treatment centres and camps. Uruvi was pleased she had rediscovered her remarkable gift. And so were those she treated. She could alleviate pain by the simple touch of her cool, steady hands. She had the knack of talking tenderly to her patients, calming and comforting them, her voice as reassuring as her touch, which was gentle and kindly. Uruvi found that by treating these people she comforted them as well as herself.

Her ability to cure was almost magical. She helped a limping soldier to walk again, she restored the strength in the hands of an archer who had lost three fingers in a battle, among many other small miracles. Stories of her healing powers were making the rounds, much to the apprehension of the royal household. Her severest critics were Dushasana and his mother, Queen Gandhari. Closer home, Shona showed his disapproval in no uncertain terms.

'I am just doing my work, which is something I love to do,' she said quietly when a visibly infuriated Shona confronted her.

'I don't want to argue with you, but what you are doing does not suit, firstly, a kshatriya princess and secondly, a warrior's wife,' Shona retorted curtly. 'I know I won't make you see sense, but frankly, you are embarrassing Radheya. I hate to see him squirm each time the topic is brought up. No one is impressed with your social work; it's ridiculed by all!'

'I agree with you on one point—you can't make me see sense because for you and your ilk, war makes sense. For me, it doesn't. I am just trying to make amends in my small way, that's all,' she said flatly, and not willing to face any more animosity from him, she got up to leave.

'No, wait!' Shona's voice cut her short sharply. 'I have never interfered with your life, Uruvi. I have no right to. But neither have I approved of you and what you stand for. Radheya has indulged you too much. I didn't like it when Radheya married you, not because you were a kshatriya but because you are an outsider. You are not one of us. You have proved it all along. When Radheya needed you most after the Raj Sabha fiasco, you ran away to Pukeya to lick your wounds. It was Vrushali who helped him through. Radheya hides it from us, his family, but all of us know that you didn't forgive him for a long, long time for his behaviour at the Raj Sabha. And what a price he had to pay! How can you be so heartless? Though a kshatriya princess yourself, you have never approved of his victorious campaigns. While the world is hailing him as the mightiest warrior in the kingdom, you show your disapproval by going to the very camps where the battles have been fought to look after the injured. Were you there by his side when Radheya was leading the Kaurava army throughout Aryavarta? Were you aware of the strategies and the coups he devised to conquer these kingdoms? Do you realize how brave and great Radheya is as a warrior and army general? Have you ever been worried about him and the danger to his life? He could have died many times over but each time you were more worried about yourself than the safety of your husband!'

That the quiet Shona masked so much anger behind his calm façade, amazed Uruvi. He raged on, 'You say you love your husband, but I say you love yourself much more! You are his wife, Uruvi—you should be by his side. Look at Draupadi—she saved the very husbands who forsook her. In spite of them staking her in the dice game, she is with them right now in the forests, suffering for their mistake, which was no fault of hers. Why do you insist on clashing with my brother? Now you are humiliating him even further.'

A faint spot of colour appeared on Uruvi's pale cheeks and her eyes turned hard and angry. A moment later, she went numb; she had never felt so many emotions rising within her in a flash of a moment—anger, pain, hurt and above all, guilt. Shona's unreserved love for his older brother made him spew such venom, she knew. In his eyes, she was a failure as his brother's wife; as a warrior's wife, she fell below standards. Even though she realized there was no point in arguing with him, she knew she had to defend herself.

There was a long pause as Shona stood shaking with anger, knowing he had been insufferably rude to his sister-in-law. 'I try but I can't help resenting her,' he told himself over and over again, trying to calm down. It was as if she had taken Radheya away from all of them. He had been secretly relieved when Uruvi had finally left his brother, but seeing Radheya's plight without her, Shona had taken back his wish that she would never come back, admitting that only she could bring a smile to his lips. So, for Radheya's sake, he had tolerated Uruvi. But he could not understand her.

Assuming that she would not reply, Shona was about to leave the room when her clear voice rang out. 'Shona, I am protecting all I have—my husband, my family, my sanity,' she said simply. 'I know you have never welcomed me here and have disapproved of me all these years. Possibly, you thought I was a threat to the peace in this house. If I was, I am sorry, but I do feel affection for this family. I know you are very protective about Vrushali but I did not seek to replace her—she will always hold a special place in Karna's heart, which I can never usurp. I am in no position to defend myself but I *am* proud of him,' she added fiercely, 'I am the wife of the greatest warrior of this generation, who has conquered the entire Aryavarta—the whole country—all alone! Karna managed to single-handedly defeat Jarasandha, one of the most valiant warriors on earth, within a matter of hours. He was the same Jarasandha whom the great Bhima took eighteen long days to kill in a wrestling combat later. I am so proud of him that it hurts me that he is winning all the glory for the wrong man, for the wrong reason. He is Duryodhana's strength and without him, Duryodhana could not have called himself an emperor. And he is doing all this for a man who doesn't have a shred of integrity nor honesty in him. He is the same man who will drag us all to a needless war. In spite of being a monarch of such a huge empire, do you think he will return Indraprastha, which is rightfully theirs, to the Pandavas?'

Shona stood silently, unable to reply. 'There are two sides in a war: the triumph and the terror,' she reminded him gently. 'I can see only the horror, the suffering, the aftermath of war. And I am sure that looking after the sick, the maimed and the crippled is not going against dharma. I don't think so, nor do my parents and Karna—and they matter most to me,' she said defiantly, lifting her head proudly.

'I am trying to protect Karna from ridicule,' said Shona, his manner abruptly defensive.

'Serving the sick and the injured is ridiculous?'

'That it is you who is serving them is!' he replied tersely.

'What does it matter who looks after the injured as long as someone does?' she sighed. 'You see war in its glory, I see its ugliness,' she stated. 'Look at that side of war, Shona, for what you see will get worse as the war is fought. And for what? For "honour"? War will pass, so will victory; but its horrors will not. To fight and kill one's enemies is the kshatriya dharma. But when you fight your friends, your teachers and your relatives, it only causes grief and endless pain.'

Shona looked at her in reluctant admiration and though she tried to turn away, she could not hide the sorrow in her large, soft eyes. At that moment, he heard the clatter of horses' hooves outside and leaned out of the window to see who had come to the palace. He saw it was Karna, who was reining in the horses drawing his chariot. 'He's back!' he turned around to tell his sister-in-law, but she was already at the door, walking rapidly, almost running, to greet her husband. A tender yet bright smile touched her eyes, making them sparkle with joy and love. Shona felt his throat constrict in sudden emotion. He remembered Vrushali's words—Uruvi loves him too much, she had said. Shona had known it, but today he wanted to believe it—for his brother's sake.

Uruvi recalled the day she first saw Karna. The details were still clear in her mind and never failed to excite her. But what had intrigued her most about him were not his good looks, his fair hair, his compelling deep brown eyes, his shy, closed-up personality, his splendid body or his magnificent skill with the bow and arrow. It was his golden kavach and kundals that had mesmerized her. Her favourite time of the day was early dawn, when she watched her husband fast asleep next to her as the sun's first rays lit up his armour and earrings.

She loved looking at the sunrays falling on his beautiful face, which took on a dreamy softness, his serene face looking almost divine. It was a precious moment that she caught every morning, basking in it. It was as if the early sunrays slanted across the room to fall on his glistening chest to embrace him, giving him a warm glow and adding new power and potency to him.

This morning, Karna was not his usual self. He pushed himself up and sat up straight, frowning slightly.

'What's the matter? Is something wrong?' she asked immediately, in concern.

He rubbed his hands over his eyes as if to drive the remnants of sleep and confused thoughts away. 'I think I was dreaming...' he murmured distractedly.

Studying his troubled face closely, she asked quietly, 'Was it a nightmare?' She recalled her own dreadful dreams, which left her tossing and wakeful each night.

'No...' he answered slowly. 'I wouldn't say it was that extreme... but it was strange.'

'Strange?'

'Why would Lord Surya visit me in my dreams to say that I will meet Lord Indra today?' he looked bemused. 'He said that the king of the gods coveted my kavach and kundals. It's all so vivid, so real! I think I am just getting a little paranoid! Or just plain tired!'

'No, you're not paranoid,' she responded. 'You are neither mistrustful, nor fearful or suspicious—in fact I'm the one who has all those sterling qualities!' she said in a lighter tone. 'Karna, please don't ignore the dream. I think it's a warning, perhaps to alert you to some danger.' As she was saying the words, Uruvi was swamped by anxiety, a gnawing fear that was a familiar feeling these days.

'Now you are giving the dream too much importance!' he said. 'But I admit it's still haunting me. All I can think of is how difficult it would be to shed my kavach and kundals—they are so much a part of me! I might have to slice them off or rip them off...hmmm, which one will it be?' he said in a bantering tone.

'Oh, stop fooling around...' she said in worried exasperation. 'Karna, war is drawing near and the Pandavas know that you will be the most difficult man to vanquish. Arjuna is your biggest rival and he has sworn to kill you in battle. Lord Indra happens to be Arjuna's father so it cannot be a coincidence that Lord Surya has warned you about him. It all adds up! Please be careful today.'

Karna smiled, trying to make light of her worry. But even when he left the palace, she mulled over the bizarre dream. Many anxious hours later, Uruvi wondered if she should tell someone about the dream but felt foolish. Should she tell Shona so that he could protect Karna? Or should she reveal her doubts to Vrushali and Radha? By noon, Uruvi was beside herself with a nagging foreboding, but told herself that she was overreacting to a mere dream.

Karna went about his morning routine of going to the Ganga for his morning bath and worshipping Lord Surya at noon. People gathered around him to request him to fulfil their wishes, and as he had vowed, he did not reject anyone. Uruvi did not expect him home till evening and was surprised when she heard his chariot arrive early in the afternoon. She rushed to meet him, her feet flying up the steps to their room.

At first, she did not see him in the chamber, hearing only the sound of someone rummaging through the chest near her bed. Hearing her footsteps, the noise stopped and Karna came into full view. Uruvi stared at him, the colour draining away and bleaching her face paperwhite. She uttered a strangulated cry, her hands clasping her mouth with horror.

Karna stood there bleeding, his chest a mass of blood and gashes. Where his kavach had once spread across his chest and back, was a lump of torn flesh and thick strips of red, bleeding skin. Blood dripped from both ears where the orbs of his kundals had once sparkled. His earlobes had been sliced off savagely.

It might have been a fraction of a moment that ticked away but at once, Uruvi guessed what had happened. She headed straight for the medicine box and a bowl of warm water.

'Let me clean the wounds,' her voice shook, but her hands were steady as she swiftly staunched the bleeding slashes and cuts. Karna stood still, as silent as she was.

'Oh, Karna, what did you do?' she whispered brokenly as she applied the antiseptic salve over the open wounds.

'I gave away my kavach and kundals to Lord Indra,' he sighed. 'He needed them more urgently,' he added with a trace of his old dry humour.

Uruvi continued applying the salve calmly, though she was shaking inside. 'He asked you for them to help his son, Arjuna. Yet you did not refuse him. And he knew you would not! Your generosity is so well known that he was sure you would not refuse to part with them. The king of the gods that he is, he knew you would be bound by the self-imposed oath of giving alms without expecting any return, without any condition,' she said softly, but her voice throbbed with pain and the anger she felt for Lord Indra and Arjuna. She hated them. 'His son is safe now! But what about you? You are completely vulnerable. The kavach and kundals made you invincible—and that was the biggest threat to the Pandavas.'

'Dear wife, my bravery was not defined by the kavach and kundals I wore. They were not my badge of honour,' Karna retorted wryly, the arrogance back in his voice. 'I fight with my capabilities, not with accessories.'

They were interrupted by an uproar at the door. It was Shona, accompanied by Vrushali, who rushed to the side of the bleeding Karna. It was a very angry Shona who confronted Karna. Vrushali, pale and quiet, quickly joined Uruvi and began making fresh bandages for the lesions all over his chest.

'I heard you did the unthinkable,' Shona seethed, gritting his teeth. 'Radheya, I warned you not to give in to any request today! But you didn't heed my words.'

So, Karna *had* told his brother about the dream but he had chosen to turn a deaf ear to Shona's warnings. Uruvi wondered, was it foolish bravery or noble generosity, or was it both?

The older brother smiled weakly, placing his hand on Shona's clenched fist to placate him. 'Lord Indra approached me dressed as a brahmin, and requested me with folded hands. He said, "I ask not for gold, or sapphire or gems as others may have desired. O sinless one, one who is so sincere in your vow, please give me the golden shield on your chest and those earrings, too. This is one gift, O chastiser of foes, that you cannot deny to me for this is one boon I need from you." I was, of course, surprised by his strange request! But I wasn't shocked for at that very moment I realized I was talking not to a poor brahmin, but to Lord Indra himself. Lord Surya had warned me in my dream that he would seek me out. I couldn't go back on my vow, so I bowed to the Lord standing in front of me and gave him what he asked for...'

Vrushali could not contain her gasp of horror. 'But they were inseparable parts of your body...' she murmured in anguish.

'Lord Indra was taken aback when I ripped them out and lay

them in front of him. He said, "Karna, no ordinary mortal would have done what you did today. I am moved by your gesture and will grant you a boon in return." In reply, I said, "If you are genuinely pleased with me, please bless me with your divine weapon, the Vasabi Shakti astra, the master weapon which can destroy any enemy." Unhesitatingly, the Lord handed me the Shakti weapon, saying that it could be used only once.'

'So you are happy that you now have the Shakti astra instead of the kavach and kundals?' Shona asked derisively.

'I had no choice, did I?' Karna answered mildly.

'No, brother, you had a choice—an informed, forewarned choice, Radheya, but you preferred to ignore it,' snapped Shona angrily. 'Why? Did your generosity make you so noble that you became self-destructive? What about self-preservation? Your large-heartedness is legendary to all by now but to be so generous at the cost of your life is…'

'Foolish! I realize that but I cannot go back on my word of honour. A promise given is never to be taken back, whatever the consequences. I would rather die than make a beggar leave my house unfulfilled.'

'How noble!' sneered the younger man. 'You gave away your most precious, life-saving armour to a god who cannot be called honourable himself! He is the one who molested Ahilya, the wife of his teacher, Rishi Gautam, disguised as her husband. Today, the same deceitful person came to you in the guise of a poor brahmin asking for your life. You are being fooled by people who do not have the best of *your* interests at heart, dear brother. In fact, the very opposite. And when at war, you cannot afford to make such foolish mistakes…'

'Stop it, Shona!' remonstrated Vrushali sharply. 'This is no way to speak to your older brother.'

'He is not always right, sister,' he said quietly, bowing his head. 'Sometimes he needs to be told that he is so very wrong. And that what he is doing will lead to his own downfall. I am simply trying to prevent that fall—but now I know I cannot avert it any more.'

And casting Uruvi a penetrating look, Shona walked away from the room hurriedly, but not before Uruvi saw the glistening tears in his unhappy eyes.

Vrushali looked wretched. 'Oh, Radheya, why is it that you—who would not hesitate to even give up your life for charity—have been deprived of honour all your life and yet have always kept your vows?' She looked at her husband in despair. He did not reply.

That night was long, stretching in the shadows of impending doom. Uruvi was restless while watching Karna sleep fitfully, his chest pale in the moonlight. The thirteen-year exile was ending—it was time for the Pandavas to return and ask for their kingdom. A war was going to be fought between the cousins—there was no stopping it—and Lord Indra's action today was a precursor of the destruction that was to come.

Uruvi heard Karna mumble uneasily in his sleep. He woke up with a start, and seeing her by his bedside, he visibly calmed down. 'You are still awake?'

'I was thinking of what happened today...'

He murmured, 'It was not just generosity which you and Shona accuse me of that made me give away my kavach and kundals,' he said evenly. 'Is Lord Indra so insecure that he wanted them in order to protect his son? His son, Uruvi, as you rightly say, cannot be defeated—and that's because he has Lord Krishna by his side. Whether I give away my kavach or kundals or not makes no difference, for the Pandavas will eventually win. The final truth is that Arjuna, through Lord Krishna, shall triumph. But by getting the Shakti astra, I have some hope for my army.'

'By making yourself powerless?'

'But, as I told you earlier, that I shall die is a certainty. You know that too, Uruvi. And that is why I did not hear the fear in your voice today. You have accepted it just as I have.'

Uruvi looked sadly at the discoloured stretch of his starkly bleached skin and a sigh escaped her lips. She found herself praying.

18

The Return of the Pandavas

Strange news filtered into the city of Hastinapur one foggy morning. Kichaka, the dreaded brother-in-law of King Virata of Matsya and the commander-in-chief of his army, was found dead, murdered in the dancing hall at King Virata's palace, his huge body pounded to a pulp. Rumours insisted he had been killed by an enraged Gandharva when he found out that Kichaka had tried to molest his wife. What made the story exciting was not its unusual goriness but the dubious report that the mighty Kichaka was killed by an unknown superhuman.

Duryodhana and Karna refused to believe the story. Kichaka could not have been killed by any ordinary mortal or a superhuman. Only two people could have killed him and those were Duryodhana himself or Bhima. Duryodhana strongly suspected that Bhima was the 'vengeful Gandharva' who had killed Kichaka; the woman in question and the cause of the butchery could be Draupadi or one of the other Pandavas disguised as a woman. As his suspicion crystallized into certainty, Duryodhana knew he had tracked down the missing Pandavas, who were in their thirteenth year of exile, the stipulated last year to be spent incognito—the agyatavasa year.

From the start of the thirteenth year, the spies of Duryodhana, under his explicit orders, had scoured towns, cities and forests looking for the Pandavas, searching for all possible hiding places, but no one could find them. But now Duryodhana knew where they were. If he could unveil their hidden identity, he could force them into another period of exile or force them to forfeit their right to the throne. It was the best time to strike.

Uruvi found Karna preparing for battle that same evening. 'Who is it this time?' she asked quietly.

'King Virata of the Matsya kingdom,' Karna replied mechanically. Knowing that she was waiting for him to expand further, he explained, 'Our ally, King Susharma of Trigarta, is Virata's mortal enemy, and with Kichaka dead, this is the best chance to seize the opportunity to attack his kingdom.'

'That's just a political pretext. The real reason is to flush out the Pandavas whom you and the Kauravas believe have taken shelter in King Virata's kingdom, is that not so?'

'Yes, you're right. I pray that it was Arjuna who was disguised as the dancing woman Brihanhala at King Virata's palace.'

'And that gives you the heaven-sent occasion to battle with Arjuna?'

'Yes, again. For thirteen years, I have dreamt of this encounter. You have all the questions but you already know the answers. Am I being cross-examined?'

She ignored his sarcasm. 'I heard about your argument with Ashwatthama—and it's not very pleasant news. Karna, he is your friend.'

'But that does not give him the right to insult me...' Karna frowned darkly. 'Uruvi, I would have taken harsh words, too, from a friend; after all, Ashwatthama is like a brother to me. But he was nasty to Duryodhana as well.' He flushed angrily. 'It all started when Guru Kripacharya mocked me, calling me stubborn and arrogant when I said that at last I had the chance to challenge Arjuna. He said that Arjuna was much superior to me. He was backed by Guru Dronacharya who, as expected, did not miss his chance to jeer at me. I know I spoke too strongly when I retaliated by telling Duryodhana, in front of the guru, that a brahmin's advice should be taken if a yagna is held and not before a war. At that jibe at his father, Ashwatthama got rather angry with me. I kept silent as I had been curt with his father but Ashwatthama then turned on Duryodhana and lambasted him. He angrily questioned his integrity as a kshatriya king and how he had usurped Indraprastha from the Pandavas through deceit.

Brahmins like his father, he argued, fight straight—not through devious games of dice. Duryodhana lost his temper and, had it not been for Bhishma Pitamaha, we would have got into a fight. The old man warned us that in the time of war, it's best we stay united and show a common front to fight a dangerous enemy like Arjuna. To diffuse the situation, I apologized to the acharyas, our teachers, so I hope it calmed down Ashwatthama too. Does it make you feel less worried now, Uruvi?'

'Karna, Ashwatthama got angry at Duryodhana for your sake. He too believes that he is not the best friend for you. You oblige Duryodhana all the time. And Ashwatthama said what I have been saying all along—why aren't you stopping Duryodhana in his destructive one-track path? He is not playing straight—no one wants the war except him. Why can't he return the kingdom to the Pandavas?' she pleaded. 'There's enough bad blood between them, let there be peace now. You know well enough by now that Duryodhana can dare to think of war with the Pandavas only at your expense. A kshatriya is one who fights only when provoked or when he cannot avoid battle. But here, Duryodhana is itching for trouble. He is deliberately starting a war. It's not going to be King Susharma versus King Virata, it's going to be the Kauravas versus the Pandavas. Let King Susharma battle with King Virata if he wants to. Why are you interfering in their feud?'

'He is our ally, Uruvi. And more importantly, he is Queen Bhanumati's brother and we owe him our support. We share a common enemy in Arjuna, who once attacked his kingdom during his victory march of north India. When King Susharma attacks King Virata from the south, Duryodhana, Bhishma Pitamaha, Guru Dronacharya, Ashwatthama and I plan to launch a surprise attack from the north to catch King Virata's army unawares.'

'So again, it's Arjuna who is the thorn in your heart?' she asked in exasperation. 'Oh, why must you try to prove you can better Arjuna? He is years younger than you, Karna. Behave like an elder and let go of it.'

'I cannot die till I battle Arjuna. And age has nothing to do with this; a warrior is not defined by his youth or age. A warrior is brave or incompetent, a winner or a loser.'

'And by challenging Arjuna each time, you are going to prove you are the brave warrior, the mighty winner?'

Like he always did, Karna baffled her with his answer. He replied softly, 'No, a loser trying to win his dignity.'

The following days saw King Susharma invade Matsya from the south and distract the army of King Virata. Meanwhile, Duryodhana, with his Kaurava army, launched a coup from the northern side, which was vulnerable as it was undefended. King Virata was soon captured and held captive by a victorious King Susharma—but not for long. The arrival of an extraordinary cook called Valala, spoilt the victory march. As Duryodhana had guessed right, the cook was none other than Bhima and the flashily-dressed dancing woman was not Brihanhala but Arjuna. It was Bhima who attacked the enemy ferociously, set King Virata free and captured King Susharma. This defeat enraged Duryodhana. In retaliation, his army then attacked the tender-faced young Prince Uttar Kumar, King Virata's son, whose charioteer was Brihanhala. Dronacharya and Karna immediately recognized him as Arjuna and proceeded to attack, with Bhishma Pitamaha and Duryodhana at their side. The crimson flag with its embossed golden palm tree—the banner of Bhishma Pitamaha—fluttered slowly, creating panic in the heart of the young prince. But the charioteer defended the prince magnificently, single-handedly tackling Karna, Bhishma Pitamaha, Dronacharya and Duryodhana. The Pandava used his weapons more skilfully than his master, Dronacharya. He stripped his most mortal enemy—Karna—of his bow and arrow and forced him to accept defeat. And finally, Arjuna flashed his hidden ace—he invoked the sammohanastra, the weapon of sleep. With his supernatural silver arrow, the Pandava prince shot a shower of the magical stardust on the Kuru heroes, their soldiers and the horsemen, and they slowly sank into a deep slumber, blissfully unaware of the ensuing battle. Some slipped on the ground, some slumped in their chariots. Arjuna watched the sea of sleeping men and told the awestruck Prince Uttar Kumar to fetch the mantles of the fallen Kuru heroes as mementos of their victory. Or better still, to deck up his sister Uttara's dolls with them! And then he blew his conch—named Devdatta—to proclaim his glorious victory.

When the Kuru heroes woke up with their Kaurava army, they knew they had been beaten. Bhishma Pitamaha declared, 'We have been stripped of our mantles, our jewels and our honour. Arjuna could have killed all of us right now, but he is too noble to kill sleeping men even if they are his enemies. We have earned enough shame to last a lifetime. Let us admit defeat and return to Hastinapur.'

A thwarted Duryodhana's rage knew no bounds. He sent a letter to Yudhishthira, which read that the Pandavas needed to go into another thirteen-year exile as they had been recognized during their agyatavasa year, before the end of the thirteenth year. Yudhishthira's answer was equally precise. The Pandavas had completed their full thirteen years when Arjuna twanged his Gandiva bow while the Kaurava army slept through the battle in ignorance and ignominy.

Arjuna's victory was like a stinging slap. Duryodhana fumed, Dushasana raged and King Dhritrashtra saw the crown slipping away again. The Pandavas were to return. And they wanted their kingdom back.

Uruvi saw Karna writhe in mental agony, forced to accept defeat by his mortal rival, Arjuna. Possibly, his shorn-off kavach could have saved him from the weapon of sleep. But Uruvi knew further talk was pointless. Her lips were sealed; her silence would be anguished, her words stifled. Karna had to see the truth for himself as the moment of his inevitable downfall was fast approaching; the end seemed near. She would watch helplessly as their lives slowly crumbled, but she could not stop the disaster any longer, so her protests died down. Just like her dreams had.

If there was any glimmer of hope for a peaceful settlement between the warring cousins, it was doused with the failure of Lord Krishna to mediate. That morning when Uruvi went on her weekly visit to Kunti, she feared it would probably be the last one before the war began. It would be a war to the death. After completing their thirteen years of exile, the Pandavas had shifted to Upalavya, another city in the Matsya kingdom, which was to become a seat of political intrigue. They sent envoys to recall their friends, relatives and allies. And amongst those who arrived there was the young, handsome Abhimanyu, the son of Arjuna and Subhadra. His arrival was doubly meaningful for he was to marry the Matsya princess, Uttara.

'Is it the last good news we shall hear?' Uruvi asked fearfully, turning to Vrushali in utter misery. Kunti had left joyfully for the grand wedding to be solemnized at King Virata's resplendent palace.

Uruvi prayed silently, 'O, give me the strength to live through the coming days...'

In the same palace, which witnessed the fabulous wedding of the young Abhimanyu with the lovely Uttara, another important alliance took place. Lord Krishna, with his older brother Balarama and his cousin Satyaki, the Yadava warrior, held a conference with other Pandava allies—the Matsya kings and princes, the Kasi prince and the Saibya ruler. They were meeting to discuss the peace initiative by the Pandavas. Also present was King Drupad with his two sons, Dhrishtadyumna and Sikhandin, and his five grandsons from his daughter Draupadi—Prativindhya, the son of Yudhishthira, Srutasoma from Bhima, Srutakirti from Arjuna, Satanik from Nakul and Srutakarma from Sahadeva. Abhimanyu was present too—his marriage did not stop him attending the important meeting.

At the same time, the Kauravas, too, held a conference to discuss preparations for war. They had spread the word and were acquiring new allies to assist them in the coming conflict. Uruvi wondered about her father and whom he would support. As an ally of the court of Hastinapur, he owed allegiance to the Kuru rulers but in principle, Uruvi knew he was for the Pandavas. Being the father-in-law of Karna made the situation more awkward for him. It would be assumed he would support his son-in-law.

'I would like to stay neutral,' he confided eventually to Uruvi.

'You won't be allowed to do so,' Uruvi responded immediately. 'One of them may attack our kingdom and we'll be forced to retaliate.'

'I like the way you say "we", Uruvi,' her father chuckled softly, though a trifle sadly. 'Pukeya has always been yours. After me, it is you who will be declared as the queen of this kingdom. That's why I am consulting you here right now!' he said grimly. 'I cannot be more diplomatic than this. I cannot bear to see the ruin of Hastinapur. Yet, I cannot take the side of the Kauravas to fight the Pandavas. The Pandavas are not asking for anything unreasonable—they simply want their lost kingdom back.'

'Yes, but some people like Karna and Balarama argue that they cannot ask for the return of something they lost as a stake. If as a king, Yudhishthira could gamble away his kingdom so carelessly, what right does he have over that same kingdom now? Does he have the moral right to be the ruler of a kingdom he so indifferently placed as a wager and eventually lost? Duryodhana has been a just king and has ruled his subjects well. They are not complaining against him. So then, why, they argue, should Duryodhana return what they lost in a wager?'

'That is just a play on words,' sighed the old king. 'The Pandavas have been punished enough with the thirteen-year exile.'

'Exactly! And that's how the Kauravas see it. The fulfilment of the conditions of the exile means only personal freedom for the Pandavas and no claim for the kingdom.'

'But the Pandavas were cheated out of their kingdom by foul means through a rigged dice game in the first place,' King Vahusha expostulated. 'This fight will lead nowhere, except to disaster!'

'But I've heard both sides realize this…' Uruvi looked pensive. 'I have heard that the Pandavas did approach Duryodhana with a peace-offering through a brahmin of King Drupada's court, after which Sanjay, King Dhritrashtra's most trusted envoy, was sent to the Pandavas to give a reply. With the resulting impasse, Krishna offered to mediate and came down to Hastinapur. He said that all the Pandavas wanted was their lost kingdom—Indraprastha—and if not that, just five villages for the five brothers. Duryodhana flatly refused and declared he would not let go of even a needlepoint of territory. What option do the Pandavas have but to fight back? Duryodhana is cornering them so that they battle out the issue. It's either quit or fight, win or lose.'

King Vahusha shook his head sadly. 'How can a righteous war be wrong? There is no sin in defending oneself against an armed enemy. If the enemy provokes their opponents into a battle, the opponents can either submit and be called cowards, or hit back with all their strength and convictions. There is no other way out.'

'To give the Pandavas their share of the kingdom would be the safest bet—and that's what the patriarchs like Bhishma Pitamaha, Vidura and Guru Dronacharya have been trying to convince both the father and the stubborn son to do,' said Uruvi. 'But Duryodhana wants the war—just like Draupadi does. She has her own reasons. She has warned her husbands that if they do not fight this battle, she will fight the Kauravas with the help of her sons, her brothers and her old father, to avenge her humiliation.'

'And Karna? What does he say? He has nothing to gain. He is so close to Duryodhana—can he not convince him not to start the war? Frankly, he is the only one who can knock some sense into the Kuru king. Duryodhana will not listen to his father, Bhishma Pitamaha, Dronacharya or even his mother Gandhari. But with Karna, it's a different matter. Why doesn't Karna dissuade Duryodhana from fighting the war?'

'The answer to all those questions, Father, would be the story of my life!' Uruvi laughed bleakly. 'Karna knows the war is doomed to end in destruction. He wants it simply because he believes it is the kshatriya way of solving the problem—to battle it out face-to-face and may the stronger side win.'

King Vahusha was about to retort that the sutaputra was a fine one to talk about the kshatriya code of conduct. Then he felt a momentary twinge of shame; he had stooped to call a true warrior a sutaputra, doing exactly what society had inflicted indiscriminately on his son-in-law.

He was troubled to see his daughter look so sad. 'Have you advised your husband against this war?' he asked her gently. 'Have you pleaded with him to discourage his friend from pursuing this ultimate folly? He has the power to do so. Child, try again and again. It is your last chance for peace.'

'I have, Father, oh, how I have,' she replied tiredly, '...but I fear I have already lost!'

✌

Peace negotiations were on, with some diehard optimists like Bhishma Pitamaha and Guru Dronacharya sincerely working for a compromise. But even as the talks continued, contingents were getting ready for war. Stealthy efforts to acquire fresh allies went on and emissaries were insidiously at work. The prime catch was Krishna, though most knew that it was the Pandavas he would support. But wanting to be fair, he welcomed both Arjuna and Duryodhana when they visited him at Dwarka.

A sleeping Krishna woke up to find Arjuna at his feet and Duryodhana waiting for him to wake up. Duryodhana claimed he had reached first, demanding that he be heard first. Krishna gently reminded him that since it was Arjuna he had seen first on waking up, he would leave the first choice to Arjuna. The choice he gave for Arjuna and Duryodhana to pick was this: either it was him, Lord Krishna, on one side, on the conditions that he would not participate in the fighting nor pick up a weapon, or it would be the invincible power of Krishna's huge army, including his tribesmen, the Narayanas at Dwarka. Arjuna selected Lord Krishna while Duryodhana went home delighted that he had so easily pocketed the huge army of Dwarka!

It was the worst act of stupidity by the Kauravas, according to Uruvi. 'I always thought Duryodhana was arrogant but not stupid!' Uruvi exclaimed to her husband. 'That man is actually gloating that he has Krishna's army and not Krishna himself! Doesn't he see he made a colossal mistake?'

'But when was he given the right to make a choice?' Karna asked with a shake of his head. 'He was never given the option, though he believes he had one! It was Arjuna who made the first move and what he selected was, yes, the best option. Duryodhana has not realized he was made a complete fool because he is under the impression that he got away with the better deal. That is why he is rejoicing over a wrong move!!'

'Arjuna knows if he has Lord Krishna on his side, he needs no army, he needs no further blessing. And that is how Lord Krishna will become Arjuna's charioteer, the Parthasarthy.'

'But that was always the case, wasn't it? Krishna would never have gone for Duryodhana anyway. It was smart diplomacy, a clever move typical of Krishna!'

'But it is not the way Duryodhana hoodwinked King Salya to support him,' Uruvi was quick to point out. 'Flattered by Duryodhana's fabulous hospitality, King Salya of Madradesh was so impressed that he deserted the Pandavas. Nakul and Sahadeva are his nephews, the sons of his dead sister Madri, and he owed them his allegiance. But Duryodhana again has made a huge mistake. Forcing King Salya to join him doesn't mean the Madra king will be a devoted supporter. He is a reluctant ally. That he was forced to submit rankles and he will see to it that he creates trouble in some way or the other.'

'Oh, he has! He has already. He is going to be my charioteer,' Karna announced with his usual composure.

Uruvi struggled for breath. 'But he hates you! A charioteer is supposed to be the warrior's best friend—guiding him, protecting him, saving him. This man will be the first one to wish you dead!' As do so many others, she thought, knowing that Arjuna and the Pandavas would spare no effort to slay her husband. A pall of gloom weighed heavily on her and she could forsee the horror of another day.

'Let's leave it to fate,' Karna said cryptically, sensing her hopelessness. 'And to Lord Krishna.' His tone said it all—he was resigned to his destiny, which he knew would run its own course.

19

Krishna and Karna

Uruvi waited all night, but Karna did not come to her room. She must have dozed off fitfully, for when she woke up it was dawn, a pale streak on the eastern horizon with a few dark, ribbed clouds hiding the peeping sun. She noticed Karna had still not returned. Worried, she wondered what she would do next, when she saw him at last, standing near the open window, against the shadows. She moved closer, unwilling to disturb the strange sanctity of the early hours of the day, but wanting to break the silence. Karna looked distant as usual. The smile had disappeared from his face since he had returned from the campaign against King Virat. But today he looked like a man who had seen a ghost. He was barely aware of her presence, staring at the horizon, the waking sun changing in the distance to a hot pink flush. She turned to where he was looking. The outlines of the distant hills were becoming clearer, but clouds were swelling into dark, thick billows against the dull rumble of the darkened sky. It started to rain.

Dread gripped Uruvi. Karna was silent, but Uruvi sensed he wanted to speak. She waited, afraid of what he was going to say. They stood quietly for a long time in the stillness of the dawn till she heard him speak, articulating each word clearly and evenly. 'I know at last who my mother is, Uruvi.'

Her spirits lifted, edging away her irrational panic. But noticing the frozen despair on her husband's face, she knew that the terror traumatizing her was not unfounded.

'I met Krishna today,' he began shortly, struggling with his inner torment.

Uruvi was puzzled. What had Krishna to do with the identity of Karna's natural mother? 'Karna, I don't understand. When, or rather why, did you meet Krishna?' she said, frowning. She sensed the strange stillness within him and knew that Karna was finding it difficult to accept an awful truth. She forced herself to be calm, and asked persuasively, 'Oh, Karna, please say it. Tell me all. Please don't hide anything from me—not now!' she continued softly. 'I am prepared to hear the worst, so say it!'

Karna leaned his head heavily against the marbled column behind him, as if the load on his mind was too heavy to bear. 'Krishna, as you know, had come to Hastinapur to mediate,' he started slowly. 'He met Duryodhana, trying to make him see reason so that the war could be avoided. All his attempts failed, and on his return to Upalavya, he came to meet me with Satyaki, his Yadava relative. He asked me to ride with him in his chariot as he wanted to talk to me,' Karna recounted, his tone suddenly monotonous. 'We drove away from the city where no one could see us. We stopped at one point and Satyaki was told to remain in the chariot while Krishna took my hand and led me away so that we could talk. I was surprised, of course, but preferred to remain silent and let him do the talking. Krishna came to the point immediately. "You are a good man, the bravest warrior. You are learned and you are generous. You know your Vedas. You honour your dharma so much so that you are the very epitome of it. Yet, why are you siding with the sinful Duryodhana?" he asked me. "Why do you back the unrighteous? I don't understand," he said.'

Uruvi couldn't help feeling vindicated. Krishna was saying what she had been trying to explain to Karna all along. Had he managed to convince Karna at last? As if reading each bit of her thoughts, Karna interposed, 'I remembered your angry words, Uruvi, and I said, "O Lord, you are correct. The righteous should side with the righteous. But although I knew Duryodhana was impelled by questionable motives, I stood by him. Because I love him too much. He is more than my friend. He is my brother who acknowledged me for what I was—an archer and a warrior. Till then, no one had recognized my worth, for I was a low-born sutaputra for everyone else.'

Uruvi supposed that Karna must have stubbornly asserted his loyalty to his friend. Not even Krishna's coaxing could have persuaded Karna to give up supporting Duryodhana. Yet she could not see the link between Karna's unquestionable loyalty to Duryodhana and his questionable birth. She was still mystified. But before Karna went on to tell her what had happened, she knew he had reasoned with Krishna just as he had once argued with her and won.

'Years ago, in this same city at the archery contest, Duryodhana gave me honour, respect and dignity as a man, as a warrior and as a friend. Guru Dronacharya refused to accept me as his disciple as I was a sutaputra. Rejected, I lied to Guru Parshurama about my identity and was cursed for the betrayal. At the contest, I was insulted by the Pandavas, booed by Bhima and scorned by Arjuna. Why? Because I was a low-caste human who had no right to string the bow. I threw a challenge at him and, since then, I have been termed arrogant! I have been jeered at for my dare and constantly reminded that I am but a sutaputra. But each time, Duryodhana supported me. I am not indebted to him for crowning me King of Anga because I have never desired kinghood. All I wanted was the dignity and honour I think I deserved—and he gave it to me every time. Touched and full of gratitude, I asked him how I could repay him and he held my folded hands, saying, "I want your friendship. Nothing else." Years have lapsed and I still remain his friend, indebted to him as I am to another person, my mother Radha. These are the two people to whom I owe everything. One saved me as a deserted baby, the other saved me from social ostracism. I live only for them because they have always supported me.'

Karna paused, as if paying respect to both Radha and Duryodhana. He said, 'Lord Krishna was quiet. After some time, he agreed that the debt of gratitude I owe to them is the most difficult to repay. And then he asked me a question: "Who are your real parents? Do you know anything about your birth?" he asked gently.'

Uruvi knew the moment of truth was drawing near and the

nervous apprehension made her feel suffocated.

Karna continued, 'I replied that I did not know who my natural parents were. But for me, my parents are Adhiratha and Radha. And I am Radheya, the son of Radha.'

"'No, your mother is a queen," said Krishna kindly, his eyes soft with compassion. "She was the princess who served Sage Durvasa so devotedly that she was granted an unusual boon. Through a mantra, she could invite any god and have a child from him. The curious girl that she was, the princess decided to try out the mantra and invoked Lord Surya, the sun god. To her dismay, suddenly, a radiant figure appeared before her. Scared and shocked, the girl tried to shoo him away, but he told her he could not go back because the mantra had come into play. And that was how you were born—as the son of Surya, you were born with the kavach and kundals which would protect you all your life. As an unmarried mother, she was forced to leave you in the Ganga, but she could never forget you, her first child."'

Uruvi felt a faint sense of unease. The story was sounding vaguely familiar; she had heard it before. His mother had been a princess... Sage Durvasa...her mind was racing back, trying to remember the story. Karna's deep baritone broke through her muddled thoughts as he continued with his narration. 'The moment Lord Krishna said my mother had been a princess, my heart leaped with surprise, joy, jubilation—I am not sure exactly what, Uruvi, but I knew at the moment that I was happy, deliriously happy; that I was a kshatriya, not a sutaputra! I could finally throw off the yoke of being a low-caste person! I turned to Krishna, my curiosity prompting me to ask more questions. "I am a kshatriya!" I almost laughed with joy. "You talk of my mother as if you know her. Is she alive? Where is she?" I pleaded. He took my hands in his and said quietly, "Your mother is also the mother of five sons who are famous as the best warriors in the kingdom. They, too, are as brave and heroic as you are..."'

'My foster mother, Kunti?' gasped Uruvi, her incredulity almost making her choke.

'Yes. My mother is Queen Kunti,' Karna pronounced this affirmation so softly that it came out as a ragged whisper. 'And I am the son of Lord Surya.'

She stared at him, dumbstruck, the shock of his disclosure leaving her numb. Her lips moved; she wanted to speak but the words stuck in her throat. She swallowed painfully.

Karna, the greatest, most honourable warrior of the Aryavarta—the great country he had established—stood tall and proud. 'At last I know who I am. I am a kshatriya, Uruvi, that identity I so desired all my life.' His lips twisted in an enigmatic smile. 'I am of blue blood *and* of celestial lineage, one of the royalty. But I am also an illegitimate son! An unwanted son, flung away by my unmarried princess-mother and a celestial god. Is this how I now introduce myself?' he said harshly. 'Suddenly I have this other family—Lord Surya, my father, Kunti, my mother, and the Pandavas, my five brothers! But no one in it whom I can actually call mine! I am yet the sutaputra. A kshatriya yet not a kshatriya!'

Uruvi realized that Krishna had revealed the truth, but it was yet not acknowledged. Karna's ambiguous identity, his shadowy parentage had been known all along to two people—Krishna and Kunti—but they had preferred to hide this truth from the man they owed it to. A hidden truth is as good as a lie. The truth had been kept a secret for reasons unknown, but the truth had to be told to whom it mattered most.

With rising bewilderment and consternation, Uruvi exclaimed, 'Why? But why did Krishna decide to tell you now after all these years? There must be a reason!'

'Because it was the need of the hour. The time to tell me was now, not earlier.' Karna sighed. 'I asked him the same question—why was I being told now when it was clear that both he and my mother had kept silent for so long. For ages, I had longed to know who my parents were. For years, I had been searching for this truth I was denied. When I asked Krishna why he had chosen to reveal it now, he said, "Because I want to save you from a certain death. I want you to live. I want you to be saved from this war.'" Karna paused, his voice thick with emotion.

'What else did Krishna say?' she asked. 'Tell me, Karna, please.'

'With his voice full of compassion and wisdom, Krishna told me, "I commend your loyalty, Karna. But according to dharma, you are the eldest Pandava, the first-born child of Kunti. From your mother's side, you are my cousin. As the eldest Pandava, you are fit to be king. You are as righteous as Yudhishthira, as powerful and compassionate as Bhima, as skilled in archery and warfare and as brave as Arjuna, as handsome as Nakul, and as wise and learned as Sahadeva. Come and join me. Be with your brothers and mother. I shall give you the kingdom that you deserve."'

'He wanted to make you the king of Hastinapur?' Uruvi cried incredulously.

Karna continued relentlessly. 'Yes. And more! I was too shocked to react. I was silent for a long time and was too taken aback at what he had told me. And then Krishna added, "Draupadi can be your wife too."'

'No!' Uruvi cried softly, shaking her head. Her mind was spinning. 'He offered you everything!' The rain outside fell with a heartless insistence, pouring straight and heavy, with an infuriating persistence.

Karna smiled mirthlessly. 'Yes, it was the ultimate temptation! I was at last getting a throne, an identity, a new family—and a wife!'

'What was your reply?' she burst out, her fists clenched tight.

'What did you expect me to say, Uruvi?' he asked quietly. 'How well do you really know me? That I would throw away everything that I have and grab what he was gifting me? Oh God, Uruvi, after all these years you still think I am pining for Draupadi, and just because he tried to bribe me by using her name, that I would take up the offer?'

'Karna, each day I live in the fear that I shall lose you...' she whispered brokenly.

'You will lose me only through death, Uruvi,' he said calmly, drawing her close. 'Through nothing and nobody else!'

She placed her cool cheeks on his chest, hearing his heart thudding wildly. She tightened her arms around him, fearful he would leave her. 'Don't talk of death,' she pleaded. 'You refused Krishna?'

'Yes, he was offering me the world, heaven, the whole universe— but why? Why now, after all this while? Not for my sake. I would get all this only if I switched sides. I had to be a Pandava to fight against the Kauravas. It was their last resort, their last means to stop the war. As the first Pandava, I would be the king of Hastinapur, and like the Pandavas, Duryodhana would have accepted this gracefully and perhaps, gladly. I know for a fact that he would have surrendered his crown to me willingly and stood by me. Just as Yudhishthira would have, I am sure.'

'Then it's all for the best, isn't it? There will be no war, there will be no feud, and there will be no bad blood any longer!' And I won't have to lose you in the war, she told herself silently. Hope laced her voice, her face brightened, but catching a glimpse of the bleak expression on her husband's face, she knew she was wishing for a hopeless dream to come true.

'Uruvi, you are such a foolish optimist!' he laughed shortly. 'You keep hoping for the most simple solutions!' Karna turned grim again and his eyes grew grave. 'I hate to disappoint you, but by revealing the truth now, they have left me defenceless. And that's what I explained to Krishna.'

He refused heaven and prefers death, Uruvi cried silently.

She heard her husband's soft words. 'I bowed to him and said, "My Lord, out of the boundless concern you have for me, you told me the truth about my parents and my brothers. Yes, by dharma I may be a Pandava. But I am Radheya first. I was brought up by my mother, Radha, and Adhiratha with selfless love and unquestioning affection. Shall I spurn their love for a mother who left me when I was a baby? She does not need me. But Radha and Adhiratha do. Neither the whole world nor the biggest kingdom can make me either leave them or tempt me away from the bonds of their love. I cannot betray them nor can I betray Duryodhana. He is the only friend I have and I am indebted to him eternally. I would rather die than be ungrateful. I have promised him my everlasting support, and I shall not take back my word. What you are offering me has all the bright glitter of a new promise, but it cannot lure me from the truth that is so dear to me. You want to save me from a certain death? I would rather face that death than turn against my friend. The Pandavas are strong because they are under your protection. But I shall face them, knowing this, and die with my friend on the battlefield.'"

The passion in Karna's voice rang true; there was a savage eloquence in his speech. He was strangely stirred, and as he spoke, she could feel him trembling against her. Uruvi wanted to ease his anguish but she allowed him to express his feelings. Outside, the pitiless rain fell with a fierce malignity.

'I have to help Duryodhana. I am his only hope. By my death on the battlefield, I shall seek release from this bondage of love, friendship and life,' Karna said hopelessly. 'I told Krishna: "I have never been Fortune's child. I have always been scorned by these very Pandavas for my low birth! Now you say that they are my brothers and that I, too, am a high-born warrior. I had sworn to kill them. By revealing the truth when war is about to begin, Lord, you have robbed me of my last weapon. Why are you destroying my life by telling me this now? Why have you chosen to tell me the secret of my birth today? I have dreamt of combatting Arjuna on the battlefield, but now, how can I fight him or any of my brothers? I know we shall lose the war, but I must fight beside Duryodhana, even if we are doomed."'

His words tumbled out as he continued, 'I said, "O Krishna! I should be angry with you but I cannot, because I know you are my ultimate redeemer. But, may I ask you for something?" And the Lord replied, "Yes. Whatever you wish for." And I said to Krishna, "You know the secret of my birth, but I beg you not to disclose this truth to the Pandavas until the day I die. They will not be able to fight me. Just like I am rendered helpless now, they, too, will put down their weapons and accept me as the oldest brother. Also, I know the noble

Yudhishthira will surrender his rights to me. He is righteous and fit to be an emperor. May he rule under your guidance. I know how this war shall end—the Pandavas will win and we shall lose and die on the battlefield. I am prepared to die. I prefer a short, glorious life and desire a death befitting it."'

Karna stared at her, not really seeing her. His great, shining eyes seem to bore right into her soul. She winced as she was hit by the finality of each word he had uttered.

'Krishna then asked me why I was so sure that the Pandavas would win. I answered, "This war of Kurukshetra is a mighty sacrifice. It is a platform for our salvation. You are the head deity and Arjuna is the head priest. The other Pandavas are the celebrants. Bhishma Pitamaha, Guru Dronacharya, the hundred sons of Dhritrashtra and I are the offerings in this sacrifice. We shall all attain heaven and one day, I hope I meet you there. We part as friends but till then, my Lord, I beg your leave." Saying this, I touched his feet. He held me by the shoulders and embraced me. I could feel the deep love, the compassion from within him. We walked slowly towards his chariot and then we parted ways. Now I am waiting to meet him again—on the battlefield of Kurukshetra.'

It had stopped raining. The sun was rising fast now, the shards of gold swiftly overcoming the dark clouds in the warm morning light, which was spreading westwards across the river. The last stars had faded, the sky turned a lovely blue, and shimmering light from the fully awake sun drenched the countryside. Uruvi felt that Karna was like the sun, his inner strength, his unshakeable resolve, his assurance, his acceptance of what was to come drying up her tears of anger and grief. She loved him. She loved him completely. For the first time probably, her admiration for him far surpassed the love she felt.

She touched his shoulder gently, 'I couldn't have loved you more!' she whispered. 'But today I can say you are my god—a god whom I treated so shabbily! A god whom I had stopped believing in, a god who brought back my faith in mankind. There can be no one more decent, kind and magnanimous than you. And I am sorry that I could hurt a man so wonderful. Oh, how can you pardon me for my insensitivity, my thoughtlessness? Oh, I love you so much! And I always will!'

'Don't! Don't love me so much!' he said thickly, and gathering her close to his chest, nestled his head in her soft neck. His body was wracked with sobs, the anguished tears, suppressed for so long, seeping into her hair. She held him fiercely close as if to protect him from further hurt, from future harm. She felt his pain, his sense of abandonment, his final betrayal. She became conscious that she was crying too—for him, always for him. She ached with his pain. Her heart bled for him and along with her pain, she felt a new emotion. It was unbridled hatred for the woman who had been the cause of this sorrow—Kunti.

Karna seemed to sense her thoughts instinctively. He raised his glistening face, the pain slowly ebbing, and he regained his customary equanimity. He was not done yet. He took her tenderly by her shoulders and looked searchingly into her shimmering eyes. 'As I told Krishna, I beg you too—promise me you shall not reveal this truth to anyone. To no one, especially to Queen Kunti. I don't want you to talk about me to her. Please.'

She opened her mouth to speak, but knowing what was coming next, Karna gently placed his hand on her mouth, muffling her protests. "No, don't say a word more. I have told you all. Today, I bared my soul to you. And there is nothing more to say, nothing more to expect. I want you to know that I am ready for my death. I am prepared. And I have no regrets—not even about my birth any more.'

'She doesn't deserve to have a son like you!' she cried. 'You may absolve her of all her actions, Karna. But I can never forgive Kunti. Never!' she repeated violently. Kunti—she uttered the name silently but with a hardened heart. She had so often addressed Kunti as 'Ma', but that name now took on a new meaning. It sounded cruelly hollow. To him—and especially, to her.

20

Bhishma and Karna

War clouds were gathering swiftly. Even the gentle Yudhishthira
had decided to leave his days of clemency behind, and preparations
were in full swing. Dhrishtadyumna, Draupadi's brother and King
Drupad's son, was chosen as the commander-in-chief of the Pandava
army. All the troops, the scattered contingents, converged towards
the great field of Kurukshetra—the battlefield for the warring cousins
and kings. A moat was constructed around the Pandava camp, and
soon, tents for all the kings dotted the camp.

The Kaurava forces, too, began their slow march towards the
sacred battlefield. Duryodhana asked his great-uncle, Bhishma
Pitamaha, to be the commander-in-chief of the Kaurava army but
it was only after Duryodhana begged him that he agreed—on two
conditions. He emphasized that he would not kill any of the Pandavas,
even if it destroyed the Kaurava army. 'The sons of Pandu and the
sons of Dhritrashtra are both dear to me. I will not kill any of them.
Only Arjuna is superior to me and may perhaps have the power to kill
me. But I cannot slay him,' said the grand veteran, who was blessed
with the boon that he would be killed by no man and the boon of
ichamaran or choosing the moment of his death.

The second condition was a peculiar one. He told his great-
grandnephew that he would only fight for the Kauravas if Karna did
not step on the battlefield of Kurukshetra.

'I almost feel sorry for Duryodhana,' rued Uruvi as she sat
with her husband in a rare moment of peace. 'No one seems to be
unconditionally on his side; he seems to be surrounded by half-
hearted, disinclined warriors. Guru Dronacharya has already said

he will only capture, not kill the Pandavas, while King Salya is the maternal uncle of Nakul and Sahadeva and an ardent Pandava supporter who has reluctantly joined the Kaurava side. Bhishma Pitamaha declares that he shall not kill the Pandavas! Karna, you are Duryodhana's sole trump card and his most fierce loyalist. But you have been crippled by the clever manipulations of Krishna. You have been emotionally blackmailed into not fighting against your own brothers. Is this war or a cruel hunting game?'

'The consequences of this war have already been decided. Except for Duryodhana, all of us know how it is going to end,' Karna cut in quietly. 'And now, it seems I won't be allowed to fight after all!' he sighed.

Uruvi was surprised when she heard his words. How could Karna not fight? Was it possible that there was still hope? She listened eagerly as Karna went on, telling her about Bhishma Pitamaha's second condition. 'Duryodhana protested vehemently when the old man said that I should not enter the battlefield. Then Bhishma Pitamaha suddenly turned on me and said angrily, "I shall not consider having you, a sutaputra, under my leadership, Karna. I have no respect for you and we have never got along. You call yourself a warrior, but you are not even equal to a sixteenth part of the Pandavas. You are no maha-rathi—instead of being a great warrior, you are an ardha-rathi, who cannot measure up to even an ordinary soldier. You are the man who fled from the Gandharvas when they took Duryodhana prisoner. It was not you but Arjuna who drove back the Gandharvas. Again, it was Arjuna who defeated Duryodhana in the battle at King Virat's capital and humbled both you and Duryodhana."'

The grand sire's unreasonable terms took everyone by surprise, even Uruvi, who had known the grand old patriarch for so long. Karna was Duryodhana's right arm and the Kaurava army's ace card, so Bhishma Pitamaha's insistence on keeping Karna out of the battlefield was suicidal. Shona was expectedly furious. 'Radheya, if you are not permitted to fight, I shall not go to the battlefield either,' he seethed. 'If that is how war ethics go, I am a sutaputra too, am I not?'

'No, brother, don't take that stance,' answered Karna levelly. 'If you do that, it will be a sign of revolt. And we cannot afford to have any dissensions now. We have to be fully prepared for the war. Get ready for it. Go!' he urged, almost pushing his reluctant brother out of the room.

The more Uruvi thought of the patriarch's harshness, the more she was convinced that it was not what it seemed. 'No, there is something wrong somewhere. Karna, Bhishma Pitamaha is the most just and gentle man I have known!' Uruvi protested earnestly. 'I can't believe that he could say such stinging words! There has to be another reason!' she said agitatedly.

'He may have his reasons,' Karna sighed. 'But I lost my temper too and called him a senile old fool who was clinging to power! I was hurt and so angry that I walked out of the room, but not before telling him: "The pleasure of killing Arjuna rests with me, not you, grand sire."'

'Which again is not true,' Uruvi said quietly. 'You may have vowed to kill him—but you won't, will you? Now your vow has lost its force because you know that Arjuna is your own brother.'

Karna turned away. 'It's such a lost cause,' he remarked wearily. 'Sometimes I wonder why I am here; why was I born? They say there is a reason for your birth, your existence. I am confounded; I have still not found mine. I was born unwanted and lived a life feeling wholly unwelcome in society. My life seems to be a series of unanswered questions, but whatever my lineage is, I have lived as a sutaputra. So what Bhishma Pitamaha said was not wrong. I am saddened, yes, not by his words, but that I cannot help my friend.'

Uruvi was secretly glad that Karna could not participate in the war, the sudden gleam in her eyes revealing her relief. She saw a new lease of life for her husband. There would be no duel between Karna and Arjuna! Karna did not miss the gleam and was a trifle amused. 'Do you seriously think anyone can stop me from fighting this war?' he smiled affectionately at her. 'Silly girl, stop dreaming!'

Uruvi wondered why the soft-spoken patriarch had acted so

uncharacteristically. Her childhood memories of the venerable old man were tender ones, of someone caring, with immense patience. Even as a child, she had often seen him getting angry at Duryodhana and Shakuni, but he had never raised his voice or used hurtful language. He could not insult Karna but for a purpose, she kept telling herself. There had to be an explanation and she intended to seek it herself.

She decided to talk to Bhishma Pitamaha. No one dared to meet the grand sire because he was an intensely private man. Very few people could muster enough courage to talk to him, except perhaps Uruvi, who was not unnerved by his monumental stature.

She was not intimidated by his hard eyes that seldom lit up. He had an uncanny way of looking through the person in front of him, with an unwavering stare so devoid of expression that many found it discomfiting. But for Uruvi, he was the kindest man, even more than her father.

When she entered the hall where he sat, she noticed with a pang that he looked feeble. His face was pale, his eyes vacant. His powerful shoulders had the dejected droop of a defeated man. He was old, but he seemed to have aged rapidly in the last few months. She hesitated for a moment; was she being impulsive as usual? She suddenly felt reluctant to broach the topic and wondered how she could slip away. But he had seen her. He gave her a long, thoughtful look and said softly, 'I hope you are not too angry with me, dear. I know I have hurt you.'

To hear the grand sire apologising to her was too much for Uruvi to take. She rushed to him and hugged him. 'No, sir, please don't humble yourself in front of me!' she pleaded. 'I know you would never wound me. I am not hurt, I am confused. I want to know why you imposed the condition that Karna is to keep away from the war. As the commander-in-chief, are you not depriving the Kaurava army of its best warrior?' she asked. 'You deliberately insulted him so that he would be forced to withdraw from the battle.'

The veteran warrior gave a slight nod, appreciating her

shrewdness. 'No, as I have told you before, I don't approve of Karna. He has been poisoning Duryodhana's ears for a long time, and I am neither impressed by his empty boasts nor his show of valour. He is nothing but a sutaputra,' he reiterated maliciously.

'You can't fool me, grand sire. You are too wise a person to label people with their caste and lineage,' she answered coolly. 'Otherwise, would you have accepted Queen Satyavati, a matsyagandha, the daughter of a fisherman, as the wife of your father, King Shantanu, and the mother of their sons, Vichitravirya and Chitragandha?' she said. 'And if Karna is a sutaputra, ironically, neither King Dhritrashtra nor King Pandu are pure-blooded royals as they claim to be. They were born to kshatriya princesses by a mixed-caste brahmin father—Rishi Vyasa, who himself was the illegitimate son of Rishi Parasher and Satyavati before she married your father. If you look at it this way, the Pandavas and the Kauravas are of mixed blood too, which you may call lowly?' she taunted.

'That's an intelligent but an irreverent argument.'

'But nevertheless true!' she retorted. 'It has never been publicly acknowledged, and therefore they did not suffer the stigma as Karna had to. You have always been liberal and I refuse to believe all those nasty words you threw at Karna! You are hiding something—and I want to know what it is!'

The old man ignored her plea and remained quiet. Uruvi would not give up; her stubborn streak would not allow it. 'Are you not the same Bhishma Pitamaha who was the first to acknowledge publicly that Karna was a formidable archer, on par or even better than Arjuna? And yet you were also the one who did not utter a word of protest when, at the same event, Bhima insulted Karna by calling him a sutaputra. Why were you silent when you saw that injustice?'

Bhishma Pitamaha did not say a word. Angered by his silence, Uruvi went on relentlessly. 'You did not intervene even when Draupadi was disrobed in your presence. How did you allow it as you presided over the Raj Sabha? You could have stopped the outrage, so why didn't you?' she demanded heatedly. 'Sir, you have earned the respect of all who know you, but you have done things that I'm sure you're not proud of! Right from how you kidnapped the three Kashi princesses, Amba, Ambika and Ambalika, for your brother, King Vichitravirya. They were forced to marry him. Were you not responsible for the suicide of Amba, who eventually killed herself because the man she was in love with refused to marry her, fearing the wrath of the great Bhishma? Kings were so petrified of you that you easily bought over their princesses and forced them to marry Kuru princes. You did it with Madri for King Pandu and with Gandhari for King Dhritrashtra. Their feelings were really never considered. You refused to practise niyoga but you allowed it to be performed by King Vichitravirya's widows with Rishi Vyasa, your half-brother.'

The old man watched her with a steadfast gaze, his face still. Uruvi pitilessly went on. 'Later, you allowed a poisonous person like Shakuni to station himself at Hastinapur, knowing full well that he had never forgiven you. You knew he would strike back and seek his revenge some day, but you preferred to keep silent as usual!' she lashed out. 'You permitted him his cunning, his deceit, his constant plotting against the Pandavas. You knew he was poisoning Duryodhana's young, impressionable mind, yet you did not bother to snatch the young prince away from his uncle's evil influence. Instead, you were a passive witness even when little Bhima was poisoned by Shakuni. Nor did you protest when the Pandavas and Kunti were duped into staying in the lac palace, which was eventually gutted in an attempt to kill the six of them. Again, you were the silent spectator as the kingdom was divided unwisely between the cousins. It was in your regal presence that a hideous crime like the gross cheating at the dice game was played out. You watched the disrobing of your granddaughter-in-law, Draupadi, by your great-grandsons, yet did nothing—how low could you allow your descendants to stoop, grand sire?'

Uruvi went on, trying to provoke the old man with her caustic words. 'And how could you see what was happening and not say a single word of anger, of protest? You are the head of the family—who would dare disobey you? Even now, at this moment, do you have it in you to stop the war between the cousins? Can you not stop the devastation that is going to happen?' she cried in frustration. 'For all your noble claims of wisdom and righteousness, you do not have the conviction to stand for the Pandavas. Instead, you side with the depraved Kauravas in the name of family loyalty. And yet you assert that dharma demands that you shall not kill any Pandava. By personally degrading Karna, you divest your own army of its best warrior. What dharma, grand sire, is this that prevents you from fighting against vice?'

Uruvi stopped abruptly; her torrent of words dried up. Bhishma Pitamaha looked at her thoughtfully, impervious to the contempt in each word she had flung at him.

He had listened with an expressionless face, but the glacial austerity on his face had melted. His voice held a rasping finality in his tone as, at last, he spoke. 'I fear my own dharma has let me down,' he began stoically. 'Like Kripacharya and Dronacharya, I, too, am bound to the Kauravas by servitude, by loyalty. I cannot switch sides as I have to protect the Kuru throne as its loyal servant who has been brought up on the benevolence of the Kuru king. Loyalty to the clan is supreme,' he said slowly. 'I have watched the dynasty crumble as young heirs like Prince Chitragandha, King Vichitravirya and King Pandu died premature deaths. I have seen queens like Satyavati, Ambika and Ambalika retire to the forests to escape the pain of watching their race die. It is my fate and my misfortune that I am alive today to see my dear ones eventually kill themselves in a mindless carnage.'

'And yet your dharma does not tell you to stop this carnage? How can you support those who are in the wrong?' Uruvi asked swiftly. 'You are Bhishma, which means "he of the terrible oath". And you are proving that your oath *is* terrible—it is your oath of lifelong celibacy and of devotion and loyalty to the king of Hastinapur, whoever he may be, even Duryodhana! How can you claim your oath is your dharma? Isn't dharma about achieving salvation by facing the world, and being accountable for every action? Isn't dharma about doing right and being right? Righteousness should rise above friends and relatives; it should not weaken because of love and affection. It has to be fair and, above all, moral. How moral is it to side with the Kauravas knowing they have wronged the Pandavas? How moral was it to be silent when Draupadi was stripped in public? And how moral is it to spurn Karna because he is a sutaputra and stop him from fighting with the Kauravas when they need him the most?'

Uruvi's temper flared again. 'How can you call Karna a sutaputra when the Pandavas are not the sons of King Pandu in the first place? They are Kunti's and Madri's sons from four different gods, not King Pandu's! They have no Kuru blood in them at all! Or is it that you are trying to protect your favourite, Arjuna, because you are scared that Karna will kill him?' she taunted. 'Does your love for Arjuna make you so weak that you deprive another person of his rights, his self-respect?'

'Silence!' roared the patriarch, his face red with fury, his eyes blazing. "I have heard enough of your nonsense! What you are uttering is blasphemy! I am trying to be fair to both sides...they and Karna are all my great-grandnephews after all!'

There was a stunned silence. Uruvi gave a triumphant smile and Bhishma Pitamaha knew he had been tricked into blurting out the truth buried deep over the years. Uruvi looked up at him with renewed respect. 'Oh, sir, you are trying to protect your great-grandnephews from certain death, isn't it? But your pretence and your feigned anger cannot save Karna any more!' she said sadly. 'If you knew all along that Karna, too, was your great-grandnephew like Arjuna and Duryodhana, why did you not give him his due right as the oldest Kuru prince? Why, oh, why, did you again keep silent and when the grossest injustice was done to him? He was a prince, but your silence let him be cursed as a low-caste orphan! You recognized Karna as your great-grandnephew at the archery contest at Hastinapur years ago, but you did not announce his true credentials—that he was a royal-born man. That he was the eldest Pandava, the eldest Kuru grandson, fit to be the scion of your royal family. If you had publicly declared that, we would not be facing the worst moments of our lives. Instead, you allowed Bhima to mock him as a sutaputra, forcing Karna to take the hand of Duryodhana in everlasting friendship. Now you talk about avoiding a confrontation between Karna and Arjuna when you had the power to do so from the very beginning.'

'How could I declare the golden boy Karna was actually the eldest Pandava? For that, I would have to cast an aspersion on my daughter-in-law, Kunti,' he said helplessly. 'Yes, I knew about Karna's true identity through Rishi Vyasa. So did Guru Parshurama and Krishna. All of us kept silent because it was up to the mother of the child to own up to the truth. We have no right to do so. It was her prerogative. Not mine. Nor anyone else's.'

Again, the onus fell on one person. Kunti. A mother who would rather watch her child die than tell the world that she had an illegitimate child.

'All of you knew the truth but stayed quiet!' she said helplessly. 'I know it now, too, so who can stop *me* from telling everyone who Karna really is! If Duryodhana and Yudhishthira realize that Karna is the true Kuru heir, it would avoid the confrontation, wouldn't it?' she asked in desperation. 'That would stop the war, wouldn't it?' she asked piteously.

Bhishma Pitamaha looked at her tenderly, the deep sorrow still in his piercing eyes. 'But you well know you can't say it yourself either! Karna has extracted a promise from you too, hasn't he?' he patted her drooping head. 'Do you think I want this war to happen? It is ripping my soul apart! Have I lived so long that I have to witness such a gory end of my own family? Two sides of my family are thirsting for each other's blood, and I can only watch them tear each other to shreds. I have to support one side because of my unswerving loyalty to the throne, but eventually, the one who sits on this throne will have his hands, his soul covered with the blood of thousands of innocents!'

'Then again I beg you, why don't you avert this tragedy?' she said wretchedly. 'Or, at least tell me a way out.'

'It is the end, dear. The war is inevitable,' the old man declared, disheartened. 'But I promise you, dear child, I shall save Karna till my last breath! I will not allow him to fight on the battlefield while I am battling the Pandavas. I shall not allow him to shoot an arrow nor will an arrow be directed towards him. But before my death, there is one person to whom I shall reveal the true identity of Karna—to Duryodhana. I owe it to him. He must realize the supreme sacrifice Karna has made for him—a sacrifice one would not make even for his own brother. I want him to appreciate the greatness of Karna.'

As the old man articulated his promise to her, Uruvi's anger gave way to compassion. The patriarch gave her a tired smile. 'You always believed I was unfair to Karna; I was harsh to him because he had so many good qualities that I feared he would become vain. He did not. I love him the most, but it is my misfortune that I never could show my affection and respect for my favourite great-grandnephew. Karna is that unfortunate young man whom I could not claim as my own, the best of them all. Though I was a disciple of Guru Parshurama, I have to admit that it is Karna who has been his best pupil, his shishya. He is the greatest warrior and archer and no one can excel him except Krishna. He is gifted, generous, righteous and brave, but doomed because of his loyalty to Duryodhana. Karna knew that this would lead to his eventual downfall as he was assisting evil against good. And that is what troubled me so much. I could not bear it and probably I was harsher to Karna than I meant to be.'

'And you are being harsher—or kinder—to him now, in your last attempt to save him?' Uruvi's voice trembled. 'This is your last attempt to save him! I guessed as much, and that is why I came to you today. But please tell me what I should do. Am I to sit quietly, knowing the truth, and watch silently as my husband gets killed in this senseless war? No! I cannot do it!' she sank to her knees, and pressing her forehead on her two clenched fists, burst into passionate weeping. The tears, which she had reined in so long, overflowed and she sobbed broken-heartedly.

'Cry, child, cry, let the tears flow...' he stroked her hair gently.

'Because soon they will dry up. There will be worse to see—and you won't be able to cry any more. My eyes are waterless now and so will yours turn dry. This was the day I wanted to protect you from, dear. And that is why I did not want you to marry Karna. Because I wanted to spare you this grief that all of us are cursed to suffer.'

'Oh, the war, the war!' he sighed dejectedly. 'I know the Pandavas don't desire it. But what do you expect the Pandavas to do, Uruvi? Take the injustice done to them silently? They have no option but to retaliate, child. That leaves Duryodhana. He wants the war because he foolishly thinks he'll win it, using Karna, Dronacharya and me. But all the three of us realize that is not how it is. We shall lose, not because we are weak, but because we are not on the side of the right, of the fair, of the good. We are fighting the war for all the wrong reasons—and the three of us know that. Even though Karna is Duryodhana's closest friend and strongest ally, he discerns the right from the wrong—but he is as helpless as we are. All I can do is try to save him! I vow to you, my dear, I shall fight for Karna's life until my last breath.'

'I know you will,' she gave him a small, watery smile through her tears. 'But, grand sire, if I tell Duryodhana about the true identity of Karna, won't he step back? I know he will. The only person he loves dearly is Karna, and for him, he will even abdicate his throne,' she said with a reassurance she was far from feeling.

'Yes, for Karna, Duryodhana probably would,' agreed Bhishma Pitamaha thoughtfully. 'But his grouse, my dear, is not against any individual. It is against the Pandavas, who he believes have no right over the throne. If you disclose the truth to Duryodhana, Karna will cease to be his friend and become the eldest Pandava and, therefore, his sworn enemy instead. Is Duryodhana's love for his friend so large-hearted that he can accept him as the eldest Pandava and the rightful Kuru heir? I wonder about that! If not, there will still be a war, but the camps will be different. It would be Karna on the side of the Pandavas against Duryodhana, but if I know Karna well, he would rather die for his friend, fight evil against good than ever betray him.

He will never fight against Duryodhana. Either way, Uruvi, Karna is destined to die on the battlefield—you cannot avert it, however much you hope and try to!' he heaved a deep sigh. 'Unless, of course, he decides to convince the Pandavas not to fight...'

'But the Pandavas would only listen to Karna if they learn about his true identity. Only then will they accept him as their older brother,' she said with a sinking heart. 'Till then, he is the despicable sutaputra who humiliated Draupadi in the Raj Sabha. Neither they nor Draupadi have forgotten the outrage. No, grand sire, they will obey Karna only if they know his real identity, which neither of us can reveal to anyone.'

'Yes, and there is only one person who has the right to reveal this truth. It is Kunti. It is her secret. And only she can disclose it. Not you, Uruvi. Nor me. Nor Krishna.'

Uruvi burst out, 'But she doesn't have the courage to tell the truth! She is more concerned about protecting her own image than the life of her eldest, unwanted son!'

'Uruvi!' Bhishma Pitamaha looked at her sternly, shaking his head at her effrontery.

'Don't be shocked by what I said—but *you* should have convinced her to do so!' she said bitterly. 'I cannot speak to her about this—I would grovel at her feet to beg for my husband's life, but Karna has forbidden me to and I am bound by my promise not to. And yet, I would break it if I were sure that she would agree to tell the world her terrible secret. Sadly, I know that she would never! Never!'

'Karna made you promise for he did not want you to take any futile step. That was his way of telling you to accept reality, because he can forsee his death,' the patriarch answered bleakly. 'Karna doesn't want anyone to know the reality of his birth, especially Duryodhana and Yudhisthira, simply because it is too late now...'

Too late now! The finality of those words were to ring through the coming, horrifying days but Uruvi could not bring herself to stop hoping...

21

Karna and Kunti

As Uruvi's love for her foster mother turned to hate, she wondered how her feelings could have changed so quickly. She recalled each moment she had spent with Kunti and wondered how the same woman who had loved her so tenderly could have deserted her own child. Kunti had always shown an enormous strength of mind and singleness of purpose—but both qualities appalled Uruvi now. It was not just anger that she felt, nor only horror and dismay, but sheer amazement. She could not believe that the soft-spoken, kindly woman she had grown up with could have been such a hard-hearted, unfeeling mother.

She now understood the meaning of Kunti's brilliant smile when she told her she wanted to marry Karna, why Kunti had cajoled her to return to Karna and why she had defended Karna when he had the audacity to call her daughter-in-law a whore. She even saw Kunti's affection for Vrishakethu as her way of loving her own son.

Seized with fury each time she thought of Kunti, she wanted to rush to ask her savagely for an explanation she owed so many people, most of all, her unwanted son. But more than a mere explanation, Uruvi wanted to plead with Kunti to announce the truth of Karna's birth to the Pandavas and save thousands of people from impending death. Kunti was her last route to rescue Karna from his doom—but she knew she had to keep her promise to Karna never to talk to Kunti about him.

Another shock awaited her. One evening, she was surprised to see a visitor at the camp where she tended to the sick and injured. The woman was sheathed in white silk, her head covered with the pallu of her sari. Was she a patient?

'What can I do for you? Are you unwell?' she asked hesitantly.

The figure remained silent, pulling the veil closer over her head. Clearly, she was trying to hide her identity.

'We can go inside,' she suggested, hoping the woman would speak.

Once inside the confines of a tent, the woman quietly removed her veil to reveal a face Uruvi had recently come to distrust. It was Kunti.

The old queen was, as always, calm and self-assured. Her face wore her usual serene composure and her pale grey eyes were unflustered. There was no sign of guilt or repentance on her face. She said sadly, 'You don't come to meet me any more! I haven't seen Vrishakethu for days...'

Her equanimity incensed Uruvi, who replied coldly, 'I am sure you have not come here to tell me this. You could have always sent me a message through your servants. So what is it you want to see me about?' Uruvi asked edgily, her eyes hard and steady. Kunti looked puzzled at the unfriendliness in her eyes and the ice in her voice, but she took a deep breath as if trying to gather courage.

'I met Karna today,' said the Pandavas' mother.

Uruvi was startled, a small knot of apprehension tightening in her heart. 'And what did you want from him?' Uruvi questioned through stiff lips, recalling, with great difficulty, Karna's promise that she was not to broach the topic of his birth to Kunti.

'I went to Karna to tell him the secret of his birth,' Kunti answered after an anguished pause.

For all her fury, Uruvi was not prepared for this disclosure. She broke into a cold sweat, her coiled anger snaking out stealthily.

'And what did you tell him?' she heard herself say. Her voice was as hard as her eyes.

Kunti was silent for a minute or two. 'I went to him because only he can stop the war from breaking out,' the Kuru queen said.

'Pray, how is that?'

'Because Karna is the real strength of Duryodhana. And Karna is the only person who Duryodhana will ever listen to,' she said. 'This war has to be stopped and only Karna can do that! Fraught with worry and overcome with anxiety, I finally decided to meet him in private. I had to talk to him! I met him as soon as he finished his noon prayers to the sun.'

'So, you had obviously gone at the right time when he grants any request that is asked of him,' Uruvi said sardonically. 'Karna is famous for his generosity. A few days back, Lord Indra, disguised as a brahmin, asked him for his kavach and kundals, and my husband, in spite of seeing through the masquerade, granted him his wish ever so willingly. What did you ask for? He must have readily agreed to give it…as he always does.'

Her sarcasm went unnoticed; the older queen was too perturbed. She continued, 'I said to him, "I am your mother. You are my first-born child,"' Kunti paused, hoping to get a response from the younger woman. But Uruvi stood still like a statue. 'I told him that the five Pandavas were his brothers but they were born much later.'

Uruvi kept quiet, trying to contain her anger. This woman was now disclosing the truth she had hidden from the world and her son for only one reason—to save her other five sons. She did not want war as she was afraid Karna would vanquish and even kill them. Yet, she would not reveal to the world that Karna was her first-born child— merely to preserve her own reputation. She would rather watch her son battle it out with the Pandavas, a mother so selfish that she had let her son suffer ignominy rather than tarnish her image as the noble queen of King Pandu.

Uruvi had never felt disgust as pure and undiluted as she did now. She looked at the woman intently, a strange gleam in her eyes.

Kunti said, 'I was afraid of his reaction, but Karna looked so happy to see me. He bowed before me and said, "I have waited for so long for this moment. What is it that you wish from me? Your wish is my command."'

'And?' Uruvi could not stop herself, her eyes glistening with an emotion Kunti could not decipher.

'I begged him to make peace with his brothers and rule the kingdom instead. I told him that as the eldest brother he will be crowned the King of Hastinapur.'

Uruvi was stunned, loathing each word the older lady was saying.

'But Karna did not agree!' Kunti cried. 'I had not expected him to refuse!' she said agitatedly. 'I pleaded with him. I begged him. I told him that as an unwed mother I could never claim him as my son. But if only he could give me one chance to redeem that wrong, I would be relieved of the guilt which has torn me all these years. All he did was look at me with his sad eyes and said, "I have always hated that mother who left me. Now I am filled with only love and compassion, but even that cannot allow me to grant you your wish. I cannot make peace with your sons. Their enemy is my closest, dearest friend whom I cannot betray. I love him too much. I would die for him rather than be a traitor."'

Uruvi stood still, as if frozen, allowing the queen mother to do all the talking. She neither wanted to interrupt her nor prompt her to go on lest her simmering rage burst out as hot as lava.

Uruvi had never seen her foster mother so distressed, allowing her calm composure to crack. The old lady was moved by an extraordinary emotion and tears ran down her raddled cheeks. 'Here I was, standing before my son and imploring him to come back to me. I wanted my son back and I was desperate with anxiety that this war would mean the loss of my sons. My only hope was Karna, who has the power to stop this war. I entreated him over and over again, and with folded hands I asked for his forgiveness. I promised him that he could have whatever he had been deprived of—his name, his right place in the family, the kingdom, and even Draupadi as his queen! Uruvi, please don't get angry, but I was ready to do anything at that moment…I just wanted him to stop the war!'

Uruvi flinched, but pressed her lips tight, restraining herself from saying a word.

'I know you will hate what I did, but I had to!' the old queen was pleading with her too. 'I had to convince Karna in some way, in any way! But even while hearing my frantic words, he seemed determined. He calmly declined again, so I paused awhile, thinking of an alternative. Then I asked him to give me two promises instead—I asked him not to kill Arjuna in battle and not to use any divine arrow or weapon more than once. Karna replied, "I shall spare all your sons, except Arjuna. I have sworn to kill him, and either I shall get him first or he will slay me. Either way, you shall still be the mother of five sons." Saying that, he touched my feet and left.'

There was a long silence between the two women; a silence filled with shattered hopes and intense emotion. Uruvi broke the silence. 'So why have you come to me now? Why are you telling me this?' she asked, her voice dangerously soft. 'If you think what you said has come as a nasty shock, it has not. I know about it. So does Karna.'

Uruvi heard the Pandava mother gasp sharply. 'Krishna had already informed Karna, and like you, asked him to switch sides,' Uruvi interposed quietly, her voice toneless.

She saw that Kunti wore an expression of complete surprise.

'But you went one step further!' Uruvi said icily. 'In other words, you asked Karna to follow a course of action that spells certain death for him. And Karna must have promised this too, knowing that fulfilling your wishes was self-destructive. By not killing Arjuna, he will be killed. And that is what you wish for—that he should die rather than your precious Arjuna!' she said viciously.

Kunti recoiled, looking as if Uruvi had struck her.

'And by asking Karna not to use a divine weapon twice ensures that you cripple him completely!' she added. 'You went to Karna to stop the war, but ironically, there is only one person who can avert it now—and that's you!' Uruvi jabbed a finger at her, pointing at her accusingly.

'If you reveal your secret to the Pandavas and everyone else, that Karna is your elder son, this conflict will stop. You have the power to end it, but you won't. You would rather cherish your wretched image and your five Pandavas! When I got to know that you were his mother, I wanted to rush to you and beg you to proclaim his true identity and stop the war, to spare his life. You have the power to do that. And I was ready to beg you. But you asked your son for his own death! You are ready to sacrifice your oldest son but you will not unseal your lips!'

Uruvi could not rein in her loathing. 'You got what you wanted!' she spat out venomously. 'You know he will not kill Arjuna, or any of your sons. You have it all. You are the winner who gave away nothing but got everything. You robbed him of his last weapon, of the right over his own life. And yet you want more. After taking everything from us, why have you come to me?' she cried in utter despair.

'To beg you to make him see reason…' Kunti implored. 'I don't want to lose him, Uruvi. He is my son too.'

Uruvi gave a short, jeering laugh. 'He was always your biological son, but was never really yours for you to "lose" him. So why now, dear mother?' her voice dripped venom. 'You came to him not to get your lost son back; you went to him to strip him of his last defence. By telling him the truth about his birth, you have effectively broken him from within. You know the intense rivalry between the two—and you were frightened of it—scared that Karna might kill Arjuna in battle! And that's why you hurried over to Karna to tell him your sob story. You went there to save Arjuna's life. Not Karna's. Because now, after what you have revealed to him, Karna will not be able to point a single arrow at any of your sons as they are his own brothers.'

Kunti felt as if she was facing a stranger, a fierce adversary who was going all out to attack her.

'Your intention was very clear. Duryodhana is your sons' enemy and, somehow, he had to be deprived of his trump card—Karna, his staunchest ally,' Uruvi uttered with reinforced fury. 'By revealing the truth to him at that exact hour, you saw to it that Karna was weakened irreparably. He is no longer a force to reckon with as you have extracted unfair promises from him. He will not kill Arjuna or your other sons. If you so desperately wanted peace, why haven't you told your sons the same story? Have you told them that Karna is their older brother? You know well enough that if Arjuna or any of the Pandavas ever discover the true identity of Karna, they would not direct a single arrow against him. You wouldn't dare to tell them, just like you have not had the decency to say so for so many years!'

'How can I tell the world that Karna is my son, Uruvi?' exclaimed Kunti. 'And even if I had, would anyone have listened?'

Uruvi was amazed at the older woman's simple reasoning. 'Did you even try? What kind of a mother are you?' she asked derisively, her face showing her open scorn. 'If you could walk into the court of Hastinapur and announce the five Pandavas as the sons of celestial gods, what stopped you from mentioning your oldest son? The moment you threw him into the river, you forgot about him as one would get rid of garbage! Did you bother to check if he was dead or alive? How could you allow your son to suffer so many years of ignominy while you preened yourself as the queen mother? You preferred to keep it a secret because it served your interests. Even now you chose to disclose the truth only because it helps you. Why don't you announce the truth to your sons? The war you dread will come to an immediate halt. Duryodhana may not want Yudhishthira to have the crown, but he would be only too happy to give Indraprastha to Karna. I am sure that like Yudhishthira, Duryodhana would voluntarily surrender his kinghood to the one person he loves most—Karna. Do you have the courage to do it?'

Kunti flushed deeply as Uruvi went on. 'No, dear queen, you have never loved nor accepted Karna as your son. But today, you have the nerve to go to him and beg for the lives of your other sons!' she said scathingly, her contempt burning in each word she uttered. 'By disclosing that you are his mother, you have so cleverly used the fact of motherhood as a political weapon to guarantee a win for your Pandava sons. You forsook Karna even today just like you did when he was born. He remains rejected even now—as he was at birth. You made him a pariah within his own family. He is today hated by his brothers only because of you! And that's why his death in this war is a foregone conclusion. Because while Karna knows that he is facing his blood brothers whom he has promised not to harm, thanks to your perfectly timed revelation, the Pandavas are thirsting to kill the sutaputra they have detested all their lives.'

Uruvi was furious, her eyes blazing. She was the spirited princess Kunti had always known her as, but this time her lashing words were directed at her. 'Such was your enormous will that though you fainted at seeing your son for the first time at the archery contest at Hastinapur, you calmly watched him being insulted by his younger brothers, Bhima and Arjuna. How could you? What are you made of? You remained silent as Karna was being publicly humiliated about his parentage. I was right next to you, but you did not give the slightest hint that the young boy who looked like a god and fought like a noble warrior was your son.'

'Did I have an alternative?' Kunti asked evenly. 'What was I to do? Yes, by his kavach and kundals, I recognized my long-lost son, but could I shout with joy and pride? Could I tell the world that he was the son I bore before my marriage to King Pandu?'

Uruvi broke into a loud, jeering laugh. 'Why not? From when has unwed motherhood been such a sin in our society?' she sneered. 'Your family has done it before—wasn't Rishi Vyasa Queen Mother Satyavati's illicit son before she married King Shantanu? Not just that, the son was given full royal respect. When her stepson Bhishma refused Satyavati's request that he should practise niyoga with Vichitravirya's widows, Ambika and Ambalika, it was Rishi Vyasa who finally performed niyoga on his widowed sisters-in-law and produced Dhritrashtra and Pandu and Vidura as heirs to the dynasty. Was that less scandalous than you announcing Karna as your son and the worthy heir of the Kuru kingdom?'

Uruvi's scornful words did not stop. 'In our society, we have a term for children who are born to a woman before her marriage—kaneena. Such incidents are not uncommon as you well know. Why even the Dharmashastras say that such children belonged to the woman's husband when she married later. Even if you had dared to tell King Pandu, who was begging you for children anyway, he would have accepted Karna. Yet, you preferred to throw your baby into the flowing river, leaving him to an unkind fate. Were you ever humiliated because of the way you conceived the Pandavas?' she asked scathingly. 'No. You were not. You were always accorded a royal welcome and blessed as a queen. Your niyoga was never considered a moral lapse. Had you revealed who the father of the child was— Lord Surya—in your list of dharma, Vayu and Indra as the Pandavas' fathers, Karna too, would have commanded the respect your other sons were given. Chances are that this son would have not only been socially accepted, but held in awe as he was born with divine signs on his body. You could have publicly acknowledged him, not only without shame, but with immense pride at the archery contest. This son of the sun god had not just the godly kavach and kundals, he had already proved he was equal, and superior, to the best warrior of his day—your other son, Arjuna. You had the chance to accept him socially. You did not. What were you scared of? That your image would be tarnished? It would not have been. Rishi Vyasa did not suffer any severe condemnation nor did his unwed mother. Both were universally respected and did not suffer any social rejection. But Karna did. And for all these years. Why? Because he did not know who his mother was! Because you did not have the courage to own up!'

Kunti cowered under Uruvi's verbal attack and two red spots rose suddenly to her cheeks. 'Uruvi, you hate me today for what I did, but I had no choice, believe me,' she appealed to her. 'I have suffered all these years, looking at him but never being able to call him my own, to hug him, to be with him. When you told me you loved him and were bent on marrying him, I think that was the happiest, most relieved moment of my life. If not me, he could have you. You would give him all that I could not. And through you, Uruvi, I experienced the joy of being near Karna! Uruvi, please don't hate me so...!'

Kunti was dry-eyed as she gazed numbly at the girl whom she had reared so tenderly. There was no love, no softness in Uruvi now. The anger she was unleashing showed that she despised her foster mother as fiercely as she loved her husband. Kunti realized that the woman seething in front of her was no longer the daughter she loved. She was the wife of her son whom she had never recognized as her own. And if not the son, the wife now demanded an explanation. Uruvi wanted to punish Kunti as harshly as she had wronged them; and the brutal truth was her only weapon to crush her.

Uruvi moved nearer to Kunti; the hunter closing in on the hunted. 'You erased him from your life so smoothly—never turning back nor looking forward to search for him,' she said. 'He could never be a part of your life, your love. You never wanted him! You gave him nothing, but yet you have made demands of him. You abandoned him not once, but repeatedly. Like you did at his birth, at the archery arena, at my wedding, at the Rajasuya ceremony, at Vrishakethu's naming ceremony—in fact, each time you met him! You could have taken any of these occasions to accept him but each time you turned your face away. A single word of your acknowledgement would have overturned the entire situation and Karna would have been the son and heir of the Kurus. Had you spoken out then, perhaps this war could have been avoided. But you favoured silence to confession. You favoured your honour for his dishonour, you favoured your five sons over him, you wanted their life and his death!' she said in a choking voice. 'All your life you have denied him a dignified life, now you are denying him even a dignified death! And you call yourself a mother? You are heartless!' she said bitingly. 'You have not given him anything but are still exacting every drop of blood, dignity and life from him. You are even more cowardly and shameless than you were that day at the arena—by begging him to spare your other sons' lives, you are making him sign his own death warrant. You are a murderess!'

Kunti's face went ashen but Uruvi was beside herself with rage. She leaned towards the older woman, forcing her to look at her. 'And that is what Karna's promise to you means, isn't it?' she breathed harshly. 'His death! You would rather watch him die than any of your other sons. And you have the effrontery to talk of your great love for him! It is a sham. Your love is as fake as you are! You are the one who pushed him towards Duryodhana and his evil ways. You are the one who, by rejecting him constantly, have hurt him always, wounding his very being. Why did he join Duryodhana and the Kauravas? Because of you! By deserting him, you forced him to turn to them. You made Karna become the heart and soul of the Kauravas—and now you want him to join you and your sons who have never even been civil to him? Karna yearned for social recognition—and only you could have given it to him. But you lied, and Karna suffered in misery all his life. You wanted to sacrifice your own son.'

Kunti gave a soft moan of horror and covered her face with her hands. Uruvi prised open her fingers and held the older woman by her wrist. 'I loathe you, not just because you are an uncaring mother but a shrewd woman who even now sees her own interests first. You extracted another promise from Karna, did you not, you heartless woman?' she demanded, her eyes shining with pure hate. 'You made him promise you that he would not use any divine arrow or weapon more than once, fully knowing that Karna had the mighty Nag astra, but which is now useless as he cannot make use of it more than once. You are cunning!' she spat virulently. 'Look at me, face the truth. That is what Karna's promise to you means, isn't it? Not just Karna's death, but worse, his ultimate disgrace—as a traitor! You are forcing Karna to betray Duryodhana, the man he trusts and loves most. Duryodhana has stood by Karna all his life and you are now asking your son to turn against him—for what? For honour, for truth, or for your sons who have run him down in the vilest of ways? By taking from Karna the promise not to kill any of the Pandavas, you are forcing your son, who has always stood by Duryodhana in his best and worst moments, to act against him. Karna, despite his supposed "low birth", has been known not just as a formidable warrior but as the epitome of loyalty, honour and gratitude. You want him to be reduced to a cheap, low ingrate! You want Karna to betray his friend, to desert him in his darkest hour of need. You, for your self-serving purpose, will make him stoop to the lowest—even in his death!'

Kunti shrank back in the face of Uruvi's rage. 'But that is what you actually are. A cold-blooded woman. Not a mother,' Uruvi enunciated each word with a savage brutality. 'You were the mother who tricked her sons to marry one woman. And you are that mother-in-law who allowed her daughter-in-law to be labelled a whore, while you maintained your spotless reputation. Why, even in this hour, you are ready to use your daughter-in-law as his ultimate temptation. You are ready to corrupt anyone for your goal.'

'Stop it, Uruvi!' Kunti stood staring at her with wide, startled eyes, her face creased in pain. Kunti's plea went unheard and Uruvi went on.

'You have got people killed for your betterment,' Uruvi hissed the words venomously as she watched the older woman hunch her shoulders as though struck by blows. 'It was your implacable will which got the Nishada woman and her five sons drunk in the palace of lac so that no evidence remained of the Pandavas' escape from the gutted palace except for the six dead, charred bodies of the unfortunate woman and her five sons. You murdered them ruthlessly to protect your sons and yourself. Now you are doing the same with Karna. Nothing and no one must touch even a hair of your precious sons and their throne. Not even your eldest son!'

Kunti was standing bolt upright with her hands to her heart. 'Uruvi, do you think that I never pined for Karna? I have suffered so much!'

'Never!' Uruvi retorted violently. 'Never as much as you made him suffer. And I cannot ever forgive you for that. Go away, go away with your son's death on your head and my misery on your conscience—if you have any! You are no mother of mine. Nor his!'

Kunti let out a soft whimper, the last cry of an animal wounded to death and hid her face with her hands. Staggering like a dying woman, she left the tent, unable to bear more.

In the midst of her confrontation, Uruvi found clarity in her mind, knowing she had forced Kunti to face the motives behind her actions. She stared after Kunti, her eyes gleaming with triumph, bright with unforgiving, unshed tears.

22

The Eighteen-day War

The last few days before the war passed slowly. The entire household at the Anga palace was uneasy, the dark future looming ahead threateningly. Karna, Vrushali, Shona, Radha, Adhiratha and the sons of Karna, except Vrishakethu, were like victims being prepared for the savage rites of a sacrifice. Her terror numbed Uruvi. She could not bear to let Karna out of her sight; her parched, dry eyes drank in the sight of him thirstily. It was only in the rare moments when he was with her that her courage came back and she clung to those moments to take her through the dark days. She had ceased to cry; the tears had long dried up. To shake off the vague terrors that assailed her, she prayed and worked fervently, spending longer hours at the rehabilitation camps. It was an escape from her ordeal, from her anguish. The endless days, one after another, dragged out their weary hours.

The war was preordained, born out of hatred and fated to wreak unimaginable tragedy. The two sides of the warring cousins summoned vast armies and lined up at Kurukshetra for the battle that was to plunge everyone into endless sorrow. The kingdoms of Dwarka, Kasi, Magadha, Matsya, Chedi, Pandya, Yadus and Kamboja allied with the Pandavas. The allies of the Kauravas were in larger numbers—besides, of course, Anga, the kings of Pragjyotisha, Kekaya, Sindhudesa, Mahishmati, Madra and Avanti in Madhyadesa joined the Kauravas, while the Kambojas, Gandharas, Bahlikas, Yavanas, Sakas and Tusharas also backed them. The army of the Kauravas was imposing with eleven divisions called Akshouhinis, while the Pandavas were severely outnumbered with a mere seven.

One Akshouhini comprised 21,870 chariots with their riders, the same number of elephants and their riders, with 65,610 horses and horsemen and a staggering 1,09,350 foot soldiers. Each Akshouhini was under a general, and all of them under a commander-in-chief— Dhrishtadyumna of the Pandava army and Bhishma Pitamaha of the Kauravas. The mere sight of four million soldiers facing each other on the battlefield at Kurukshetra struck terror in the people of the Kuru kingdom who waited fearfully for the war to begin.

On the first day of the Kurukshetra war, Dushasana led the Kaurava army and Bhima the Pandava side. The bugle signalling the beginning of the battle ripped the air with its terrible finality. Against the clamour of rumbling trumpets and reverberating conches, the horses neighed and the elephants trumpeted impatiently, eagerly waiting for the war to begin its deathly carnage.

Death bared its fangs as never before, stinging each family and soldier with its venom. Thousands were butchered that day and in the next seventeen horrifying days. Strangers killed strangers, brothers slaughtered brothers, cousins murdered cousins, uncles killed nephews and nephews massacred uncles. The learned gurus and the shishyas—the teachers and the pupils—learnt bloody lessons of murder and mayhem. The skies were torn with the wails of mothers, daughters, sisters, wives and orphans. Prowling jackals and watchful vultures ripped apart the slain soldiers and dead animals.

On the very first day came a terrible blow. It was the death of Shona—at the hands of Nakul. Radha was almost out of her mind with grief. Seeing her plight, Uruvi wondered how Radha, Vrushali and herself would be able to bear the news of Karna's death one day.

Karna was inconsolable, ridden with guilt, and reproached himself bitterly for being the cause of his younger brother's death. 'If it were not for me, he would not have been fighting a war—he would be safe, leading the life of a charioteer.'

'Even if he were a charioteer, he would have gone to war. He died a hero's death!' Uruvi said gently, trying to console him. Karna, in deep and bitter reflection, buried his face in his hands, in hopeless surrender.

'How much more are we to suffer?' he sighed in a hoarse whisper, hot tears trickling steadily down his weary face.

Each day brought worse tragedies. The death of the gentle Vikarna made even the Pandavas sad. Bhima was said to have wept uninhibitedly, moments before he killed his favourite cousin. 'I can never forgive myself!' he cried in mixed pain and bitterness.

On the tenth day of the war, the unthinkable happened. The mighty, invincible Bhishma Pitamaha was felled by an arrow from his great-grandnephew, Arjuna. Everyone on the battlefield stood shocked, not believing that the man who had been blessed with the boon to choose the time of his death could not escape a mortal's fate.

As the grand sire had promised, he did not hurt either the Kauravas or the Pandavas. Duryodhana had often accused the old man of being biased, berating him for not actually fighting for the Kauravas after all. 'But he was the strongest barrier protecting the Kaurava army from impending defeat,' said a crestfallen Karna, recounting to Uruvi what had occurred the previous night.

The war was stuck in a stalemate with both the sides suffering equal losses. The tenth day was a threshold—it was a do or die moment and the grand sire took it upon himself to force a decisive battle. 'I shall fight like a lion, and this time, either I will kill Arjuna or I will make Krishna break his promise not to wield any weapons himself during the war,' he promised Duryodhana, with Karna silently witnessing every word of that vow.

That day, there was a fierce battle between Bhishma and Arjuna. Although Arjuna was formidable, he was helpless under the frenzied attack of his grand sire. Bhishma Pitamaha viciously shot arrows which smashed Arjuna's armour and broke his Gandiva bow. Arjuna was simply powerless before the wrath of the old veteran.

'As Bhishma Pitamaha was dangerously close to killing Arjuna with his deluge of arrows, Krishna threw down the reins of his chariot and jumped onto the battlefield. He lifted a chariot wheel and charged towards Bhishma Pitamaha, breaking his promise that he would not pick up a weapon in this war,' recounted Karna, his voice toneless. 'Arjuna finally managed to convince Lord Krishna to stop, but he explained that to protect his protégé, he would readily break his own promise. Krishna returned to the chariot only when Arjuna vowed to redouble his determination and effort in the fight.'

Uruvi listened in horror as Karna continued. 'Knowing that the grand sire was vulnerable only against a woman, Krishna, on the tenth day of battle, brought in Shikhandi, Draupadi's transvestite brother, as Arjuna's charioteer,' he said. 'Lord Krishna knew that the patriarch, if faced by a woman in battle, would cease to fight and not lift weapons against her. And the Pandavas agreed to this ploy to vanquish the grand sire. Using Shikhandi as his armour, Arjuna shot a slew of arrows at Bhishma Pitamaha, piercing his entire body, and finally, the grand sire gave up the fight.'

'But that's unfair!' cried Uruvi, aghast at the treachery of the Pandavas. 'I thought the Pandavas were upright warriors!'

Then she recalled the plethora of unfair means that had been shamelessly used before the war. The feud of the cousins, the burning of the lac palace to murder the Pandavas and Kunti, the unfair division of the kingdom, the rigged game of dice, the shaming of Draupadi in the royal court, the exile, the deceitful way Karna was shorn of his kavach and kundals, the last desperate attempts by both Lord Krishna and Kunti to sway Karna against Duryodhana, and the vilest of all, revealing the terrible truth of his birth to Karna, thus stripping him of his last vestige of dignity. 'Why are we talking about morals and fairness?' she asked defeatedly. 'This war is, in itself, an unethical one.'

Bhishma Pitamaha lay in the bloodied battlefield, his entire body held above the ground by a bed of arrows. It was a sight that humbled even the gods who watched from the heavens, revering and blessing the dying warrior, who had given up the fight but not his last breath, waiting for the auspicious moment to give up his body.

Uruvi was invaded by another emotion. Mingled with her sorrow over the old patriarch's fall was the fear that his death would mean the end of Karna. He had promised her that he would save Karna until the last moment of his life, and by forbidding him to enter the battlefield, the grand sire had done his utmost to protect his great-grandnephew. Now, with the fall of the powerful Bhishma Pitamaha, the protective shield had vanished and Karna was vulnerable again. If Karna stepped onto the battlefield, it meant certain death for him, Uruvi realized with a heavy heart. From that hour onwards, Karna would be living on borrowed time.

The fall of Bhishma Pitamaha spelt the Kauravas' nemesis and for the first time, Karna joined their army in the battlefield. He announced his intention on that day, 'The grand sire, who possesses all the qualities of a good man and a great warrior—intelligence, prowess, honesty, self-restraint, humility and modesty—is now lying on a bed of arrows in the battlefield. Without his leadership, what is the use of so many Akshouhinis in the army? With the fall of Bhishma, Duryodhana has lost everything!' cried Karna. 'The fall of Bhishma Pitamaha occurred even while all of you were on the battlefield. He fell with a mighty crash, like a mountain would. But do not worry. I will save you and your forces. I shall attack Arjuna. I will vanquish the Pandavas and the entire Pandava forces, and ensure that Duryodhana is crowned as king. If I fail to do so, I will meet Bhishma Pitamaha in heaven. This is my promise,' announced Karna.

While his words relieved Duryodhana, Uruvi despaired at the finality of her husband's words. That evening, Karna told his worried wife, 'I need to meet Bhishma Pitamaha and beg for his forgiveness. With his blessings, I shall take part in the war from this day onwards.' He left her in the camp, where she tended to the wounded soldiers, some dying, many screaming in agony.

Hours later, she saw an inconsolable Karna returning to the tent. Only a sliver of the sun's ray pierced the purple darkness as another dawn was about to break. Karna's golden sunset eyes had darkened with trouble and anxiety, pain and bitterness. He stood tall, but no longer proud. His broad shoulders were slouched in a defeated droop. He looked utterly crushed.

'He, too, knew who I am,' Karna said, looking sadly at her. 'He blessed me as Kunti's son. He hoped that with his passing, the enmity between the cousins would end and that I would return to my Pandava family…oh, Uruvi, how much more do I have to suffer?' Karna sighed in bleak hopelessness. 'I told him that though I know that I am Kunti's son and not a sutaputra, I could not turn my back on Duryodhana. I had to be true to him and his friendship, to my own lineage and to my convictions. I would repay with my life for all my mistakes in word and deed.'

Uruvi touched Karna's hand soothingly. He continued, 'Bhishma Pitamaha looked infinitely sad but blessed me with these words: "O Karna! With your support and help alone is Duryodhana safe. You are considered his brother, but friendship is greater and deeper than any relationship by birth. You bear the entire burden of this Kuru dynasty. There is no difference between Duryodhana and yourself. You both are equal to me. Command the Kaurava forces and achieve victory! You are as dear to me as Arjuna and Duryodhana. In fact, you are dearer, as great injustice had been meted out to you. Don't ask for forgiveness from me—I ask for your forgiveness, child." Hearing those words from the grand old man, Uruvi, I died a thousand deaths! I have never felt happier, more pained, more ashamed! I was happy that he loved me and respected me as a warrior, but the pain was because it came so late…everything's too late now! Can even death release me from this misery?' he said hoarsely, grief etched on his face. 'And is this the same misery I shall bequeath to you and our son?'

He looked fixedly at her for a long, indeterminate moment, his glance searing through her soul, staring past her. Strong emotions crossed his face as he smiled sadly and walked away.

On the eleventh day, Karna entered the battlefield, but not as the commander-in-chief. He requested Duryodhana to choose Guru Dronacharya as the new chief to command the Kaurava army. Though reluctant, Duryodhana did not disagree with his friend. The focus of the Kaurava attack was now to capture Yudhishthira alive, so that they could win the war as early as possible. But with Arjuna fiercely protecting his older brother, this seemed too ambitious a strategy, as several unsuccessful attempts proved.

The twelfth day saw the beginning of doom. The placid, mild-mannered Lakshmana, the only son of Duryodhana, was killed by Abhimanyu. Uruvi recalled the honourable, honest prince, loved dearly by everyone. She remembered how each day the young prince, the unlikely son of a father like Duryodhana, would meet the people of Hastinapur and try to alleviate the suffering of the needy. He was more of a saint than a prince but destined to die the death of a brave warrior.

Bhanumati was numb with shock and Duryodhana was devastated. 'I shall give the Pandavas half of the kingdom now,' he wept, as he knelt near the motionless body of his young son. 'I did not want this gentle boy of mine to fight the war because, like you, Uruvi, he hated war and bloodshed. I did not want him to die—he was the heir to my throne! He was the only young survivor of the Kaurava family. Uruvi, remember how he, Bhanumati and you had begged me not to allow Krishna return empty-handed from the Hastinapur court when he had come to mediate between us and the Pandavas? Lakshmana had implored that we give the Pandavas at least two villages, but I did not listen to him or Bhanumati. Oh, now I would give them the kingdom if it could bring my boy back!' he cried heartbrokenly.

It was the love of a father in all its poignancy that spoke, but Uruvi wondered if Duryodhana really had any desire to stop the war and give away the kingdom. However, she conceded, in his time of grief he had at least owned up to his responsibility for waging the senseless war.

The Kauravas mourned the death of the young prince and vowed revenge on young Abhimanyu, clamouring for the killer's blood. But the brutality with which Arjuna and Subhadra's sixteen-year-old son was butchered shocked everyone. A new strategy was opted for on the thirteenth day. To distract Arjuna and get him away from Yudhishthira, who was to be captured alive, Guru Dronacharya and Duryodhana made the Samsaptakas' division, consisting of warriors from the kingdom of Trigarta, attack Arjuna fiercely, pushing him away from the main front. Meanwhile, the full Kaurava army concentrated on capturing Yudhishthira by rearranging the army in the chakravyuh pattern, a defensive formation in the shape of a lotus. The teenaged Abhimanyu was called for help as he was the only one who knew how to penetrate the labyrinth of the chakravyuh besides great warriors like Krishna, Arjuna, Karna, Balarama and Pradyumna, Krishna's son. Abhimanyu had dared to enter the chakravyuh at Yudhishthira's request, but he could not retreat and got stuck in the midst of a pack of bloodthirsty fighters.

Jayadrath, the King of Sindhu and the husband of the only Kaurava princess, Dushala, had cleverly cut off Abhimanyu's back-up assistance from Yudhishthira and his army by surrounding them at the entry point of the chakravyuh. Surrounded by six fearsome warriors—Guru Dronacharya, Kripacharya, Karna, Ashwatthama, the veteran Brihatbala and Kritvarma, the Bhoja king and cousin of Krishna—the young lad died fighting, sacrificing his life as he tried to protect the life of his uncle, Yudhishthira.

Kritvarma had been Abhimanyu's teacher, but could not forgive his pupil's one transgression. His son, Matrikavat, had been killed by Abhimanyu and the unforgiving father had finally exacted his revenge by joining in the gory killing of the Pandava heir.

Uruvi was filled with dismay. When she met Karna at the end of the day, she asked him sadly, 'How could you, as a decent human being, a noble warrior yourself, kill Abhimanyu in that merciless way?' Her heart cried out more in revulsion than in pain. 'He was but a child, a little older than our Vrishakethu. All you great warriors pounced on him like wild animals! I knew war was a killer, but does it turn men into such hideous fiends?'

Shame clouding his eyes, Karna bent his handsome head abjectly. 'I have no justifications, Uruvi. You are my conscience, but all I can say is that I followed my commander-in-chief's instructions,' he said impassively. 'That was my duty—I could not disobey him. As guided by him, I aimed at the reins of Abhimanyu's horses and cut them off, forcing the lad to the ground. After that, it was mayhem. He was attacked from behind, his bow was broken, and his horses and charioteer killed. He stood on the ground alone, with just a sword and a shield in hand. Guru Dronacharya broke his sword, and I his shield,' Karna continued, closing his eyes as if to blank out the horrific image. 'Arjuna's son then took up a chariot's wheel as his only weapon and whirled it like a discus, trying to ward off our arrows. Finally, exhausted and spent, he was overpowered by Dushasana, who came up from behind and closed on him in combat. Both fell down and Abhimanyu struggled to get up, but before he could stand up, Dushasana crushed his head with a blow from his mace.'

Karna paused, his voice thick with emotion. He could not go on for the sight still haunted him. He forced himself to continue. 'And then Dushasana and the others danced around his lifeless body, shouting in glee. I couldn't bear it any more and I turned away but it was Yuyutsu, the Kaurava prince, who eventually shouted at them to stop that horrible victory dance. Uruvi, I stand guilty again. Oh, God help me, how many more sins am I going to be accountable for? And like I said before, Arjuna deserves his revenge and I deserve the death that will fall on me.'

Uruvi gazed at her husband. His face was ghostly in its pallor, his eyes bleak. She asked herself what torment he must be going through. His hopes had been destroyed and despair had broken his spirit.

Karna did not look at her. His vacant eyes rested on the distant battlefield in the still of the moonless night. He was a crushed man, a still figure in his silent, heartbreaking anguish. He made no protest and showed no resentment. He seemed to accept life's stinging blow as the ordinary course of things. Life had extracted everything from him, shred him limb from limb and then hurled him cruelly on a bloodsoaked battlefield. Uruvi recalled his high spirits, his vitality, his wry humour, his sardonic, lopsided smile and his confidence in his future, and she wept silently for him for she knew all her love was no balm for him.

In revenge for the vicious killing of his beloved son, Arjuna proclaimed that he would kill Jayadrath, the Sindhu king and Duryodhana's brother-in-law, by sunset that day. His announcement sent chills of apprehension through the Kaurava army. It was an open challenge; Arjuna twanged his Gandiva bow and Krishna blew his Panchjanya conch. The fourteenth day was the bloodiest day of the Kurukshetra war with Arjuna, impassioned with anger in his grief, single-handedly killing lakhs of warriors who tried to protect Jayadrath.

And true to his word, Arjuna's oath was fulfilled. The entire Kaurava army, with its great warriors, converged around the Sindhu king to protect him all through the day, and when the sun set, cheered in triumph that Arjuna had not been able to keep his vow. But the sight of the sun setting against the reddened sky was a mere illusion cast by Lord Krishna, immediately catching the Sindhu king and his protective shield of soldiers off guard. Using the Pashupata astra of Lord Shiva, Arjuna shot a shaft from his Gandiva bow straight and true, striking the Sindhu king's head, which rolled down to the ground, severed completely from his body. Jayadrath, the man responsible for his son's death, lay dead on the battlefield before the sun had set. Arjuna's oath had been redeemed, forcing Uruvi to recall another terrible vow sworn by Arjuna—that he would slay Karna on the battlefield of Kurukshetra. Each day was like a sword waiting to fall, stretching its hours towards the deadly end.

That same evening of the fourteenth day, another hero plunged to his death. Ghatotkacha, the son of Bhima and his wife Hidimba, was a rakshasa, a demon, but a brave one and a master of illusory weapons. He could even grow into an awesome size by his own will. Using his sheer height, he had destroyed entire divisions of the enemy, duelling fiercely with veterans like Ashwatthama and Karna and even defeating warriors like Duryodhana. He wreaked such terrible havoc that Duryodhana finally pleaded with Karna to use the Shakti missile which Karna had reserved to use on Arjuna during the final, fatal confrontation between him and the Pandava prince. It was that divine weapon gifted to him by Lord Indra in exchange for the kavach and kundals. Karna took up his position and, in one mighty throw, hurled the mighty missile at Ghatotkacha. The young demon fell at once with a resounding crash on an entire division of the enemy, killing more than four lakh warriors.

The Shakti astra was meant for Arjuna, but was destined to kill the unfortunate Ghatotkacha instead. Krishna had cleverly used the demon son of Bhima as a sacrifice to save the life of Arjuna, once again resorting to a ruse. Uruvi counted each rule flagrantly broken by the so-called righteous side; her anger seethed from day to day as the restraints of dharma were discarded in many vile deceptions.

The killing of Guru Dronacharya was the ultimate breach of trust, reeking of treachery. On the eve of the fateful fifteenth day of the war, Guru Dronacharya, smarting under Duryodhana's allegation that he was a traitor and biased towards the Pandavas, decided to use the deadly Brahmadanda weapon, which was more powerful than the mighty Brahmastra—but the guru had not imparted the knowledge of how to use it to either his favourite pupil, Arjuna, or his beloved son, Ashwatthama. This knowledge made Dronacharya invincible that day.

There was no one who could defeat the guru and the only hope was taking advantage of his sole weakness—his son, Ashwatthama. Krishna knew that once he heard that his beloved son was dead, Dronacharya would voluntarily desist from battle, throw down his weapons and give up his life. That would be the moment of the great kill.

But for this deed, someone would have to mouth the terrible lie that Ashwatthama had been killed. Krishna told Bhima to kill an elephant named Ashwatthama, and then announce that he had killed him, using only the animal's name, so that Dronacharya would believe that his son was dead. Yudhishthira was told to say his first lie ever by seconding Bhima's assertion. So Bhima slaughtered the elephant and went up to Dronacharya, saying with glee, 'I have killed Ashwatthama!' Shocked with disbelief, the guru turned trustingly to the most truthful man of all, Yudhishthira. It was then that the

Pandava king admitted the half-truth. 'Yes,' he declared. 'Ashwatthama ("the elephant," he said in an undertone) is dead!'

Stricken with sorrow and believing his son was dead only because the news was uttered by the honest Yudhishthira, the guru quietly gave up his weapons, surrendering his will to fight and to live. In a grief-stricken trance, he sat down to meditate. Seizing the moment when the guru was defenceless, Dhrishtadyumna, the prince born out of fire for the sole purpose of killing Dronacharya, climbed onto the guru's unmoving chariot and unsheathing his sword, beheaded him in one fell stroke. And so it was that yet another rule of war was flouted.

Karna bowed to the guru's lifeless body, and after a long pause, commented unemotionally, 'We get what we deserve. The flames of the fire once started are going to burn you some day. We shall all die a death we deserve. We shall die as we lived—in deceit and duplicity. I know that Guru Dronacharya was killed treacherously, but this was the same noble warrior who had ordered Abhimanyu to be attacked from behind and killed when he was vulnerable. All our deeds have come full circle; it is the order of things that we have perpetuated. So be it. Death would be a mercy. It would be everlasting peace!'

It was as if Karna was waiting for his turn now.

23

The Death of Karna

The night of the sixteenth day of the war was unusually still and starless. After the passing away of Dronacharya, the Kaurava army seemed splintered but with Karna as their new commander-in-chief, hope surged afresh. Uruvi was filled with a new dread; fresh and strong, it stoked her worst fears. Duryodhana wanted Karna to kill Arjuna on this day. But would Karna return to her alive? The thought tortured her as she tended to the wounds of the injured whose number had swelled dramatically in the last few days. Even medications were in short supply. Cries of pain heralded death. Would Karna come back to her in the same condition as the soldiers dying in her camp? This morbid thought would not let go of her, churning in her mind all through the weary night.

She finished wrapping the compress on the burning forehead of yet another young injured soldier. In a few hours, the dawn would break to begin another day. She got up abruptly, with one single thought—she had to meet Karna. Would this be their last night together? The thought plagued her, driving her into a silent frenzy.

Karna was amazingly calm when Uruvi came to him. Like her, he seemed to know what peril the day held for him but unlike her, he was stoical.

'Are you not tired?' he asked gently, noticing her dull eyes, red with strain on her wan face. 'You must have had a long day...'

'I wanted to be with you.'

He sat close to her, his arm going round her waist. She rested her head on his shoulder. She slipped her hand through his and held them tight. She felt, with immense sadness, how there could be so

277

much love and peace in just holding hands. She did not want to let go of his warm hands; she didn't want to let him go away from her, ever. He was silent, so was she. They did not want to talk any more. She closed her eyes, wanting to savour this short moment of bliss, wishing it could last forever.

After a long time, she felt Karna disengage himself from her. He had got up, standing tall and handsome as ever. Was this their final farewell? She lowered her eyes quickly, feeling tears threatening, her grief silent. He kneeled down by her and kissed her softly, kissing the unshed tears away.

'Look after Vrishakethu,' he whispered, breaking away from her. 'And my mother and father. And Vrushali. I hope she can forgive me for what I did to her. Tell her on my behalf that I am truly sorry. I had no right to take away her sons, too, away from her.'

She knew that his sons could be killed on this day and that Karna had the same premonition.

She nodded, she could not speak. Her throat was thick with emotions and she said piteously, 'I will always love you, come what may.'

'You have always been strong. You are my brave soldier, fighting for and protecting all of us. Look after the family for me. And I will be there for you. Always, my little woman.'

And he abruptly turned away from her, to stride out rapidly towards the dawning day.

It was the beginning of the most unforgettable day of Uruvi's life. Each moment of that cataclysmic day was recounted to her by the loyal Ashwatthama—who was by Karna's side on the battlefield. Till his very end.

Ashwatthama told her of how it began, as Duryodhana pleaded with King Salya with folded hands. He said, 'Karna is going to kill Arjuna today. And Arjuna's biggest advantage is that he has a marvellous charioteer like Krishna. The only person who can offset that advantage is you, King Salya! You are the only one who is equal to Krishna and you can be an even better charioteer. Karna is sure to kill Arjuna, but that will be possible only if you would consent to be his charioteer.'

But King Salya flew into a temper. 'How dare you suggest that I, a king and a kshatriya, be a charioteer for a sutaputra? I am a maha-rathi, a great king. You are asking me to serve a low-born man?' Duryodhana pleaded again 'My lord, I cannot dare to demean you! You are far too superior to all of us. My only request is that you guide Karna's chariot, so that he can kill Arjuna. Even Lord Brahma once took up the reins of Lord Shiva's chariot in a battle.'

King Salya was pleased with Duryodhana's humility, and finally, gave in.

Karna knew that King Salya actually hated him and also knew about the promise King Salya had given Yudhishthira, his nephew, that he would run Karna down relentlessly till the very end. But despite knowing King Salya's intentions, Karna thanked the king respectfully. King Salya prepared a chariot for Karna and brought it before him. Karna, following the tradition, went around the chariot three times to perform the ritual of pradakshina. Karna then looked towards the sun and bowed deeply.

'He was saluting his father,' Uruvi wanted to tell Ashwatthama, her heart breaking.

Duryodhana had come to see off his friend. He hugged Karna close and told him that he wished to see him come home victorious by sunset.

'It will be either Arjuna or me who dies in the battlefield today,' Karna had said solemnly. 'If he dies, I win; if I die, he wins.'

It was as if Uruvi could almost hear Karna's voice, as Ashwatthama went on with his narration. Karna knew the outcome; he knew that Arjuna would kill him and that Bhima would vanquish Duryodhana. Karna was certain that he was walking towards his own death and she had known it in her heart when she saw Karna refrain from picking up his celestial bow, Vijay, even for a single battle during the eighteen-day-long Kurukshetra war. Karna never used his bow because he had accepted the fact that he would not live by the end of the war.

'You shall win, my friend! I shall await my hero's return,' said Duryodhana, and embraced Karna again.

Karna bowed respectfully to his friend and they walked together towards the chariot. He allowed King Salya to enter the chariot first and they headed towards the battlefield.

'Karna had organized his army brilliantly that day. The fight started in all its fury. Karna had decided that it would be a fight unto death,' said Ashwatthama. 'Arjuna advanced alone. He saw that Karna's sons Sushama, Satyasena and Vrishasena protectively stood around their father's chariot. The warriors ranged against Karna were Satyaki, Dhristadhuymna, Shikhandi, the five sons of Draupadi, Bhima, Nakul and Sahadeva. But they could not check the might of Karna as the fierce battle began. Eventually, Bhima killed Satyasena and two more sons of Karna were wounded.'

Uruvi paled as she listened to him. Vrushali would have to be a very brave woman to bear the death of her sons. Witnessing the death of a child is probably the cruellest thing a parent has to endure, a tragedy too terrible even to contemplate.

'The army of the Pandavas was no match for Karna,' continued Ashwatthama. 'He blew them away like flimsy clouds in a storm! As the head of the Pandava army, Yudhishthira faced Karna and fought belligerently. Karna was wounded right at the beginning of the battle, but he fought back, defeating Satyaki and others who came to help Yudhishthira. He smashed the chariot and the bow of Yudhishthira to pieces. Then, with an arrow, Karna pierced his armour too. When Yudhishthira stood helpless and at his mercy, Karna touched him with his bow and said, "O Yudhishthira, you are the noblest kshatriya but more a brahmin at heart. Do not challenge your superiors! You had once commented that as a sutaputra, I cannot fight a kshatriya. But, my lord, you have failed to act as a kshatriya as well. Go to Arjuna! You can never defeat me in a single battle!"'

'Saying that, Karna turned his chariot to the other side of the field.'

Uruvi knew he did not mean those words for he was only trying to save his brother's life, but she could not voice her thoughts to Ashwatthama or to anyone else. Karna was bound by the promise he had given his mother, Kunti.

'Bhima was livid when he heard Karna's words and suddenly charged at him,' Ashwatthama continued. 'Bhima injured Karna so grieviously that Karna almost fainted. I wanted to rush to him but Arjuna stopped me by locking swords with me in a duel. I was routed.'

'And then I saw Arjuna veer towards Karna. King Salya saw the chariot of Arjuna hurtling towards Karna, who could barely stand. It was a different Salya—seeing the sheer bravery, heroism and generosity of Karna, King Salya was deeply impressed and realized his mistake in considering Karna a mere sutaputra. He bowed his head, folded his hands to Karna and said, "I can see now that there is no one in the battlefield that can equal your excellent qualities, my lord! Forgive me my arrogance! I am overcome by your devotion to duty, to your king and to your friend! Now the time has come to kill Arjuna. He is our biggest danger. He is wiping out our army single-handedly and he must be stopped. It is only by his death that the Pandavas will lose the war. And now I know only you can kill Arjuna, great warrior! I am no ordinary fighter myself and I know full well the greatness of Bhishma and Drona, but this I can say—no one can stand up to you!"'

'Hearing these words, Karna's eyes filled with gratitude and he replied, "O sir, you have made me the happiest person in the world today! I am determined to kill Arjuna today so, sir, kindly take me to him."'

'And King Salya led Karna towards Arjuna, his powerful horses fiercely galloping through the length of the battlefield. On the way, their chariot was stopped by Bhima and Satyaki. Sushama, Karna's son, rushed to his father's rescue but in one swoop, was killed by Satyaki.'

Sushama was dead too—how would Vrushali bear it, Uruvi wondered in despair.

'Karna killed the son of Dhrishtadhyumna. But he was facing five great warriors—Shikhandi, Janmejaya, Yudhamanyu, Uttamaujas and Dhrishtadhyumna. Seeing Karna surrounded by yet more warriors, Duryodhana rushed to his friend's help with his brother Dushasana. But Bhima interposed and attacked Dushasana. They fought a horrible duel. "By coming to fight with me, you have given me an opportunity to repay a debt to Draupadi. You had pulled Draupadi by her hair and dragged her to the Raj Sabha. Today I shall kill you for that deed!" So saying, Bhima smashed Dushasana's chariot and his bow with a tremendous blow. He picked up the fallen Kuru prince and in one slicing sweep, cut off his hands and threw them on the ground. "I had promised Draupadi that these wicked hands which touched her would be torn from your body and flung to the ground!" he screamed in fury and ripped the chest of Dushasana mercilessly, making the blood spurt like a fountain. Then in a frenzied way, Bhima put his lips to it. It was the most horrendous sight! "I have fulfilled my oath, O Draupadi!" he shouted in devilish glee. "Your brother is dead, Duryodhana, and now it is your turn!"'

'Karna was sickened by the ghastly way Bhima had killed Dushasana. His eldest son, Vrishasena, seeing his father in danger, distracted Arjuna by advancing towards the Pandavas' army. But he did not stand a chance as the sharp arrows of Arjuna killed him while Karna looked on helplessly. "Now you know how I felt when you killed my Abhimanyu!" shouted Arjuna, and Karna, wild with fury and grief, charged at the Pandava prince.'

Uruvi clenched her fists, preparing herself for the worst.

'The two greatest warriors were facing each other, with only Death separating them. Their duel began—first with ordinary arrows, and then with the divine weapons, the astras of Agni, Varuna, Indra— each neutralizing the astras of the other. When the duel reached a feverish pitch, Karna picked up the terrible Bhargavastra, a special gift of his guru, Parshurama. Seeing this, Krishna asked Arjuna to invoke the Brahmastra or it would not be easy to kill Karna. To protect Arjuna from Karna's astras, Krishna leapt onto Karna's chariot and pressed it down, making it sink six inches into the ground. Meanwhile,

Karna had aimed at Arjuna's neck, but his astra hit Arjuna's crown, the famous Kiriti, which rolled down to the ground. Arjuna was unharmed yet again. Thrice Vasudev Krishna had saved Arjuna from Karna's deadly arrows—the Shakti which Karna was forced to use on Ghatotkacha instead of Arjuna, the Bhargavastra and finally, the Nag astra. Karna could have used the Nag astra again but I wonder what came over him because he refused to pick it up again.'

Uruvi recalled the condition Kunti had forced on her helpless son—that he would not use any divine weapon more than once. It was not Karna's righteousness which forbade him to use the divine astra the second time, but the unfair promise his mother had asked him to make, Uruvi thought bitterly.

'Then Karna was left with no powerful astra to protect himself. He was completely vulnerable, but he continued fighting,' continued Ashwatthama, the admiration for his brave friend evident in his voice.

Uruvi knew she was now listening to the story of the approaching death of her husband. Each word of Ashwatthama was like a vicious stab. She was shrivelling inside, dying slowly.

'Fate suddenly started working against Karna. All at once everything seemed to go wrong for him! The earth under Karna's chariot crumbled and the wheels stuck deep in the soil. He couldn't move and Arjuna shot another astra—the Aindrastra—at him. Karna could have invoked the invincible Brahmastra to counter it but he suddenly froze. It was as if he had lost all his ability to think! I tried to distract Arjuna so that Karna could have time to retaliate, but it was futile. It was as if no one stood between them now—it was just Karna and Arjuna. It was their fight to death!'

'Karna then asked Arjuna to give him time to set the wheels of his chariot right. "That is the rule of righteous war," he reasoned. Krishna scoffed at this and said, "Talk of righteousness does not become you, Karna! You were part of all the evil designs of Duryodhana, including the disrobing of Draupadi in their court. You were part of the unrighteous killing of Abhimanyu. And you talk of righteousness!"'

Krishna's words hurt Uruvi as deeply as it must have hurt Karna.

And much more, for Uruvi knew that Karna must have realized what Krishna said was painfully true. At that time, Karna had the choice to make a decision between right and wrong, and he had chosen the wrong, not because he lacked in judgement but because of his blind loyalty to his friend—but he had stood by his choice, stubborn in his convictions to the bitter end. The thought nagged Uruvi's troubled mind—did Karna really have to take the wrong path to help his friend? It had helped no one but had precipitated a dire chain of events, leading everyone to their doom.

'Krishna taunted Karna about his righteousness, but how could he forget how often Karna had spared Arjuna's life?' cried Ashwatthama in anger. 'Karna had defeated Arjuna earlier too, but saved him by pulling back his arrow so that it would strike Arjuna only after sunset, the official end of the day's battle. Later, when Duryodhana questioned Karna about this gesture of generosity, Karna had replied that he would always adhere to the rules of war. Moreover, he did not want future generations to point a finger at him and say that the sutaputra Karna killed the kshatriya Arjuna by deceit. But, in turn, that is exactly what the kshatriya Arjuna did—he killed Karna through treachery!'

Ashwatthama paused, his voice faltering, 'Karna continued struggling with the wheels of his chariot even as Arjuna's arrows rained on him. Karna stood up again and resumed fighting. Swiftly, Arjuna set forth the Agni, Varuna and Vayu astras, but Karna, defenceless, stood tall, taking all the arrows while grasping at the wheels of his chariot.'

Uruvi shut her eyes; she could imagine the scene in vivid detail. O Krishna, could you not have helped him? But Krishna had helped him die instead, Uruvi reminded herself dully.

'Krishna urged Arjuna to kill Karna quickly. And then, the great, noble Arjuna committed the most heinous act!' Ashwatthama's voice shook with pain, his face pale with fury. 'While Karna was down on his knees, writhing in pain and struggling desperately with the stuck wheels, Arjuna, from behind, aimed the Vajra arrow, the weapon of Indra, at him. It struck Karna on his back, and it was then that Karna finally fell, unable to defend himself because he was attacked from behind. Uruvi, I must tell you that even in his last throes, he did not lose his splendour. He was staring at the distant sun, as if trying to absorb the last rays, his body glowing strangely. He died before my eyes! And then I saw it—a flash of bright light left Karna's body at the moment of his death.' Ashwatthama's voice wavered and he broke down completely.

Uruvi stared at his weeping form and felt an unbearable pain blaze through her. She couldn't breathe any more. She gasped, the pain choking her, and buried her face in her hands, her fists digging deep into her burning eyes. She could not cry any more; her screaming agony refused to spill over. Karna was dead. And now there was nothing left for her.

Everything stood ominously still. The sun sank, drowning in grief, folding the world in darkness. But the all-enveloping darkness could not blot out the agony that coursed through her.

Uruvi could barely register what was happening around her. All she could hear were Karna's last words to her. That she had to be there for Radha. For her old, broken father-in-law. And, most importantly, for Vrushali. Would she have enough strength in her to face Vrushali to inform her of the death of her husband and all her seven sons in this war? And in that instant, it hit Uruvi that the agony stinging her was unparalleled to the torment Vrushali was going to suffer.

If Uruvi had never been convinced of Duryodhana's sentiments for Karna, she was forced to retract her estimation in their shared hour of grief. Seeing Salya with Karna's broken bow and the treacherous chariot, Duryodhana fell apart. To see the egotistic king fallen to his knees, weeping unreservedly, was a sight Uruvi had not been prepared for. The Kuru king could not reconcile himself to the fact that Karna was dead. Deep in despair, his tears flowing relentlessly, he was unable to speak. Where was that arrogance and his famous show of temper and wicked words? The anger, the pride, seemed to have seeped out of the king. He was a completely shattered man. And in that moment, all her resentment against this man she had disliked for so long, dissipated swiftly. In the pain and loss she shared with him, she found the will to forgive.

Ashwatthama had left, inconsolable in grief and anger. But she had not expected Duryodhana to visit her. She was shocked to see him in the middle of that night, outside her tent.

'May I come in?' he asked, his silhouette dark against the sky. The man who entered the tent was not the Duryodhana she had known all these years. The man standing before her was a ghost, pale and deathly.

'I have just returned from talking to Bhishma Pitamaha. He told me everything!' he murmured hoarsely. 'Oh, Uruvi, why didn't you tell me about Karna? Why didn't you let me know that Karna, Radheya, was actually a Pandava? Were you afraid I would have hated him? That I could have disowned him? No! No, Uruvi—I now have Karna's death to bear!' he gave a muffled cry of pain.

'Bhishma Pitamaha told me the story of Karna—his birth as a result of Lord Surya's visit to Queen Kunti before her marriage, his subsequent abandonment by her in the river Ganga, how he was rescued and brought up by the charioteer, Adhiratha and Radha, his quest for knowledge, his rejection by Guru Dronacharya, the learning he acquired at Guru Parshurama's ashram, the curse of Parshurama, the curse of the brahmin, his gifting away of his kavacha and kundals to Indra, and his meetings with Krishna and Queen Kunti. Uruvi, he was my friend, my mate, and he kept me in the dark while forfeiting his happiness, his life! I pushed him to a certain death!' he cried, completely distraught. 'Karna was above any caste, any social order—he was unique, too special! I always believed that Karna was a kshatriya; his actions, his thinking were those of a true kshatriya! I always owed him everything, but now, in his death, I am forever indebted.'

'Karna wanted it that way,' Uruvi said wearily, an ache persistently gnawing at her heart. 'He did not want you to know the truth of his birth because he thought that would be an act of betrayal on his part.'

'But if you had told me, Uruvi, I would have never allowed him to fight his own brothers...!' he exclaimed. 'Or did you think that I would pit brother against brother and snatch the crown?' he looked at Uruvi and knew he had just confirmed his doubt. Uruvi had believed the worst of him. 'I wouldn't have done that. Not to Karna. Never!' he said vehemently. 'Karna was the rightful heir to the Hastinapur throne—I would have gladly given him that crown had I but known! Uruvi, did he think I was so unscrupulous that he did not trust me with this decision? For him, I would have forsaken the war and the throne. I owed it to him! But if this is what Karna desired, I shall respect the wishes of my friend. I will never reveal this secret to anyone—though I would like to shout out to the world how great my friend was, how fit to be king and more!'

Uruvi was full of wonder. These were his very words when he had fought for Karna's self-respect at the archery contest at Hastinapur. His words *had* rung true though it was only now that she realized that he had been sincere.

'Do not grieve, Duryodhana!' she tried to console the devastated friend. 'I have always thought ill of you. But not now! All my hatred for you is gone, Karna is gone!' she choked. 'Karna wanted to die like a warrior. He was one, he acted like one and he died like one,' she said finally.

'How can I not grieve for the greatness of my friend?' he cried. 'How can I not weep for his extreme devotion to me and our friendship? Karna knew that he was the eldest Pandava, yet he did not go to his brothers and chose to remain with me. He gave away his life for the sake of our friendship while fighting against his own brothers. Oh, why was I not killed instead of him?' He kneeled at her feet, the tears streaming from his anguished eyes. 'The greatest friend, my supporter, has fallen because of me! The war means nothing to me now—it was all so futile!' he wept.

'You can still stop this madness,' she told him gently. 'Make peace with the Pandavas and give them back their kingdom.'

'I would, Uruvi, I would. I have lost everything! I don't want Hastinapur any more. But the time has gone. Too much blood of our loved ones has been shed. I shall not let it go waste. I cannot surrender to escape death. By doing so, I shall be branded a coward by all! I know the outcome of this war. The Pandavas have won. And I have been defeated—but not by the Pandavas. I have been defeated by the selflessness of Karna. I did not deserve his friendship. And for him, I want to die too—I want to die on the battlefield. Like a kshatriya. Like Karna.'

It was the day of Karna's funeral. Duryodhana was wracked with grief. So was Vrushali. She had quietly slipped into her room and kept herself locked in, trying to gather some semblance of her shattered life. She had cut herself off from the outside world. Adhiratha and Radha were inconsolable in their sorrow, and when they were eventually told the truth of Karna's birth, they broke down completely. 'Who am I supposed to cry for? My Radheya? My Shona? I was lucky to have two such good sons. But Radheya was the ideal son and till the end, he never gave up on us!' wept the old man.

The night was long; the sun refused to rise the next day. Before daybreak, Uruvi dared to go to the battlefield, the place she loathed with her entire being. It was a heaving mass of humanity as funeral after funeral took place. She didn't hear the shrieks in the air, didn't see the blood flowing by her feet, she didn't notice the stench of dead bodies heaped on the ground as she made her way through to look for Karna in the darkness.

And then she saw him lying slumped against the wheels of his chariot. She went closer to his prostrate form. Karna had always a luminous quality about him, and even in death, his body shimmered, his face reflecting an inner serenity, a certain tranquillity never visible before. The angst-ridden man was free of his yoke of torment at last.

She saw a shadow behind her. She turned quickly. It was Krishna and behind him stood the five Pandavas with their mother.

'Yudhishthira wants to light the pyre for his elder brother,' Krishna told her gently.

Uruvi looked searchingly at him. He nodded slowly. Her gaze went past him to the elderly lady standing behind, hunched and unsure. Kunti seemed to have aged dramatically in the past days. The five brothers were close together, their heads bowed, looking clearly uncomfortable.

Uruvi slowly shook her head. She heard Kunti gasp.

'As his brother, it is Yudhishthira's duty to light the funeral pyre,' Krishna reminded her softly. 'Are you still angry with them, dear? They acted out of ignorance. Now they know the truth.'

Uruvi looked at Karna's still face, his broken body. 'Is that wretched truth supposed to change anything now? Isn't it all too late? Anyway, I don't wish to say more on this...but it was Karna's last wish that it would be you, my lord, who would light his funeral pyre. If you don't think it presumptuous, I would be thankful if you would oblige,' she said stiffly, speaking with difficulty.

Krishna placed his hand on her head. 'Yes, I shall and I consider it an honour. Karna was a hero and died a hero's death. In this world of greed, power and betrayal, only one man—Karna—has followed the path of righteousness. Not even his other brothers could do it. And I am mourning the death of this great man of all the three worlds,' said Krishna.

Uruvi heard Kunti give a small sob, but she did not turn around. Krishna turned to the weeping mother and said, 'Kunti, your son was so upright throughout his life that even in his last hours, the goddess of righteousness herself sought to protect him! The only way to kill this good man was to deprive him of all his righteousness. I tried. You had tried earlier too, Kunti, but both of us failed.'

'On the battlefield, I tried again. When Arjuna was attacking the fallen Karna with his shower of arrows, I went to him in the guise of a poor brahmin and told him that I had come all the way to ask him for a favour. The ever-generous Karna, despite his pain and the fact that he was close to death, said, "All I can give you now, sir, is my life. I shall happily give that to you!" I said, "Of what use is your life to me?" Karna replied, "Please, sir, ask for anything you want."

'"I am a sinner and I need all the righteousness and dharma you have to save myself from going to hell. I need the fruits of all your good deeds."'

'And without thinking twice, the injured Karna cut his abdomen and spilled his virtuous blood on my hand, saying, "O brahmin sir, you have given this sutaputra an opportunity to redeem himself."'

The others stood in silence and in shame as Krishna continued, 'Karna, by this last selfless act, was deprived of the last quality that separated him from the lesser mortals—his righteousness. And touched by his generosity, I showed him my original, universal form—my Vishwaroop—and asked him for a boon. He replied, "Although I can request you to give victory to Duryodhana and bring his slain army back to life, I shall not do so. I wish for just two things—that upon my death, Queen Kunti should declare publicly that I was her son and that I am no longer a low-caste man."'

Uruvi now turned to look straight at the cowering figure of Kunti. She had buried her face in her hands, unable to bear the message of her dead son. Nor could she bear to suffer the scornful stares of Uruvi and her five remaining sons. Even in his last moments, Karna had almost begged his mother to publicly acknowledge him as her son. Uruvi felt rage leap at her throat. She wanted to lash out at this heartless woman who had forsaken her son and refused to accept him even in his death. Would she ever stop hating Kunti? Uruvi looked contemptuously at her now, wanting to mock her for at last having the courage to divulge the terrible secret to her sons. Oh, how she hated this woman!

Krishna, looked at her and shook his head. 'The second boon Karna asked of me was to fulfil a wish of his that he had not been able to carry out himself—that of annadanam—his wish to distribute food to others so as to liberate his soul from the cycle of births. That was one wish he regretted he could never carry out, as people avoided eating in the house of a low-born man. Karna's third request was "Please light my pyre on the most barren part of the earth so that no man may suffer the pain I did." Respecting his wishes, I am here, Uruvi, to do the needful.'

Krishna made arrangements for Karna's funeral with the help of the Pandavas. When the ceremonies were over, he lit the pyre, acceding to the last wish of Karna. Ashwatthama was there with King Salya. Uruvi was surprised to see Draupadi join the mourners, her head bowed low, hiding the expression on her face. But her bent head and her shoulders cut a figure of quiet grief.

Uruvi stood a distance away from the Pandavas. Kunti tried to approach her but Uruvi's frozen look stopped her. Uruvi noticed the genuine sorrow on the faces of each of the Pandavas. Yudhishthira and Arjuna looked the most wretched. She wondered how the Pandavas had reacted to their mother's revelation. Two brothers hating each other all through their lives, two brothers the most bitter rivals, two brothers always ready to kill the other. All because of a mother who kept her secret selfishly locked away and let it all happen. Uruvi turned her face away, wanting to turn away from these people, unable to forget how each one of them had hurt her husband throughout his life. Had Karna forgiven them? She still could not bring herself to even think of forgiveness!

Uruvi stared into the rising flames of the pyre, feeling a similar fire raging through her. She did not know if it was pain or wrath but it seemed as if the flames were licking her and engulfing her swiftly.

And so, the funeral of Karna was conducted in solemn grandness as would befit a Pandava. And ironically, it was at his funeral that Karna gained legitimacy—something he had craved for all his life. He had eventually earned his rightful place.

24

Pandavas' Hastinapur

For the first time, Duryodhana was not looking forward to the battle the next day. It was the eighteenth fateful day of the war—and ended as swiftly as it had begun.

When King Salya was felled by Yudhishthira and the last generals were killed, the Kaurava army lost all hope. And among the ruins of his army and all his dead brothers, stood a lone Duryodhana, who fought to the death. Overwhelmed with grief, and having lost his will to live, Duryodhan was almost suicidal. As he burned with hate, anger, pain and repentance, he went into a pool to cool his body. The Pandavas, searching frantically for their last enemy, found him there and surrounded the pool, jeering at him and calling him a coward for hiding in the water to escape certain death at the hands of Bhima. With them was Krishna.

Duryodhana stepped out of the water, his mace held high. 'I am not hiding like a coward as you claim. I am cooling the fire burning in me for so long. I have no fear in me now—because I have no fear of losing. I have lost everything already! Yes, I shall fight you. I am alone, but I will fight the five of you together.'

Reminding him of all the injustices inflicted on them, Yudhishthira taunted him about the young, hapless Abhimanyu who, alone and defenceless, had been killed by a band of great warriors like him. Duryodhana heard him out, then snarled, 'Enough of talk! It's time to fight once again!'

Then, leaping at Bhima as his first opponent, Duryodhana began his last combat. The duel was long and protracted as they matched each other in strength and skill—until the moment Krishna spoke the fateful words that were to decide the outcome of the fight. He reminded Bhima of his oath again—of how he had said he would smash Duryodhana's thighs, the same thighs on which Duryodhana had dared to invite the helpless Draupadi to sit. Hearing this, Bhima gave an infuriated war cry as memories of the outrage surged back. Then, in his rage, he smashed his mace below Duryodhana's waist and ripped his thighs apart mercilessly. Duryodhana's groans thundered as he writhed in pain. Placing his foot on the head of the prostrate Duryodhana, Bhima would have trampled him to death had Yudhishthira not stopped him.

Leaving him to die a slow, agonizing death, the Pandavas left their cousin, who was still seething with anger and hate in his last dying moments. 'Oh, Krishna, I will die as a true kshatriya. I was a noble king and a brave warrior. I shall die in a few moments and meet my friend Karna and my brothers in heaven. But you and the Pandavas will live and suffer!' he said, spitting out hate and venom for the man he believed was the cause of his destruction.

And that was how Ashwatthama, Kripacharya and Kritavarma—the three survivors of the holocaust—found him a few hours later. The gentle Ashwatthama, enraged about the brutal way his father and Karna had been killed, promised a terrible oath to the dying Duryodhana—that he would kill all the five Pandavas the same night, before the dawn of the next day.

He went away to fulfil his promise and returned in a short while, triumphantly announcing, 'The Pandavas are dead!' When Duryodhana heard these words, he opened his eyes for a moment, more peaceful after hearing that his enemies were dead at last. Then, he declared Ashwatthama as the next supreme commander of the Kaurava army. He eventually died in the arms of Ashwatthama, who did not know that he had perpetrated a more heinous crime than the devious murders of his father and his best friend.

The very night he had promised the dying Duryodhana that he would kill the Pandavas, Ashwatthama had set fire to the Pandava camp. He had attacked the seven ill-fated men sleeping inside, kicking and stamping them mercilessly to death. At the break of dawn, Ashwatthama realized that it was not the Pandavas but the five sleeping sons of Draupadi and her two brothers, Dhrishtadyumna and Shikhandi, whom he had heartlessly trampled to death. When they learnt what had happened, the grieving Pandavas bayed for Ashwatthama's blood. They searched high and low for him but he could not be found.

Uruvi was told about Duryodhana's excruciating death by Ashwatthama himself. The war had officially ended, Bhishma Pitamaha had breathed his last, but the search for the murderous Ashwatthama was still on.

Three weeks after the war was over, it was she who found him, or rather, it was he who came searching for her. Uruvi was gathering medicines at the camp and locking up the supplies when she saw a shadow against her tent. Knowing no fear, she stepped out to face the gory, bleeding visage of a tall man. She started violently and barely managed to stifle her cry of horror when she recognized the voice of the injured man, who said, 'I want some medicine, sister. I am hurt!' It was the soft undertone of Ashwatthama, the man who had painfully recounted each detail of Karna's last day and how he had died. Ashwatthama, the man whom Karna was closest to besides Shona and Duryodhana. The man who was Karna's everlasting friend.

She took him inside. Ashwatthama's face was wet with blood, which made it difficult for Uruvi to find the source of his wound. And then she saw it. Right in the centre of his forehead was a huge hollow from which he was bleeding profusely. It was the very spot where a glittering pearl once lay, the precious gem Ashwatthama was born with that blessed him with immortality. The gem was to protect him from death, disease, hunger and war—but it could not protect him from the wrath of the Pandavas.

Uruvi slowly started cleaning the wound as Ashwatthama rasped, 'They eventually tracked me down in the forests! They couldn't kill me as I am blessed with this wretched immortality but they prised away the gem from my head to give to their grieving wife, Draupadi!'

'Draupadi, whose five sons and two brothers you mercilessly killed!' Uruvi shook her head in dismay. 'Yet in the grief and pain you caused, I've heard she has forgiven you. But have you forgiven them—or yourself?'

'I got what I wanted!' he answered feverishly. 'The Pandavas have no heirs now! I killed them all!' he breathed.

'Oh, Ashwatthama, what has happened to you?' cried Uruvi. 'You were the kindest, the gentlest and the most just of them all! You were the man who could harm no one, think ill of no one, and yet today can you recognize yourself? You are what Duryodhana was, burning in the never-ending fire of hatred and fury. Why? Why did you allow yourself to become such a monster?'

'You call me a monster, sister?' he cried in frustrated fury. 'And were not the Pandavas more terrible demons to murder my father in that heinous way? Was Arjuna not a monster when he killed my friend Karna while his back was turned and he was grappling with the wheels of his stuck chariot? They were the ones who made me a demon! They talk about righteousness but were they ever fair themselves? I wanted to kill the Pandavas but I killed their sons instead…and I have no regrets! I am ready to bear Krishna's curse of finding no release from this life!'

'You murdered them in their sleep!' said Uruvi sadly. 'You killed each one of them and Dhrishtadyumna and Shikhandi by trampling them to death! You, gentle Ashwatthama, who hated it when anyone lashed even a horse! What has the need for revenge done to you?'

Ashwatthama looked hard at her and finally said, 'You were the most fiery lady I ever met—how can you so easily forgive the death of Karna? He didn't deserve to die that terrible death!'

'And is that why you are hitting back? Would Karna have been happy to see you in the state you are today? No, brother; hate and anger are corrosive—they only allow evil to flourish. And the worst evil you have inflicted is on yourself—you have made the good man in you become evil.'

The same words hold true for me as well, thought Uruvi, abruptly pausing in her statement. Had she, too, got so corrupted with hate, anger and resentment that she had forgotten how to grieve for what she had lost? Had she lost Karna as well as her innate faith in goodness? Would she end up being a bitter wreck, wallowing in antagonism and animosity all her living moments? Staring at Ashwatthama's distraught eyes crazed with utter hatred, Uruvi felt a prick of fear. She was afraid of herself now; she feared her virulence and her vindictiveness. Her face flushed with embarrassment as she recalled her abominable behaviour at Karna's funeral—hard and unforgiving as she was now, three weeks later. She shivered and it was not because of the cold wind outside.

Swamped by her own uncertainties, Uruvi heard herself cautioning Ashwatthama, 'Yes, Karna died by deceit, but by hating Arjuna, will I get my Karna back? I cannot spoil the sanctity of Karna's memory with rage and rancour. It would defile all that he stood for. Could you not have respected his memory?'

Ashwatthama flinched but Uruvi persisted, swabbing the wound stubbornly. 'You were the son of Dronacharya and today you are a fugitive, running away from the world! You tried to kill the unborn baby of Abhimanyu in Uttara's womb by targeting it with the dreaded astra of destruction. But fortunately, the baby survived—and he was born as Parikshit. So, the Pandavas have their heir, Ashwatthama. You could not save your father or Karna but try to save yourself now. Ask for Draupadi's forgiveness and you shall seek redemption. You have come to me to heal your wound. I have done as much as I can but I cannot stop the bleeding from this gaping wound in your mind. It runs too deep. It will bleed forever. Go to Draupadi—only she can help you.'

Uruvi turned around to apply some balm on his cleansed wound. But he was not there. He had left some time ago.

~

Uruvi could not sleep any more. Each time she shut her eyes, she saw the image of Karna standing tall against the battlefield. It was him again, with his thick mane, his sunset gold eyes, his twinkling earrings, walking towards her, with his gold armour blazing against the raging fire behind him, burning everything, everywhere. She saw the blood-spattered battlefield, with headless corpses heaped in the centre, the cries of those mortally wounded screeching against the sunless skies.

She realized she had been dreaming, but the dream was no different from reality. Dreaming about the terrible war, she was only seeing, in the harshness of waking, the senseless carnage, the blood and the pointless deaths of all those whom she loved and revered. There had been little reason for this meaningless war, the futile bloodbath and the hopeless future it harbingered. She vividly replayed the death of her husband and a shudder ripped through her. She was senseless with grief, she couldn't think any more and she wished she could escape from her everyday torment. How would she survive without Karna, without his affectionate laugh, without his teasing smile, without his reassuring kisses? No, she screamed silently, I cannot live without him, I see him everywhere, and I feel him near me. I can feel his breath, I can smell his scent, I can see his deep eyes laughing up at me, I can hear his soft laugh, I could just sink into his arms…

Lulled by the lovely vision of her husband when he was alive, she thought she heard voices below her balcony. Vrushali's was the loudest. Uruvi sat up with a start. Why was the soft-spoken Vrushali talking with so much intensity? Vrushali had been almost mad with grief ever since her terrible losses, so Uruvi hurried out of the room to see what was troubling her afresh.

The sight she met with stopped her in her tracks. Vrushali was arguing with Krishna, not allowing him to enter the palace. Trying to console her was Draupadi and looking on helplessly were the Pandavas and Kunti.

'Vrushali!' Uruvi said urgently, rushing to her sister-in-law's side. 'Let them come inside.'

'I don't want them here, Uruvi!' Vrushali said shrilly. 'I don't want any of them anywhere near us ever! They are murderers! They killed my Radheya, Shona and all my sons! They have heaped enough pain on us. What more do you want from us?' she rounded fiercely on the guests, her eyes glittering with unsuppressed fury.

'I have lost my sons too,' Draupadi interrupted softly. 'And my brothers and my father. My loss cannot be your solace but all of us are suffering—no one has been spared!'

Uruvi thought Vrushali would lose control on hearing Draupadi but the raw anguish in Draupadi's voice seemed to calm the frayed nerves of the older woman. Draupadi was unusually quiet, more temperate than before, the fire in her completely quenched. She was more like ash after a devastating fire. Her eyes were dull, her face lined, and her long flowing mane was tied in an untidy knot. She stood stooped and lifeless, wretchedly unhappy.

Vrushali looked suddenly exhausted. 'I wish we had never come to Hastinapur! I want to go back to Champanagari!' she said plaintively. And she swept out of the room in a flurry, unmindful of the guests she had just been rude to.

'Please don't mind her,' Uruvi murmured apologetically. 'She has still not recovered…' she allowed her voice to trail off deliberately. She bowed low to Lord Krishna and said formally, 'What is the reason for your visit? The fact that all of you are present means it must be something important.'

It was Yudhishthira who stepped forward and said reverently, 'We have come to take you home, Uruvi.'

'Home?' she repeated, almost stupidly. And then what they were asking of her sank in. 'No!' she said fiercely. 'This is my home! This is Karna's home; this is our home with his memories in every corner! This is my sanctuary!'

'No, I cannot leave this place,' she said more calmly. 'I can't live with you at Hastinapur. I am happier with my family here. In this house.'

'Please, Uruvi, won't you ever forgive us?' broke in Arjuna urgently.

He looked into her pale face, her sleep-deprived bleak eyes shadowed by pain and anxiety. She had a pinched look, making her wistful loveliness more fragile than before. Her eyes were vacant, but he sensed a silent accusation in them. Or, possibly it was his own sense of culpability making him imagine it. He could not rid himself of the guilt ripping him. He had killed his own brother. He had made this woman he once loved, a widow.

'Can you ever pardon me, Uruvi?' he pleaded. 'I can never say that to Karna, but please make me feel better. Help me to regain my pride. I have repented for the awful crime I have committed—I have killed my own brother in cold blood! However much Krishna and my mother try to convince me that Karna was a doomed man and that he had faced death because of six other people, I can't forget how I alone was responsible for his death!'

The pain was familiar; she was acquainted with the self-flagellation, the self-castigation. It was guilt that was tearing Arjuna apart. She recognised the torment in his eyes and desperately wanted to end his suffering. 'But Arjuna, what Lord Krishna says is true. Karna was betrayed by other people, all of whom were responsible for his death, not just you!' she said softly. 'It happened six times. First, at his very birth, his mother disowned him, keeping her honour above the self-respect of her first-born child. As a young, unwed mother, she cast him into the river, forsaking him and leaving him to a certain death. Karna was killed the day he was born. And he died each time his mother refused to acknowledge him.'

Draupadi gasped at Uruvi's brutal forthrightness, but for a moment, a gleam of triumph flashed in her eyes. Uruvi had uttered the words that she had wanted to fling at her mother-in-law ages ago, time and again.

'Please stop, Uruvi, don't punish me any more! How can you demean me in front of my sons now?' cried the queen mother of Hastinapur, raising a protesting arm as if to ward off the hurtful truth.

'I am not condemning you,' Uruvi shook her head. 'Can't you see your sons suffering? Is your honour more important to you even now that your sons have to suffer a senseless guilt that is killing them slowly?'

'Yes! I am being made to suffer for that single mistake of my life. I am asking for your forgiveness, but forgiving oneself is probably the most difficult task—and I haven't pardoned myself for that one fault of mine. But when can it be made right? I have already lost one son!' she sobbed.

'So has Bhanumati. And Radha lost both her sons. Draupadi's five sons were killed in this war and Vrushali lost seven,' she said impassively. 'Each one of us has lost someone most dear to us. That is exactly what I am trying to explain to Arjuna,' Uruvi said quietly. 'Arjuna, you need not suffer from needless guilt. Karna was destined for that death. The three curses of the angry brahmin, the earth goddess and, most importantly, Guru Parshurama's curse that Karna would forget the incantation of the Brahmastra when he needed it most, would be the second reason. The third time was when your father, Lord Indra, used deceit to rob Karna of the kavach and kundals. Again, for the fourth time, your mother was responsible for my husband's death when she revealed the truth of his birth at the time that suited her—just before the war. She crippled him with that truth, knowing that he would not raise a finger against his blood brothers. Moreover, she extracted a promise from him that he would not kill any of your brothers, except you! Likewise, that he would use a divine weapon only once against you!'

Arjuna recoiled, recalling how he had escaped Karna's fatal Bhargavastra and the Nag astra. Bhima gave a cry of pain and turned to Yudhishthira in despair, 'That is why he told us to go away. And I taunted him with my outrageous words! What terrible truth is this that we do not have the strength to face it?'

'That is a truth we were denied so long but have to live with even longer!' said Uruvi. 'The fifth time was when King Salya did not help him when the wheel of his chariot got stuck. And lastly, when all of this failed to kill my brave, hapless husband, it is Krishna himself who conspired to make sure Karna was killed. You, Arjuna, have killed a man already killed six times before by his own people!'

Uruvi halted briefly, filling the silence with her impassioned words, but her eyes were soft and melting, clouded by a deep sadness.

Krishna, his face solemn, nodded his head in quiet agreement. 'Yes, Uruvi, I admit I made Arjuna kill Karna. But that was only because Karna, though the best of men, was helping the wrong side. And he was the sole danger to Arjuna. I regarded the mighty Karna not as Arjuna's equal but far superior to him. And that is why Karna needed to be killed with the greatest resolve. In energy, Karna was equal to Agni, the god of fire. He had the impetuosity of the wind, the speed of a shooting arrow. In anger, he could be the destroyer himself and anyone who turned against Duryodhana earned his ire. He was as brave as a lion, he was a hero! Not even the gods could have killed him! He had to be killed by treachery.'

Uruvi's voice was gentle, almost kindly, as she spoke to Arjuna. 'Don't grieve for what you did, Arjuna. You are a warrior and Karna was your enemy. He had to be killed. If not him, it would have been you who would have died. And that would have been terrible too! Karna decided to accept his destiny, never losing his immense pride. His strength of inner conviction came from his self-belief. Despite what Krishna warned him about, he did not bend. In fact, Lord Krishna, he was one person who never succumbed to your appealing charm!' Uruvi said with a slight smile.

It was the first time she had smiled since the death of Karna and Uruvi found herself a little surprised. She felt the last of her bitterness dissolving; it was almost like physical pain ebbing away. She felt relaxed suddenly, a certain soft light glowing within her. It was the radiance of forgiveness, of hopefulness.

She walked up to Yudhishthira and folded her hands, 'Please don't take me away from my duties. I am needed here. It is not that my refusal stems from anger or hurt or spite,' she said evenly. 'My place is here—with Radha, with Vrushali, and with the sick and the maimed. I can't think of going anywhere else! They need me.'

'Uruvi, you are needed at the palace,' said Yudhishthira with slow deliberation. 'Karna, as the eldest Pandava, was the rightful King of Hastinapur and as his wife, you need to be there. And Vrishakethu, as the son of Karna, is the heir apparent to the kingdom. He will wear the crown. And that is why you have to come with us. We want you to be with us. Please.'

Uruvi took each word uttered by Yudhishthira calmly. Krishna added, 'Don't say no, Uruvi. The Pandavas and Vrishakethu are the new hope for the people now. Hastinapur today resembles a city of the dead. We need to rebuild it, bring hope into our lives again. The end is the new beginning. And Vrishkethu and you are part of this new life.'

'Vrishakethu probably, not me,' she said with a slight shake of her head. 'I do not want to involve myself with any kingdoms and politics. I have refused to return to Pukeya too, even though my father was very insistent! I am too tired of it all—I would rather devote myself to what I always did—trying to heal people. That is my way of healing myself.'

'And Vrishkethu?' asked Arjuna and Uruvi heard the genuine concern in his voice. 'He is the son of the finest archer and the greatest of warriors, don't forget that, Uruvi. He needs to be properly trained. Until now, he was under Karna's tutelage and I hear he has all the makings of a great fighter. I would like to mentor him from now on. Please let me take him under my care. Krishna and I shall make him as fine a warrior as his father was. He will be my second Abhimanyu,' he said simply, his voice heavy with emotion.

Yes, Uruvi thought, it would be a new beginning…Arjuna was pinning all his aspirations and ambitions on her son. She knew that it was a tremendous gift for Vrishakethu to be trained by none other than Lord Krishna! She felt a wrench at the thought of parting with her son—he was her lifeline now. But she recalled the discussion she had had once with Karna, about how he regretted that he could never be Krishna's disciple. His son today had the good fortune Karna had been deprived of. But did she want her son to go through war and fighting and bloodshed? She did not, but for Karna's sake, Uruvi forced herself to be pleased about Arjuna's offer. He would have wanted his son to be under Krishna's care. He could not have asked for more. Picturing Karna's face glowing with pride and pleasure in her mind's eye, Uruvi found her resistance melting away.

She smiled again; it made her feel lighter. 'I agree with Arjuna that Vrishakethu needs proper guidance and patronage—and who could be better than you and Lord Krishna?' Uruvi assured them with a smile. 'Yes, I am gratified.'

She saw the quick look of relief flash between Arjuna and Krishna. Kunti looked pleased.

'But I cannot accept Yudhishthira's offer,' she continued. 'Vrishkethu cannot be king. Neither will he be the heir apparent of the Hastinapur throne. You have been blessed with a grandson— Parikshit, Abhimanyu's son, and only he is entitled to the crown.'

'How can you say that?' Arjuna demanded. 'Vrishakethu is the older grandchild. And more importantly, he is the son of Karna, the eldest Pandava, making him the rightful heir!'

Uruvi shook her head decisively. 'No! I cannot accept this reasoning. It's the same story being rerun. I don't want history being replayed! We are paying the price for what happened three generations ago—and I couldn't bear a repeat of the same mistakes. There will be no future tussle and bloodshed for power! I want peace, not even the tiniest hint of a potential war!'

'You are overreacting, Uruvi! You are depriving your son of his royal rights over an irrational fear!' reasoned Arjuna, then added more kindly, 'Parikshit is just a new-born baby—how can you plan for him now when you are not making a proper decision for your teenaged son? History will not repeat itself. I will take care of your son, Uruvi, I promise!'

'I know you will. And I am sure so will all of you—and that's what I am so apprehensive about! In your misplaced affection for your nephew, Arjuna, you just might neglect your grandson. I won't let that happen! If not Hastinapur, some day my son shall be King of Pukeya—I am not depriving him of that! But I repeat, I shall send

Vrishakethu to you only on the one condition—that he will never be made king,' she said resolutely, her words steeled with a firm finality that Kunti knew no one in the room could combat. Not even Krishna, who was unusually quiet throughout the conversation.

'So be it, Uruvi,' he interposed quietly. 'Vrishakethu will not be the heir apparent. But we shall take him under our wing and do the best we can for him.'

Kunti looked at her nephew in surprise; Krishna must be as disappointed as they all were right now but he did not show it. She looked at him narrowly, almost certain that he had some other plans. But Uruvi was not taken in by his quick acquiescence either.

'No, Lord Krishna. I want a promise. And I want it to be kept.'

'Dear, you just said you don't want history to repeat itself and here you are starting on a new series of promises and conditions!' he smiled. 'I assure you, I shall comply wholly with your wishes. We shall leave now,' he said. 'But remember, dear, the more you want to go the other way, the path that you were destined for is the one you will have to follow.'

He was as charmingly cryptic as always, Uruvi acknowledged with a small smile.

As they were leaving, Uruvi noticed Draupadi lagging behind. She came close to Uruvi and said simply, 'Thank you.'

But in those two words was a wealth of emotion. What was Draupadi thanking her for? To have kept her secret intact? Or was it because Uruvi had given her Karna's son to look after? Or because Arjuna had left this place a happier man? Draupadi pressed her hand with gentle fingers and Uruvi returned the gesture, feeling the sorrow flow through both of them. They had loved the same man; both had lost him forever and now they would be mothers to his son.

Uruvi watched the cavalcade of the Pandava chariots leaving her home. She stood motionless, feeling bereft. This was the same place on the balcony where she used to stand, watching Karna leave each morning. The same place where she stood waiting for him to return every evening, hearing his chariot coming down the path. She felt dry tears gathering behind her eyes and her throat tightening.

Suddenly, she heard a movement behind her. She swung around, the anguish naked in her eyes. In front of her stood Kunti.

'When will you stop hating me, my dear?'

Kunti stretched out her arms and Uruvi did not hesitate any more. She rushed into them, burrowing her face deep into her foster mother's shoulder, trying to wipe away the hot wave of sorrow and shame that overwhelmed her. She raised her head and looked mistily at Kunti, who had held her warmly so often but whom she had confronted so angrily and hated for such a long time.

The barrage of tears burst at last. Uruvi felt the wetness of tears soaking her skin, her soul. Kunti gathered her in her arms and Uruvi collapsed in her lap, sobbing unrestrainedly, weeping her anguish out, grieving for all she had lost.

She inhaled the familiar fragrance of Kunti's warm body and felt consoled, comforted. She knew now what it was to forgive. It was leaving hell and touching heaven. It was divinity.

Epilogue

Even though Uruvi kept her promise to Karna to look after Vrushali and found the inner strength to give her solace, Vrushali, in a final fit of despair, killed herself, unable to bear the grief of the death of Karna and her brave sons. After the death of Radha and Adhiratha, Uruvi decided to go back to her childhood home. In Pukeya, she looked after her old parents and continued tending to the sick and the wounded.

Under the patronage of the Pandavas, her son Vrishakethu became a great warrior like his father Karna, filling Uruvi with pride. Bowing down to his mother's wishes, Vrishakethu refused to accept the crown of Hastinapur, content with being the King of Pukeya after his grandfather's death. King Yudhishthira ruled Hastinapur for thirty years and then handed the throne to Parikshit, the grandson of Arjuna.

Vrishakethu often accompanied his uncle Arjuna in battles, including the military campaign that preceded the Ashvamedha yagna, the sacrifice Arjuna held to mark his victories as a king. In this sacrifice, a horse was let loose and the territories it wandered into then came under the rule of the king, to mark him as a conqueror. Vrishakethu fought bravely in the battle against Babruvahana, the Naga son of Arjuna. During that campaign, Vrishakethu, with his uncle Bhima, fought King Yavantha, who ruled a kingdom to the west, and the young King of Pukeya won King Yavantha's daughter as his bride.

It is believed that Arjuna developed a strong, unflagging affection for Vrishakethu and taught him skills with the bow and arrow that made his nephew the most formidable archer in the country. Vrishakethu's other teacher was Krishna, just as Karna would have wished.

Vrishakethu was the last warrior on earth who knew how to use the deadly weapons, the Brahmastra, Varun astra, Agni astra and Vayu astra. With the age of Kalyuga, the era of corruption and the downfall of morality, approaching close and fast, Krishna warned his devoted disciple not to pass on this knowledge to anyone else as it had the power to cause mass destruction.

Vrishkethu kept his promise to Krishna and did not reveal it to any other person. It remained his secret, showing he was a worthy son of his father Karna, who always kept his word, and his mother Uruvi, a healer until the last days of her life, who had hated war but who lived through the bloodiest of them all.

Acknowledgements

I decided to write this book on an impulse, one which, unlike many others, I have not regretted. At the back of my mind were my mother's encouraging words, echoing over several decades, ever since I graduated from penning unpublished short stories and illegible essays. Evidently unimpressed with my journalistic writing, she wished that I would write a book of poems or a novel someday. Belying my name, I chose the latter. Thank you, Aai.

And there are so many others who have been an undeniable part of this process.

C. Rajagopalachari's unforgettable *Mahabharata* that I first read thirty years ago and re-read subsequently for reference.

My editor and the Rupa team for being patient with me and bringing out this book, thank you.

I was touched and pleasantly surprised by the number of well-wishers who generously helped me in some way or the other, even though I barely knew them. Always graciously yours, thank you.

Prakash—my friend, confidante and husband whose loyal support and unwavering conviction in my capability egged me on to undertake many things that my lazy bones and indolent mind would have avoided. However, he has still not been successful in making me join the gym.

Kimaya and Amiya—my teenage daughters who deigned to agree to read the book—if it ever gets published. I thank them for their support—not once did they rush into the room and chatter while I pored over my work.

Biswadeep Ghosh—my friend and ex-colleague who read the first draft of the manuscript. After (im)patiently perusing through the tome, he decided to edit it, and in the process, got to know much about the Mahabharata. It was the second draft that went to the publishers.

My dear, irrepressible friends—Niloufer, Priya, Amina, Ash, Jyoti, Anahita, Samata and Roshan without whose timely inputs and opinions, the novel would not have progressed from the title to the epilogue!

My cousin Shaila who helped me with my homework and vernacular literature.

My sisters—Asha and Radha, who promised that they would buy the book and not borrow it from me or the library.

And Dharmanand Bharne—my father, my guru, my mentor, my guide, my philosopher and my best friend without whom I would not have taken up writing. Or anything else.

Lastly, I thank God whom I hope I never fail.

Forthcoming from KAVITA KANÉ

Sita's Sister

In Videha, there lived four lovely princesses, Sita, Urmila, Mandavi and Shrutakirti. Beautiful, intelligent and kind, they were bound together by love and happiness but lived in fear that one day they would be separated by marriage. And the time did arrive: the four princesses got married—all on the same day—to the four handsome princes of Kosala in the biggest wedding ceremony ever. But, unfortunately, they did not live happily ever after.

As Sita prepares to go into exile, her younger sisters stay back at the doomed palace of Ayodhya, their smiles, hope and joy wiped away in a single stroke. And through the tears and the tragedy one woman of immense strength and conviction stands apart—Urmila, whose husband, Lakshman, has chosen to accompany his brother Ram to the forest rather than stay with his bride. She could have insisted on joining Lakshman, as did Sita with Ram. But she did not. Why did she agree to be left behind in the palace, waiting for her husband for fourteen painfully long years?

The Ramayana invariably brings to our collective minds the characters of Ram, Sita, Lakshman, Bharat, Kausalya, Ravana, Mandodari, and even Kaikeyi and Manthara, but not Urmila. This is the story of Urmila, the neglected wife, the most overlooked character in the Ramayana.